ABOUT THE AUTHOR

After ga... ...isto... ...ni Keer embark... on a career in contract flooring before settling in the middle of the Suffolk countryside with her husband, an antique-restorer. She valiantly attempted to master the ancient art of housework but with four teenage boys in the house, it remains a mystery. Instead, she spends her time at the keyboard writing women's fiction to combat the testosterone-fuelled atmosphere, with #blindcat Seymour by her side. She adores any excuse for fancy-dress, and is part of a disco formation dance team.

JENNI KEER

The Hopes and Dreams of Lucy Baker

avon.

Published by AVON
A division of HarperCollins*Publishers* Ltd
1 London Bridge Street
London SE1 9GF

www.harpercollins.co.uk

This paperback edition 2019

First published in Great Britain by
HarperCollins*Publishers* 2019

A catalogue copy of this book is available
from the British Library.

ISBN: 978-0-00-830969-5

This novel is entirely a work of fiction.
The names, characters and incidents portrayed
in it are the work of the author's imagination.
Any resemblance to actual persons, living or dead,
events or localities is entirely coincidental.

Typeset in Birka by Palimpsest Book Production Limited,
Falkirk, Stirlingshire

MIX
Paper from
responsible sources
FSC® C007454

This book is produced from independently certified FSC™ paper
to ensure responsible forest management.

For more information visit: www.harpercollins.co.uk/green

To Lauren for starting me on the journey, and Linda for helping me get there.

Chapter 1

'**B**loody hell. There's a cat back here.'

A voice reverberated from the depths of the red and white removal van as Lucy Baker approached. It had been blocking in her tiny yellow Fiat for nearly two hours and despite popping out at regular intervals to check on progress, she saw it was still there. The Hobbycraft centre would be closing in half an hour and she wanted to pick up some more balls of the Candy Crush double knit while it was still on offer.

She peered around the side as a pathetic almost-meow echoed off the van walls. A cautious black paw appeared from behind an upright double mattress at the far end, followed by a tiny pair of luminous yellow eyes.

'Don't just stand there. Pick the poor sod up,' said the older man to his younger, spottier companion, who grunted and made a sudden lunge for the cat.

Startled by the movement, the bony creature dashed down the centre of the van and leaped from the back, bypassing the ramp. It caught Lucy's arm as it jumped and pelted up the pavement.

'Idiot,' the older man muttered and turned to Lucy. 'You all right, love?'

She nodded mutely and rubbed her arm as a noise to the left made her turn. In the open doorway of the newly occupied number twenty-four stood an *extremely* tall, suited man. Not too shabby on the eye, with a look of self-assurance, he was enough to get any heart fluttering. A subconscious hand went to her hair. Things were looking up if this was the new neighbour. Perhaps she could forgive him for failing to warn the residents of Lancaster Road it would be blocked for most of Sunday afternoon. After all, everyone deserved a second chance.

'You own a cat, mate?' the removal man called over to the suit.

'God, no. Allergic to the damn things.'

The zooming rocket of attraction, which had shot into the sky as she'd appraised the fine figure in the doorway, floated gently back to earth like a downy white feather. His second chance evaporated, along with the initial appeal she'd mistakenly conjured up based purely on his muscular frame and a pair of serious, dark eyes.

'Well, we either brought him with us up the A1, or he's local and we nearly took him home. Shame Liam here scared the poor bugger off. Let's hope there's not some broken-hearted kid pining for it this evening.'

The suit strode over to the van. He was dressed terribly formally for someone who had spent the day moving house. Perhaps she'd got it wrong and he was the estate agent.

'I hope the bloody thing hasn't left cat hair all over my mattress or I'll be up all night sneezing and rubbing my eyes.'

Damn. It appeared Lancaster Road was stuck with him.

'I don't think it's from a loving home,' ventured Lucy. 'The poor creature was in an awful state. It looked more like a stray to me.'

The young lad finished unstrapping the mattress from the cargo rail and shuffled it forwards. 'You take it on then,' said the suited man, 'if you feel so sorry for it.'

'Oh no, I can't.' Lucy's eyes were wide. 'My landlady doesn't allow pets.'

They stood facing each other for an awkward moment.

'Right,' he finally said. 'So then you're loitering at the back of the removal van because...?'

'Um, I'm just waiting to get my car out,' and she pointed to her Fiat.

'We'll be done within the hour,' he replied, not bothering to look across at Lucy's trapped vehicle.

'Great.' Her smile was forced and her heart sank to the bottom of her flip-flops. The Hobbycraft centre would be closed by then.

The suit cast his eyes around the few remaining items of furniture and returned to the house, closing the front door firmly behind him.

Manhandling the wobbly mattress down the ramp, the removal men momentarily rested it on the pavement between them. The older guy looked over to the closed door and sighed, just as another front door was flung open. They heaved it up again and walked towards the house.

'Okay, what's going on?' asked Brenda, the elderly lady who lived between Lucy and the new arrival. 'Honestly, Lucy, your aura is all over the place. I could sense your frustration from the pantry.'

Not exactly a conventional pensioner, Brenda's purple-streaked, silvery hair fell down her back in a tidy plait, and her slightly hunched body was swathed in a rainbow of cotton garments. A silver locket was swinging from her neck but she tucked it out of sight as she walked towards the road. Her sharp eyes focused on the young lad and he wriggled uncomfortably. Juggling mattress and doorknob, the pair wrestled their way into number twenty-four.

'You told me you were going to the retail park this afternoon, Lucy. Have you been waiting for the van all this time?' Brenda ran her fingers back and forth through the purple buds of lavender growing in the narrow border down her path. Lucy caught the aroma and felt calmer.

'It's not a big deal. I can pop over after work next week.'

'Nonsense. It would have taken them two minutes to shift the van across and let you out. Honestly, I do believe you wouldn't have said anything if they'd parked it in the middle of your living room.'

The family from across the road tumbled out their sunny yellow doorway; the harassed mother clutching a baby to her hip, and the little girl giving Brenda and Lucy a cheery wave. They waved back with equal enthusiasm.

'I must finish those crocheted flower brooches for the preschool fête,' Lucy said. 'Chloe came over with her mother last week asking for tombola prizes. I have so many scraps of wool to use up, I feel I'm killing two birds with one crochet hook.'

Brenda chuckled. 'She's not easy to refuse, is she? With that cheeky grin. She's cleared me out of blackberry and apple preserve.'

The family piled into their people carrier and Lucy couldn't help but feel slightly jealous at the ease with which they pulled away from the kerb and trundled into the distance. If only the stupid removal van had parked three metres further down.

Brenda peered over the low wall as the front door to number

twenty-four finally clicked shut. 'I glimpsed our new neighbour walking past earlier – quite the stud muffin. Good enough to eat and go back for seconds.' Her hand went to her throat and she played with the silver chain. 'A bit of male companionship would do you the world of good, young lady. Knitting needles and assorted buttons do not a fulfilling life make.'

'Oh no you don't.' Lucy crossed her arms and stared at her dear friend, a woman most locals considered something of an enigma, but whom Lucy adored unreservedly. It wasn't that people didn't like Brenda, they loved her, but she made them feel uncomfortable. They would happily stop by for one of her herbal remedies if they had a migraine coming. Or the lotion from the doctor couldn't clear up their intimate rash. But they didn't like to stop for tea. It didn't taste quite right... 'I don't need you to start matchmaking, and I certainly don't want you chanting incantations at midnight in a potato sack in the hope the universe shifts slightly to the right and lots of non-existent chakras align – or whatever it is you do.' Brenda was prone to floating about and pretending to be mysterious, and Lucy happily indulged her friend. It was harmless enough and Lucy suspected Brenda was playing out an elaborate theatrical charade purely for her own amusement. 'You'll make me drink something from a glass vial and three days later I'll wake up with a headache, naked in a wheat field, surrounded by journalists.'

'Tish. You do talk nonsense sometimes. I'm merely an enabler. And if we search deep enough inside ourselves, it's amazing what can be summoned from within.' She closed her eyes, her body rising as she inhaled slowly and put out her hands, palms upward. 'Anyway, it's pointless to protest, because things are afoot without any intervention from me. He's already arrived,' Brenda said, opening her eyes and looking serious.

'Yes, we know all about his arrival: three hours blocking the road without so much as a note through our doors,' said Lucy.

'Not the sexy neighbour. The cat. I had a feeling there was one on its way.'

'How on earth...' began Lucy, but she had given up trying to find answers for the mysterious things that happened around her friend. Because if Brenda Pethybridge had been expecting a cat, Lucy suspected the universe wouldn't dare fail to deliver.

Chapter 2

Lucy spotted the stray in her tiny square of garden later that evening, weaving its way in and out of the assorted pots of straggly begonias and half-stacked piles of bricks. The poor little thing was all jutty-out limbs and tufty black fur, and had no more meat on its bones than a Lowry matchstalk cat.

Her efforts to coax it out were met with catty indifference and the nonchalant wipe of a chin along the edge of the battered metal watering can, so she changed tactics and five minutes later the nervous scrap was in her kitchen, peering up from the edge of a saucer of tuna.

'Don't look at me like that,' Lucy begged. 'I'd give you a home if I could.'

There it was again, the feeling her stomach was doing a series of inelegant roly-polies. Realistically, there was no way her landlady would drive all the way out to Renborough for a spot check on a mid-May Monday evening, but Lucy couldn't escape the nagging possibility, even if statistically it was more likely that the Prime Minister would stop by for a Jaffa Cake and a quick chat about the state of the NHS.

As the tiny creature licked up the last flake, Lucy swiped open her phone and googled local cat rescue centres. Renborough Animal Rescue was the nearest, but it was overflowing and under-resourced. There was a heartfelt plea on the website for people to consider offering a forever home to one of their twelve black cats as they were either considered unlucky or boring; the cute kittens and striking ginger toms were always chosen first. If the centre took Lucy's neighbourhood stray on, it would be number thirteen and that made her feel even more uncomfortable.

Reluctantly, she dialled the number as the cat halted its post-banquet ablutions, cast her a catty glance and attempted to meow in protest. A pathetic squeak came out.

'Sorry, sweetheart, I don't have a choice.'

The centre was closed but the answerphone invited her to leave a message or dial another number if it was an emergency. Lucy looked over to the cat, who was strutting up and down the kitchen and sniffing the stretcher rail of a chair. It hardly qualified as an emergency so she hung up.

Fetching a hand-crocheted blanket through from the living room, she folded it to make a temporary bed on one of the mismatched pine kitchen chairs, but the curious cat had wandered into the hallway, so she scooped up the creature and returned it to the kitchen. Carefully closing the door behind her, she went into the living room to pick up her knitting. Not a skill mastered by many twenty-five-year-olds but the only real talent Lucy believed she had. Such a shame there wasn't a great deal of demand for it in a professional capacity, knitting Shreddies for Nestlé aside, and she was fairly certain you had to be a nana for that.

Later that evening, in the middle of a complicated bit of shaping, there was a genteel knock at the front door, followed by a cheery 'Co-ee!'

Lucy's heart didn't exactly sink but it certainly didn't do a joyful skip as she opened the door to reveal her elegant mother; the sort of woman who coordinated everything from her soft furnishings to the contents of her fridge and expected everyone else to do the same.

'Darling. Stand up straight. We don't slouch.' She double-kissed the air either side of Lucy's face and took in her daughter's resigned expression. 'Aren't you pleased to see me?'

'It's *always* lovely to see you, but you could have rung first. I might have had company or been out somewhere.'

Her mother laughed at the joke Lucy didn't know she'd made.

'I'll have a coffee please if you're offering, but only if you've got the decent ground coffee in. Your father has driven out this way to collect an oily engine part from some eBay person for that damn BMW of his, and I said I'd come along for the ride so I could tell you about my simply *marvellous* plan for September.'

Lucy gave her mother a blank look, the significance of September momentarily eluding her.

'My Big Birthday,' her mother prompted.

'Oh.' An uneasy feeling began to ripple across Lucy's body. 'I thought you'd decided to go for something low-key?'

'I know I said I didn't want to advertise the fact I'm turning fifty, but after that poor woman across the road dropped down dead with an undiagnosed brain tumour at fifty-nine, it started me thinking. Life is precious and I want to celebrate that. Plus, it will be a wonderful excuse for a party. I rarely get the opportunity to dress up these days. You know what your father's like with social occasions. And it's not like I'm going to be buying another wedding outfit any time soon.'

9

Lucy felt a bubbling panic rise in her chest. 'I'm hardly an old maid.' She had enough insecurities without the announcement of a forthcoming event where they could be bandied about by her less than subtle mother, in front of an intimate gathering of close family and friends. This was not *a simply marvellous plan*; this was a total and utter catastrophe.

'Emily was married for two years and expecting her first child by the time she was your age.'

Deliberately not responding, Lucy walked towards the kitchen to hunt for the packet of Colombian ground coffee she kept in especially for these visits. Not a coffee drinker herself, except in emergencies, she'd never quite got around to mentioning it to her mother.

'I'm not saying motherhood is for everyone, but perhaps *that's* where your strength lies. Perhaps you are a homemaker rather than a breadwinner?'

Again, Lucy didn't comment. Even though she loved Emily dearly, she wasn't in the mood for a soliloquy about the virtues and achievements of her big sister. They had always been close, despite a five-year age gap and sixty miles between them, but her sister's high-flying career and two adorable daughters were the bright orange carrot her mother periodically waved in front of her, even though Lucy wasn't sure carrots were her thing.

As Lucy swung open the kitchen door, a black head poked out from under the cluttered table.

'Oh darling, not a cat. They bring in dead things.' Her mother scrunched up her face. 'Mind you, anything left on this table wouldn't be discovered for weeks.' She moved a pile of knitting patterns to the side and put her Jasper Conran handbag down.

'I'm only looking after it until I can get in touch with the rescue centre in the morning.'

'You mean it's a stray? Lucy! It will be riddled with fleas and goodness knows what. You really don't think these things through. Sometimes I despair of you.'

Yanking the cafetière from the back of the cupboard, Lucy nearly knocked over several precariously balanced mugs in the process. As she began making the coffee, her shoulders slumped and her mother was perceptive enough to notice.

'Oh sweetheart, I know it seems I am constantly scolding you, but it's only because I care. You've got this lovely cosy flat now, and the little job at the toy shop, or whatever it is. You're right, you're still young. I love both my girls so much and you know how much I... Eurgh, it's coming towards me. Make it go away.'

Lucy plunged the cafetière with too much force and the coffee gurgled in the glass jug. Okay, so perhaps she wasn't a successful regional manager living in a chocolate-box house, deep in the Hertfordshire countryside, but she enjoyed her job at Tompkins Toy Wholesaler and felt at home in her cluttered little flat.

She poured two strong coffees and persuaded her mother to decamp to the living room, closing the door on the malnourished cat.

'You've knitted some more of those dolls. Very, erm...accomplished. Perhaps you should pass them on to the girls to play with,' her mother said, referring to her granddaughters, 'because you're running out of seating in here.' She piled the knitted figures up on one end of the sofa and sat down.

'They aren't toys, they—'

'Boy dolls too, I see. How very modern.'

Lucy let out a tiny but audible sigh. 'So, this party then?' She steered the conversation away from her knitting and back to the party in order to gauge the extent of the inevitable horror that was a large social function.

'Yes, Emily thinks it's a simply *marvellous* idea. I thought it would be a splendid opportunity to gather all the family. Uncle Ted can fly over from Ireland, and all the cousins could come. Then there's family friends, the bridge club, your father's work colleagues at the bank...'

'Exactly how big is this party going to be?' Lucy's eyes were dinner plates, never mind saucers, and her voice came out in a squeak.

'That's the exciting bit. I've booked Mortlake Hall for the *entire* weekend. I've got that money from Aunt Freda and I thought: why not, Sandra? One in the eye for Stuart's snotty mother.' Stuart was Lucy's brother-in-law and, as far as her mother was concerned, he was the sprinkles on the six-foot-high, frosted cupcake of her eldest daughter's many achievements. Lucy felt like a stale digestive biscuit in comparison. 'And I was thinking you could keep your father amused while I undertake the socialising he so loathes. The pair of you can mope together in the corner.'

'I might have a boyfriend by then. Stranger things have happened.' For a fleeting moment Lucy reconsidered her new neighbour, purely to get her mother off her back, but then dismissed the idea and took a tentative sip of the bitter coffee. Although boyfriend acquisition was top of her mother's agenda for Lucy's life, it wasn't high on hers. Of course, she hoped to be part of a fulfilling romantic relationship one day, but her immediate dreams were more small-scale: doing well in her job and conquering her debilitating lack of confidence – although she suspected both were linked.

'Oh, do you think you could?' Her mother smiled in delight and leaned forward to put her hands up to her daughter's cheeks. 'It would make the seating on the top table so much easier. And it would stop that uncle of your father's continually hinting that boys aren't your thing.' She sat up straight and clapped her hands together. 'It would be simply *marvellous* if you could manage to find someone. I've always said you have the potential. And I've often thought how ironic it is Emily got the dark hair when it's the blondes, like you and me, who are supposed to have all the fun. Smarten yourself up a bit and get out there instead of playing the wilting wallflower. If only there was someone *suitable* who wouldn't mind.' She raised a hand to her mouth and tapped her top lip. 'I'll have a word with Emily...'

As Lucy waved her parents' car into the distance an hour later, she had a vision of her mother introducing her to everyone at the Big Birthday as her twenty-five-year-old spinster daughter who had a *little* job in a toy shop and spent her spare time knitting dolls.

Returning to the hallway, Lucy heard scratching from the kitchen. The cat was clawing at the back door and she realised there was nowhere for it to do its catty business. She wondered whether she could improvise with a seed tray and some garden soil, but as she opened the back door to investigate the contents of the rickety shed, the cat made a dash for freedom and was through her legs before she could stop it. Momentarily stunned by the speed of its escape, she froze on the back step. But the night-black cat had vanished completely into the cat-black night.

Chapter 3

All thoughts of the bright yellow eyes and narrow vulpine face vanished from Lucy's mind as Adam presented her with the usual list of crises before her bottom hit her swivelly chair at Tompkins Toy Wholesaler the following morning. There was a product recall for My Pretty Princess vanity cases, as the mermaid blue eyeshadow had caused an allergic reaction in a couple of isolated incidents. Three packs of the Hear Me Growl Tyrannosaurus Rex had been dropped off to an independent toy shop, instead of the three *pallets* they'd ordered. And fifty-six Water Fun Super Soakers had been delivered to the wrong branch of TopToys.

Lucy subconsciously fed each of the polished agate stones on her bracelet through her fingers like rosary beads. She so desperately wanted to make her mark at work, but life kept jabbing twigs in the wheels of her bicycle and sending her flying over the handlebars.

'Come on, Lucy, we can do better than this,' Adam said, resting an overly familiar hand on her shoulder. 'I need you to be one of Adam's Little Angels. Drill down and see if you can't get these problems sorted by ten. You ladies are always so good at dealing with these pesky hiccups. Must say though, I'm surprised you let that dinosaur order slip through. Tut, tut.'

'Sorry,' mumbled Lucy. 'I'll get straight on it.' She was fairly certain that she'd put through the T-Rex order as pallets but she also knew the guy who picked for that delivery route was in the middle of a vicious divorce and it wouldn't be the first mistake he'd made in the last few weeks.

'Appreciated and all that. I'm so rushed off my feet at the moment, otherwise I would happily help you out, but I'm sure you understand the pressures I'm under. You can't have an office of worker bees without a queen.'

There was a titter from the other side of the partition.

'It's an analogy, Pat.' Adam gave an exaggerated sigh. 'You know we don't do queer jokes in this office. I'm fully aware that we need to promote a politically correct and professional work environment. I read the memo.' He rolled his eyes at Lucy. 'And we don't do fat jokes out of respect for you, Pat, so let's leave the gays alone. Eh? Right, I must crack on. Time and tide...' Adam walked over to his immaculate, empty desk and began colour-coding his paper clips.

In contrast, Lucy's desk was a jumble of Post-it Notes, stacks of brochures from manufacturers and scruffy note-books that she used to record every order she took. It looked a complete dog's breakfast, dinner and tea, but Lucy could usually locate the things she needed. Eventually.

She stared absent-mindedly at the floor – a random jumble of carpet tiles in primary colours, as if to remind the staff they worked in an industry geared towards children. The internal line flashed on her phone.

'Don't let him make you feel like any of those problems are your fault or your responsibility,' whispered Pat. 'It's obviously another warehouse cock-up. Let them take the flak.'

Pat sat at the desk opposite Lucy, but the partition, painted in what Adam referred to as a Motivational Yellow, meant unless they stood up they might as well have been in separate offices. A large lady who kept her tightly permed auburn head down and barely raised her voice above a whisper, Pat had only ever spoken about three sentences to Lucy's face, yet conspiratorially contacted her via the internal line on a regular basis.

'It's not a problem,' said Lucy. 'Hopefully I can smooth things over with the customers. I'll tackle TopToys first.'

Surveying her muddle of a desk, and accidentally sending a nodding fluorescent orange alien flying, she located her computer mouse under a bundle of Beach Barbie promotional leaflets. She pulled the company details up on her screen and prayed she'd get the friendly older lady and not the ranty man who had a tendency to launch into a tirade listing every error made by Tompkins in the last twenty years whenever something went wrong.

As she dialled the number, she gazed about the office and let out a slow and deliberate calming breath. It was hard to feel gloomy for long in an office where a one-legged parachuting Action Man dangled from the ceiling over the filing cabinet, and Igglepiggle was rogering Shaun the Sheep on top of the water cooler.

By lunchtime, Lucy had managed to persuade a driver to return to TopToys to sort out the water pistol crisis, issued a product recall for the faulty vanity cases and arranged for the missing dinosaurs to be couriered out.

Jess was impressed.

'I bet you didn't even get a thank you from Adam. Why he couldn't sort out the problems himself, I don't know. He's supposed to be the sales office manager.'

Jess was upstairs pretending to query an invoice, but in reality wanted to snatch five minutes with her best friend, their fair heads ducked below the partition to avoid detection.

'He's not so bad,' said Lucy. After the short-tempered boss at her previous job, who regularly launched his telephone across the room when things got stressful, Adam was a welcome relief.

'Honestly, he can't even manage his trousers, never mind a sales team.' Jess glanced across at the two inches of fluorescent socks that highlighted how short his trousers were as he completed another circuit of the office and approached them. Rumbled, Jess stood up and tried to look businesslike, shuffling through the folders she had in her hand and pretending to tick things off.

'Ah, the Terrible Twins...'

'Having the same colour hair hardly makes us the female version of Jedward.' There was a pause as Jess considered the implications of this. 'And if you start calling us Juicy, I swear I'll stamp on each and every one of your newly sharpened pencils.'

Adam threw an anxious glance at his pencil pot and then pulled his shoulders back. 'Jessica Ridley. Riddle me this and riddle me that.' He put his hands on his hips, like an unamused teacher. 'What exactly are you doing upstairs in sales anyway? Haven't you got numbers to add up and...divide by four, or something?' He tried to avert his eyes from Jess's slender legs, but the short, cotton skirt she was wearing made it difficult. 'Back to accounts please and save the socialising until after work. My ladies are very busy.' There was a muffled cough from Connor, often overlooked because his desk was tucked around the corner of the L-shaped office, and a definite squaring of the shoulders from Jess.

'Actually, I was compiling a spreadsheet analysis of our fiscal input and was sent upstairs to access some computerised data from Lucy as she knows our CDAs. But if you've got five minutes, perhaps I can run it by you?'

'Well, erm, I'm quite busy and Lucy is probably the best person, as you say. I think she has a handle on the CDAs, but make it quick. With Sonjit off today we are a *man* down.'

One of the younger sales girls called Adam over and he immediately lost all interest in nomadic accounting staff.

'So, what exactly are CDAs?' Lucy queried.

Jess shrugged. 'He deserved it for ogling my legs again.'

'I thought the whole point of a short skirt was for men to admire your legs?' Lucy hadn't worn anything above the knee since her year eleven gym skirt. 'I'm not sure you can be picky about who gives you the appreciative glances.'

'It's part of my arsenal to lure the young, wealthy, single men.'

'Like Dashing Daniel?'

'Just give me a little more time, hon.' She gathered up her manila folders, tapped the wobbly head of the bright orange alien balanced precariously on the edge of Lucy's desk and gave her friend a cheeky wink. 'Definite work in progress.'

Chapter 4

'Can I help you?' Lucy asked as she peered around the door.

It was rather late for house calls, but she answered the knock because a confused Brenda had called very late one evening the previous week, thinking it was early morning and clutching a bundle of borrowed Regency romances. Lucy was relieved to discover this visit was not from her disorientated friend, although was unsettled to discover the formally dressed man from number twenty-four on her front steps.

'Cat,' he said.

'Pardon?' Had her new neighbour really barked a solitary word at her?

'That damn cat from the other day is hiding in the utility and my eyes are swelling up faster than popcorn in a sodding microwave.'

'The removal van stray? Oh, I was wondering what happened to it.' She'd kept an eye out for it the previous night, periodically sticking her head out the back door and calling 'cat', but it hadn't reappeared.

'It's backed itself between the washing machine and the tumble dryer and I don't know how to get it out, short of shooting it and pulling the corpse free with the end of the broom.'

Lucy narrowed her eyes and hoped this was just his dry sense of humour.

'Sorry,' she said, 'I can't take it on and wouldn't know what to do with it if I did.'

Never allowed pets as children, Lucy and Emily had made do with a stuffed Scooby-Doo (great at the sit command – rubbish at fetch). Their mother wasn't one for the mess and inconvenience that invariably came with animals: stray clumps of hair, unhygienic food bowls and muddy paw prints on her immaculate white tiled kitchen floor. But there was something about cats that appealed to Lucy. They were independent yet loving. They didn't demand much apart from a lap and they didn't judge you on your silly comments or untidy nature.

'Fine, but it's the third time I've caught it in my house and I'm losing patience, so I'm going with the shooting option...' He shrugged his wide shoulders. Was he joking? And could she live with herself if he wasn't?

'Okay, I'll find my shoes and come over,' she sighed.

'Right,' he said.

'You're welcome,' Lucy mumbled under her breath as he walked out through her front gate.

A few minutes later Lucy was at his front door. After some clumping and huffing, it swung open and he stood back for her to enter. When she realised she wasn't going to get a word out of him, she stepped inside and followed him down the long hallway.

As he strode away, the musky scent of Paco Rabanne lingered long enough to make her head turn like a hungry Bisto kid. Cross with her nose for leading her mind astray, she tried to peek through the open doors as she followed him without being obvious. There was nothing dotted about; no ornaments, no photographs, no personal objects whatsoever. What little furniture there was looked brand new and insubstantial. Goodness knows why it had taken the removers most of the day. Perhaps he hadn't finished unpacking yet, although there weren't any boxes lying about.

'Through here,' the slightly scary bear of a man said as he gestured to a door at the end of the corridor.

Lucy walked into the utility and looked in the direction he was pointing. She bent down in front of the washing machine. Two of the yellowest, widest eyes blinked back from the dark.

'Come here, sweetheart.' Lucy put her hand tentatively between the two machines and made kissy noises.

'Huh. It will take more than that. I've been here half an hour and all I've got is an allergic reaction for my trouble.' To make his point, he blinked his puffy eyes. 'I've had to abandon the contacts and I'll be damned if I can find my spare pair of glasses.'

No one was more surprised than Lucy when the cat, head low and ears back, came towards her.

'Well, I'll be...' He reversed like a cartoon elephant backing away from a mouse as the cat emerged from the gap. 'We clearly have a Doctor Dolittle in the neighbourhood.'

Lucy coaxed out the small black streak, but it bypassed her and walked over to the homeowner, rubbing around his legs and purring softly, even as he stepped away. Looking down at the animal though, his expression changed from alarm to compassion. He stopped his retreat and let it have a moment of contentment getting to know his trouser leg. His hand twitched, as if he was considering bending down

21

for a stroke, but then Lucy heard him sniff. Reminded of his allergy, his whole body stiffened. She walked over and scooped up the cat.

'So, just you in this great big house?' she asked, hoping for more than a one-word answer.

'Yes.'

She persevered. 'My house has been divided into three flats and I rent the ground floor. It gives me a bit of garden and the couple on the top floor are never there because they travel...'

He looked at his watch, bringing it Mr Magoo-style close to his face. A combination of no contact lenses and the allergic reaction, she assumed. 'Right. Look, I don't do small talk. Nothing personal. Only child thing. Probably why I choose to be *on my own*,' he said pointedly.

'What a shame. You have no one to chat with about your day. No one pleased to see you when you walk through the door...'

'Yeah, well, sometimes company isn't all it's cracked up to be.' It wasn't an aggressive response, more a contemplative one.

'Nonsense. Even one of these darling creatures would make a great companion,' she said, snuggling up to the cat. 'Shame I'm not allowed pets at the flat. Even a goldfish can be a good sounding board when life gets stressful.' She turned her attention to the bag of fur and bones she was holding, scrunching up her nose like a squirrel and wiggling her face in close. 'I would have given you a home. Yes I would. I would have cuddled and snuggled you, and rubbed your fluffy, little tummy...'

A dismissive snort came from the man, but the deepest,

rumbliest purr came from the cat as it rubbed its tiny head on Lucy's chin.

'Aww. It's such a friendly, trusting little thing.'

'I'm sure it's the loveliest creature ever to grace this earth, but I'm *really* struggling here.' He rubbed his fingers underneath his bloodshot eyes, trying to alleviate the itchiness without adding to the irritation. 'So perhaps...?' He waved towards the front door and walked out to the hall, obviously expecting Lucy and the cat to follow. It was clear they'd outstayed their welcome, not that either of them had been particularly welcome in the first place.

'Of course. Sorry. I'm Lucy Baker, by the way,' she said, turning back as she reached the front door with her refugee.

'George Aberdour.' He nodded briefly and then firmly closed the door on them both.

'A thank you would have been nice. I mean, it wasn't even my cat.'

Lucy was filling Brenda in on the details of her visit to George's house as she handed over a small bag of shopping she'd picked up for her friend after work. Although Brenda would happily trot into the town centre, both the large supermarkets were on the outskirts, and you needed transport to get to them – which Brenda no longer had.

This close friendship, which began in earnest after bumping into each other near the Mills and Boons at the local library and giggling over the bare-chested men on the covers, quickly became important to them both. The yawning age difference meant nothing to two lost women in need of companionship. Lucy's youthful energy and altruism complemented Brenda's assertiveness and wisdom, each looking to the other for qualities they wished to possess.

'But despite his manner, there's karma at play,' Lucy continued, 'because no sooner had I walked up his path than the cat wriggled free and ran to the back of his house. If he so much as opens a window, the cat will be back inside like a dieting woman to an opened bar of Galaxy.'

'Agreed,' said Brenda, as she stepped into the hall, allowing Lucy space to enter. Lucy stopping for tea and cake after delivering the shopping was a given, established the previous year as Brenda's way of saying thank you. 'That little fellow is on a mission and George is the goal. I think our little stray has found a home there.'

'I find that highly unlikely. Mr Aberdour is definitely not a cat lover.' Lucy shook her head gently, thinking of his less than complimentary descriptions of the cat.

Brenda smiled. 'Oh, the universe is cleverer than you give it credit for, my dear.'

'Now I know you're losing the plot,' Lucy joked, but an uncomfortable silence followed.

They lingered in the long hallway, surrounded by the ticking and tocking of Brenda's many clocks. Every time Lucy visited, she had the strange feeling they were collectively counting down to something, but she hadn't quite worked out what. A small pile of brown paper packages sat on the Shaker table by the front door awaiting collection and a potent mix of rosemary and tea tree drifted out from the kitchen. Whether it was the fragrant scents, the rhythm of the clocks or merely being with a good friend, Lucy felt more at ease in this house than she did anywhere else in the world.

'As it's such a pleasant evening, I thought we could have

the tea in the garden,' said Brenda, rallying. 'I wanted to talk to you about...' She frowned. 'It will come back to me in a minute. And perhaps today we could try the valerian and chamomile?'

'That sounds lovely.' Lucy was in no hurry to return to her flat, but wished she'd thought to grab her knitting. There was something rather fun about having Poldark across your knee, even if he was in 4 ply.

Ten minutes later, the pair stepped through the back door and delicate chimes tinkled as the door swung shut behind them. Lucy carried the tray of tea and placed it on the cast-iron bistro set on the patio. Like her garden, Brenda's was small, but it was overflowing with flowers, herbs and unrestrained trees and somehow managed to look about four times the size of her own. A light breeze toyed with Lucy's hair and she smiled as a group of starlings perched around the birdbath stopped their chatter in deference to the kindly old lady who kept their drinking water so efficiently topped up.

'So how has your week been, my darling?' Brenda asked, pouring the highly scented tea into garish Sixties bone-china cups.

'It started well. It was my niece's birthday on Monday and she was delighted with the foldaway kitchen I sent – one of the perks of working at a toy wholesaler. Emily helped her Skype me to say thanks and it was hilarious. She dressed up for the occasion, even donning a tiara, and sat on a beanbag, all serious and formal. It was like watching a mini version of the Queen's Speech. And then little Gracie walked across the screen and merry hell kicked off.'

'Awww, I know how much you love those little girls. Shame they don't live closer.'

Lucy often talked to Brenda about her nieces and showed her the Facebook pictures of their latest exploits. They'd both been in hysterics recently over a short video her sister had posted of Rosie trying to hula-hoop. Every single time, the hoop slid gently to the ground whilst an exuberant four-year-old thrust her hips backwards and forwards like a demented Mick Jagger. How she hadn't snapped the hoop in half at the end out of utter frustration was a mystery.

Lucy moved on to talk about the upcoming birthday party, Brenda studying her face intently the whole time.

'I don't know why it worries you so much,' Brenda said, tipping her head to the side. 'You needn't pretend with me – I see that troubled expression. It's obvious you aren't looking forward to it one bit.'

Lucy sighed, realising she was more readable than a large-print library book. 'Whenever we visit family, my mother can't stop gushing about Emily and how proud she is of her career and lifestyle, and I sit there, wanting to put up my hand like a schoolchild and shout, "what about me?" But, of course, I don't.'

'Sometimes, you need to be a bit more forceful, young lady. Put a spin doctor head on those young shoulders of yours and shout about your strengths. Tell people how much you enjoy your job and want to get on in life. How kind you are, and that you have so many friends in the neighbourhood. Talk about your beautiful knitting—'

'My knitting?' Lucy was confused.

'Absolutely. Can Emily knit?'

Lucy smiled. 'She wouldn't even know which end of the needle to poke in the wool.'

'Well there you go. You underestimate yourself and your

abilities. Look at the beautiful things you create from a couple of balls of wool and your effortless dexterity – they are real masterpieces.'

'It's just knitting.' Her woolly Poldark was hardly Turner Prize-worthy.

'It's not *just* knitting. It's a definite skill. Oh, how I wish you could see what others see. You are such a beautiful, intelligent and kind girl, who deserves recognition, success and love...' Brenda's voice trailed off and her bright button eyes pinged wide as she slapped her hand on her thigh. 'I remember what I wanted to talk about now,' she said. 'I wanted to do something about you and that young man.' Lucy's stomach tightened. 'And I have something that will help...'

With some difficulty, and refusing Lucy's help, Brenda stood up and shuffled back to the house. Lucy assumed she was having another distant moment (*what* young man?), but she returned clutching something to her chest.

'Close your eyes and put out your hand,' she instructed.

Lucy reluctantly did as she was told and felt cold metal slide into her palm.

'Sometimes we all need a little help along the way. I want you to have this because I've become incredibly fond of you, and I know you'll use it wisely. Besides, once he gets to know you, I've a feeling the pair of you will get on like a house on fire,' and she giggled to herself. 'You can open your eyes now.'

Lucy looked into her open hand. Nestled in her palm, with a chain coiled around it, was a silver locket. It was oval and had the circumference of a small egg. There were engraved flowers and swirls on the front face and it had a beautiful filigree edge.

'I can't possibly take this, Brenda, but thank you.'

'If it opens for you, I *insist* you take it. It's a very special locket and doesn't open for everyone.'

Did Brenda mean there was some trick to opening it? Or merely that it needed a good squirt of WD-40? Lucy studied it closer. On the side facing the hinges was a tiny button, so she pressed it and the locket popped open. Inside, instead of the usual space for photographs or a lock of your beloved's hair, were two silver panels. Each side was engraved with words in an ornate script. Lucy tipped the locket towards the sun, trying to make out the inscription, but Brenda knew the words by heart:

'Deserved of love, this locket finds you
Use these spells to forever bind you.'

'I don't understand,' Lucy said, looking over to her friend.

'It means that the locket finds its way to a deserving person and using the spells will help you be with your true love.'

Brenda was off again, with her mumbo jumbo.

Humouring her friend, she turned the locket over, but there were no further inscriptions. 'What spells?' Lucy asked.

'You'll see. The locket isn't ready to tell you yet, but it will. When the time is right.'

'I'm really grateful that you've entrusted this beautiful locket to me but—'

'Do you think I'm some doddery old lady who is losing her marbles, Lucy?' Brenda gave her a challenging stare.

Lucy swallowed. 'No.'

'Then take it. And do what it says. And I'm telling you, that great big scary man from next door is the one you should be aiming for.'

'George?' Lucy coughed out the word. 'He's not really my type,' she said. The locket really would have to be magic to break down his defences, but she knew deep down it was merely a pretty trinket, something Brenda was trying to persuade her was more special than it was.

'Nonsense. With a body like that, even the Queen would have trouble keeping her majesterial hands to herself. I know I struggled when I met him on the pavement yesterday. Can you imagine being enfolded in those arms? His magnificent biceps either side of your body as he pinned you to the bed? Heaven...' Her crinkled eyes scrunched up tight with the thought, and a grin spread across her face.

Despite not wanting a mental image of George pinning her to the bed, it did momentarily flash up and a little shiver pulsed through Lucy. She was clearly reading far too much Mills and Boon than was healthy.

'Well, I'm absolutely certain I'm not *his* type.' She crossed her arms.

'Double nonsense. A pretty thing like yourself. The man would need glasses not to notice you.'

'Funnily enough, he does need glasses, especially since that stray cat has been paying him uninvited visits. But, honestly, I didn't warm to him at all.'

'That's often how the best romances start. Haven't you noticed?'

'Only in films.' Lucy smiled and let her arms fall back to her sides. Of course she wanted there to be a special someone in her life – her previous special someones had turned out to be mediocre at best. And perhaps that was what was missing? A person in her life to make her feel loved and to cheerlead team Lucy as she strove her to reach her potential

– not in a motherly or neighbourly way, but in a sexy, you're all woman and the yin to my yang kind of way.

'I strongly suspect there's a great big softie under there,' Brenda said. 'I'm sensing a reason for his odd behaviour. He's had a great deal of unhappiness in his life.' She scrutinised her young friend for a moment, as if mulling something over in her mind. 'There's something else you need to know about this locket; the wearer will be imbued with an inner confidence. It won't make you do unsuitable things, like run naked across the cricket pitch at Lord's during a test match, but it will enable you to project a confidence that you wouldn't otherwise have. You'll notice, as I did, how much bolder you feel when you have it around your neck.'

'But—'

Brenda put out a thin hand to silence Lucy. 'Think of it like this: it's enabling a side of you that already exists to come to the fore. I thought about passing this on to you many times, but I feel the time is finally right. Let the locket boost your confidence at work and treat it like training wheels. It won't be long before you're free-wheeling.'

As Lucy put the chain over her head, a warm sensation flooded her body. She dismissed the notion it was anything to do with the locket, satisfied that it was merely the glow you experience when a dear friend shows their love and concern. She would wear it to please her friend, but it would be tucked somewhere for safekeeping the moment she got back to the flat.

Brenda wandered over to a pot of mint and nipped off the top few leaves, crushing them in her fingers and bringing them up to her nose. Her eyes seemed to lose focus and she looked rather lost for a moment. A blackbird swooped over the wall in front of her. She blinked and shook her head.

30

'Do you have time for another cup before you have to see to the horses?' she asked, looking over to Lucy.

It was about the third time in recent weeks Brenda momentarily thought she was talking to her long-dead sister-in-law – a keen horsewoman, with a small stable yard attached to her property, and a great friend to Brenda in years gone by.

'I work at Tompkins, remember? Jess got me the job after all those redundancies at the council last year.'

'Oh yes, silly me.' The old lady's face scrunched up and then she plastered her usual bright smile back under her anxious eyes, as she bent forward to pull up some faded blooms.

'So sad these flowers have gone over,' she said. 'The pretty blue, with the startling yellow centre. They always were favourites of mine. Oh, why can't I remember what they're called?'

Lucy looked at the abandoned brown stems of the once glorious forget-me-nots, as Brenda fiddled with the end of her thin plait, muttered to herself, and shuffled down the flagstone path to her back door.

Chapter 5

Richard Tompkins, a silver-haired, quietly spoken man, waited for absolute silence before his low, throaty rumble commanded complete attention.

'As you all know, Vernon retires on Friday, having been with the company for nearly thirty years, so make sure you all take the time to sign the card that's going around. Pat has kindly taken the reins with regard to his leaving party and has organised a buffet at the The King's Arms by the waterfront on Friday evening.' Pat's cheeks flushed as she looked at her feet and shuffled the wheels of her office chair slightly backwards. 'Please make an effort to attend, especially as the company will be providing a case of wine to get the party started.' A ripple of surprise ran through the office and a few people decided they might tip out for poor old Vern after all. 'I can also confirm that our replacement general manager, Sam Mulligan, will start first thing Monday. Sam has a solid background in the retail toy market and has been contracted specifically to give the company a bit of a shake-up. I am fully aware we are lagging behind the times and we need to embrace the twenty-first century. Changes and economies are likely.'

'Is that code for redundancies?' someone asked from the back.

Lucy's heartbeat quickened and she stared hard at her sensible shoes. Surely she couldn't be unlucky enough to be made redundant twice?

'I won't lie to you, it's a possibility. She successfully reversed the fortunes of the failing Toy Box chain, but she had to cut out a lot of dead wood. As you know, it's now one of the leading online retailers in the country.'

'She?' repeated an incredulous Adam. Lucy also lifted her eyes in surprise.

'I'm not sure Sam Mulligan's gender should have any bearing on the matter, because I can assure you it will make no difference to her competence. Or is it that you have a problem working for a woman, Adam?' asked Richard.

'No, no, of course not. I just assumed...'

'Never assume,' said Mr Tompkins. 'Right, I have some phone calls to make. Thank you all for your time.'

Lucy's heart gave a little skip. A female boss. All the managers at Tompkins were currently male and had been so since time immemorial. But then it was a traditional firm. It was only five years ago the sales team had stopped posting hand-written order forms down a huge drainpipe for the warehouse team to pick. A shake-up was certainly needed and she was excited to think a woman would be responsible for it, as long as Lucy wasn't part of the dead wood Mr Tompkins had alluded to.

As Richard left the office, there was hushed discussion.

'Dearie me, not looking good for you, Lucy-Lou. Last in, first out,' Adam said, stroking his chin and finding a small patch of whiskers missed by his razor that morning.

'She wasn't last in,' said Jess, putting her hand on Lucy's knee. 'There are warehouse staff who only started at Christmas.

Lucy's been here a year. And she's bloody fantastic. This new manager would be a fool to lose her.'

Lucy smiled at her friend but coloured at the attention.

'Out of my hands, I'm afraid,' said Adam, adjusting his cuffs and brushing imaginary fluff from his tie. 'Back to work now, team. Our customers need us like books need worms. Accounts back downstairs please. The phones are calling.'

'Someone needs to tell him his expressions are rubbish,' whispered Jess.

'Don't you dare spoil our fun.' Connor leaned forward, poking his head between Jess and Lucy. 'I'm compiling a book of them. We need some entertainment to get us through the day.'

An afternoon of customers chasing late deliveries and grumbles from the warehouse went by quickly, but Lucy wasn't as focused as usual. The meeting had unsettled her. Jess's job was safe as there were only three of them in accounts and they were always overworked. But this new manager might decide to make economies in the sales office, as there were often times when Adam paced the floor liked a caged, novelty-sock-wearing lion. If he wasn't always fully occupied it meant they were overstaffed and Lucy suspected the disorganised girl with the messy desk might not make the final cut.

After an unsettled week at work, with everyone trying their best to ignore the redundancy-shaped elephant in the room, the last thing Lucy felt like doing that evening was attending Vernon's retirement party. As she wrapped her sausage sandwiches in foil and grabbed a yoghurt from the fridge, she saw the skinny black streak of cat leap up onto Brenda's fence. Not having seen it since that night at George's, she'd assumed it had moved on to pastures new, but if it was still hanging about, then it was still homeless, and this was something she had to address.

Checking she had ten minutes to spare, Lucy rang the rescue centre for advice, hoping to catch someone in their office. The plight of the cat, with its kamikaze-esque homing device, was weighing on her mind. She was in luck. The cheery gentleman on the end of the phone offered to come out to the neighbourhood and look for the cat later that morning as he had a home check in the area.

'We can bring the little fella in and scan him for a microchip, but in ninety per cent of cases, these are ferals. I find they make the best pets anyway – ferals. Don't have the expectations of the domestic. Lovely animals if you take the time to gain their trust. Another black one though, poor little sod might have a long wait for a forever home.'

There was an inaudible twang as one of her heartstrings was plucked.

'You might like to try having a poke around number twenty-four,' Lucy suggested. 'The owner will be at work, but the cat seems to head for him every time.'

Knowing it was less welcome than a ravenous fox in a hen coop full of fat chickens, she could only assume the cat was a reincarnated former acquaintance of George's who had come back to exact some form of twisted, allergy-related revenge.

The King's Arms public house sat beside the River Douse as it wound its playful course around Renborough town centre and out into the countryside. In the summer, the large riverside beer garden was a major attraction. In winter, an open fire proved equally appealing. Whatever the season, the view across the river was stunning and, even in inclement weather, large windows offered the same impressive view, albeit from behind the glass. It was always bustling with people and the evening of Vernon's retirement party was no exception.

Pat, in her whispered and unobtrusive way, had been pushing for all company employees to come dressed as children's toys or characters. Tompkins was, after all, a toy wholesaler. People responded with varying degrees of enthusiasm. Vernon had merely donned a Mr Men tie, while others had taken the trouble to cobble together home-made costumes of superheroes or characters from nursery rhymes. Jess was a particularly adult Little Red Riding Hood, complete with a black laced bodice and strangely erotic white, thigh-high stockings. Lucy was a vague approximation of Tom Baker's Doctor Who but was relying totally on her accurate facsimile of his trademark scarf for identification. And one of the men from the warehouse had hired an expensive Buzz Lightyear costume. He spent a lot of the evening waving his laser gun in people's faces and Connor threatened several times to send *him* to infinity and beyond if he didn't pack it in.

Adam had come as Chucky.

'So, I'd like to end with a toast for old Vern,' Adam said, his fake scars already having petrified a small boy who'd accidentally wandered into the function room looking for the toilets. 'A man of few words, and even fewer talents. Ha ha. So, ladies, gentlemen and Pat – only kidding there, Pat-a-Cake...' Pat's head sank even further into the hood of her teddy bear onesie. 'If you would kindly raise your glasses to Vern.'

'To Vern!' Everyone stood to toast the man who had given the company the best years of his life but had only been given a stomach ulcer and a novelty clock in return. (Adam had persuaded a local toy manufacturer to make a bespoke Magic Roundabout clock, as Vern had a soft spot for that particular children's programme.)

'God bless him and all who sail in him,' Adam continued, still waving his glass about. 'And as we're on the subject of ships, have you heard the one about the old sailor and the prostitute? He put on his uniform—'

'Thank you, Adam.' Richard Tompkins stood up. 'Your fifteen-minute toast was most eloquent but perhaps we should let Vernon take the floor?'

Vernon spoke for less than a minute and then returned to his seat – his verbal brevity one of the reasons for his popularity. He looked quite moved by the clock and kept stroking Florence and Dougal when he thought no one was looking, but Lucy noticed. It had been a thoughtful idea of Adam's. He did have them occasionally.

Now that the formal presentation was over, people lined up to pile their tiny white tea plates ridiculously high with assorted buffet food. The pub had done a lovely spread and Pat had been in earlier to hang Happy Retirement bunting and scatter silver helium balloons.

'I see Mr Tompkins has brought a hot date along,' said Sonjit to a table of female colleagues.

'She's not all that,' huffed Jess, whom Lucy suspected had a tiny sugar-daddy-type crush on their boss.

'I think this one's a keeper,' Sonjit continued. 'Apparently, he took her to Belgium over Easter, when he went on that extended business trip. She's very glamorous – quite the trophy girlfriend.'

'Aww, that's lovely,' Lucy said. 'Everyone deserves to find love. He's been single for years.'

She craned forward to assess the lady concerned, but her view was largely obscured by a nervous Pat, bobbing about in front of the couple, waving platters of smoked salmon vol-au-vents and vegetarian sausage rolls.

'Hrmph,' Jess muttered. 'I spoke to her in the ladies' earlier and she was rather too gushy about it all for my liking. All lipstick and liposuction. She's after his money. I know the type...'

After a small glass of Prosecco and a wobbly feeling in her knees, Lucy tucked herself in the corner to sip lime and sodas as everyone mingled around her. She loosened her scarf and wafted it in front of her face to cool down. Jess was near the bar, throwing her head back and laughing as though she was with the funniest man this side of the Watford Gap, even though it was only the young lad who drove one of the forklifts. Moments later, collecting her third large glass of wine, she glanced across at Lucy and beckoned her over, but Lucy shook her head, content to be tucked away from the hordes.

'Lucy? All alone? Room for a little one? Budge up, budge up.' Adam was clutching a bottle of house red by the neck and tried to add a measure to Lucy's empty tumbler.

'Not for me.' She tried to cover the top of her glass but wine dribbled over her fingers.

'Come on. You don't have to play Miss Goody Two-Shoes with me. We're not at work now. What happens in the pub, stays in the pub. You know me? Well, not in the biblical sense, but there's still time. Ha ha.'

Lucy briefly closed her eyes but unfortunately he was still there when she opened them.

'I don't like to talk shippety-shop on a night out, but well done for sorting those problems earlier in the week. Deftly done. I'll make sure I big you up to Sam-the-Man on Monday.'

'Except, of course, she's a woman.'

'Yes, yes. You don't need to take me so *literary*.'

Lucy cast a desperate glance across the room at Jess and wished she'd thought to put the locket on, to give her the nerve to tell Adam where to stick his problems, if nothing else – not that she believed it possessed special powers but at that desperate moment, it would have been worth a try.

'So, anyway,' Adam said, leaning in closer. 'There was this old sailor who visited a prostitute...'

Chapter 6

Sunday evening, as Lucy cut out a crescent shape from thick cardboard to support the blade of Poldark's scythe, there was an impatient rapping at her front door. She reached for the remote and turned down the sound on the Create and Craft channel, abandoning her project temporarily.

Several years ago she'd knitted a two-foot-high Harry Hill on a whim, and it was shown on his *TV Burp*. Encouraged by her best friend Jess, she'd been producing knitted celebrities ever since. Not many people could boast Ed Sheeran, Harry Potter *and* Wolverine on their sofa. Currently mid-Poldark (a bare chest, tricorn hat and scythe), she rather thought he might end up on her bed.

She opened the door to a sulky-faced George – heavy-framed glasses magnifying his puffy eyes. Lucy was surprised how much they suited him. Clark Kent George wasn't as intimidating as Superman George.

'The scrat-bag is back.' There was no hello, or how are you.

'Scrat-bag?'

'The cat-thing.'

'The adorable, homeless, half-starved cat?'

'No, the bag of fleas that insists on wedging its scrappy backside up between my washing appliances and smells like a dead badger.' Was that a microscopic twinkle in his eye or had she imagined it?

'Would you like me to come and remove it?' Why he felt she was his personal cat-catcher was beyond her.

'I'm hardly popping by for tea and cake.' He noticed her nostrils flare and softened his tone. 'It must have slipped in between my legs this morning as I was leaving for work. I thought I saw something but I wasn't sure and didn't have time to investigate. Forgot all about it. Came back tonight, after a particularly long day up at the NEC, flicked on the TV, fell asleep and woke up with it nestled in my lap.'

'Hence the eyes?' she asked, thinking a dozy George with a bony cat nestled in his lap was an adorable image.

'Hence the eyes. And these damn glasses are causing me all sorts of problems, not least because I keep misplacing them.' He wiggled them Eric Morecambe style and left them balanced wonkily across his nose. Although there was still no smile, Lucy was beginning to suspect he had a Jack Dee approach to humour where a straight face was all part of the act. Both his eyebrows shot up as though he was waiting for an answer to the question he hadn't actually asked. The glasses slipped back into place.

'I'll come over, but I *really* can't take it in again.'

'I'm not asking you to take it in. I'm asking you to get it out. Look.' He tipped his head to one side, as if that would make him seem more reasonable. 'I've had a long day. Eight hours talking about cardboard boxes and printing machines, and a two-hour drive each way. I want to walk into my utility room and be able to breathe. If you can't take it, perhaps you could palm it off on the old lady between us?'

'Um, no, I don't think she's—'

'Well, whatever, *Lisa*, could you get it out of my house before my eyes swell up so much I can't see to put one foot in front of the other?'

'Okay, but this is the last time.'

She waited for a thank you but was disappointed.

And it's Lucy, not Lisa, she added silently.

Monday morning and Lucy was ready for work with a full half an hour to spare. She'd slept badly, having spent two hours worrying about the new general manager and the possible consequences of the planned company shake-up. For most of the night she rolled restlessly around the bed, tangling her legs in a knot of sheets and her mind in a knot of worries. But by the time the milk float rattled its way down Lancaster Road and daylight punctured the bedroom in long, thin shafts, Lucy decided the changes at work were the kick she needed. *New boss – new me*, she reasoned.

Brenda was right, it was a matter of confidence, but she didn't need a bit of fancy jewellery to bring it to the fore. She enjoyed working at Tompkins more than she could have imagined when she first started and, somewhere in the back of her mind, her mother's birthday waved its immaculately manicured hand and gave her a determination to embrace the new and not look back.

Sam Mulligan was a petite thirty-something woman with short, cropped black hair, power-dressed to maim, kill and take no prisoners. Her no-nonsense approach meant smiles were harder to come by than tickets for a Beyoncé concert. The contrast of her black tailored suit with the bright red of her glasses, matching manicured fingernails and glossy scarlet lipstick reminded Lucy of a black widow spider. It was an image she couldn't get out of her head for the rest of the day and one that seriously hindered her plan to be more confident around the new boss.

Richard Tompkins gathered most of the staff upstairs to formally introduce Sam and then retreated to his glass-fronted office to conceal his golf clubs in the corner cupboard and shuffle papers. The set of poseable Marvel superheroes that usually graced the back bookshelf in unfeasible sexual positions had also been evicted before the arrival of the new manager, Lucy noticed.

Sam took the opportunity to set out some ground rules.

'I'm not Vernon and I work differently, so there will be changes. For a start, I am moving my desk into the sales office, at least to begin with. I want to be in the thick of it with you, not tucked away behind a glass door and only sought out when there is a problem.'

Anxious glances were exchanged and Adam tugged at his tie as though he needed more air. Vernon had been a hands-off manager who trusted his team to get on with things. Now it seemed the office supervisor was going to be supervised.

'Before I begin to tinker with the engine, I need to see how this machine is running. Then I can establish which components are squeaky and need oiling, and which are beyond repair. I plan to spend some time in all the departments, including the warehouse and a couple of days on the road with the delivery drivers and the reps, so I can get to know this company inside and out.'

Suddenly Adam wasn't the only one fiddling with his clothing.

'I want you to carry on with your jobs as if I'm not there.

I can assure you no major changes will be implemented until I've apprised myself of the current running of the company.' She paused and smiled. 'Talk to me, I'm here to get the best from you all and ensure Tompkins Toy Wholesaler becomes the leading supplier of toys and games in this region. I would prefer if people called me Sam. There's no need for formality. I consider input from the staff essential if we are to work efficiently as a team. Don't be afraid to speak up as I come from a retail background so there are a lot of areas within distribution that are new to me. Right, let's streamline this machine and see if we can't turn it into a Formula One winner.'

Adam began an enthusiastic clap but stopped when he realised he was giving a solo performance.

'Well said, Sam.' He flashed her a smile and gave her a conspiratorial wink, as though she was his best buddy. 'And I, in turn, would like to say a few words and welcome you to our little family, because I think of my team as family. You'll find I run a tight ship, but it's full of happy sailors and...'

'I swear, if he wheels that joke out again...' muttered Connor.

'Thank you for the welcome, Adam, but I think we need to press on.'

'Absolutely, *mon capitan*.' The smile remained on his lips but had fallen from his eyes.

'That said, if you would come with me?' and she motioned for him to follow.

Moments later they were heaving the dated, solid pine desk out from her office and setting it up in the corner of the sales office.

Absent-mindedly counting the agate beads on her bracelet

through her fingers, Lucy tried to concentrate on the order she was processing, but she felt hot and her left foot was repeatedly bouncing up and down over her right. According to Brenda, agate was a stone of strength, courage and calm. As her fingers worked their way frantically around the bracelet, she remained unconvinced.

'Thank you, Adam. Now I can start to assess the company from the ground up.' Sam settled into her chair, pulled out an A4 notepad and, occasionally glancing around the sales team, she made copious notes. Everyone, including Adam, was head down and focused.

She's good, thought Lucy. *I don't stand a chance.*

Exhausted, Lucy threw her keys on the coffee table and collapsed into her squishy armchair. It had been a long day. She kicked off her shoes and they landed at odd angles across her stripy fireside rug. Leaning back, she stretched her arms up to the ceiling and yawned. For a moment she was painfully aware of the silence. There was no one to ask how her day had been or to make her a much-needed cup of tea.

As she stared at nothing and wished she had at least a cat of her own to come home to, the locket caught her eye. It was next to her keys on the low coffee table where she'd abandoned it, slightly concerned her unpleasant neighbour might rugby-tackle her to the ground and proclaim undying love if she wore it. It sat in a shaft of early evening sun, catching the light and reflecting a beam back at her.

'What's so special about you then?' she asked the locket as she fingered the delicate filigree edge and let the chain run through her fingers. It felt warmer to the touch than metal should – almost glowing. Flipping it open, she squinted at the ornate, tiddly writing, and angled it towards the light to get a closer look. That couldn't be right...

Although she had only been half-focusing when Brenda recited the words, she was pretty certain the inscription in the locket had changed.

Chapter 7

'Come in, come in,' Brenda chirped when she saw Lucy at the door. 'Tea? I still have some of the valerian and chamomile and I'm sensing you might need it. There's some fruit cake in the tin as well.'

While many of Brenda's visitors were in and out before you could say, 'thank you for the package', Lucy enjoyed stopping by for the unusually flavoured teas that came from sweetshop-sized glass jars, with faded labels proclaiming Aphrodite's Blend and Shaman's Brew in a spidery hand. She loved listening to tales of Brenda's unorthodox life; from being on the road in the Sixties with her late husband's band, to her passion for all things natural and home-made. It was a two-way friendship that their different backgrounds and more than fifty-year age gap only enhanced.

'Tea would be lovely.'

She followed Brenda into the exotic-smelling kitchen, hooking her bag over the back of a rush-seated chair tucked under the central table. The gift she'd ordered for her dear friend had arrived that morning and the brown padded envelope containing it was poking out the top. Walking over to the large, old-fashioned gas stove, she peered into the aluminium saucepan bubbling away merrily and offered to stir the colourful contents.

'Only if it's anticlockwise and not more than three times,' said Brenda.

Lucy did as she was told, first glancing at the kitchen clock to work out the direction of her stir.

Smiling to herself, Brenda arranged the colourful fine bone-china cups and saucers on a tea tray. Lucy finished stirring and returned the wooden spoon back to the spoon rest. She looked over for reassurance that she'd done everything correctly.

'I was teasing, you ninny,' Brenda said. 'How can it possibly matter which direction you stir a pot? I worry about you sometimes. Mind you, I worry about me sometimes...'

Lucy blushed and offered to carry the tray into the living room. Brenda shuffled in behind her with the cake tin and collapsed onto the sofa with a weary sigh, straightening a cream lace antimacassar as she did so.

Lucy slid into her favourite chair. It had wooden arms and a straight back, which should have made it uncomfortable, but it was a chair that Lucy often found herself reluctant to leave. Brenda was choosy about who sat it in, but it was always offered to her.

'You're certain this chair hasn't got a hidden heated panel?' she asked for the umpteenth time. 'I swear it heats up as soon as I sit in it.'

Brenda smiled. 'No, it's just a kindly, old chair who looks after people it likes,' and she placed the tin on the table. 'So, tell me what has been happening.'

Lucy slipped the locket from her bag, flipped the catch and showed Brenda the inscription.

'Take a beeswax candle, carve true love's name
Sit through full moon 'til end of flame.'

'When you handed it to me last week, I thought you were reading out the inscription. Didn't the locket say something about finding me and binding me to my true love?'

Brenda chuckled and picked up her cup and saucer. 'Oh, how I love this bit. So exciting,' she said, avoiding Lucy's question. 'You must follow the instructions to the letter to guarantee success.'

'Did you swap the locket over when I was asleep?' Lucy asked, clutching at wispy straws.

'Do I look capable of standing on a garden bench and feeding myself through a tiny top bathroom window?'

'Knowing you, I shouldn't be surprised if you had the ability to walk through the exterior wall.'

'Well, I didn't do either, cheeky madam.'

Brenda's words reassured Lucy she'd completely misunderstood, but she still wasn't happy that her elderly friend wanted her to undertake a ridiculous ritual to attract a man. It was no better than the girls at school playing around with a Ouija board. She knew Fiona Carter had deliberately manipulated the glass to get some boy's name to come up, because she admitted as such several years later. It was all silly nonsense undertaken to amuse bored minds.

'I'm really grateful you've entrusted the locket to me, but I want to sort my life out by myself. I'm perfectly capable of attracting a boyfriend without your dodgy jewellery, and I love my job and the people I work with. I realise I have to stand up for myself a bit more, but it's still a challenging and fun environment, and one I want to succeed in. All the accessories and all the colours...'

'Ah, colours, how they light up this grey world of ours. The grey never truly goes away, I'm afraid. We must try to mask it with our kaleidoscopic clothes and colourful smiles.' Brenda stirred the fragrant tea she still hadn't sipped, whilst Lucy looked down at her beige long-sleeved top and plain navy blue skirt.

'Exactly. And since my mother has decided to hold this stupid party in September, with a guest list to rival a royal wedding, I'm going to make her proud of me by knuckling down and being more organised at work. I might even consider Mr Sneezy-pants as my plus-one for my mother's do, if he starts to behave,' joked Lucy.

Brenda put her tea down and pushed the saucer away as though it was finished. 'Excellent decision, if I may say so.'

'But I'm going to do it without any of your hocus-pocus.'

'Now you listen to me, young lady. There's not a spell in the world that can go against the natural order of things. They can help bring out what is already there and calm muddied waters, but it makes me cross when people believe all this Harry Potter nonsense. If there were invisibility cloaks and levitating spells, trust me, I'd be using them.'

Hmm... thought Lucy, *flowers don't naturally turn away from the sun and face the house of a mysterious old lady*, but she kept the thought to herself. It had always unnerved her how the birds all seemed to congregate on Brenda's ridge tiles and how everything in the old lady's garden grew taller, faster and stronger than anywhere else. If George thought she was a Dr Doolittle, he'd be staggered at Brenda's affinity with the natural world.

Feeling in need of cake, Lucy leaned forward and prised opened the cake tin, only to find a selection of pencils and a wrinkled carrot inside. Not wanting to embarrass her friend, she slipped it down the side of the chair and changed the subject, relaying the tale of removing the unwanted cat from George's house.

'He's a funny one. Can't make him out,' said Brenda.

'I think he's rude.' Lucy thought about his monosyllabic sentences and offhand demeanour.

'No, that's not it. So many shades of yellow. Look in his eyes. There's a tale there, to be sure.'

'Yes, he's allergic to cats.' She knew she was being flippant, but George Aberdour didn't bring out her charitable side.

Brenda patted Lucy's arm with her fragile hand, and she noticed the transparent skin and pale liver spots. Was Brenda eating properly? Or was it all part of getting older: losing weight and becoming more forgetful? It was difficult when you saw someone regularly, but she was sure her friend was beginning to look more gaunt. There were times Brenda seemed momentarily unaware of what was going on around her and it was beginning to worry Lucy. Her glorious, technicolour friend had tiny flickers of grey, almost invisible to the casual observer.

'Well, I certainly wouldn't kick him out of bed. In fact, I'd be tempted to tie him to it. If I was twenty years younger, I'd be knocking on his door asking to borrow a cup of sugar. Probably in a silky negligee.'

'Only twenty? You'd still be nearly sixty.'

'I'll have you know I hit my sexual peak in my early sixties. That's probably what did for Jim. Oh, pop your eyes back in your head, child. I'm only joking. The athletic sex probably gave him an extra five years. I can still touch my toes, you know?'

Lucy envied her friend's wild tales, thinking she'd have nothing more to tell her own grandchildren other than she'd helped to knit the world's longest scarf for charity.

As she collected her bag from the kitchen later, Lucy remembered the parcel and handed it to Brenda.

'I've got you a present – a book by Elliott Landy, the famous photographer. It's a collection of his work focusing on the rock music scene in the Sixties and contains some unseen prints. Jim's in there. I checked.'

'How wonderful.' Brenda slid the book from the envelope and clutched it as if she'd been given the moon.

Lucy shrugged. 'I saw it online and knew you'd appreciate it. It's just a little something to let you know I was thinking of you.'

'But, my dear,' Brenda said, reaching for her hand, 'sometimes a little something can mean *everything*.' And a happy tear trickled down her cheek.

'What a lovely sentiment,' said Lucy, and she watched Brenda begin to scan the pages for photographs of precious memories.

Lucy's mum rang that evening, as she did every Monday, Wednesday and Friday, at exactly seven o'clock.

'Hello, darling. How are things since we popped by? I've hardly seen your father since he bought that bit for the silly old car. Straight home and in the garage without so much as

52

a by-your-leave. Mind you, he's been generally uncommunicative since I put him on that strict diet, but I refuse to buy him a new suit for September until he's shifted some of that weight. I don't want people thinking he's letting himself go. I'm so glad we booked the venue when we did. I would have hated to settle for somewhere not quite so prestigious, and Mortlake Hall is *very* prestigious. It was used for that BBC period drama last year. Emily told me. And talking of your sister, she rang with simply *marvellous* news. Has she rung you yet?' Her mother paused for breath.

'You know we don't call each other much. Facebook and text messages generally keep us in touch.' Once Emily became a mother, the long chatter-filled phone calls the sisters used to share were replaced with less immediate forms of communication. By the time Lucy was home from work, Emily was up to her elbows in the bedtime routine, and when Emily was free, Lucy was with Brenda, at Knit and Natter, or leafleting for some community event – always keen to help out as long as it didn't involve drawing unnecessary attention to herself. Facebook messages were the perfect compromise.

'I'm sure she won't mind me telling you – she's expecting again. I do hope it will be a boy this time. I know Stuart would like a son, as much as he loves the girls.' And another generous handful of sprinkles fell from the ether onto Emily's cupcake of life.

'That's fantastic news. I'll give her a ring.'

It was exciting to think another gorgeous, pink, talcum-powder-scented being would soon exist. Lucy adored her nieces to distraction, especially the tiny baby phase when they fell asleep across you in an instant, trusting and content. A doll-sized hand gripping your finger tightly as a tiny baby-grow-covered chest rose and fell in the slow rhythm of sleep. But she also enjoyed the challenges that came with vocabulary and attitude. She must visit them all again soon. It had been far too long.

'Perhaps send her a little congratulations card, darling. I doubt she'll have time to chat, what with the girls and the pressures of work.' Emily had fallen straight into a retail management job from university and continued to scale the career ladder, giving birth to two children merely a small hiatus on her ever-upward climb. At thirty, she was now troubleshooting for WHSmith and their mother refused to patronise any other stationer or bookseller to demonstrate her support, convinced her eldest daughter would be running the company within five years. 'I hear she's working on a failing store down in London. It's probably all due to the multicultural workforce, but she'll soon pull it round. She's been working such long hours recently that I suspect there's another promotion in the offing. You've got to admire a woman who is that career-driven yet still finds time to be such a *marvellous* mother to her little girls.'

'Mmm...' Lucy's words got caught in her throat.

'The baby is due in November and I must admit I was secretly relieved it wasn't any earlier. It would be terribly inconvenient if she'd been due around my birthday because I have great plans for Emily to give a speech. I felt it was appropriate, what with her being my eldest child and everything.'

Lucy knew it was nothing to do with age but everything to do with Emily's superior speech-making abilities, and was thankful her mother hadn't asked her to perform a similar duty.

'I should think that will be their family complete then, unless it's another girl. You need to hurry up, young lady, or they won't have any cousins of the same age. And if you do the whole baby thing with Emily, she can guide you through. She's a natural. You only have to look at the girls to see how bright and well adjusted they are. And you can keep up your hobbies; maybe knit some little cardigans or something?'

Lucy was not an academic child, much to the despair of her mother, but Sandra did at least acknowledge Lucy's creative flair, actively steering her away from the messier crafts as a child and encouraging her knitting, purely on the basis that it didn't leave sticky patches everywhere or stain the tablecloth.

'Mmm...' Lucy mumbled again and got through the remainder of the call by making encouraging noises in the appropriate places.

Her mother updated her with every possible detail about the fiftieth party and she was reminded it would be terribly helpful if she sorted her outfit sooner rather than later so any unfortunate close family colour clashes could be avoided.

Lucy put the phone down knowing that she was loved, but possibly not understood.

Chapter 8

The next morning, Lucy ambled into her living room and heaved back the faded green velvet curtains, determined to embrace a bolder version of herself. Standing in the middle of Lancaster Road, wearing not much and holding the battered, floral-patterned cake tin, was Brenda.

Seeing the movement of swishing curtains from the corner of her eye, the old lady looked across to the window but registered no recognition. Almost looking through Lucy, she returned her gaze to the tin and shook her head as if she was trying to focus.

It was then that Lucy noticed the rain – a drizzly mist, not proper splashy raindrops, but enough to get a scantily clad old lady wet and cold, even in May. A creeping panic swept through her body. It was the first real and frightening embodiment of her recent fears concerning her neighbour. Not pausing for thought, or to even change out of her pyjamas, Lucy dashed to the front door, but Brenda was already scuttling towards the junction with Tudor Avenue.

Dashing past number twenty-four, Lucy paused as she noticed George's incredulous face peering out the window. He stared at his pyjama-clad neighbour, bouncing around on the pavement in front of his house, gesturing something at him.

The next moment she was banging at his door, hoping to enlist him on her search and rescue mission.

'Brenda's gone walkabout and she's dressed completely inappropriately,' she blurted out.

'Unlike your good self.'

'Seriously, she's in a thin, cotton nightie. She's seventy-nine. Please help.' She swallowed back a sob. Her priority was finding her friend.

The mocking eyebrow dropped and he nodded, noticing her genuine distress.

'Of course.' He grabbed his keys and mobile from the otherwise empty side table next to his front door.

They eventually caught up with Brenda near the postbox at the bottom of the avenue. Lucy reached out for her friend's shoulder and made eye contact.

'Brenda? It's me. Lucy.' She gently took her neighbour's hand in her own. It felt cold, and the drizzle was now turning to heavy rain.

'Jim forgot his lunch again. I have to get to the school and give it to him...' Brenda's eyes were frantic.

'It's okay. Let's get you in the warm and I'll deliver it for you.' The way the old lady's eyes narrowed as she looked into Lucy's face broke her heart, as she realised there was no sign of recognition. She bit back tears and forced out a gentle smile.

Brenda started to shake with the cold, so Lucy put an arm around her and rubbed her bare shoulders to try and warm her up. George, who was only a couple of paces behind them, started to pull his smart, grey V-neck jumper over his head, but as he did so, his shirt untucked itself and rode up his body with the jumper.

Lucy stood motionless for a fraction of a second and tried

hard not to focus on the narrow trail of dark hairs that disappeared into the waistband of his navy blue suit trousers. And she *totally* failed not to gape at the muscle definition across his abdomen. There was an almost imperceptible flash of nipple as the shirt slid back down his body.

'Put this over her.'

Lucy snapped her mouth shut and wriggled the jumper over a protesting Brenda. Between them they cajoled and coerced her back up the street and through the front door. Lucy collected a towel from the downstairs cloakroom and patted her down, aware of a strong smell of wee now they were inside. The orange and purple patchwork blanket Lucy knitted two Christmases ago was draped over the back of the upholstered wing chair, so she wrapped it around the shivering lady and finally caught Brenda's eye. A trembling hand reached out and gripped her own, squeezing it for reassurance. Lucy squeezed back.

'Everything's okay, Brenda,' she said. 'We're home. We're safe. There's nothing for you to worry about.'

A hovering George beckoned her into the hall, as Lucy felt more treacherous tears building. He studied her face for a second and then briefly reached out to touch her shoulder. At a moment when she felt everything was collapsing, it gave her the strength to pull herself together. His hand dropped back to his side.

'I don't want to interfere, but I think she needs to be seen by someone as a matter of urgency.'

'I agree. I'll try the surgery. Could you grab my mobile from my kitchen table? I don't want to leave her. My front door isn't locked.'

George nodded and returned with her phone two minutes

later, handing it over just as his own started to buzz. He turned away to answer it.

'No, I hadn't forgotten... Has he? Oh, for goodness' sake... I'll have to sort it then...' George covered the phone with his hand. 'I need to go.'

'I can manage. She's much calmer now. Honestly. It's fine.' Brenda looked tired, her thin fingers stroking the blanket, and her eyes closing.

'Give me a contact number. I'll ring later to see how she is, but there's an emergency at work.'

She gave him her mobile number. 'Thanks for your help. I wouldn't want you getting into trouble with the boss.'

'Yeah, bit of an ogre.' He put the phone back to his face. 'With you in ten,' he said, then slid it back into his trouser pocket. 'Bye then, Grandma,' he said to Lucy.

Lucy followed his eyes and remembered she was wearing her Keep Calm and Carry on Knitting pyjamas.

'Russell Crowe knits,' she said, indignantly.

'Oh, you mean you actually *do* knit? I thought the pyjamas were ironic, or a gift, or something.'

'It's a very therapeutic pastime.'

'Yeah, if you're about ninety.' He ran his hand through his thick brown hair, ruffling it up without realising. Brenda watched him from the living room and smiled. She looked at Lucy, who was sporting a cross face, and smiled even more. Then she clasped her hands together and let out a happy sigh.

'The cat?' Brenda called out to George. Lucy couldn't work out if it was a question or a reminder. Or even if she knew who George was.

'Oh yes. Did the rescue centre find it? They said—' Lucy began.

'It's all in hand.' He nodded at Brenda to signal his departure and the front door clicked shut. There was a pause and the old lady noticed the battered tin by her feet. Bending forward, she prised open the lid enough to see the contents. Lucy waited for her to comment but she didn't.

'A cup of tea will warm us both up,' Lucy finally said. 'I'll nip upstairs and get you some more suitable clothes, if that's okay?'

Brenda nodded slowly, although Lucy wasn't convinced she understood what she was agreeing to.

'You stay there under that snuggly blanket and keep warm.' She tucked the sides around her friend to keep it from falling. 'I won't be long. Just need to make a quick call.'

'Use the phone in the hall, dear. Mind the flex though. It's dreadfully frayed. Jim will keep playing with it and putting his fingers through the fabric, but he says we can't afford a replacement, and it still does the job.' Her eyes looked glazed but she suddenly became aware of the blanket on her knees again and started to pick at the threads.

Lucy's heart heaved, but she pulled herself together and went into the hall. Brenda's phone was quite a modern walkabout one and the base unit was in the kitchen, not the hall, but the number to the surgery was on her mobile contact list so she used that.

Lucy explained the situation to the receptionist, trying to keep her voice low so she didn't alarm Brenda, who was now singing 'The House of the Rising Sun' quietly to herself. Establishing Brenda was calm and safe and that Lucy could stay with her for as long as necessary, the helpful lady asked her to hold and said she would see if she could catch Dr Hopgood before he started surgery. Lucy popped her head around the living-room door whilst she waited. Brenda looked drowsy and her singing had slowed to a mumble. The surgery hold music stopped and the phone line clicked.

'Given everything you said, including the possibility your neighbour is currently incontinent, Dr Hopgood suspects some sort of urine infection. They can lead to spells of delirium in the elderly and are quite common. He's put her down as a priority house call and she'll be first on the list. If you are happy to stay with her, he'll be out to you just after twelve.'

'That's not a problem, thank you.' Although Lucy was starting to suspect there was more to this than a simple UTI.

'He also suggested getting some fluids into her, as UTIs tend to go hand in hand with dehydration. See if you can get her to drink some water, or even some tea.'

After hanging up, Lucy tried the office, but the out-of-hours answerphone was still on. Because recording messages made her feel self-conscious, she decided to wait until the phones were manned and explain the situation properly.

When she returned to the living room, Brenda was asleep, so Lucy took the opportunity to run up the first flight of stairs and find her friend some clean clothes. Even though she'd been up to the third floor on numerous occasions, she hadn't been in the master bedroom before. Like the rest of the house it was cluttered but in a welcoming, lived-in way. The imposing mahogany wardrobe stood with one door open, and a rainbow of clothes hung on old-fashioned padded hangers. There was a thick brown and orange geometric rug on the floor next to the bed and the room had a strong lavender smell. Like all the other rooms in the house, this one also held a noisy clock, its steady ticking adding to her feeling of unease. She grabbed a pair of wide-legged cotton trousers and a red loose-fitting top, remembering to pick up some clean underwear at the last moment.

In the bathroom she found a small plastic bowl, a flannel and a bar of home-made rose petal soap. Last year, whilst she sat in Brenda's kitchen knitting clothes for premature babies, her friend melted tallow, added rose-hip-infused lye and a handful of petals (informing Lucy how good rose hip was for ageing skin) and finally poured the silky mixture into small lined bread tins to set. It had been left for a few weeks to age and then Lucy had been given a bar, tied in raffia with a dried rose tucked in the bow. It was some of the nicest soap Lucy had ever used and she understood Brenda's passion for the natural and the home-made.

Whilst the old lady continued to sleep, Lucy dashed home for some clothes of her own, not wanting to deal with the doctor in her pyjamas. After locking her front door, she nipped into Brenda's kitchen and made herself a much-needed cup of tea. It was a room that resembled an old-fashioned apothecary, with racks of jars and tins on every wall, but then Brenda was running an apothecary in all but name.

Finally, with the hot tea by her side, she sat down near her softly sleeping friend and tried to make sense of events. Something was wrong – very wrong. Brenda had never before displayed such unsettling behaviour. Putting the pieces together, she realised this wasn't a simple and inevitable case of ageing – physical deterioration and a slowing of thought – but escalating issues with memory and confusion, highlighted by this episode. And there had been no husband or children to pick up on the signs or seek the necessary assistance. This dear old lady, who'd spent a lifetime helping others with her herbs and potions, now needed help herself. But, although she had no family, Brenda had one very special friend, one close at hand who would step up and step in, and that was Lucy.

As she wondered how much and how soon the care would be needed, and if she could work it around her job, she remembered the office. With all the running about, it had completely slipped her mind. Adam was unimpressed.

'Where the hell are you, Lucy? We're up to our earlobes here. Two members of sales are off for half-term and Sam has mentioned your unauthorised absence several times. Hope you're going to come up with something better than the dog ate my homework?'

'I tried earlier but the phones weren't manned,' she mumbled.

'Then the reason for your no-show had better be good, Lucy-Lou, like decapitation or death. Are you *actually* dead?'

Lucy told him about her traumatic morning. 'I don't like letting everyone down, but I think I need to stay with her until she's been seen by a doctor.' She was aware her voice was wobbling but there were bigger things at stake here than her job. Her friend had disappeared into a world Lucy couldn't follow her into, and it was heartbreaking. Getting her back was paramount. 'I'm sorry, but Brenda is my priority. You can dock my pay, or make me work late all week, or take it from my holiday, or—'

'Okay. Okay. I get the picture. Leave it with me,' he huffed, and ended the call.

Chapter 9

Dr Hopgood was a young man who had more stubble around his face than hair on his shaven head. It was very Vin Diesel, and obviously done to combat the prematurely receding hairline, but it suited him. He was wearing a loud pink shirt and a dazzling black and white spotty tie – one where the spots jumped about if you looked at them for too long. Answering the door and escorting him down the hall, Lucy quickly filled him in on the situation, mentioning she'd now washed and changed Brenda, and how drowsy her friend had been since the episode.

As they entered the room, Brenda stirred. The doctor walked over to the wing chair, knelt down next to the fragile old lady and put out a hand to her knee, gently teasing her for being somewhat of a stranger at the surgery.

'And what's all this I hear about you practically putting me out of a job with all your alternative treatments? Don't get me wrong, my own grandmother is a fan of home remedies and she is one of the healthiest people I know. She still starts every day with two tablespoons of apple cider vinegar in hot water...'

For someone who didn't like doctors, Brenda managed a surprisingly flirtatious smile.

Dr Hopgood then established that although Lucy wasn't

family, his patient was happy for her to stay, and began to assess Brenda in earnest. Lucy stood at the back of the room, uncomfortable intruding on a personal consultation but aware Brenda needed the support.

'Give me your hand and I can do a little test to see if you've been drinking properly, young lady.' He gently pinched the skin on the back of her hand and then jotted something down in his notes. 'Okay, I'm going to need a sample. Do you think you could manage that?' At ease with this softly spoken man, Brenda nodded and, with Lucy's help, managed to produce the necessary sample. A urinary tract infection was diagnosed with a simple dipstick test.

The young doctor then asked Brenda a series of questions: what was the day? The month? The year? Who was the Prime Minister? Could she count backwards in twos? Her answers were vague and she was distracted and sleepy, worn out by the whole sample palaver.

After the consultation, and with Brenda's eyelids drooping again, Lucy offered to see the doctor out.

'When she's on the mend, and with her permission, we can arrange for you to be listed as next of kin. She's clearly fond of you.'

Lucy felt a lump rise up her chest and lodge in her throat.

'I'm going to put a community admissions avoidance team in place,' he continued. 'She's made it perfectly clear that she doesn't wish to go to hospital and I respect that. They should be in touch within twenty-four hours and will help with her hygiene and so forth. They'll make some general observations, check her blood pressure and pulse, and we can keep an eye on her condition. In the meantime, could you pick up this prescription for the antibiotics and keep up the fluids? You might like to try her with Dioralyte sachets. They are available from the pharmacy, and she should start to improve over the next day or so.'

'And then she will be back to her old self?' Lucy was hopeful but realistic.

'The episode this morning was triggered by the infection, but the questions I was asking earlier were to help me assess her long- and short-term memory. I will refer her to a memory clinic when the infection has cleared up, but, taken alongside the things you mentioned earlier, I can't rule out the early signs of dementia. We'll see what happens a bit further down the line, but it may be a case of reviewing her long-term care. It's a big, old house for her to manage, with lots of stairs, and no one immediately on hand if there is a problem. I know you are happy to help, but it's those times when she's home alone I'm worried about.'

Even though he was only voicing the thoughts that had been gathering in her head, Lucy momentarily closed her eyes. Dementia was a scary word, and one that never came with a happy ending.

'But she doesn't want to end her days anywhere other than this house. She's talked about it many times and insists the only way we'll get her out of here is in a wicker casket.'

'I understand how fiercely independent she is, but, in all likelihood, there will come a point where she won't be able to live alone any more, irrespective or not of a dementia diagnosis.'

Although Lucy understood it was Mother Nature's way – people got old and simply wore out – this wasn't how it was supposed to be for Brenda. After all, Mother Nature was her close personal friend; surely she could have pulled a few strings and let Brenda live to a hundred and three, still proudly clutching all her marbles, then have her slip away quietly one night in her sleep.

'She'll hate that. People in her house and being told what she can and can't do. I will look after her for as long as I can before we have to involve outside agencies. I appreciate it won't be easy, but she's one of my dearest friends and I'll find a way.'

'She is very lucky to have a friend like you, Miss Baker,' said Dr Hopgood. 'Some people don't even have family who care enough to do that.'

Both Adam and George contacted Lucy that afternoon: Adam to tell her she was to take as much time off as she needed and he would write it off as compassionate leave, and George to check on Brenda. Adam's call took her by surprise. She had expected some sort of reprimand, and possibly an inappropriate joke, so was relieved when he offered neither. George's call was brief and he was still calling her Lisa, but it was thoughtful of him to ring.

She popped home for her knitting and her current Regency romance and, fitting in a bit of housework for Brenda, spent a quiet afternoon watching over her friend. A neighbour called not long after the doctor had left, expecting to collect some lotion or other, but when Lucy explained Brenda was unwell, she offered to pick up both the prescription and a bit of shopping. Lucy had been troubled to discover Brenda's fridge contained very little except for a lump of cheese and three pairs of soft-top socks.

By the evening, and after sleeping much of the day, Brenda made herself a pot of herbal tea, having refused the Dioralyte, insisting on warm water and honey with a pinch of salt instead.

She asked for Jim several times and held some strange horse-related conversations with Lucy, clearly confusing her with the dead sister-in-law again. But after two doses of her antibiotics and lots of fluids, she seemed generally less muddled and agitated.

A strong waft of rosemary caught Lucy's nostrils as Brenda swirled the loose tea in her bone-china cup. She'd picked up enough in the last two years to know that it was a memory enhancer. *She knows*, Lucy thought to herself, unable to approach such a delicate subject with her friend.

The sun had all but gone, gracefully retiring to the other side of the world, and the tassel-edged, gold standard lamp in the far corner was on, giving the room a soft glow. Brenda was quietly snoring in the armchair as Lucy drew the dated gold floral curtains and sat down. She felt at home here because it reminded her of her own untidy living room. Everywhere you looked something new caught your eye. It seemed much friendlier and more welcoming than the impersonal spaces of her childhood home, where the general clutter of life was kept to a respectable minimum. This was a room filled with scatter cushions, dried flower arrangements and animal statues, where strange symbols graced the spines of books, the pictures on the walls and the mystical ornaments. In contrast to her own mother, Lucy found the proliferation of objects calming, not stressful. What did it matter if there was a sprinkling of dust? Or no clear surface to put your cup of tea? She was surrounded by a sense of belonging, even if she didn't quite understand what it was she belonged to. Tucking her legs underneath her, she settled into her favourite chair and let her book fall open where the embroidered bookmark nestled between the pages.

The Duke of Darkness eventually reached a satisfactory if predictable conclusion, although she wouldn't have forgiven his scandalous affairs, regardless of his damaged childhood. Lucy looked at the cover one last time, those shadowed eyes and that resolute jaw, and tucked the book into her knitting bag. It briefly crossed her mind that George would make a passable Duke of Darkness. He certainly had the looks, but the Duke remained well mannered and courteous throughout, however annoyed he was by the behaviour of the heroine. So perhaps not.

After helping Brenda upstairs, Lucy made a temporary bed on the long, upholstered sofa, switched off the standard lamp and wondered if she'd ever be able to fall asleep with the myriad of clocks chatting to her from every corner of the house.

Five minutes later she was floating in a world of passionate dukes, black cats and grumpy neighbours.

Chapter 10

The community admissions team arrived the next morning, but as Lucy was on hand, there wasn't much they needed to do. Two bustling ladies with mumsy figures and cheerful smiles checked Brenda over and seemed generally happy she was back on track, even though she was still sleepy and having muddled moments. Not long after they'd left, Dr Hopgood telephoned to check for signs of improvement in Brenda's condition. Lucy discussed with him her intention to become more of a carer for Brenda by calling in on her more regularly but in an unobtrusive way, and Dr Hopgood was supportive of her plans.

At eleven o'clock, there was a knock on the door and a young Interflora delivery girl handed over an enormous, and very expensive-looking, bunch of flowers.

'Oriental lilies and yellow roses. How lovely, but who on earth would be sending me flowers? It's not my birthday,' said Brenda. 'Is it?'

'Not yet. Soon. July,' Lucy reassured her.

Lucy put the arrangement on a raffia mat in the centre of the occasional table near the fireplace. She handed Brenda the card, who read aloud 'George'. Brenda turned the card over but that appeared to be it. So his written messages were as brief as his conversations, thought Lucy.

'Do I know a George?' Brenda asked.

'From next door. He helped us yesterday. Remember?' Lucy prompted.

'Not really, dear. But I don't want to talk about yesterday. Oh look, they're in a pretty crackle glass vase.'

'It's a very generous gesture,' said Lucy, never having seen such an impressive bouquet before.

'Hmm... Some might say it's worth more to have half an hour of someone's time than a lavish present,' Brenda said, as she reached out for Lucy's hand. 'I remember George now. The sexy one with the strong arms? I think the boy means well; he has a few lessons to learn, that's all.'

Lucy huffed at Brenda's casual dismissal of George's lack of manners.

'You can take that look off your face, young lady, because I have a feeling you'll be the one to teach him.'

The following day was one of those glorious May days that heralded the departure of spring and the arrival of summer. Collared doves cooed from the trees and late cherry blossom fell like confetti at the slightest breeze. Drawing back her curtains, Lucy decided it was the sort of morning you should walk to work – be outside and inhale the aroma of cut grass and scented flowers and feel the warmth of the sun on your skin. It would take forty minutes to get across town by foot, rather than twenty minutes in the stop-start traffic by car, but worth the extra journey time. She'd already rung Brenda to check she was okay, but even with the planned walk, she had time to pop over and share breakfast together, something Lucy decided she needed to do more often.

An hour and a half later, Adam welcomed her in his own

inimitable style as she stepped through the sales office door.

'Two men down and we don't seem to have been able to steer the boat through the unusually busy traffic jam of problems we've encountered in the last two days. I won't lie to you, Lucy-Lou, it's been particularly stressful, what with half-term and everything. You need to apologise to old Starchy Knickers over there.'

He gestured to Sam, surveying the office over the top of her elegant red-framed spectacles. She had a phone to her ear and was thoughtfully tapping a silver Parker pen on the edge of her desk. Adam swung his chair to face Lucy and crossed one leg over the other, exposing a particularly splendid pair of Spider-Man socks and far too much groin.

'And then perhaps you'd deal with this latest crisis? Four hundred Fizz, Boom, Bang chemistry sets shipped out in the last three months and it's taken until now for someone to spot that despite the inclusion of a detailed instruction manual, including a section in bloody Estonian, *none* of the translations are in English.'

Lucy sighed. She was straight back in to solving other people's muddles.

'I'll make it my priority, but surely it's just a matter of contacting the manufacturer and asking for a translation. We can add them to the units we have in the warehouse and those still out with our retailers. Hopefully, consumers will contact the manufacturer direct when they realise.'

'Yeah, well, I'm sure it's straightforward if you have the time to focus on it properly, but I have other, more pressing matters to deal with. She's got me running around like a squirrel on speed. So much for not interfering.'

Lucy walked over to the general manager's desk and waited

72

for her to end the call, before apologising for her unauthorised time off work.

'You should have contacted us as soon as you became aware of the problem. My biggest issue is we didn't hear from you until nearly ten o'clock.' Sam was multitasking, even as she answered Lucy she scribbled notes in her jotter. 'Although I'm still not convinced helping out a neighbour justifies a two-day absence.'

'Sorry. She wasn't well and went for a wander in her nightie, taking a packed lunch of cream crackers and toothpaste to her dead husband—'

'I don't want to hear your excuse, although I must say it's more creative than some I've heard.' Sam didn't look up. 'I want you to be at your desk by nine or ring in to notify us promptly that you will be delayed.'

'I tried to ring several—'

'The personal apology is appreciated, and Adam has backed you one hundred per cent, so let's move on. Has Adam filled you in on the science sets crisis?' Lucy nodded. 'Could you get straight on it please? He's been fiddling about all morning and I haven't seen much progress.'

Lucy slumped into her chair and switched on her computer. Poor Adam was obviously stressed. It must be hard running the sales office, especially when his staff let him down. She'd stay late to make up for it.

'Thanks for your support,' she said to Adam later as their paths crossed on the stairs. She was heading downstairs to the photocopier; he was returning with a box of ballpoint pens.

'Yeah, well, it's a one-off, so keep it up your jumper. I don't want people thinking I've gone soft.'

'And you're sure that's what the words said when she first gave it to you?' asked Jess, a few days later.

Lucy had finally confided in her about the locket as they both stood in the staff kitchen doing the tea round for their various departments. Lucy had no choice. Adam decided it was a job for the new girl and a year on Lucy hadn't questioned it. Jess volunteered in accounts because she knew Lucy was lumbered with the task on a daily basis.

Disconcerted by the possibility the words in the locket had changed, Lucy was searching for a rational explanation. Jess, who had to ask Lucy to pop the catch because her long nails made it impossible to press the fiddly button, had the locket in her hands and was inspecting it closely, much like Lucy had when she'd discovered the candle spell.

'It's difficult to be sure, as the letters are so small, but I assumed Brenda was telling me what they said, to save me squinting. But thinking back, I'm almost certain the first word started with a flouncy old-fashioned "D".'

'You've told me often enough that your old lady friend is a bit odd, how her whole house seems alive and she heals people with funny old lotions and potions. I thought we'd decided she's some sort of white witch.'

Perhaps Jess, who devoured TV shows like *Merlin*, *Angel* and *Once Upon a Time*, wasn't the best person to turn to for logical explanations.

'No, it's ridiculous,' Lucy said, as much to convince herself as Jess, and refusing to be drawn on what exactly Brenda was or wasn't. 'Unless I had a midnight visit from a particularly generous cat burglar who happened to have an almost identical locket in his pocket, I must have imagined it.' Lucy didn't know why she'd involved Jess – whose eyes were baby-seal-wide and was now holding the locket reverently in both hands, like she was delivering myrrh to the baby Jesus. She placed it carefully back on the central table.

'Let's do the spell thingy anyway? It will be fun – like that time we made a love potion for the new boy at school.'

'That wasn't fun; he was sick all over my school bag and we got a detention. Plus, I'm not sure *we* made or administered the potion. I was an innocent bystander – one who had to buy a new school bag.'

'Oh come on, writing a name on a candle and letting it burn out is simple enough,' Jess persevered. 'Lots of old charms and spells use candles. They light the way and dispel the forces of darkness. The ancient Egyptians used them, and just about anyone involved in any hocus-pocus has jumped on the bandwagon. Churches buy them by the barrow-load. Very symbolic.'

Lucy remembered Jess's passing white witch phase well. Jess did lots of activities in phases. There was the gym phase (she had a massive crush on one of the personal trainers), the knitting phase (in solidarity with her friend – but she was all fingers, thumbs and bad language) and currently the beauty therapy phase (self-taught via YouTube and a bit random). No explanation for that had been forthcoming but Lucy suspected it was a combination of trying to win over Dashing Daniel from work and her plans to earn some extra money on the side giving facials, manicures and a bit of intimate waxing.

'And even though I haven't met this George of yours—'

'He's *not* my George.'

'—this George your dotty neighbour's got earmarked for you, I think I should give him the once-over. If he's got potential, we're definitely doing this candle malarkey, because even if he *was* your type, you'd live next to him for twenty years and never have the guts to ask for so much as a cup of sugar.'

'That's not fair. I've already been in his house. And practically seen him topless. I even got a flash of nipple.'

Jess spat out her mouthful of Diet Coke and wiped her dribbly chin with her free hand. She didn't drink tea or coffee, which made her volunteering to do the tea round seem even more magnanimous.

'You're one secretive bunny, Miss Baker. This bloke has been in your neighbourhood for a whole fortnight and you've only told me about him today as an aside to your locket conundrum. You do know best friends are supposed to text each other this stuff on an hourly basis, right?'

'You know I'm not that sort of person, and anyway, seeing him topless was a by-product of Brenda getting caught in the rain. Nothing happened.'

'Nothing? You've seen his nipples! I think you may have missed out great chunks of this tale – the juicy chunks. Come on girlfriend. Spill.'

So Lucy went back to the beginning and told Jess about the allergy-inducing cat. And the wandering neighbour. And the nipples.

'Right, I'm coming home with you tonight, so I can suss out this George for myself.'

'You can't just invite yourself over. I might have plans.'

'Yeah, right. The only plans you'll have are to watch non-stop *Craft and Create* on TV with your gang of knitted friends, as you run up a quick Aran sweater with your size twelves.'

'Number fives,' muttered Lucy.

Chapter 11

'I'm so jealous of all this,' Jess said, abandoning a hastily collected overnight bag in the middle of the hall and curling up on the sofa next to Thor. 'There's no one watching you, clocking when you go out or come back in. I couldn't bring a bloke back to our flat. Mum would either embarrass me or start flirting with him. But it's what I need, Luce. Someone to whisk me away from it all. Preferably a bit of a looker, not short of a bob or two and with his own place.'

'I don't know why you love it so much. My flat is a mess,' said Lucy, defensive about the state of her home and painfully aware of her shortfalls from the comments her mother made every time she visited.

'But everything is so woolly and welcoming. It's full of colour and knick-knacks and it doesn't smell of takeaways or stale smoke. Because, seriously, if the gin doesn't get my mum, the fags will.'

Lucy started the meal, leaving the chilli to simmer, and returning to her friend in the living room. She picked up her knitting and chatted away without once looking down to see what her fingers were doing. Jess was impressed with the half-knitted Poldark and pushed Lucy to consider setting up a website, as she'd done many times before.

'I've told you people would pay good money for them. I bet I'm not the only one who would buy a knitted sex god. Got to be better than an inferior flesh one. They don't answer you back or make you sleep in the wet patch, but you still get a cuddle. Think about a Facebook page, at least.'

'I don't think they're good enough, but thanks for the vote of support.' Lucy added Poldark's second nipple, double-checking it was level with the first.

'So when does the monosyllabic giant return home from work?' Jess said, leaping up to peep around the living-room curtains. She'd clearly been expecting George to be conveniently striding around his front garden, possibly topless, when they arrived so that she could suss him out.

'It varies.'

'What does he even do?'

'I think he makes boxes. Brenda said he'd mentioned E.G.A. Packaging to her. It's that huge factory on the industrial estate near the old airfield.'

'Oh, well…' Jess almost sounded disappointed. 'He'll do nicely for you. You can sit and knit bed socks while he tells you all about the benefits of cardboard over bubble wrap.'

'Gee, thanks.'

'I didn't mean it like that.' Jess, with her limited attention span, came away from the window. 'Let's eat. It must be nearly ready because I can smell delicious aromas drifting down the hall and garlic always makes me salivate. We can crack open the cheeky little bottle of red that accidentally fell in my overnight bag on the way here.'

The girls ate a spicy beef chilli together; Jess appreciatively hoovered up every last morsel while Lucy pushed forkfuls around her plate like a croupier moving the chips on a roulette table. Jess being there made her nervous. She generally admired her friend's enthusiasm and energy except when it was being directed at some aspect of her own life. She hadn't forgotten the enforced make-over last month. Horrible, horrible experience. A blob of mascara and a smattering of face powder usually sufficed.

'So are you going to do the spell?' Jess asked

'To be honest, I'm not sure I want Mr Aberdour launching himself at me.' Lucy curled her top lip. Although, and she would never admit this to Jess who would happily add two and two and make sixty-seven, she was intrigued by this solitary man. There'd been no visitors since he moved in, and he came across as brutally abrupt – but she was certain he'd picked up on her distress when Brenda had gone for her wander. His fleeting touch of concern had given her goose bumps.

'At the moment, honey, I don't think you are even the tiniest green dot on the edge of his radar, so doing one simple spell won't do any harm. And if you think it's all mumbo jumbo, what does it matter? Let's pop in on the old dear next door and get the low-down. It's about time I was properly intro-duced to your other bestie.'

There was much more colour in Brenda's cheeks, thought Lucy, looking across at her friend. The antibiotics were doing their job and Dr Hopgood was happy with her progress. The community admissions avoidance team meant well but were simply not needed. It was almost as if the wandering incident had never taken place.

The girls sat together on Brenda's pale green, squishy sofa, Jess having tried Lucy's favourite chair but quickly hopping out and moving next to Lucy after being jabbed by an arm.

They were sipping overly sweet blackberry and apple gin from Seventies sherry glasses; each decorated with a different-coloured geometric design. Brenda insisted it was late enough in the evening to have a little stiffener and the girls were happy to indulge her, especially Jess who was disappointed the bottle of wine she'd brought over was nearly gone and Lucy didn't keep any in. Didn't she know sleepovers were supposed to involve excessive amounts of alcohol and a cathartic session of truth or dare?

'So how long have you known Lucy?' Brenda asked. 'I forget.'

'Yonks, since we sat next to each other in year seven French,' said Jess.

'The clincher was you thumping that girl for tripping me up in the maths corridor.' Lucy smiled, remembering how Jess stood up to the girls who teased Lucy because she was quiet, how she was kind to the nerdy kids, and how she spoke to boys as though they were ordinary human beings and not scary aliens from another planet.

'Surely you girls would rather be catching up on gossip and giggling about dishy movie stars? Much more fun than sitting with a daft old lady,' said Brenda, leaning over to top Jess up.

'Nonsense, Mrs P,' said Jess. 'We see each other at work every day, and besides, I need your help. I want Lucy to take the locket seriously.'

'You didn't say it was a secret,' Lucy gushed, glad she had at least brought the locket with her, having left it abandoned in a wooden bowl on the mantelpiece pretty much since Brenda had given it to her.

'It's not, my dear. But not everyone believes.'

'Lucy doesn't,' said Jess flatly.

'I didn't say that exactly. I'm not sure I need a locket to make someone like me, that's all.'

'Quite right too,' said Brenda. 'But in Lucy's case, I felt the locket calling to me.'

'Wow. So you really are a spiritual person? Can you contact the dead and all that? I was a white witch once, you know.'

Brenda smiled at Jess who had shuffled so far forward to the edge of the sofa, her bottom was barely gripping the edge.

'Interestingly, I was told later in life that my mother was a white witch, but I never really knew her. She was killed in a bombing raid in 1940. I was tucked safely in Aldwych tube station with my aunt and she was supposed to join us.' There was a pause. 'She never did.'

'Bloody hell. What happened?' Jess asked. Lucy knew the story – she had heard it a few times over the last two years, but she was conscious it was a painful subject for Brenda.

'She was helping an elderly neighbour. The house collapsed on them both.'

No one said anything for a moment. By now even Jess was aware how difficult this was for Brenda, who had gathering tears.

Brenda rummaged up her sleeve and fished out a folded cotton handkerchief to gently blot her eyes. 'I was only a child, but I remember her smile, and her kindness.'

'So did she, like, pass on the locket and tell you its history and all its mystical properties?' Jess asked, trying to move away from the memories she had unwittingly unleashed.

'The locket was nothing to do with her. It was given to me by someone I met when I was a lovesick young groupie, trailing around after The Yellow Crows. It's how I got my Jim. And he was the love of my life.'

'Yellow Crows – like the Sixties band?' she squealed.

'The very same. Jim was the drummer.'

Jess's eyes expanded faster than inflating balloons. 'You married a pop star?'

'They were more rock than pop, but yes, and I have so many fond memories of our years together.' Brenda's eyes were brighter now that the subject had changed to a happier topic – her life with Jim.

In fact, Brenda had crammed most of her escapades into one decade. Falling in love with the drummer of The Yellow Crows, and finally accepting that they would not be blessed with children; Jim and Brenda had spent several years on the road with the band and partied their way through the Sixties in glorious technicolour and a drug-induced haze. It was during this period of her life, helped by the chemically enhanced freedom of mind, that she discovered her unusual gifts and established a connection with Mother Earth.

'Brenda has all his drum kits and sound equipment up on the third floor,' said Lucy. 'The whole floor is a bit like a studio, with posters and album covers on the wall.'

'That's awesome. You're so cool for...'

'For an old lady?' Brenda volunteered.

'Yeah.' Jess smiled. 'For an old lady. A white witch married to a pop star.'

'I said *my mother* was a white witch. I don't follow any particular doctrine. I am what I am and don't label myself.'

You are certainly unique, thought Lucy to herself. She took a hasty sip of her gin and instantly regretted it. Her whole body tingled as the alcohol made its way down like a slow electric pulse.

'So, everyone knows "London Lady" and "Give Me Some

of your Lovin'", but what happened to The Yellow Crows after that?' Jess asked.

'There were some minor hits in the late Sixties but they disbanded in… Oh, I forget.'

'Seventy-two,' reminded Lucy.

'That's right, and after the tragically early death of the lead singer there was never any chance of them reforming. Jim trained as a music teacher, albeit an unorthodox one. Although he was a drummer, he was competent on the keyboard and guitar.'

'You never told me all this stuff,' Jess said to Lucy. 'You have a really funky neighbour.'

'Friend,' corrected Lucy and got a cheeky wink from Brenda in return.

'Anyway, Luce said that the words inside the locket had changed,' said Jess, swinging the conversation back to the locket.

'Yes. They do that.' It was said so matter-of-factly that Lucy felt herself physically jolt. Brenda was sitting there, telling them that the engraved words in a silver locket had said one thing the day she handed it over and another a few days later. Totally impossible. She must be stringing Jess along; after all, Jess was lapping all the white witch tales up like a thirsty cat.

'So what happens now?' Jess asked.

'There are some simple spells for Lucy to follow. If she carries them out, she has the power of the universe on her side to get her man. And if she wears it…' Brenda gave Lucy a stern look '…there are other benefits.'

'Fab,' said Jess. 'And after she's got her man she can pass it to me?'

'There I must disagree. The locket chooses people. Lucy

will know when to hand it on and to whom. I've had it for sixty years and only passed it on once before, although it came back to me for safekeeping after it had done its job on that occasion.'

'I wonder how old it is?' said Jess, undeterred. 'Probably Victorian because they were into a lot of charms and superstition and all that stuff. It looks kind of twiddly and old.'

Brenda smiled. 'Older than you would believe, and Lucy will be the next success story in its long and interesting history...'

As Brenda closed the front door to them half an hour later and they started to walk down the path, Jess tugged Lucy's sleeve.

'What car does George drive?' she asked, springing about like an excitable puppy.

'Some big black thing with this year's plate, but I don't know the model.'

'Is it that bloody huge Audi A4 parked outside number twenty-four?'

'Oh, he's home.' This was not good news. And Jess was far too enthusiastic for Lucy's liking.

'Great, let's pay him a visit.' Jess turned left and walked towards George's house.

'You can't just knock on his door,' but her friend was already bounding towards his house.

'Watch me.'

Lucy hovered in the background, a position she was used to, as George's dark green front door swung open. She loitered behind a low-growing, purple-flowering hebe as if this knee-high shrub would somehow conceal her.

Jess, who normally had no problem launching into conversation, stood on his front step momentarily dumbstruck.

'Yes?' an impatient George snapped.

Jess smoothed down her hair and gave a small cough. Perhaps she was also intimidated by the size of him. Up close, there was an awful lot of George Aberdour.

'We wondered if we could borrow, erm…a cup of sugar. We're making cupcakes and we've completely run out.'

'Sugar?' he sighed. 'Really?'

'Yes, really,' Jess said, levelling up to George. Well, levelling up to the wide expanse of his firm chest. Lucy knew it was wise not to pick a fight with Jess; George clearly had that lesson still to learn. 'If you don't have any, or you're too mean to lend a neighbour some for the cakes they are baking to raise money for the orphaned, disabled children, who have recently had their orphanage repossessed – then that's fine. We won't bother you any more.'

'Orphaned, disabled *and* homeless?' His top lip twitched.

Jess put her hands firmly on her curvaceous hips, and Lucy saw his eyes survey the petite waist and slender legs of her friend for longer than she thought was strictly necessary.

'Yes.' Jess folded her arms across her push-up-bra-enhanced bosom and tapped an impatient foot.

'In that case, I'll have a rummage. Wouldn't want to be responsible for them starving on top of all their other misfortunes.' He looked past Jess, noticing Lucy for the first time as she half bobbed behind the shrub. 'Did Brenda get the flowers?' he called over.

'Um, yes, she was delighted. It was kind of you.' She gave a half-hearted sniff of the hebe bush to make it appear her unnatural stance had a purpose.

'Nonsense, it was only a phone call, but on this occasion I picked them out myself. Normally my secretary does that sort of thing for me. Right, sugar.' George strode down the hallway.

'Oo, get him. "Normally my secretary does that sort of thing." Does she wipe his bloody—' Jess stopped mid sentence as he loomed into view.

'Keep it. It's a spare.' He thrust an unopened bag of granulated at Jess. 'And my secretary happens to be male, so I have to wipe my own backside.' He nodded at Lucy, merely an acknowledgement she was there, and closed the front door between them.

'A cup of sugar?' Lucy repeated as they walked back to her flat.

'I panicked.'

Jess was sprawled across the sofa, wiggling her scarlet toenails and clutching the last glass of wine.

'He's got a certain something, that's for sure. Absolutely not my type, but I can see where Brenda's coming from. And all that monosyllabic rubbish, I mean, doesn't he realise it makes him more attractive?'

'Does it? I'd rather he was pleasant and generally more chatty.' Lucy looped the wool around her hook and slipped off the stitch. She was finishing the last of the crocheted brooches for Chloe's preschool fête.

'Nonsense. It's a touch of the Darcy. You're the one who reads all those historical romances. Those dukes and viscounts are always offhand and aloof until the feisty heroine comes along and tames them. You should *so* be the one to tame him, Luce.' Jess looked at her bemused friend and gave her an enormous grin. 'Come on, let's do this candle thing. It'll be payback for being so up himself. You can sweep along to that posh thing of your mum's in his fancy black Audi to get her off your case. By that point he'll be so under the spell he'll be all like, "Oh, I love you, Lucy Baker. Marry me?" And you can be all, "No way, loser. Back off."'

'Don't you think I can bag my charming neighbour without resorting to Brenda's dodgy locket?'

Jess coughed as she sipped from her glass. 'Sweetie, you hid in a bloody bush just now. There was no eye contact and certainly no physical contact – both of which tend to be my opening gambits. A stoke of the arm and a lingering look work wonders.'

'I'm a slow burner. I don't want to swamp the poor chap. I talked to him about the flowers.'

'Your slow burning hasn't even ignited the wick.' Jess shoved Thor, Ed and Wolverine to the edge of the sofa and leaned forward. 'And talking of wicks, and in anticipation of your excuses, I stopped at that hippy shop on the way here.' She rummaged in her bag and stood a six-inch beeswax pillar candle on the low coffee table between them. 'You'll be letting Brenda down if you don't at least give it a go, and I know you're keen to keep the old dear happy. The woman in the shop said it should burn for at least eight hours, which will do nicely for your all-night vigil, and it will give off a lovely natural honey scent. It's a full moon next Saturday, so you have no excuse and a whole week to psych yourself up.'

Chapter 12

Lucy's heart sank as she entered the sales office balancing a tray of tea in one hand, and wrestling the door with the other. Dashing Daniel, the East Anglian Area Sales Rep, was loitering by her desk and fiddling with a decapitated teddy bear. Daniel unsettled Lucy as much as he excited Jess.

'Hope you've made one for me, lovely Lucy?' Daniel's voice was loud enough to ensure she became the focus of the entire office.

'Erm...I didn't know you were coming. I'm sure there is enough water in the kettle if—'

'Just playing with you, Lucy. Grabbed a Costa on the way in.'

Lucy felt her cheeks burn and turned away to distribute the beverages.

'Still got you doing the tea round? Old Dickie-boy needs to invest in a decent drinks dispenser for you all.'

'That's highly unlikely since he brought old Starchy Knickers in to cut our overheads to the bone,' said Adam, walking up to Lucy and helping himself to his I Like Big Cups And I Cannot Lie mug.

Lucy shot a panicked look to the far end of the office, worried that Adam and Daniel's less than respectful nicknames might get overheard, but Sam was nowhere to be seen, and Mr Tompkins (who had never invited anyone at the workplace to address him as anything other than Mr Tompkins) was safely behind his office door flicking through golf magazines.

'She Who Must Be Obeyed is out with Derek today,' said Adam, following her gaze. 'You should have seen his face when he turned up at half five this morning to find a bright and breezy Sam, complete with her Marks and Spencer Moroccan-style Fruity Couscous and Vanilla Bean and Maple Syrup Smoothie, ready to hit the road. All hopes of stopping at Meg's Diner for his usual mid-morning fry-up flew rapidly from his mind.'

'He's allowed a break. He's not doing anything wrong by stopping there,' said Lucy.

'Yeah, but would you take *her* into a greasy spoon caff?'

'She's only doing her job.'

Lucy had noticed that things were already running more smoothly with Sam around. Yes, she was tough, but you didn't get to the top by making friends. Richard's golf magazines had only come out because she was off site. Everyone was making more of an effort and knuckling down when she was around.

'That's right, Lucy. You stand up for your boss. Girl power,' said Daniel.

'I am her immediate superior, Daniel, and therefore I am her boss, not Sam. In fact, as I am technically in charge of sales, you're also answerable to me.'

'In your dreams. And talking of dreams, you featured in one of mine recently, Lucy. You were wearing a black, lacy basque with a notepad in your hand, offering to take something down for me...'

'Excuse me. I have work to do.' Her already red face was now positively aflame as she tried to manoeuvre past the two men.

'Don't make inappropriate remarks to my ladies, Daniel. We run a PC office and we like to think of ourselves as a caring family in here. Besides, Lucy is hardly likely to wear a basque. She's not got the figure. You need curves to pull something like that off.'

However hard she tried, Lucy could not make herself invisible or these embarrassing men disappear. She squeezed past them and slid the tray under her desk, not bothering to return it to the kitchen as she knew full well she'd be making the afternoon tea. Slipping on her headset, she hoped they'd get the message and move on to annoy someone else.

'Talking of which, Lucy,' said Adam. 'Could you get straight on to The Toy Depot? They want to know if we can get some outdoor games for the under-fives to them by lunchtime. They've massively under-ordered garden toys this year – like the rest of us, they probably weren't expecting the summer to start so early – but most of our warehouse stock is spoken for. Perhaps you could rustle up some pavement chalks, or buckets and spades for them in the meantime?'

'Hold it right there, Adam,' said Daniel, tossing the headless bear onto Lucy's desk. 'I've specifically popped into the office for Lucy's help, so you'll have to join the queue.' Lucy's heart sank to her sensible shoes. Being wanted by Daniel was not a good thing, unless you were Jess.

'You don't get to breeze in here and monopolise my staff. She needs to sort out this problem for The Toy Depot.' Adam squared up to Daniel. The only thing in his favour was his height, but it didn't faze Daniel. Nothing much did.

'I thought it was the sales office supervisor's job to sort the problems,' said Daniel.

'It's okay. It's probably my fault. I didn't order enough because we had all that stock left over from last summer,' Lucy said, aware the tension was escalating.

'Far be it for me to question your priorities, Adam, but I've managed to negotiate with a major supermarket chain to stock the ClickIn that we import exclusively, and it's all systems go. After the price hike of Lego since Brexit, there's quite a lot of interest in compatible building bricks. But if you want me to wait until she's sorted your little trauma...' He shrugged, dismissively.

ClickIn had been developed by a personal friend of Richard Tompkins – a plastics manufacturer based in Belgium. It was a quality product with a growing range and was doing well in mainland Europe. Mr Tompkins had secured exclusive UK distribution rights, so if it took off, it would be a major coup for Tompkins. Daniel knew he'd won the round, Lucy knew he'd won the round, and even Adam knew he'd won the round.

Daniel pulled up a spare chair next to Lucy and started to run through the details with her, as his final presentation would need to be faultless. Adam hitched up his trousers and sulked back to his desk, muttering something about bloody reps breezing in and thinking they owned the place.

'Right, I'm off to have lunch with a lovely lady from The Wooden Toy Company,' Daniel announced, an hour later. 'Strictly work.' He winked at Lucy. 'I'll be back later for those ClickIn promotional starter sets. I know there was a box delivered last week and I'll need some for the supermarket directors to play with.'

'Um, okay. I'll sort them out for you.'

Daniel sauntered out towards the door singing 'Stand and Deliver' at an unnecessarily loud volume.

'Adam?' he said, as he stopped in the doorway.

Adam looked up from fiddling with his stapler, pinging a strip of staples across the room as he did so.

'Look after your Ants,' said Daniel. His hand swept the office by way of explanation and then he ran two fingers across his eyes, fired two imaginary flintlock pistols and popped them back in their equally imaginary holsters.

'That man spends too much damn time driving around the countryside listening to bloody Radio Two,' said Adam.

Chapter 13

Adam finally sat down to access his computer late that afternoon, having spent most of the day looking over people's shoulders and spouting random motivational comments, including, much to Connor's delight, 'You'll never climb to the top the mountain, Sonjit, if you don't prepare the way with a lawnmower.' She'd only asked if the warehouse needed to do a manual stock check of fidget spinners for a bulk order.

Adam fiddled about with the mouse and Lucy watched his face go from confused to frustrated to angry. Connor was eventually called over to cast his slightly more technically knowledgeable eye over the problem. It took him seconds to work out someone had stuck a Post-it over the laser. Adam was straight on the phone.

'Ha bloody ha, Daniel... Because who else would it be? I don't need proof. I know it was you... Oh yeah, like the time you offered me an Oreo with toothpaste in the middle? I wasn't bloody laughing... Deny it all you like, but I'll catch you in the act eventually and then we'll see who's got the biggest smile on their face.' The phone was slammed down with considerable force. 'Did anyone notice Daniel near my desk this morning?' Adam addressed the whole office, but

Lucy and Pat avoided eye contact. 'Don't try and cover for him, ladies. He's a wolf in fox's clothing. He's sneaky like a fox and I don't trust him. He comes in here all charm and flattery, but mark my words, turn your backs and he'll gobble you up and spit you out for breakfast.'

The phone conversation with Daniel reminded Lucy she needed to dig out the ClickIn starter sets, and with the clock heading towards half five, she headed downstairs to locate the box.

The stationery cupboard was jokingly referred to as the Tardis by the staff, partly because of its cobalt blue door and partly because certain people (who placed great importance on their stationery upkeep) seemed to disappear in there for decades. It was a cupboard by virtue of having no outside windows but was, in fact, room-sized. As well as stationery and the large, old-fashioned photocopier, it housed all the promotional literature from their suppliers and any free gifts or samples for customers. Lucy found the ClickIn box dumped behind a more recent delivery of photocopier paper, but as she leaned over to pull the heavy box out of the way, she caught a precariously balanced box of Biros with her elbow. It tumbled to the floor and one hundred 0.1mm black ball-point pens spread themselves out behind the stacked boxes. Oh, why was she so clumsy?

She bent over the boxes to try and retrieve the scattered pens. As she did so, the door opened behind her and someone flicked the lights out as the door swung shut.

'Well, hellooo,' said a Leslie Phillips-style voice.

Lucy froze as the footsteps got nearer.

'I spy, with my little eye, a rather shapely behind. Ding-dong!'

Lucy turned around to confront Daniel with his hands on his hips, but before she could react, the door swung open again. The smile fell immediately from Daniel's face and, although the figure in the doorway was just a silhouette, there was no mistaking Sam's authoritative voice.

'Do you really think the workplace is appropriate for this type of behaviour?' she asked.

The question was obviously rhetorical because she didn't wait for an answer but instead grabbed a ream of white paper from the shelf near the door, and said, 'My office, Daniel. Five minutes,' as she spun on her patent leather heels and walked off.

Daniel, unusually, seemed as uncomfortable as Lucy.

'Bloody hell, Lucy. Don't go making allegations of sexual harassment or anything. I thought you were Jess. I'm really sorry.'

Only because you were looking at me from behind, she thought. If you looked at the girls from the front, the differences were more obvious. Jess knew how to maximise her assets by wearing push-up bras, figure-hugging outfits and generally exposing the bits of her that men liked to look at. She drew attention to her lovely fair hair, letting it swish from side to side and twisting it around her fingers as she talked. Her almond-shaped blue eyes were accentuated by the clever application of make-up, and she had a voice and made sure it was heard.

Lucy, by contrast, dressed down, usually with knitted accessories that never quite worked. Her hair was often swept up in a ponytail. She wore very little make-up and her posture was far from that of a catwalk model. She liked comfortable, she liked home-made, and was very much a curious mixture of both.

'It's okay.' It wasn't as if he'd groped her.

'So we're cool?'

She nodded.

'And these are the promotional starter sets?' he asked, pointing to the box with the ClickIn logo emblazoned across the side.

She nodded again.

'If you slide it into the hall, I'll grab it on my way out. Better face the music. Sorry again, Luce,' he said as he walked away singing Elton John's 'Sorry Seems to be the Hardest Word' to himself. Why Jess had a thing for him was beyond her. She was sure his constant singing alone would drive her mad.

It was only after Daniel had disappeared up the echoey stairs, his last notes debating whether they should think it over, that she realised he wasn't apologising for his actions – he was apologising because she wasn't Jess.

Chapter 14

Lucy decided to eat her chicken salad al fresco as it made her feel like she'd gone out for a meal, even though she was technically still at home. She'd checked on Brenda earlier and was now popping in a couple of times every day. Brenda always welcomed her, even if it took a few moments to place her, but she was largely back to her old self and Lucy often felt redundant. There was the occasional odd comment, muddling Lucy with someone from her past, or misplacement of items that tended to turn up later in bizarre locations, but the wandering incident seemed far behind them.

Jess had bailed on their usual Friday night pub date, saying something had come up, but Lucy wasn't stupid. Dashing Daniel had been singing 'I Gotta Feeling' by the Black Eyed Peas as he left the building. She even spied him trying out a couple of disturbing hip thrusts in the staff car park.

Like Daniel, Lucy had been pulled into Sam's desk-less office briefly after the Tardis incident. (Sam still used it for confidential conversations, but her desk remained firmly in sales.) She wanted to make certain Lucy was okay, so she assured her boss it had been a harmless joke. Sam muttered something about conducting an urgent review of company policies, with sexual harassment being top of the list.

Balancing the salad on a low pile of bricks, Lucy pulled a rusty wrought-iron chair out from a tangle of brambles that had ensnared it while no one had been looking. Brushing dust and leaf debris away with her free hand, she angled it to face the last of the sun. Although her patch of garden was small (the length of the tiny gardens in Lancaster Road in complete contrast to the three-storey buildings), she felt lucky to be on the ground floor. Although Lucy was not really a gardener, there were a few pots dotted about and some low-maintenance shrubs in the thin borders, and she couldn't imagine not having access to an outside space.

It had rained earlier in the afternoon, but it had been a warm rain. Now, the static clouds hung in the sky, dirty grey underlined with the orange-reflected light from the disappearing sun. As she reached for the bowl of salad and tried to spear a slippery piece of lettuce with her fork, Lucy noticed the neighbourhood stray behind her begonias again. Well, she thought it was the stray, because it was black, underweight and had the same glowing yellow eyes, but this cat had a smart blue collar.

She made kissy noises and put out her hand in a gesture of friendship, trying to encourage it over. It *was* the same cat – it gave the same pitiful meow and had the same twitchy demeanour. Perhaps it hadn't been a stray at all and its owner had replaced a lost collar? But to let it get into that state was wicked. Or maybe someone had given it a home. Not Brenda, because she would have mentioned it, and not the taciturn George because he definitely didn't have a lifelong membership of International Cat Fanciers' Association.

Almost able to touch it now and hoping to read the collar to work out its identity, there was a sudden crash from next door and the cat and Lucy jumped apart like guilty lovers.

'Bugger, damn and blast,' Brenda's voice came over the wall. The cat sped away in one direction and Lucy ran in the other. She was round Brenda's within the minute and greeted by a worrying sight.

'What are you trying to do?' Lucy asked. 'Kill yourself?'

Brenda had tried to move the stone birdbath and it had toppled over. The broken bowl lay next to her feet.

'I was trying to take it to the bottom of the garden.'

'ON YOUR OWN?'

'When I bought it from the garden centre a few years ago, I carried it in from the car by myself. Of course, I still had the car back then…'

'You should have asked me to help. It wouldn't have been any trouble.'

Brenda cast her eyes downwards and started to rub her anxious hands together.

'I don't like it, Lucy.'

'Like what?'

'Not being able to do the things I used to be able to do. Not being able to remember details as sharply…' She sunk into the cast-iron garden chair near the herb border. 'The other day, when you and George were in my house, I'd been wandering, hadn't I? The doctor said I had.'

'You had a moment, that's all, because of the infection, but you're better now.'

'I don't remember any of it until you were rubbing me down with a towel, and that frightens me. The appointment for the memory clinic is tomorrow. A lady from Tudor Avenue is driving me. She said it was the least she could do since I sorted out her recurring migraines last year. Everyone has been so kind.'

Lucy waited for her to continue but Brenda decided that was all she was going to say on the subject.

'Oh God, Lucy. Don't ever get old.'

'I've heard it's better than the alternative.'

'I'm not convinced,' Brenda said, shuffling up the path to her back door.

The radio was playing a rousing anthemic Coldplay song. Lucy was on her iPad looking at images of Poldark and humming slightly off-key. She was trying to work out how to knit the breeches for the nearly finished figure, when there was a knock at the door. Expecting the burly George and another cat crisis, she was surprised to find a power-dressed Emily.

'I've been in your neighbourhood for most of the day at the Renborough WHSmith,' Emily said. 'It's been struggling, despite the introduction of a Post Office concession. So I wouldn't be much of a sister if I didn't stop by to say hello. Luckily Stu's mum has got the girls and, unlike the child-minder, she doesn't charge by the hour. You've got me for a quick cup of tea before I have to head back. Sorry it's not longer.'

After the fancy air-kissing thing most of the family insisted on since becoming part of Stuart's extended family, the girls hugged. Lucy was conscious of her sister's expensive perfume and the feel of her soft cashmere cardigan as Emily clung to her for an unprecedented length of time.

'Come in and I'll have a rummage for some cake.'

'Oo, yes. Cake would be good,' said Emily, closing the front door behind her. 'I don't think I thanked you properly for using your staff discount to help me buy Rosie's birthday presents last month – really appreciated. And talking of the kids, I have some news...' Emily deposited a smart leather briefcase and Mulberry handbag in the hall.

'Oh?' said Lucy, glad her sister couldn't see her face as she followed her into the kitchen.

'Mum's told you, hasn't she?'

'Erm...'

'It's okay. It's not a secret, but I haven't posted it online or anything yet. I don't want to tempt fate until I hit thirteen weeks.'

'It's wonderful. I meant to send you a card, but you know how organised I am.'

'I know. I'm still waiting for a Christmas card.'

'How's the pregnancy going?' Lucy asked. She bent down and started to riffle through the cupboards for a box of Mr Kipling's finest that she was sure she'd seen loitering behind the cereals, but it was nowhere to be seen.

'There's not been so much morning sickness with this one, but I'm incredibly tired all the time. Honestly, I could fall asleep on one of your upturned knitting needles and I'm not kidding. I said to Stuart how different it is from the first two and now he's convinced I'm carrying a boy. God, Luce, I'd better be. I'm not going through this again for anyone.'

A packet of Jaffa Cakes was discovered in the tinned food cupboard and the sisters decided they counted as cake.

'Let's take these into the living room,' Emily said, casting an eye over the cluttered kitchen table and the chair backs draped with laundry. 'I need a comfy chair. Besides, I love that room. It's so cosy.'

'Untidy, you mean, compared to your show home, which always reminds me of something from a photo shoot in *Hello!*'

'Yeah, well, keeping it like that takes a lot of work. Sometimes I think the girls are afraid to even play in it in case they mess it up. Stuart's overly pedantic about things like cushion placement for a bloke. Serves me right for marrying an older man. He had it all his own way for too long. Would you believe it takes me fifteen minutes to make the bed every morning? Honestly, two heads do not need eight pillows. We had to get a cleaner when I had the girls. Can you imagine trying to keep on top of all that with two small children?'

'Oh, poor you. How dreadful to be forced to get a cleaner...'

Emily whacked her sister's shoulder with the back of her hand. 'You know what I mean.' She nestled herself amongst the crocheted blankets and knitted figures and let out a contented sigh. 'You really should think about selling some of these. There's definitely a market for them. Have a look at Etsy and Folksy. These little beauties would go down a storm.'

'Maybe,' Lucy said, nibbling the edges off her Jaffa Cake.

Playing with a pile of Regency romances on the floor with her foot, Emily picked one up and glanced at the blurb. 'I spent my childhood dreaming of a big house and a wealthy man sweeping me off my feet.' Emily looked at the handsome lord on the front cover and stroked his face with her thumb.

'You got your dream then?'

'Yeah.' Silence.

She looked tired, Lucy thought. Tired and ill, but that's what pregnancy did to you. She'd pick up in the second trimester.

'So tell me all about you, sweetie. How are things?' Emily eventually asked.

Hastily swallowing her mouthful, Lucy sighed. 'If you must know, my mother is turning fifty in September and is arranging a function at Mortlake Hall to rival the royal wedding, with over a hundred guests. She will probably arrive in a horse-drawn glass coach, and I fully expect a swan ice sculpture, a dramatic firework display and Tom Jones to be flown in to sing for the evening.'

'What a coincidence. *My* mother is arranging a similar extravaganza in the same month. Only last week, I was asked to give a speech. The following day the suggested wording was emailed to me – all seven pages of it. She's even advised me on outfits for the girls, who she's now expecting to recite a poem about how special grandmas are. They are two and four, for goodness' sake. What makes her think they are going to be able to stand in front of everyone and recite a poem? Neither of them can even read properly yet.'

'I think all she requires of me is to turn up with a suitable boyfriend and still have a job. Neither of which I can guarantee at this stage,' Lucy said. And the girls exchanged a look they had shared many times over the years when discussing their mother.

As Lucy waved her sister off through the living-room window later, the skies still overcast and heavy, she saw George pull into the kerbside space Emily had just vacated. She was concerned for her sister, but hoped it was just the pregnancy making her look so drawn. Emily said all the right things, but then she was good at that – much better than Lucy. It would be a good idea to keep a closer eye on her, as it was easy to forget the caregivers needed care too, and she hoped Stuart was pulling his weight.

Her eyes were drawn back to George, who'd obviously been indulging in a bit of retail therapy after work, as the car was full of shopping. She watched him carry a couple of M&S food bags into the house. Then he came back for what looked like a suit bag, but then she'd only ever seen him in suits.

Finally, and rather surprisingly, he manoeuvred a tall, bulky object out of the boot. It comprised a long pole with various platforms. There was a string-covered scratching post on the base, a carpeted tube halfway up and a dangly ball attached to one side.

He cast his eyes around, as if he was concerned he might be spotted, and a bright red ball on a string bounced along the pavement behind him as he walked to his gate.

Chapter 15

The headless teddy, now sporting a mismatched head and bright red bow, was sitting on Lucy's desk when she walked into the office. She knew it was Pat, probably to cheer her up after last week. It wouldn't bet the first time Pat had taken pity on a damaged toy.

The sales line rang as she connected her headset and entered her password.

'Tompkins Toy Wholesaler,' she sung, eager to start the day on a bright note.

'Luce, just the girl.' It was Daniel. Her heart sank. 'Don't know about you, but I've had my knuckles rapped, whipped and grated for our cupboard shenanigans.'

Really wanting to pull him up for the use of the word "our", she merely said, 'I reassured Sam it was a silly joke...'

'Yeah, well, she implied I could get into more hot water than a freshly diced carrot if I didn't pull back. Apparently, I'm on a warning and if anyone makes a formal complaint I'm sunk. Luckily no one at Tompkins thinks like that. You all love my cheeky-chappie nature and don't take the banter seriously. Am I right, or am I right?'

Lucy said nothing.

'I reckon she's got to be seen to follow these things up –

something to prove in the new job, that's all. Anyway, I wanted to let you know your pert behind is safe from my wandering hands...' He paused. 'You aren't going to report that comment are you? I'll keep my comments totes PC from now on – honest.'

'Did you just ring to establish the future safety of my bottom or is there something I can do for you?' Lucy wanted this unnerving call to be over as quickly as possible.

'Ah, yes, can you get on to ClickIn and see if you can't wangle us another free box of those starter sets? I might have a rival chain interested – there's a baby doll.' The new PC Daniel had lasted less than ten seconds.

'Wouldn't it be more appropriate for Adam to ring them? He carries more weight than me.'

'I don't care if he's the newly appointed Chief Executive of the Universe, people warm to you, Luce. Adam rubs people up the wrong way and doesn't stop rubbing until there are friction burns.'

Flattered, but feeling Daniel's faith in her abilities was misplaced, she agreed.

'New me,' she told herself under her breath as the call ended and a cry came from Adam's desk.

'WHAT THE...?'

Everyone looked up. Lucy could see he'd logged onto his computer and was staring at a screen saver that would have even the warehouse lads blushing.

'Adam?' said Sam, walking to his desk with a manila file in her hand. 'Can I ask if... What *are* you doing?'

Adam was leaning back on his desk, trying to obscure the offensive image from his boss yet remain casual and not alert Sam that anything was wrong. He wasn't really able to pull it off.

'I, erm...I'm stretching my back before I settle for the long haul. You know? Busy day ahead. Expect I'll be stuck to the desk like a butterfly to glue.'

Unable to resist casting a quick glance behind her, Lucy saw Connor reach for his rapidly expanding book of Adam's more imaginative expressions.

Sam walked to the side of Adam's desk and placed the file on the corner. He swivelled awkwardly to mirror her journey. 'I want to discuss the stationery needs of this office with you. We seem to get through an awful lot for such a small company. But perhaps you should finish your pre-work yoga session first? Have a look through these numbers and see what you think. Come to me when you've got some input.'

'Absolutely,' he said, arching his back and rotating his shoulders backwards.

Sam returned to her desk and Adam, tilting his screen away from prying eyes, slumped into his chair.

'Connor? Have you got a minute?' he called across the office.

'Where's Pat?' Lucy asked Sonjit, who was near the water cooler and removing Shaun The Sheep from Igglepiggle's unwanted advances. It was a pointless exercise, as they would be reunited before the day was out.

'All I can say is if old Pat-a-Cake has gone down to the Tardis hoping someone wants to play Postman's Knock with her, she's in for a long wait. Ha ha,' Adam said, wandering over to join in the conversation. Lucy's heart started a slow thud. If Adam knew, *everyone* knew. She braced herself for an afternoon of inappropriate jokes.

'Sometimes you can be such a jerk,' said Sonjit, as she filled a paper cone with ice-cold water and took a sip.

'I am muchly sorry for any offence I caused.' Adam placed his hands together in prayer and bowed.

Sonjit drank the last of her water, threw the cone in the bin and put her hands on her hips.

'Do you *want* me to file a case of racial harassment?' The expression on her face remained blank. It was a conversation they had on a regular basis, but it was a futile one. Sonjit would never make a fuss because, whatever unfortunate things spewed from Adam's mouth, he'd been incredibly supportive when her mother had been terminally ill last year.

Adam weighed up the possibility of her carrying out her threat and decided to brave it out. 'Do you want me to file a lack of humour report? Honestly, some people can't take a joke.'

'Some people work for one,' said Sonjit, but Lucy noticed her gentle smile as she walked away.

'I reckon it's about time to lubricate the old tonsils,' said Adam, sidling up to Lucy.

'But I'm right in the middle of a complicated—'

'Time and tide make the thirsty man dry.' He tapped his watch. 'Chop, chop. It's nearly quarter past three and I'm as dry as a desert-bound sailor. And I'm sure I'm not the only one. It's important to keep the troops fed and watered if you want them to go into battle.'

Sighing, Lucy slid her chair back.

'I'm not busy at the moment if you want me to do it?' offered Connor.

'Don't be silly. It's more of a woman thing. Lucy never complains. And she does make a sterling cup of tea.' When

Sam finally started on those company policies, Daniel wasn't the only one in for a shock, thought Lucy.

'I tried.' Connor shrugged, as Adam sauntered over to see whether Sonjit needed more highlighters. He was, Lucy noticed, very attentive to Sonjit's stationery needs.

'It's okay,' said Lucy. 'I'm feeling sorry for him after the screen-saver incident, so I'll let it go. Who did it? Even he can't blame Daniel this time. He wasn't in today.'

'Wanna bet? Guess who Pat saw leaving the office car park as she pulled in first thing?' said Connor.

At the end of a long week, Lucy reversed her bottom out of Brenda's gate, having passed a pleasant hour knitting a twiddl-emuff and supervising Brenda's meal. Worried about her friend's persistent memory muddles despite the infection clearing up, she'd been researching dementia online and come across these fabulous knitted muffs for sufferers – something to keep their hands busy and quieten their minds. Visiting the dementia ward at the hospital one evening earlier in the week had been an eye-opener, but she was keen to prepare herself for any eventuality. It wouldn't make the clouds gathering above number twenty-two disperse, but it made Lucy feel she was doing *something*.

She waved at the young mum who lived opposite and watched her struggle to strap her sulky pigtailed daughter into her car seat. As she turned back to latch the gate, a striding George rammed into the back of her and nearly knocked her to the pavement.

'Sorry. Sorry,' she repeated, hoping he wasn't about to shout at her.

He was staring into his iPhone and clearly hadn't been looking where he was going.

'Do you always apologise for things that aren't your fault, Lisa? It's an annoying habit of yours.'

'Sorry.' Her cheeks flushed hot.

He raised an eyebrow, pressed something on his phone and flipped the case shut, but it buzzed and he flipped it open again.

'How is Brenda?' He nodded at her front door but kept his eyes on the screen.

'Okay, I think.' Lucy told him about the UTI and the referral to the memory clinic. From the few details she had been able to prise from Brenda, she gathered there had been more memory-related questions and that Dr Hopgood would be contacted with the results. Brenda refused point blank to consider a CT scan or further blood tests, because she no longer needed proof of her condition.

'They've indicated she's displaying the very early signs of dementia and she's not taken it very well.'

He took his eyes off the screen and looked at her. 'Well, no one is going to greet that news with party poppers and balloons.'

Did the man have to be so consistently blunt? She changed the subject.

'Brenda and I were wondering what happened to the stray. Someone must have taken it in. I'm sure I saw it with a collar on the other day,' Lucy said.

George avoided her eyes and pretended to be engrossed in the message he was typing.

'And then I saw you unload a cat activity centre...'

He pressed the screen and looked up.

'Yes, well, it's only temporary. A curious young lady I met recently reminded me that it's not healthy to be alone and pointed out cats make great companions...' Their eyes locked for a moment but both pairs darted in opposite directions as soon as contact had been made. Curious was as good an adjective as any, she decided. Gorgeous would have been preferable, but at least he hadn't plumped for bonkers or unhinged. 'Anyway, couldn't bear his pitiful little eyes staring at me all the time. Worse than a demanding woman... Joke,' he clarified.

'*His* pitiful eyes?'

'Took him to the vet. Scratbag is unequivocally a boy.'

'Scratbag?'

'The vet insisted on a name when I registered him and that was the first thing that came to mind. Which reminds me...' He fished about in his pocket and dangled a door key in front of her face. 'I was going to pop in on you later. Flying visit to sign some ridiculously important, have-to-be-signed-on-a-Saturday-because-the-Europeans-seem-to-work-all-week, type papers with a pulp and paper manufacturer in Germany tomorrow and realised I'd forgotten about Scratbag. Could you?'

There was a pause. There was also a tiny part of her that wanted to say no because he'd still failed to grasp that the word please on the end of a sentence was a real game changer.

He glanced at his watch and then back at her face.

'Nice scarf,' he added, noticing the colourful knitting in her hands as though a belated compliment might sway her decision.

'It's not a scarf. It's a twiddlemuff.'

He managed to keep a straight face. 'Right. Well. The food and all the bits he needs are in the utility. Had a local man fit a cat flap in the back door this week. Didn't do that whole keeping him in thing as I figured he knows where he's well off. I'll feed him first thing, but if you could throw some food at him tomorrow night?' There was a pause, which George clearly took as her agreeing to feed his cat. 'I'll be back early Sunday morning. My flight lands at three in the morning. Ridiculous really, I'll be longer in the air than on German soil. Keep the utility door shut. I'll be shattered enough as it is, without cat hair on my pillow keeping me up for what's left of the night scratching and sneezing.'

She waited for the magic and highly elusive word. It didn't appear.

'No problem,' she sighed.

'Great. You may as well hold on to the key for future emergencies.' He thrust the key ring at her and walked off.

Chapter 16

A spring clean was in order, even if spring was making way for her more sultry, and emotionally unpredictable, relative. Lucy spent Saturday morning cleaning and tidying, and by lunchtime she'd given the living room a good going-over; sorted out miscellaneous bags of wool, wobbly piles of books and a scattering of knitting magazines.

She grabbed a sandwich for lunch and settled down to a new book: *The Duke's Dangerous Secret*. Goodness, how this taciturn duke reminded her of George, even more so than the duke from the last book. They both needed a good shake, but while the spirited Lady Eleanor might have taught this duke a lesson or two, Lucy hadn't even been bold enough to correct George over her name. Her eyes darted to the locket on the mantelpiece – it still made her feel uncomfortable and the impending full moon wasn't helping.

At seven o'clock, Lucy decided to feed George's temporary lodger. Thinking he might like a bit of company, she tucked a book under her arm with the idea of sitting with him for a while. Knitting, she decided, and more specifically the ball of wool, might be too much of a temptation for a cat.

As soon as she'd turned the key in the back door and pushed it open, Scratbag jumped down from the worktop and started to weave between her legs. He tried to meow a greeting but it was still a pathetic effort. Lucy looked around for the food.

'All the bits he *needs*,' she repeated to herself. Good grief, some serious money had been spent here. The plush igloo-type cat bed next to the radiator and the four-storey deluxe cat activity centre she'd seen George unload from the car the other day were just the start.

Lucy didn't profess to be an expert, but as she opened a sachet of Gourmet Perle cat food, she felt certain Scratbag would have been just as content with a tin of supermarket own label. Surely gourmet cat food was for owners with more money than sense? But then George, whom she noticed also had a trouser press standing in the corner, probably fell into that category.

'Would sir like to sample the salmon and whole shrimp?' She bowed as she put the dish on the floor and swept a dramatic hand over the food.

Whilst he tucked into his meal, Lucy washed out the previous bowl, changed his water and wiped down the hair-covered worktop. She then sat on the floor next to Scratbag as he began his post-banquet ablutions.

'*The Duke's Dangerous Secret*,' Lucy announced to the cat. 'I'm on chapter five but you'll soon pick up the gist of the story.' She then proceeded to read chapters five through to nine to a contented Scratbag, who didn't blush at the explicit sex or comment on the excessive use of adverbs. He sat curled in the middle of her crossed legs, quite a convert to romantic historical fiction.

'George will be back to feed you in the morning,' she

reminded him, and then she locked up and returned home. She couldn't put the locket off any longer.

Taking the locket from a wooden bowl on the mantelpiece (it was safer to return it to the same place because, whilst she didn't want to wear it, she also didn't want to misplace it), Lucy read the inscription again. She was relieved to find the words hadn't changed. If it mattered to Brenda that she followed the spells, then follow the spells she would, even if she felt a total twit doing so. It wasn't that she anticipated them having any effect, but there was a tiny part of her that suspected if she didn't do them, Brenda would somehow know.

She peered out the kitchen window and saw the reflection of the full moon on the algae-speckled glass of the tiny shed window. Thank goodness it was a Saturday, as she didn't fancy struggling through a day at work after a night-long vigil. She could sleep in tomorrow. Sundays were supposed to be lazy days.

Despite previously begging Jess to come and keep her company, her friend declined and made a vague comment about being busy. Lucy assumed she was referring to the not-so-mysterious boyfriend, and was peeved she was doing this alone as Jess had guilt-tripped her into doing it in the first place. However, it was simple enough; all she had to do was carve George Aberdour into the side of the candle and sit up with the silly thing until it had burned through.

Kneeling beside her low coffee table, she tipped her knitting bag upside down to look for her yarn needle.

Out fell the ball of double-knit brown wool and Poldark's half-finished breeches, a recently completed twiddlemuff and the fluffy blue pencil case of scissors, knitting needles, pins and stitch holders. As she gave the bag a final shake, the sought-after yarn needle fell to the floor.

She bundled everything back in the bag, picked up the fat beeswax candle and scratched George's name along the side. It was tricky as the candle kept rolling away from her, but when she'd finished the name was at least readable. She went into the kitchen to look for something heatproof to stand the candle on and to search for the matches, eventually finding a small saucer that had lost its matching cup. The matches took a while longer to locate until she remembered she'd used them in the bathroom to burn some oak bark incense sticks Brenda had thrust upon her last month to increase her feelings of power and inner strength. With no instructions about the locket itself, she put it on, feeling it somehow needed to be part of the process.

Her watch told her it was gone nine and Jess had said the candle should burn for at least eight hours, which would see her through until five o'clock. She flicked the match down the side of the matchbox. It gave a crackle and burst into flame. She lit the wick, blew out the match and sniffed the strangely intoxicating smell of the sulphur before resting it on the edge of the saucer.

Okay, now what? Sit and stare at it for eight hours? That was going to drag, especially as she wasn't sleeping much since the changes at work. She gazed at the orange flame, dancing and flickering to its own music. A faint honey smell emanated from the hot wax, and she scrunched up her eyes to summon up a mental image of George, in case that somehow made the magic that she didn't believe in more potent.

Hypnotised by the light, and repeating his name in her head, she hoped that Brenda's instincts were right and he had a softer side, because if this ridiculous ritual worked she might find she'd let herself in for more than she could cope with. It wasn't that he was unattractive – far from it. He had large, soft brown eyes and lips that had the potential to form a pleasant smile if he would only let them. He'd looked so scary and businesslike the first time she'd met him, but the recent addition of the glasses suited his features and softened that intimidating look, somehow making him slightly vulnerable and more human. She thought about all the money lavished on the little scrap of cat that he hadn't wanted but that had wormed its way into his heart. Perhaps he was lonely. There didn't seem to be evidence of a girlfriend, and there were still no visiting friends or family.

After a while, Lucy noticed the candle had burned down to the start of the G in George. Nearly three-quarters of an hour had passed. Perhaps the night wouldn't be such a drag after all. She reached for her jumbled knitting bag and took out Poldark's half-finished breeches and her needles started to click away to a backdrop of mindless television.

By three o'clock in the morning Poldark was finally complete; a resplendent two-foot-high topless figure in a tricorn hat and holding a knitted scythe. Once the breeches were finished, it hadn't taken long to sew him up and stuff him. The candle was now down to the last bit of George's surname but still had a couple of hours burning left.

Lucy was at the point where she was fighting to stay awake. The television had long since been turned off, as early-morning programming left a lot to be desired: *24 Hours in A&E* and re-runs of *Traffic Cops* weren't really her thing. She needed to focus on something or she'd be on the first train to Sleepy Town. It was too late to embark on another knitting project, so she decided to read for a bit. There were two back issues of *Knitting and Crochet* lying on the floor in front of her huge wool basket. She picked them up and flicked though them, but they'd been well and truly thumbed, so she tossed them onto the table, making a conscious effort not to treat the floor as a tabletop. They skidded across the wooden surface and landed too close to the candle for comfort, so she moved them to the middle of the table.

Feeling that she needed to be engaged in something that would hold her attention, she went on a hunt for *The Duke's Dangerous Secret* but couldn't remember where she'd put it, so grabbed a handful of books from the pile by the bed to flick through. The problem with being disorganised was that both the books she'd read and the books she was planning to read were randomly stacked together. What she ought to do was separate the ones she'd finished with to take over to Brenda. She carried all of them into the living room to go through the blurbs and find one she hadn't read. Kneeling by the coffee table, she selected *Her Benevolent Master* from the pile; *Lord Fullbroke offers refuge to the fleeing Cassandra but will her dark secret destroy them both?* She pulled some cushions down from the sofa and put them behind her back, still preferring to sit crossed-legged on the floor.

After a while, Lord Fullbroke and his bulging trousers were not really doing it for her. She found herself nodding off, and there were a couple of horrible moments when she felt like she was free-falling as sleep tried to grab her. She jolted herself awake and readjusted her position, sitting on her knees and resting the book on the edge of the table. The lights were dimmed after Poldark had been completed, but there was still enough light to read by. Her concentration was wandering and she found herself rereading lines and skipping words.

The candle looked close to burning out, so she only needed to stay awake for a little bit longer...

Chapter 17

There was a loud banging noise. In Lucy's dream the errant Lord Fullbroke was risking all to prove his love for her, but he wouldn't open up about his tragic past. If only he wasn't so devilishly handsome. The castle was on fire and she realised the jealous Cassandra was trying to burn her alive in her bed.

Bang, bang, BANG.

Lucy forced her eyes open as her senses finally got through to her brain. There was a bitter, smoky smell and she realised the shouting and banging were both very real.

The room was filled with smoke and she could see a low, flickering flame on the coffee table. Her heart thudded. Her hands started to shake. The open book, which she must have nudged across table as she'd fallen asleep, had pushed the pile of discarded books and the magazines into the candle. They were on fire. *Really* on fire.

She screamed.

'Lisa? LISA?'

Someone was kicking her front door.

Adrenaline pumped to every extremity of her panicked body. Should she deal with the fire or answer the door? Her flight instinct was considerably stronger than her fight instinct. She opened the living-room door, ran into the hall and took the safety chain off. As she pulled the door inwards, George came bolting through it and flattened her to the ground. He must have taken a run-up to shoulder the door, expecting to meet with solid wood, but instead met with a distraught Lucy. They landed with a clump together on the carpet. His enormous frame and weight constricted her chest and pinned her down like Wile E. Coyote under a boulder. Despite the drama of the situation, all she could focus on for that instant was the musky smell of his aftershave and an extreme close-up of his stubbly chin.

The fire alarm decided now was the time to draw everyone's attention to the escalating crisis.

'That damn alarm should have gone off before now,' George grunted. Scrambling to his feet, he headed for the kitchen. 'But the fire brigade are on their way.'

She could hear the cold tap on full blast. George shouldered past her carrying a plastic bowl of water to douse the flames. There was a loud sizzle. She stepped to one side as he pushed back out into the hallway and through to the kitchen for more water.

The second bowlful extinguished the flames completely and they stood together in silence as the bitter, black air swirled around them. They looked at the ash-strewn, water-logged table as a single scorched page fluttered to the floor. She saw George glance around. Now that she looked at it from someone else's perspective, and despite the tidy-up, she realised there was an awful lot of wool-based items in her living room: crocheted blankets, knitted ribbed cushion covers and the oversized log basket to the right of the mantelpiece overflowing with oddments of wool. Wolverine and Thor stared straight ahead, both paralysed with the fear of what might have been. Poldark was face down on the carpet. In the distance a siren approached.

'Are you okay?' George asked.

She coughed to clear her lungs. 'I think so.'

'Let's get outside. The air in here isn't going to do either of us any good.'

As they stepped out on to the pavement, the flashing blue lights and whining siren appeared. Two men in bright yellow helmets leaped from the cab before it had even pulled to a halt. They rushed passed as George flung a resigned arm towards Lucy's flat, and the pair of them slumped onto the low wall in the front garden. The young lad who lived directly above her stumbled out into the night in his pyjamas and with splendid bed hair to watch the proceedings. Luckily, the couple who owned the top flat were in Barcelona. A babble of concerned neighbours established the quiet, helpful girl from the flat at number twenty was okay and then drifted back to their beds.

Lucy glanced across at George, who looked unusually morose and ashen-faced, but then he had just dealt single-handedly with a potentially catastrophic event. He chose to sit at the far end of the wall, distancing himself from the midnight arsonist. Neither spoke and there was a period of frenetic hustle and bustle, the beep of radios and the stomp of heavy boots running in and out of the flat as the firemen assessed the situation.

An ambulance arrived not long after the fire engine, and a stern-faced paramedic, who was more beard than face, examined Lucy and fitted her with an oxygen mask. Her vital signs were checked and after a few minutes it was decided she didn't need to be admitted to the hospital. The oxygen had done its job and her airways were clear.

An older fireman, and clearly the one in charge, finally appeared after his inspection of her flat.

'It was the candle. Looks like it caught some papers on the table.'

'Books,' Lucy volunteered. 'And a couple of magazines.'

'That'll be your black smoke then, love. Glossy mags are pretty toxic. We've ruled out any further hotspots with the TIC.' He waved a black hand-held piece of equipment at her that looked a bit like a tiny television on a stick but was clearly some sort of thermal imaging device. 'Smoke alarms all in good working order. Shame the living-room door was closed or that might have gone off a bit sooner. You were fortunate that a neighbour realised what was happening, young lady. And you were also extremely lucky there was nothing else combustible near the flames or the whole house could have gone up. If a spark had flicked to the curtains or the basket of wool you'd be in real trouble right now.'

'Unbelievable.' George stood up and walked over to her. His big frame obscured the glow from the street lamp. 'You were playing with candles at five o'clock in the morning? Do you realise how totally irresponsible your behaviour was? You could have been killed.'

So much for the spell bringing them closer. He clearly thought she was a total idiot.

'I... I was...'

'I don't want to hear it. I've seen the damage a fire can do and it's not something I take lightly. You have NO IDEA how angry I am, right now.' And he stormed off towards his house, his striding figure disappearing in the shadows of the night.

Having collapsed into bed within minutes of the fire brigade departing, and fallen asleep within seconds of her smoky hair touching the pillow, it wasn't until later that morning Lucy could assess the damage from her antics the night before.

There was no real harm done, apart from the badly scorched coffee table and the acrid smell. She'd been lucky. If George hadn't woken her, the fire could have spread, with horrific consequences. She had some serious apologising to do.

'These are for you.' She thrust a bunch of black tulips at a confused George, hoping they were a suitably masculine floral choice, but was unable to meet his eye. 'I wanted to say a proper thank you for what you did this morning.'

'I don't want flowers.' He frowned.

'Oh, sorry. Are you allergic to them?'

'Not particularly. Just everything else on the damn planet. Look, I'm hardly ever here to appreciate them. It's a waste.'

'Please take them. And these.' She handed him the gift bag containing a couple of bottles of wine.

He looked inside. 'I don't want anything. You're just lucky Scratbag was on the ball.'

'Scratbag?'

'Yeah, it was almost as if he knew. He did that rubbish meow and wrapped himself around my legs. Then he trotted to your door, pausing to see if I was following. I picked up on the smell of smoke, and as I got level with your front window I saw a flicker of flame. You should be buying him the catty equivalent of these gifts. Perhaps a bunch of mice and a couple of bottles of distilled catnip?'

Lucy looked at his face as he made the joke, but again there was no trace of anything resembling a smile – no crinkling of the eyes or upturn of the mouth.

'Please? I've written you a card,' she persevered.

'Okay,' he sighed, as he reluctantly took her offerings. 'But don't *ever* do anything so stupid again.'

Feeling severely chastised, Lucy returned to the flat and rang Jess for some sympathy and understanding.

'Yes?' Jess snapped.

'It's only me.'

'Oh, Luce... Sorry. Your call woke me up and I'm in a foul mood so give me a wide berth, but don't ask because I *really* don't want to talk about it.' There was a rustle of bedding and a scraping noise. 'Bloody hell, is that the time? I've slept for longer than I thought.'

'I wasn't exactly up with the birds myself this morning.'

'Yes, the candle thingy. How did it go?' She heard Jess stifle a yawn and fidget in the bed.

Lucy relayed the disaster from the previous night and Jess, picking up on her friend's feelings of despondency, decided they should meet in town for a lazy Sunday afternoon drink and some girlfriend time. After she'd put some clothes on, of course.

Sitting in the crowded pub garden of The King's Arms, overlooking the meandering River Douse, Lucy nursed a gin and tonic as Jess worked her way through three large glasses of house white. If Lucy was worried she looked rough after her candle all-nighter, Jess looked a hundred times worse. There were telltale red rims to her eyes, a glow to her nose suggesting repeated blowing and dark circles under each eye that probably matched her own. But Jess had nailed a smile across her face and was dealing with whatever had caused the tears in her usual way – by slapping on plenty of make-up and getting on with it.

The busyness of the pub gave them an anonymity that suited them both. Inside was so packed, there was barely a place to stand, never mind sit. Outside, the Heineken-parasoled hexagonal picnic benches had been taken over by families out for a late Sunday lunch and older couples returning from day trips to National Trust properties and open gardens. The sun was out and the air was a hunger-inducing combination of yeasty beers and fatty chips.

Jess and Lucy found a space on the wall near the riverbank, the bricks uncomfortably cold on the backs of their bare legs. Dangling their feet over the slow-moving river and watching the fast-food debris and serene waterfowl float past, they soaked up the sun and chatty atmosphere. Jess was wearing a strappy lemon-yellow sundress and her designer shades, and looked like a blonde Victoria Beckham. Lucy was in T-shirt, shorts and a floppy cotton hat, and looked more like a female Worzel Gummidge.

'I can't see how the whole candle episode can have any positives. All it's done is reinforce his perception of me as inept and ditzy. And because I fell asleep, I technically didn't even sit through the full moon until the flame went out, or whatever it said. I tried, but perhaps now I can get back to living my uncomplicated, knitted life. I told you it wouldn't work and, quite honestly, I'm relieved that it didn't.'

Jess tried to smother a yawn but the infectious nature of yawns, plus her own ridiculous lack of sleep, meant Lucy quickly followed.

'But Brenda said *spells* – plural. You've only done one, even if it was a total failure. Didn't she say the locket would reveal them to you? Have you even checked it since setting fire to your Regency book collection?'

Lucy rolled her eyes. What was Jess expecting? It was a silly old locket, made by a bunch of superstitious Victorians, to amuse and entertain. Did she think the words were going to change? Honestly, Jess was so gullible.

Lucy rummaged around in her bag, having taken it off that morning, but now feeling bereft when she didn't at least have it with her. She flipped it open.

'Blimey, girl. You must have done something right,' said Jess, leaning over her shoulder. 'You'll have to accept the locket is magic now. The words have changed again.'

Chapter 18

*'Pluck three strong hairs from your head
And place beneath your true love's bed.'*

'**O**h, you're kidding me?' Lucy sighed.
     'You can't give up now. My arms have gone all goose bumpy. This is real. The magic is real.' Jess was wriggling around like a three-year-old who needed the toilet. 'I didn't know whether to believe Brenda before, but even you can't still think it's just an ordinary locket?'

Lucy's insides were churning faster than a washing machine on repeat spin. It was like being told you'd won millions on the lottery – that creeping sense of disbelief at the unfolding events – especially when you knew you hadn't bought a lottery ticket in the first place. How could this be happening?

'You can't back out now. You've absolutely got to see this thing through,' her friend persisted.

Lucy folded her arms across her chest, deliberately turning away from the bouncy Jess and focusing on the trailing branches of a weeping willow that were being tugged downstream by the river. *I'm being pulled too*, thought Lucy. *Can I fight it any more than the willow can?*

'C'mon, Luce. Brenda would be pleased to think you'd taken

her seriously. And you can keep her updated and involve her in it all. Give the old girl something to think about other than her bowel movements.' Jess knew exactly which heartstrings to tug.

'Freaky word changes aside, it's not that I mind doing something to keep Brenda happy, more that it involves potential humiliation on my part.'

'But there's no real harm in it if you don't believe magic can make someone fall in love with you. All it means is you are going to have a lot more contact with George, and he's hardly a chore. Some people would consider him fit.'

'It's not positive, "she's an intriguing girl I want to get to know her better" contact. It's "get that bloody bonkers knitting obsessed pyromaniac out of my sight" contact.'

'Nonsense. I bet he's warming to you and your quirky nature. You've got nothing to lose.'

'Apart from my dignity – which I'm pretty sure went up in smoke this morning anyway.' But Jess didn't break her gaze. Lucy dropped her eyes to the ground, defeated. 'Okay, then tell me how I'm supposed to get three of my hairs under his bed? I've already managed to inadvertently enlist the help of the Bedfordshire Fire Brigade. Next it will be the police force arresting me for breaking and entering.'

'Sometimes you are so naive, Luce. How can it possibly be breaking and entering when he's given you a key?'

Sam spent Monday morning in the warehouse. She turned up at eight o'clock in some sort of boiler-suit with ironed creases down both legs and bright white trainers with deep purple flashes along the sides. Given the level of dust and dirt on the concrete floor, they wouldn't be bright white by the end of the day.

Lucy was hearing all about it over lunch. As she was on a different lunch hour to Jess, she increasingly found herself sitting with the warehouse workers in their staffroom. In many ways, she felt more comfortable among these men, who reminded her of her down-to-earth dad, than she did with those from her own office. The two younger girls talked relentlessly about clothes, and Pat said nothing at all.

Lucy's dad was her ally and the person who had made her teenage years bearable. Her mother and Emily were the strong ones, the clever ones, the driven ones. Lucy and her dad sort of muddled through life. Paul Baker had turned Sandra Wallington's head not because he was a blue-eyed, gentle man with a good heart, but because he drove a bright red MG convertible and worked in a bank. Sandra had wrongly believed he was as career-driven as she was on his behalf and that he would be headhunted by Goldman Sachs before he was thirty.

But after years of nagging him to take promotion, she had to accept that Paul Baker would never rise above the position of operations manager at their local Barclays. He was happy looking after his small team of 'essential managers', or what he still stubbornly referred to as cashiers when the branch manager wasn't in earshot. He didn't want the stress and could live quite happily without the pay rise. He was a simple man, with simple pleasures but an extremely complicated wife. And while Sandra and her eldest daughter reached for the stars, Lucy and her dad had always been content to watch them twinkle from the ground and appreciate the things around them. Although Lucy had recently noticed her hand was starting to twitch.

Her dreams had always been tiny, manageable; she wanted

to be better organised, be able to stand up to her mother a bit more, find a pretty dress for the office Christmas party... But now, with the locket dangling a wealth of possibilities in front of her, she realised she had inner ambitions lurking deep in her unfulfilled soul. These aspirations were unexplored: to have a career, to find love, to be able to walk up to men like Daniel and give as well as she damn well got.

Listening to the warehouse workers' grumbles and moans, she nibbled on her cheese and grilled aubergine sandwiches. She didn't always agree with their opinions but liked their banter. In turn, the motley collection of mainly older men enjoyed having the attractive, youthful Lucy sitting with them. It made them feel young again. Roy had even taken to slipping a comb in his overalls pocket since she had been joining them.

'That bloody woman has already been in here and rolled her eyes at the calendar,' one of the forklift drivers mumbled. The bikini-clad, curvaceous girl who graced the wall above the fridge didn't bother Lucy. The screen saver on her laptop at home was the semi-naked scythe-swinging Ross Poldark, so who was she to judge?

'Yeah, well at least you weren't shut in a six-foot cab with her for the day,' said Derek, who was back early from his run but was scheduled for another shortly. 'She smelt of bloody eau-de-pretentious-female and I swear she looked down her snobby nose at me all day. Telling me how to reverse the lorry and questioning my decision to take the A134. I've been doing the damn job for eleven years. I think I've got the route cracked by now.'

'Careful, she'll hear you,' warned Lucy, anxiously turning to the door.

'Nah, she's collared Roy. Poor sod has been stuck with her

all morning in that back corner where all the damaged stock gets dumped.'

At that moment Roy swung the door open and collapsed into one of the plastic chairs at the end of the table.

'Bugger me. She's doin' my head in.'

'Stressful morning, Roy?' one of the younger lads teased.

'Managers should be upstairs managing, not watching over perfectly competent staff. But enough about me, what's this I hear about you and Daniel fooling about in the Tardis?'

Five pairs of eyes swivelled in Lucy's direction and her cheeks flushed.

'I wasn't... I didn't...'

'Lucy! He's a ladies' man, albeit a charming one,' said Derek. 'You can do much better than him.'

Before Lucy could protest any more, the door swung open a second time and Sam walked in.

'Ah, Lucy. I've been looking for you. What on *earth* are you doing in here?'

'Oh, erm, I'm having my lunch.'

'When do you finish?'

'One, but I can come now. It's no trouble. I've finished my sandwiches.' Lucy bundled her half-eaten packet of crisps and gooseberry yoghurt back into her lunch bag, scraped the chair back and moved to get up.

'No, no, you're fine. But come and find me later. I'm down the back of the warehouse assessing our returns and over-ordered stock. There are six pallets of Teletubby-themed stock that have been in the racks for years, and I'd like to see if we can do something with them, especially since the revival of the television series. I feel certain we could use that storage area more efficiently.'

'Of course.'

Sam glanced around the tiny kitchenette, her eyes lingering pointedly at the calendar. 'Ah yes, must print out the updated sexual harassment policy and, after some of the things I've witnessed this morning, review the health and safety policy as well. Right, see you in an hour, Roy,' she said as she left.

'Oh great, that's my afternoon bollocksed up then,' huffed Roy.

Lucy found Sam heaving boxes of ride-on Noo Noos out of the industrial racking. As Lucy approached, Sam glanced at her watch and wiped her dusty hand across her forehead, leaving a dirty smudge.

'You're early.'

'I'd finished so I didn't mind. Have you stopped for lunch?'

'I grabbed a coffee earlier.'

To give the woman her due, she wasn't a slacker. Lucy walked over to help.

'No, don't you get mucky. I'm happy doing this. I need you to chase up each item and find out why we have it. Is it faulty stock? Damaged? Or just over-ordered? As long as the manufacturer isn't waiting for us to return the pallet in order to credit us – you'll need accounts' help for that – we can brainstorm what to do with them. I'm reluctant to dump perfectly good items. If Roy and I work on a stock check of this area, could you give some time over to putting together some sort of report? Tell Adam I've told you to come off the phones. And if he complains he's a man down, tell him to pick up a headset.'

That would go down well. Why did she have to be nominated to pass that information on?

'And while I've got you, I wanted a word about earlier.' Lucy swallowed. 'Is there a reason you don't eat in the upstairs staffroom? I would have thought it was more appropriate. Girls of your own age, less swearing, more hygienic...'

'Is it a problem?'

'No, you can eat your lunch where you like, within reason.'

Another black mark in her copybook.

Sam turned back to the shelves but then hesitated. 'The other women aren't unkind?'

'No. They're fine.'

'Okay. Because I won't tolerate bullying in the office.'

'Honestly, they're fine.'

Chapter 19

'I've failed again,' Lucy said to Brenda over a chamomile-scented tea and a malted milk biscuit.

Brenda had been quite agitated when Lucy first arrived, fretting over the name of the Prime Minister, like it was the most important thing in the world that she should be able to recall it. But she was happier now that her dear friend was with her and was eager to hear about her day.

'Eating with the warehouse workers is obviously unacceptable,' Lucy continued. 'I'm amassing whatever the opposite of house points are by the day.'

'Hovel points?' Brenda smiled.

'Probably, because that's where I'll be living if I lose this job. The rent is already squeezing me dry.'

Brenda patted her hand. 'Things often turn out better than you think they're going to. Too many people spend a lifetime worrying about things that never happen. Sometimes you remind me of my younger self: uncertain of my path and lacking in confidence. If you've been wearing that locket, you'll start to notice a difference in your confidence levels.'

Lucy felt her face flush. 'I haven't,' she admitted. 'But I will. I'm sorry. I thought I could sort this out myself.'

Brenda smiled to herself. 'Jim was the person who taught

me to believe in myself and grab the things I wanted in life.'

'And the locket,' Lucy reminded her.

'Erm, yes, that as well. But the love of a good man does wonders. And, on that note, how are things going with that lovely young man from next door? Jerry? Jeffrey?'

'George. Not so good…'

And Lucy, pleased Brenda was having a good day and really needing a friend, finally filled her in on the candle catastrophe, as Brenda had clearly slept through the whole disaster.

Brenda tittered to herself all the way through the tale. 'I said you two would get on like a house on fire.'

'Please don't tell me you knew I was going to set my books alight?'

'Not exactly,' Brenda admitted, and giggled again.

'It's not funny,' said Lucy, although secretly she was delighted to see her friend in such cheery spirits – even if it was at her expense.

'My dear, if you can't look back at life's disasters and see the funny side how can you move on?'

'Okay then, it was a bit comical. Especially when he came charging through the front door.' Lucy's legs felt a bit fuzzy as she remembered his stubble and his aftershave, both in closer proximity to her than she would have liked.

'How sexy to have that great hunk of a man draped over you. It's all very Mills and Boon. Which reminds me, you said I could borrow some of those new Regency romances of yours a while ago. There's no hurry, but I'm still interested, when you've got the time to look a few out.'

Lucy's heart sank.

'I dropped them to you a couple of weeks ago. Don't you

remember? You finished *The Nobleman's Daughter* because we had a laugh about the bath scene.'

'Did I? Oh, silly me. Yes. Quite right. They'll never beat a Betty though.'

Brenda, who had devoured Mills and Boons since she was a girl, had a soft spot for Betty Neels and her laughingly chaste heroines. Ironic, given Brenda's less than chaste lifestyle before, and apparently after, she met Jim. (Lucy had been shocked to learn car keys in the fruit bowl was not an urban myth, and even more shocked that Brenda had participated, considering Jim was the love of her life.) One of the many reasons for their friendship was a shared passion for a taciturn doctor from the Seventies or an egotistical viscount from 1815. Lucy often passed books on to her friend, hiding a paperback under her cardigan or carrying a few over in an unmarked carrier bag. Brenda would smile and remind her she wasn't trading in illegal drugs, but then Brenda hadn't spent a lifetime being teased for her choice of reading material.

'Get Emily to lend you some *decent* books,' her mother pleaded. 'Instead of all that silly, dreamy nonsense. You need to get your head out of the clouds and focused on a career.' What she didn't know, because Lucy wasn't a telltale, was Emily read romances and enjoyed them just as much as Lucy did. Emily was canny enough, however, to leave the latest Man Booker prizewinner casually out on the sideboard when her mother was babysitting her little darlings.

'So, back to our hunky neighbour...' Brenda was deftly moving the subject away from her forgetfulness. 'If you've completed the candle spell, that cheeky little locket will have something else up its sleeve.'

137

The locket was still in her handbag from Sunday when she'd gone to The King's Arms with Jess. She bent over to fish it from her bag, looked at it sitting innocently in her hand and thought about her resolution to be bolder. Nothing had changed. She still wasn't standing up to her mother, was still pushed around at work and was still letting George call her Lisa. Perhaps she did need some help, after all.

She poked her head through the chain and the locket slid down her chest, nestling between her breasts. A soft glow seemed to spread through her entire body. She took a slow breath in and then exhaled, feeling calmer about everything somehow. Flipping the catch, she read out the latest spell: the three hairs under his bed shenanigans.

'Ah, I remember. I had to enlist the help of Jim's younger sister with that one. It cost me a shilling and a bag of penny sweets to bribe her. So how are you going to sneak some of your hairs into his bedroom? I don't suppose you can pay off Scratbag with a couple of fresh herring?'

'Jess has a plan.'

'Oo, good.' Brenda rubbed her pale hands together. 'You will tell me how it goes, won't you?'

Lucy nodded. Jess was right; her journey with the locket was breathing new life into Brenda and following the spells cost her nothing but her time. 'I'd better head back now and get myself something to eat, but I'll be over again later.' She stood up, conscious of the locket swinging as she moved.

'It's kind of you, but I don't need constant checking.' Brenda stood up and walked over to wind up the Edwardian wooden mantel clock. 'I'm more sorted for what is coming than you think, Lucy.'

Chapter 20

Lucy stood on the pavement outside Brenda's, taking in everything around her; from the cheerful pink and lilac aquilegias nodding their bell-shaped heads in the front gardens, to the lazy butterflies, sunning themselves against the crumbling red bricks of the boundary walls. She noticed Scratbag perched on the warm bonnet of George's car, and was convinced he winked at her. He looked first at his owner's front door, then swivelled his head back pointedly to look in her direction as if to say, 'What are you waiting for?'

She pulled her shoulders back and turned towards George's house, head high, but as she put up her hand to knock, the door swung inward.

'Ah, Lisa, just the woman. I was about to pay you a visit as I believe this is yours.' He handed her the bookmarked copy of *The Duke's Dangerous Secret*. 'Unless Scratbag has nipped out for a library card when I wasn't looking. More of a classics man myself, but I expect it has merit, if you're into that kind of thing.'

'Lucy,' she corrected, placing her hand across her chest where the locket lay beneath her T-shirt. Was she imagining it? Or was the locket almost buzzing?

'Oh, I could swear your name was Lisa.'

'Well, it isn't. It's Lucy. It's always been Lucy. There was never a time in my life when it wasn't Lucy.' Surprised at her confidence with this intimidating man, she felt her heart rate double and her mouth go dry.

'Right. Erm, I was actually coming round to ask a favour...'

Lucy crossed her arms, hoping it made her look in control, but also to muffle the thudding from her chest.

'There is a final meeting with the German pulp and paper manufacturer, so I'm flying over Wednesday evening. I'll be back late Thursday afternoon. Scratbag needs feeding. Not that I plan on keeping him long-term, but I couldn't see him homeless.'

'If you say please, I'll think about it.' It was a revelation to Lucy to realise she had the upper hand. He wanted something from her, and she had the power to say no – not that she would, but he didn't know that.

George, who had been standing legs apart and chest out, dropped his shoulders slightly.

'Of course. Did I not say please? I thought I had.'

'You most certainly did not.'

'I apologise. *Please* would you feed Scratbag while I'm away, Li— Lucy?'

'Of course.'

'Unfortunately, I've got a lot of work commitments coming up that will involve staying away...'

'It's not a problem. As long as you ask nicely and give me a bit of warning.'

'I'll pay you, naturally.'

'Don't be ridiculous. I don't want payment. But perhaps you could do a similar favour for me in return?'

'Don't tell me your knitted pals need feeding? What do I

give them? Kapok?' Lucy was close to telling him where to stick his kapok and he sensed this. 'Sorry. Uncalled for. They look very...technical. I'm sure my fat fingers couldn't manipulate the needles to knit so much as a scarf. All credit to you for having a creative hobby.'

Lucy narrowed her eyes and tried to assess how genuine the apology was.

'I was going to ask if you'd keep an eye on Brenda when I visit my parents the weekend after next. She insists she doesn't need looking after, but I'm trying to check in on her a couple of times a day. Now the UTI has been treated, it's only a case of making sure she eats and drinks properly and giving her some company. She can be a bit forgetful, that's all.'

'As long as she doesn't turn me into a toad, or anything.' He raised an eyebrow. Clearly the misguided neighbourhood whispers regarding Brenda's dubious practices had reached him.

'Is that a yes then?'

'Not sure she particularly likes me, but of course I'll do it.'

'Oh, she likes you.' Lucy thought back to Brenda's various comments about what she would like to do with his supposedly irresistible body. 'Much, much more than you think.'

'So, I had this simply *marvellous* idea and thought, as you are quite crafty, you could make up one hundred napkin swans for the tables?'

There was another thudding in Lucy's chest.

'Erm, no, I don't think so, Mother.' She twirled the locket chain about her fingers.

'Sorry? Did you say no?' Lucy could almost visualise her mother removing the receiver from her face, giving the phone a withering stare and putting it back to her ear.

'That may have come out wrong, but I really don't want to spend hours and hours folding napkin swans. I've made them before and they are quite complicated. I have more important things to do.'

'Like what?' Sandra said in a tone that implied she couldn't possibly imagine her youngest daughter having priorities that took precedence over her napkin swans.

'I'm in the process of setting up a website for my knitted figures.' It wasn't true, she hadn't done a thing, convinced no one would buy them, but it was the first thing that sprang to mind. 'It's taking up all my spare time at the moment. I'm calling it, erm...Nicely Knitted Celebrities. Depending how that goes, I might not have a lot of spare time by September.' *Plus, Brenda might need more care by then*, she thought to herself, and she knew which activity she gave priority to.

'So you think people will *actually* pay for them?' her mother asked.

'Emily thought so. She's been very encouraging.' Perhaps she would speak to Emily and Jess about setting a website up as they were both huge supporters of the idea. Even if it didn't take off, the anonymity of an online site meant her failure would be low-key.

'I was about to say she's the person you should talk to, what with all her experience.'

'Yes, I'm sure her years of experience selling books and pens gives her an excellent insight into the market for knitted dolls. I mean, she's practically Alan Sugar.'

'You are in a funny mood tonight,' her mother said. 'Perhaps I'll ring again tomorrow when you are in a more agreeable frame of mind.'

* * *

'You're finally wearing the locket,' said Jess.

'Brenda was keen and it is a pretty thing.' Why had it taken her so long to accept she couldn't do this by herself? The effect had been almost instant and enabled her to stand up for herself with George. Once she'd put the locket around her neck, something had taken over, given her a self-assurance she could never have summoned alone.

'So when's the Not-Jolly-At-All Green Giant off next?' Jess asked Lucy, as they chatted in the staff car park, enjoying the slow-building heat of the morning and delaying entering the air-conditioned chill of the office. It was June and summer had finally nudged spring out of the way and persuaded her to take the unseasonal rain in her suitcase. She wrapped the country in warm temperatures and bestowed upon it long, lazy days with cooling evening breezes. The weather was absolutely perfect. But this was England; it wouldn't last.

'Tonight. Some important meeting in Germany. I really don't understand the business world. Germany is a place I would go for a week, not an afternoon. He's returning tomorrow.'

'Then I can come over and help with the spell. Shoving a couple of hairs under his bed should be a breeze, especially as you have a key. I'm glad we aren't going to have to resort to my lock-picking skills. They're a bit rusty.'

Not sure if that was a joke or not, Lucy moved the conversation on. 'It feels a bit dishonest. He's given me a key to feed the cat, not to go snooping about the house.'

'Oh, for goodness' sake, Luce, live a little. You might find you enjoy yourself. The most daring thing you've ever done was knit in 2 ply when the pattern said four.'

'You're not funny, Jessica Ridley.'

'No, but I'm right.'

'Come on, Polly,' said Adam.

Lucy looked up from the floor where she was kneeling; fliers advertising bargain Teletubby stock spread out across the colourful floor tiles and the locket swinging as she moved.

'Put the kettle on. It's eleven o'clock. Time for the morning coffee round. Can't have my team *flailing* at the last post.'

She was about to get to her feet, but hesitated.

'I'm dreadfully busy, Adam. I need to get these out today. Could you please ask someone else?'

'But you always do it.' Adam placed his hands firmly on his hips.

'Exactly. So I think it's someone else's turn, don't you? Perhaps a rota would be fairer?'

Adam huffed but didn't push it any further. 'Pat, be a love,' he said.

Lucy heard the wheels of Pat's chair squeak as she rolled it away from the desk and saw her reluctant auburn head bob up.

This being-confident lark was proving so much easier than Lucy could ever have imagined. Saying what she felt and standing up for herself had always seemed such a scary prospect. She had wrongly assumed it would lead to conflict and confrontation. Two things she had generally spent her life trying to avoid.

'If you need to pop out more often than usual today, just say,' Adam said, walking past her desk with an armful of folders and pulling a conspiratorial face with a huge pantomime wink. Lucy frowned. 'You know? To the ladies'? I completely understand about you women and your monthlies.'

That evening Jess was at Lucy's doorstep with her overnight bag and two bottles of Chardonnay.

'Jess! We'll never get through both of those.'

'Perhaps it's time you let go a bit, Luce. Honestly, you are about the only person I know whose face doesn't light up like a Belisha beacon when they see an unopened bottle of the old vino.' She threw her overnight bag into the hallway and stood the bottles inside the door. 'Right, let's get it over with.'

'You want to do it *now*?'

'Why not? Lucy Baker, you think about things too much.'

'I'm not dashing over to George's yet. It's too early to feed Scratbag and the man only left two hours ago. The neighbours will think it's odd.'

'What? Odd that we're going over to feed the neighbour's cat, which you've been asked to do anyway?' Jess glanced at her friend's saucer-like eyes and tutted. It probably was too early for Scratbag's supper, but Jess was a doer not a ponderer like Lucy. 'Fine, fine. We'll start on one of these,' and she grabbed a Chardonnay by the neck. 'And don't you dare say it's too early for a drink.'

Jess had ordered Lucy not to get anything special in for dinner. She was happy to take pot luck. A random cook, Lucy was the sort of girl who opened the fridge, selected a handful of ingredients and whisked something up with a flourish. Considering she was as disorganised with food preparation as she was in most other areas of her life, she had very few failures – the pea and banana risotto being the only one in recent memory.

They ate a simple pasta dish and sank the first bottle without much trouble. Deciding to eat in the garden, they enjoyed the intoxicating scents that drifted over the wall from Brenda's medicinal jungle and chatted about work.

'Bloody Sam's still got one more day in accounts. You should have seen Margaret yesterday – she was flapping about like a bat tied to a tree. At one point she was so flustered she dropped a stack of invoices and they cascaded across the office floor like a pack of playing cards. It took us twenty minutes to put them back in date order,' complained Jess. 'I don't think she'll cope with another day of Big Brother watching.'

'Accounts will be okay. I can't see Sam losing anyone in your office.'

'Not worried about that. More worried about the changes she's making. She's talking about updating our system just when I've got the hang of the current one. She's implied on more than one occasion that we are massively behind the times, but if it ain't broke, I'm not sure she needs to be fixing it. Fancy software is all very well until it crashes.' Jess waited for a reaction but clearly didn't feel Lucy was looking suitably sympathetic. 'You needn't look so smug. She's got her eye on your system as well – says it's all outdated and we need to encourage more online orders, email promotions to customers rather than printed leaflets, set up a company Facebook page, that kind of thing.'

'Poor old Adam,' Lucy said, although she thought Sam had an excellent point about the old-fashioned nature of the company, especially as the Teletubby fliers had taken her half a day.

Jess glanced at her watch and put her wine glass down on the kitchen table.

'Right, enough faffing, missus, it's action o'clock. Let's see what clues we can gather about this mystery man of yours. I mean, let's feed George's cat.'

Chapter 21

Scratbag began weaving in and out of their legs as soon as they unlocked the back door. Lucy fed him and changed the water in his bowl.

'Okay, let's do this.' Jess swung the hallway door open and walked into the main part of the house. She turned back to check Lucy was following. 'What *are* you doing, Luce? Please don't tell me you are actually on tiptoe?'

'I don't want anyone to hear us.' Her heart rate was through the roof.

'He's in Germany. He'd have to have supersonic hearing. Walk properly, you muppet.'

Lucy fumbled about and fished the locket over her cotton top, clutching it in her left hand. Her breathing slowed and she dropped her heels to the floor.

Jess opened the door to the living room. It was identical to Lucy's in proportion but considerably less cluttered. And without any knitted companions.

'Oo, loving the black and white furniture. Very chic.'

'We don't need to go in there.' It was bad enough they were going in his bedroom, she didn't want Jess poking about anywhere else.

'Don't you want to know a bit more about him? I do. On your behalf.' Jess flicked the light on.

'Jess!'

'Chillax, hon. I'll be quick. Real leather. Classy.' Jess stroked the furniture as though she was caressing the arms of a lover. 'A man of taste. Not many knick-knacks though are there?'

'I know. None of the usual clutter most people accumulate,' she agreed, trying to placate her friend and get her out of the room as quickly as possible.

Bobbing down on her knees, Jess started poking about in the large white, fitted cupboards either side of the fireplace.

'Come away from his personal stuff, Jess. I'm warning you.' Lucy was mortified that her friend was now riffling through his possessions. Not that he had many, but it was the principle.

Jess closed the cupboard door, but not before she'd opened another one and had a look inside.

'These cupboards are empty, Luce. This man has *nothing*. Do you reckon he's on a witness relocation programme or something? 'Cause this is seriously weird.'

'Perhaps he's not a hoarder.'

'This is more than the result of a tidy mind. Everyone accumulates things: books, photographs, silly tat that you buy on holiday and unwanted presents you get from family at Christmas. It's what happens. It's almost as if he's never lived a life before moving here. Perhaps my witness relocation programme isn't such a wild idea.' And Jess meandered back to the hall, her hand trailing over the furniture along the way.

The girls went up the first flight of stairs and worked out which was George's bedroom as it was the only one furnished, but it looked more like an impersonal hotel room. It had a

149

large double bed with coordinated bedding, some basic storage in the form of a chest of drawers, a matching bedside table and a fitted wardrobe that ran the length of the room. And it was so tidy. No odd socks scattered across the carpet or abandoned books. Just a phone charger, a solitary photo and a pair of perfectly positioned black leather shoes next to the bed.

'A photo at last. Guess we're right about this being his bedroom then.' Jess pointed to the black and white photo of an older man with a strong genetic similarity to George on his pine bedside table.

'Okay, let's get it over with,' Lucy said. She pulled a few hairs from her head and counted out three. 'So where do I put them? Under the pillow?'

'Better put them under the bed itself, like the spell said. Give them here. I'll do it.'

'I'm not totally useless.' Lucy knelt beside the bed and bent down to get underneath. 'There. Done. Let's go.' She swivelled back to face the room. 'Jess! Will you stop being so nosy?'

Jess stood in front of his open wardrobe, running her hand along the row of coat hangers.

'Nice clothes. What there are of them. This is a man with a sense of style and a wallet to finance it. I'm loving the Hackett polo shirts. I wondered if the Audi might be a company car, but after looking at his furniture and his clothes I'm thinking he has some serious money lying around. Things are looking up – for you, I mean. It will be nice to have a boyfriend who isn't short of a euro or two.'

The girls were halfway down the stairs when Jess stopped. 'You keep going. I've got to go back and see if I closed the wardrobe doors properly.'

'You did. I checked.'

'It's no good. I have to be sure. You go down and make sure nothing is out of place in the living room.'

'We wouldn't need to do all this checking if you hadn't poked around in places you had no right to be poking around in.'

'Okay, okay. I'm sorry. You were right, but just do it will you? I won't be a sec.'

Jess was a good couple of minutes and Lucy was about to call up to her when, horror of all horrors, she heard a key turn in the front door. Her heart doubled its pace and she went hot and cold all at once. What was George doing back?

She ducked into the utility and closed the door softly behind her. Oh no, Jess was going to be discovered and he was going to be furious.

'What on earth are you doing in here?' George's booming voice echoed down the hall. It was all over. He'd found Jess. How embarrassing. He'd confiscate the key and never let her feed Scratbag again. 'Did that ditzy girl let you out of the utility? I specifically asked her not to. I don't want you clawing the sofa or weeing on the bed...'

Ah, not Jess. They'd inadvertently let Scratbag into the main part of the house. She tried to exhale the pent-up breath quietly.

'Come here, my beautiful boy. Better dose up with the antihistamine if I'm back again. Are you surprised to see Daddy? Daddy's a bit surprised to be back home himself. He's had one hell of an evening.'

Daddy? Lucy smiled to herself. The softer side Brenda had been so convinced was lurking underneath the blunt exterior

151

was clearly only reserved for the cat. And a cat he had professed to barely tolerate at that.

Footsteps clumped down the hall and into the adjacent kitchen. A cupboard door opened and closed again. The tap was turned on briefly and then silence.

Time ticked by and Lucy wondered what her best course of action might be. Should she make a run for it or wait for Jess? If she left now she would have to lock up after herself and that would definitely lead to the discovery of her friend. But if she waited around and he entered the utility she would be found, unless she climbed into a cupboard or hid behind the trouser press. Neither option was realistic.

Further clanking in the kitchen made her glance at the utility door in expectation. Then she heard the fridge open.

'Come on, fella. Let's have a boys' night in front of the TV.' George's voice carried through the wall. 'I'll just nip and put the television on while the tea brews.' There were footsteps down the hall and then the distant drone of music from a television being switched on.

Aware of a warm sensation across her chest, Lucy looked down at the locket. This was ridiculous. Why was she hiding in his utility room when she had a legitimate reason to be here? She swung open the door to the hall and met George returning to the kitchen.

'Hi,' she beamed her widest smile at him and then looked down at Scratbag, weaving in and out of George's legs and purring louder than the exhaust of a teenager's souped-up car. 'I was just about to feed him, but it appears *Daddy's* home early. What a lovely surprise.' She bent down to pet the cat, who walked up to her hand and nuzzled his tiny head against her outstretched fingers.

George coughed. 'Yes, well, I obviously didn't realise we had an eavesdropping visitor. Not sure why I slipped into baby talk, probably because I'm exhausted, not to mentioned severely pissed off. My meeting was postponed at the last minute as their CO came down with food poisoning, but I didn't find out until I was in the damn departure lounge.'

'You don't have to apologise to me for showing your cat affection,' Lucy said. 'Anyone would think you were afraid of people seeing your nice side.'

'What do you mean? I'm always nice.'

Lucy raised an eyebrow.

'Okay, I'm sometimes nice. In fact, I've just made a pot of tea. Would you like to join me? It was remiss of me not to have offered before.'

Aware poor Jess would still be lurking upstairs, and seeing a chance to allow her friend to escape, she accepted. 'Just a quick one then.'

He directed her to the living room and disappeared to make the tea. When he returned, they stood awkwardly by the mantelpiece, clutching their mugs as a detective drama played in the background. Lucy heard soft, paddy footsteps down the hall and the utility door close. George didn't appear to hear anything, and stood awkwardly, trying to make small talk as Lucy practically downed the hot tea in one.

'Right, I'm off.' She thrust the empty mug at him.

'Oh. Thought you were going to stay for a bit?' George furrowed his brow.

'Sorry, gotta dash. I'll see myself out,' and she left an open-mouthed George, looking more bereft than she'd expected.

'Oh, bye then,' he mumbled.

*　*　*

'That was close,' Lucy said, as the girls tumbled into the hallway of the flat together.

'You have no idea. I had to walk past the stupid cat. It swivelled its inky-black head as I passed and gave me the evils,' said Jess.

'It's okay. We can bribe him with tuna steaks and he'll keep your secret safe.'

'Good job I don't have any secrets then.'

'Apart from Daniel, you mean?' said Lucy.

Chapter 22

As soon as the words left her mouth she regretted them, but that was what a large glass of wine and a confidence-boosting locket did for you.

'What makes you think I have a secret concerning Daniel?' Jess asked, avoiding eye contact.

Lucy was forced to relay the Tardis incident, astonished the company gossip hadn't made it into the accounts office. Everyone else had been teasing her about it for days.

'If he was only apologising because he'd cornered the wrong person, then he was clearly assuming the right person wouldn't have minded. And then you cancelled on me. And Dashing Daniel was strutting around the office and singing even more than he usually does. You could have told me, you know? I'm pleased for you. You've had your eye on him for months. Perseverance clearly pays off.'

The dejected look on Jess's face didn't sit well with a girl enjoying those exciting early stages of a relationship. Her posture crumpled and she shook her head.

'Oh, Luce. I've made such a fool of myself. We all know he's a flirt, but he's a good-looking one and he drives a nice car. He didn't want a girlfriend. He wanted a good time.'

Lucy looked at her remorseful friend. 'Oh, sweetheart.'

Jess turned away and picked imaginary fluff from her skinny jeans. 'An expensive date at some posh place in Bedford where there was enough cutlery for four people. A night in a Travelodge the following Friday because I'd held out on the first date. And *then* he decided it wasn't a good idea to be dating someone from work. I'm not stupid. He was never interested in me as a long-term prospect. I was just another number in his iPhone.'

'I'm sorry, honey.' She was furious on her friend's behalf. Next time he asked for help with the ClickIn starter sets, she might just tell him where to store them.

'I'm the one who should be sorry. He made a move on you.'

'Barely. He switched the light off, went a bit Leslie Phillips on me, and then Sam opened the door. So, on top of all her concerns about my competence, she now thinks I'm the office bike.'

'When in reality it's me?' she sniffed.

'No. It was just Daniel being Daniel and muddling us up.' She put her hand on Jess's knee. 'Will it make things awkward at work?'

'No. I've drawn a line under it and put it through the shredder. He was nice enough, very apologetic and all that, but clearly wasn't looking for the long-term relationship I had in mind.' She flicked away a burgeoning tear with her thumb and broke out a dazzling smile. 'But you know me? Onwards and upwards. I have a Plan B. There is someone else on my radar.'

Lucy looked at her friend expectantly.

'It's just a possibility at the moment. I don't want to rush and get burned twice in a row. But if things pan out like I hope, then I'll tell you all about it.'

'Okay, but I want to be the first to know if there might be a romance on the horizon. And if I bag horrible old Mr Sneezy Pants, we could be double dating before you know it.'

Jess didn't answer.

Early the next morning, while the girls were munching on slices of toast and peanut butter before the commute to work, there was a heavy knock at the door.

'It's George,' Lucy sighed. 'I'd know his hammering anywhere. I can't possibly answer in my T-shirt and pants.'

'I'll get it.' Jess jumped up from the table.

'But your nightwear is skimpier than mine.' The hem of her silky chemise barely covered her bottom.

'He's not come here to look at me,' Jess said, reaching for the latch.

Lucy slunk behind the kitchen door and peered through the gap.

'Is Lucy in?' George asked, in his usual blunt manner.

'Can I take a message? She's...indisposed.'

'She left the spare key at mine yesterday.'

'Ooo, at that stage already? She'll be moving in before you know it.' Jess gave him a cheeky nudge of the elbow. She was swishing her hair around and her voice was bubbly and slightly breathless, but Jess was like this with everyone – even the postman.

Looking around for the locket, Lucy found it near the kettle where she'd taken it off the previous night. She slipped it over her head, even though she was aware it was slightly odd to accessorise Hello Kitty nightwear with Victorian silver jewellery.

'Ignore her,' Lucy said, stepping forward and tugging at the hem of her T-shirt. He'd seen her in bedwear before, but she'd been wearing bottoms when they'd run down Tudor Avenue together in the rain. Although she knew Jess wasn't after George, poor George didn't know that, and she needed to stop him being used as a temporary ego boost after the Daniel disaster. 'She's only teasing. She knows full well it's so I can feed Scratbag.'

Lucy slid past Jess and stood directly in front of George. Gosh, he was extremely tall when you stood up close.

'Lucy.' He nodded, but his gaze didn't linger as long over her body, she noticed.

She tried to make eye contact, remembering Jess's tips for attracting men, but he looked away, so she swished her hair. It became tangled across her face, and in desperation she reached out for his arm. There was a moment of silence when George looked down at his arm, Lucy looked down at his arm, and she squeezed his firm muscles for want of something to do with her now embarrassingly redundant hand. She cleared her throat and took a step back. Jess made this flirting malarkey look easy, but it wasn't.

'Coffee?' she ventured, trying to remember where she'd stashed her mother's Colombian ground coffee.

'I'll pass.'

'Okay. Another time?'

'Hmm....'

And he was gone.

As the girls were getting in their respective cars and heading off for work, Chloe's mum from opposite called over to them.

Although not a close friend, Lucy had got to know her when they both volunteered to help with the Renborough summer fayre the previous year. Bolder than Lucy, she'd dressed up as Madame Zelda for the fortune telling. Lucy stuck to behind-the-scenes help: knitting a rodent for Splat the Rat, folding endless raffle tickets and washing up in the refreshment tent.

'Don't suppose you've seen a tiny, white lop-eared rabbit about?' she asked.

'No, sorry. Have you lost one?' asked Lucy.

'Chloe left the hutch door open last night and he's gone missing. He shouldn't be too hard to spot as he's only truly camouflaged when we have snow.'

'I can check my back garden now for you, if you like? What's he called?'

'Turnip. That's what you get when you let a four-year-old choose the name. Thank you. I've asked all the neighbours to keep an eye out and I put up some posters with my number on. Poor Chloe is really upset. Spread the word.'

'What is it with your neighbourhood and lost animals? Are you like a Bermuda Triangle for mammals or something?' said Jess, as they rummaged around in the begonias and peered over the wall into Brenda's garden. But there was no Turnip to be found and with time ticking on, the girls gathered their bags and headed to their cars for a second time.

Thursday was sunny, but Friday was wet and windy, the sudden drop in temperature making Lucy dig out a cardigan. As a rule, people looked forward to Fridays at work. They were certainly a damn sight better than Mondays, but for the sales office at Tompkins Toy Wholesaler it meant the intimidating presence of Sam back in their office.

Adam was having what Jess called 'A Mare' and made sure everyone suffered as a result.

'Can I have a volunteer to get the initial order for the new Norwich Cheeky Monkeys Toy Shop sewn up by ten? They open in two weeks and if we cock up their first big order, they won't place another one. Come on, ladies...' Connor's sigh drifted out from behind his partition. 'We need to show them we're made of *metal*,' Adam said.

'That's a totally unrealistic ask, Adam,' Sonjit said. 'Have you seen how much there is to do?'

'Look, I'm going to be deep in the doo-doo of a dog if we can't pull this off. I told her it was no biggie.' He jerked his head in the direction of Richard Tompkins' office, where Sam was running through the monthly sales figures. 'So don't make me look like an idiot.' Lucy bit back the obvious retort. The locket may have been increasing her self-confidence, but she wasn't totally suicidal. 'We don't want the old crow thinking we're slackers,' he added.

'She looks more like a black widow spider to me,' Lucy mused. 'All that black with a splash of red.' She instantly regretted her comment because she was warming to her new boss, but the locket was poking its oar in.

'The Black Widow. Nice one,' said Adam in a loud voice.

'Shhh...' Lucy didn't want everyone to know what she thought of Sam's wardrobe.

'Don't sweat it, she's in with old Dickie boy, so unless she's got *supernatural* hearing, I think we're safe.'

'We could divide the workload up into sections,' Lucy ventured, returning to the problem in hand. 'Rather than someone wrestling with the whole order.'

160

'If you think you can do my job, then be my all-expenses-paid guest, Lucy-Lou, because I'm stressed to old bollocks over here. She's trying to squeeze magic from a very overworked wand.'

Can I do this? Lucy asked herself. *Probably*, her new braver self answered. So she took Adam at his word, collected the order from his desk and cast her eye over it to assess the nature of the beast. Then she divided it up into the different categories (wooden toys, preschool age, electronic, outdoor games, and so on) and photocopied sections for Pat, Sonjit and herself to focus on. The office still needed to run as normal, but with three of them off the phones, they could wrap it up for Adam's deadline. Pat and Sonjit were heads down immediately, working on the sections Lucy had allocated them and didn't question her assumed authority.

'So where are we with the Cheeky Monkeys order?' Sam asked as she came out of her finance meeting with Richard Tompkins a little while later.

'Nearly diddly-done, your majesty.' Adam did a theatrical bow as Sam walked past. 'I've got Sonjit, Pat and Lucy working together and they are just doing a final check. We wouldn't want any errors, would we, girls? It's been intense, but we're almost there.'

'Excellent delegating, Adam. Well done. I'm impressed.'

'Oh, it was nothing. We thrive on the pressure up here in the sales office. As I always say, if you can't ride a bumpy storm on a weathered horse, then what sort of man are you?'

'Indeed,' said Sam, dropping into her seat and sliding her glasses from the top of her head to her nose.

Lucy shot Adam an angry stare. He had the grace to look uncomfortable, and Lucy had the grace not to make an issue of it. Although she could feel her confidence growing, she wasn't prepared to make a big announcement in front of her boss or undermine Adam. After all, he'd supported the time off she'd had for Brenda.

Later, however, as he sidled up to her to ask if she could nip downstairs to do some photocopying, Lucy looked him straight in the eye and told him she was busy. He walked around the desk to Pat and bent down, and she heard a long sigh escape from Pat's side. Her chair wheels squeaked and the auburn head bobbed up.

By the afternoon, and under Sam's watchful eye, the office was running smoothly. The South-West area rep secured a large Tramp'O'Bounce order and Adam successfully negotiated a better discount with a supplier. (Talking the talk over the phone, Adam could do. Paperwork, not so much.) At four o'clock, Sam left them to investigate a complaint regarding a faulty foam blaster that had shot the soft bullet out with so much force during a customer demonstration that it had smashed the main shop window. Although everyone continued to work hard in her absence, the atmosphere became noticeably more relaxed.

'So, what's the word on the street?' Adam asked, wandering over to the back of the office where an animated discussion was taking place.

'Do you mean what are the ladies talking about?' Connor said. 'Not sure it's your bag, to be honest. Girl stuff.'

'Unless we're talking about freaky sexual fetishes, I'm probably right there with you. Ha ha. Has anyone got any freaky fetishes? Sonjit?' He looked at his colleague with hopeful eyes.

Sonjit's cheeks flushed briefly and she held Adam's gaze

for a fraction too long. 'We were discussing romantic comedies.'

'Well, then you've misjudged me, my fair and pleasant maidens. Don't mind a romcom myself. In fact, we have quite a collection of them at home.'

Connor looked disappointed not to be backed up. 'Really?'

Adam coughed. 'Of course, I prefer a violent war film or a gritty thriller. But real men are in touch with their feminine side, Connor. Plus, I read you are more likely to get lucky after you've sat through the soppy crap with a woman. It gets their hormones going or something.'

Sonjit rolled her eyes and put her hand to her headset as a call came in. The friendly chatter dried up and Adam started to wander back towards his desk, getting caught up in the cord from the blinds as it snagged on a cuff button. Everyone immediately pretended to be busy.

Lucy's internal line buzzed as Adam sat down at his desk and ran his fingers randomly up and down the keyboard. It was Pat.

'Adam said "we". Do you think he's got a girlfriend?'

Chapter 23

The phone call from Lucy's mother that evening was more cautious after the napkin refusal, allowing Lucy to have an equal share in the conversation. She chatted to her mother about what was happening at work and was pleasantly surprised to find the conversation was a two-way affair for a change. Feeling buoyed up by her mother's encouraging comments, she even dared to suggest there might be a man on the blurry horizon. The idea the spells would work was ridiculous, but she was at least getting closer to George, and he was starting to grow on her.

Feeling positive after the phone call and her successful day at the office, Lucy continued her mission to be organised in other areas of her life and decided to tidy up the kitchen. She emptied out the cupboards onto the now clear kitchen table and tried to organise them in a more logical manner. Grouping cleaning products and washing powders together, she placed them under the sink. Tins and packets went in a low cupboard, plates and bowls in another. The high cupboard over the kettle now held all the cups and glasses, along with the tea, her mother's ground coffee, sugar and special chocolate sprinkles for her hot chocolate – and maybe one day soon her own cupcake of life.

As she closed the last overhead cupboard, she noticed something moving about outside in the pots by the shed. She leaned over the sink to get a better look and noticed a patch of white fluff. Turnip? But he was too high off the ground to be a dwarf rabbit.

Scratbag crept from the begonias with a mouthful of white. 'Nooo!'

Lucy rapped on the window and the cat stopped dead. He turned his head, white bunny swinging in his jaws, and gave her an indifferent catty stare. She rapped louder and then dashed to the back door, fumbling to unlock it. Scratbag knew he'd been caught red-handed and dropped the bundle to the ground before making an elegant getaway over the wall into Brenda's garden.

Kicking on her turquoise Crocs, Lucy rushed to the white, fluffy, inanimate pile. Turnip had nibbled his last bundle of hay and lay on the grass a matted mess of blood, fur and mud. Poor Chloe.

She gently picked up the rabbit, respectfully wrapped him in an old towel and nipped out the front to copy down her neighbour's number. A phone call would be easier than a face-to-face.

'I'm sorry but I've found Turnip this evening in my garden. It looks like he was erm...got by a fox, but I'm sure it was quick and painless.'

'Oh dear, Chloe will be so upset but thank you for letting me know. It's been a fraught two days. I guessed something like this had happened.'

'Shall I dispose of him for you?' Lucy looked at the grubby bundle and decided it wouldn't be kind for Chloe to see him in that state.

'She'll want to bury him properly. When we lost our other rabbit, she tied flowers around his head and put pictures in with him. It's what you do when you are four. Shall I come over and collect him?'

'Erm, I'll pop him over in a bit. I'm just in the middle of something.'

She tenderly washed the tiny bundle and placed it on a towel. As she grabbed her hairdryer from the bedroom to dry poor Turnip off, there was a knock at her front door.

That knock.

She dumped the hairdryer on the kitchen table and walked down the hall.

'The offer of coffee from earlier, does it still stand?' George asked, as soon as she opened the door.

'It's a bit inconvenient at the moment.' Bloody man. Although she was running around like a crazy thing trying to get him interested in her as a romantic prospect, his timing was awful.

'I wanted to explain why I was so rude after the fire.'

'Oh, okay. Come in.' Maybe he was going to apologise.

George, with his huge shoulders slumped forward and head low, followed her into the hallway, where they both lingered for a moment. George's nostrils flared slightly and he pulled a troubled face.

'Yes, there's still a whiff of smoke. I think it's in all the furnishings and I can't seem to shift it,' Lucy said.

'No, you won't. The smell will linger for weeks.'

She turned to the kitchen but George stopped. His huge frame blocked out the light from the glazed front door and made Lucy feel small and fragile.

He cleared his throat.

'Look, I realise I'm a difficult and insular man. I don't have adequate social skills and I say what I think, whether people want to hear it or not. I can't dress up my sentiments with flowery words and I really do call a spade a spade. It's how I am. But I'm not intentionally rude. I'm so busy with work that it's become my life. I forget people exist outside of the factory, and when I come across them I don't know how to speak to them.'

'This being your cardboard-box-making factory?'

'It's rather more involved than that,' he huffed. 'We supply packaging for the food industry, and since we acquired a major supermarket deal I'm all over the place and rarely work from the office. There's a lot going on at the moment and I find it difficult not to let my work eat into my private life.'

She suddenly felt a bit sorry for him. At least she had a good group of friends. 'Let the big boss worry about all that. Try and switch off when you come home.'

'I am the big boss.'

'You *own* the company?'

He nodded.

'When we first met and you said you worked in packaging I thought you meant on the production line or something.'

'I have done in my time. It's important to understand all the processes involved, and every aspect of the company, in order to be able to oversee it properly. Effective management can't be confined to an office.'

Lucy thought of Sam and her hands-on approach.

'But sometimes I wonder what it's all for,' he continued. 'Do I really want to work for the next thirty years and drop down dead with a heart attack, like my father?'

'I'm sorry. I didn't realise you'd lost your dad.' She thought back to the black and white photo by his bed but was not quite brave enough to reach for his arm.

His eyes went dark and his voice was quieter. 'E.G.A. Packaging was his baby: Edward George Aberdour.' He shrugged. 'But if the pressure gets me in the end, what good is money in the bank to a dead man?'

'Do you enjoy your job?' she asked.

'Yes, but I don't have a life outside it. I don't have a social life or even a hobby.'

'You're not seriously considering learning to knit?' she joked, leaning her bottom on the hall radiator and sticking her chest out the teeniest bit, in an attempt to look alluring.

'Absolutely not. I don't care if Russell Crowe is a proficient knitter; it's a girl thing. But it's why I took on Scratbag temporarily. He's something to come home to, even if I am sneezing within minutes of coming through the front door. Meeting you has made me realise I need to start getting out there, making friends...'

Lucy wondered if perhaps there was something to these locket shenanigans after all. She fluttered her eyelids and flicked her hair over her shoulder.

'It would be good to have a friend who gives me more than a rubbish meow in response and who doesn't view me as a romantic possibility.'

Or not.

There was an awkward pause. Lucy shifted from foot to foot, conscious of the bitter smoke smell, and of George taking up more than his fair share of this small space and making her feel vulnerable.

'But we're digressing. The real reason for my visit was to explain my disproportionate reaction to the fire. When I realised you were still inside, and knowing how quickly a fire can rage out of control, I was worried. And then it transpired you'd been careless with candles and I saw red. You could have died.' This time his tone wasn't as angry as the night of the fire. It was almost as if he cared.

'I know. I'm sorry.' Lucy moved towards the kitchen, as being this close to George was unsettling. Her insides flipped as he followed.

'I've had a tricky couple of years and had to learn the hard way that people aren't always what they seem. It's made me suspicious and even less likely to open up than I was before.' George said as Lucy flicked the kettle on. 'But talking to Brenda, she obviously thinks you are a sensible and trust-worthy person, so I thought it was a good idea to tell you about...' George stopped mid-sentence as he noticed Turnip lying prostrate across her kitchen table. 'Are you...' He paused, searching for the right words. 'Are you in the middle of hair-drying a dead rabbit?'

'Umm...' she said, her voice rising in pitch as she tried to choose suitable words.

'Do I even want to know why?' George folded his wide arms across his chest.

'Possibly not.'

'It's the missing rabbit from the posters, isn't it? I saw one pinned to the lamp post when I got home yesterday.'

'I'm afraid so, and the little girl who owned him is very upset.'

'So you're styling him? Giving him a quick cut and blow-dry?'

'I found him in the back garden and I didn't think the little girl would want him back in this state.' She gently stroked

Turnip's velvety ears as he lay across the towel, and she decided not to tell tales on Scratbag.

'Is pet mortician another one of your bizarre hobbies?'

'At least I have hobbies. And friends.' She regretted her tone. This was not how to win someone over.

'So be honest, wrap him in the towel and tell the mother it's not a pretty sight. It seems ridiculous to pretend otherwise. I understand it's upsetting, but that's life. The rabbit was obviously killed by a fox, but nature is cruel. I thought the whole idea of pets was to teach kids this stuff.'

Sanctimonious git. How dare he criticise when she was trying to do a kind thing?

'Not when they're four, for goodness' sake! I can imagine you'll be the sort of parent who responds to a question about death with a PowerPoint presentation depicting the various stages of decay occurring in the human body – maggots and all. What does it matter if the toddler has nightmares for years and ends up in therapy? At least they know the truth, right? Let's not even start on Father Christmas.' Lucy glared at George.

An eyebrow rose to meet his thick, dark hairline. 'Look, I didn't come here for an argument, I've had enough of those to last a lifetime, so let's take a rain check, shall we?'

Lucy backtracked. Not only did his cross look send a thrilling ripple of something through parts of her body that had lain dormant for far too long, but her mother had been so thrilled her spinster daughter might be bringing a date to the Big Birthday that it would be foolish to alienate him at this stage. After all, she didn't have to actually like him, just convince her mother she did.

'It's no trouble. Look, the kettle is already starting to boil.'

Steam was rising from the spout, but George was already in the hall.

'I'm not sure I can face a cup of tea with a corpse in the room. Think I'll be off. But thanks.'

'Another time?' she called.

'Yeah, perhaps,' a distant voice called back before the front door closed.

'Thanks for that, Turnip,' she said.

Chapter 24

After returning Turnip to the mum across the road and finding Chloe bouncing around doing an Olympic gymnastic display across the sofa, seemingly not too distressed, Lucy knitted a quick twiddlemuff to vent her frustration over George's visit. The hospital had been so pleased when she'd dropped some off earlier in the week, she'd asked the Knit and Natter to help her make some more.

As she pondered the bad timing that seemed to plague her attempts to create a good impression in front of George, she realised she hadn't checked the locket since placing the hairs under his bed and that was days ago. Now wearing it every waking hour, and finding she felt quite bereft without it, she slid it over her head and opened it up.

> *'Give myrtle, honey and feverfew*
> *To clear his head for dreams of you.'*

She hadn't heard of either myrtle (apart from Hogwarts' Moaning Myrtle) or feverfew, so immediately googled both, without even questioning why she was now happy to follow the locket's bizarre instructions or her acceptance that engraved words on a solid object could change with no rational explanation.

Myrtle, she read, was a flowering shrub from the Mediterranean with fragrant leaves and small, white flowers. Sacred to Aphrodite, it was symbolic of love and immortality and often used at weddings. Apparently a sprig from Queen Victoria's bouquet had been planted at Osborne House on the Isle of Wight, and stems from the original plant had been used by the royal family ever since, with both Kate and Meghan having myrtle in their own wedding bouquets. Unlikely to find it growing locally, Lucy sourced the oil online, noting the repeated warnings that it was to be consumed in small quantities. She hoped one or two drops would be enough to invoke the magic.

Feverfew was also a herb of love and protection but, unlike myrtle, was common in the UK. It was used to prevent migraines and once she saw an image she remembered Brenda scrunching up the delicate, frondy green leaves and smelling them to relieve headaches. She was certain her neighbour's garden would yield this plant.

Honey she had in the kitchen cupboards and thanks to her recent sort-out knew exactly which cupboard it was in. It never went off and had been discovered in ancient Egyptian tombs, still edible. Googling further, she realised honey in spells had a long tradition, especially if you wanted someone to be sweet to you. All the ingredients made sense to her as part of a love spell, so all she had to do was mix them up and persuade George to drink them.

And make sure there were no dead animal carcasses lying around when she did so.

Adding hot water to the office coffee cups Monday morning, Lucy was hit by the pleasantly pungent smell of the bitter, roasted beans. It was a shame it never tasted as nice as the aroma promised. She poured water on her teabag, fully aware she was a rebel for drinking tea in the morning. Jess nibbled on a Bourbon, her legs crossed at the ankles as she sat on the worktop in the staff kitchen, leaning back against the cupboards. Adam had drawn up a rota for the tea and coffee runs since Lucy had been brave enough to speak up, although it had taken him practically a day and several visits to the Tardis to complete it. But she was happy to take her turn, and still coordinated with Jess when she did so.

'Mr Tompkins' fancy piece was in accounts first thing,' Jess said.

'Oh?' Lucy bent down to retrieve a carton of milk from the fridge.

'Told you it was serious. He's added her to his company car policy and she was speaking to HR about altering his summer holiday dates. She was chatting to me for ages; all loved up and over made-up. There's a wedding on the cards, I reckon. Mark my words.'

'It's great he's found someone. I could never understand why he was still single.'

'I suppose,' Jess huffed. 'Talking of love, have you got the next bit of the spell yet?'

'Yes, and it's a list of ingredients I need to make the taciturn George drink, or possibly eat. It wasn't specific about the administration.'

'Oo, what are they?'

'I doubt you've heard of them, but it's all under control. You'd be proud of me.'

'Let me see? You know I'm interested. And it was me who got you to follow all this when you dismissed it as rubbish.'

174

'I'm still not convinced. George isn't exactly throwing himself at me. Not that I'd know what to do with him if he did.'

'I could give you some pointers.' Jess grinned. 'For a start, I'd go with the gruff, monosyllabic, alpha-male thing and ask him to put on a white vest. Then I'd dirty him up a bit and get him to handcuff you to the bed—'

'Thank you. I get the picture.'

Lucy took the locket off and passed it to Jess, who was all fingers, thumbs and long, pointy nails.

'Myrtle, honey and feverfew.' Jess wriggled her phone from the back pocket of her tight, denim skirt and started tapping away. 'It says here you can make a tea from feverfew.'

'I thought I might bake some cupcakes with the ingredients.'

'Feverfew, myrtle and honey cupcakes are a bit experimental, even for you, love. Besides, according to Wikipedia feverfew tastes bitter.'

'It will be fine. I'll mask it with another strong flavour.'

'Okay, but don't expect me to eat one. I'm still haunted by your courgette and peanut butter cookies.'

Adam was supportive when Lucy asked to leave early Tuesday afternoon to accompany Brenda to her GP appointment. Dr Hopgood suggested Brenda didn't attend alone, which naturally worried them both, but it was pretty much information they already knew. He had the results from the memory clinic and confirmed that Brenda, despite refusing a CT scan, was showing the early signs of dementia. He took his time, going through diagnosis and prognosis slowly and gently, finally passing over a bundle of relevant leaflets.

Lucy wanted to burst into tears, but Brenda, staring straight ahead and not so much as breaking eye contact with him, gave her the strength to blink them away. Of course, the signs were there, it wasn't shock news, but she'd privately hoped for a miracle.

'Now, Mrs Pethybridge, I'd like to touch on the subject of lasting power of attorney, which would enable someone you trust to act on your behalf in legal and medical matters should there come a point you were no longer capable of making such decisions for yourself.'

'A discussion for another time, doctor,' Brenda said, and he didn't push it. 'Let's see what the next few weeks bring first.'

'Okay, but looking to the future, I want to talk about the various medications that will help slow the progression of the illness. We have a number of options—'

'We're done for today. Thank you for your time, but I have things to do.' Brenda stood up and thrust out a hand to shake his. 'And it's lemon balm tea you need, young man.' The doctor looked blank. 'To help with your anxiety and insomnia.'

She walked out the door, leaving an open-mouthed Dr Hopgood staring after her.

'I haven't even confided in my wife about the insomnia,' he said.

'Yes. She's good, isn't she?' said Lucy.

Later in the week, Brenda's missing television remote turned up in a cut-glass vase. She hadn't been concerned by the loss as she wasn't watching much television, but her digital radio in the kitchen was often on, playing the middle-of-the-road music of Radio Two more and the spoken word of Radio Four less. It hadn't registered with Lucy at the time, but her friend had stopped listening to *The Archers* several months ago, due to what Brenda had called the 'muddly nature of the storylines'. Lucy now recognised that it was the listener who had become more muddled.

Occasionally, Lucy was still confused with the long-dead sister-in-law when Brenda was telling an involved tale, but having done her own careful research after the diagnosis, Lucy was happy that life would be manageable for them both for a while to come. And with Brenda's general good health, Dr Hopgood had suggested the deterioration might be slower. Lucy even noticed a couple of Alzheimer's Society leaflets kicking about, tucked under a pile of Mills and Boons, which reassured her that her friend was taking a sensible approach to the future. A future that Lucy hoped would be long and largely happy.

Lucy didn't see George that week, despite hoping she would bump into him on the road, or that their paths would cross in the supermarket. He was really starting to get under her skin, in a good way: his brutal but endearing honesty, the heady scent of his expensive aftershave and his concern for her the night of the fire. But George remained elusive, although Scratbag often came out to meet her when she returned from work, rubbing a soft head against her bare legs or standing on his back feet to headbutt her outstretched hand. He gave her catty stares that seemed to suggest he knew more than he should and certainly more than you would want him to. But he was friendly and affectionate, and finally starting to put on some much-needed weight.

She rang her sister to check how the pregnancy was progressing, but all Emily wanted to talk about was whether Lucy had gone online with the knitted figures. Their mother had reported back to Emily about the website and Lucy was forced to admit it was somewhat of an exaggeration.

'You should have something up and running by now. They are so clever and I know at least a dozen parents at Rosie's preschool who would order Little Mermaids and Elsas from you in a blink of their neatly plucked, Botox-enhanced eyes.'

'They aren't strictly celebrities,' Lucy pointed out. 'And I'm not sure I'd even know what to charge.'

'How long does each one take to knit?'

'About a week, if I do it during my lunch hour and the occasional evening.'

'Then don't you dare charge less than twenty pounds for each one.'

'Twenty pounds? They aren't worth that much.'

'You need to do some serious research, honey. I think you'll find people are prepared to pay for something unique and hand-crafted. But mind it doesn't take over your social life.'

'I've never had one of those so that won't be a problem.'

Spurred on by Emily, Lucy decided to take the plunge. She asked Jess over later that week, to help set up a shop on Etsy – a website for hand-made and vintage items. Looking on the site, she was surprised to find what some people were prepared to pay for similar-sized knitted dolls, and hers had a quirky twist (and a lot more sex appeal). She realised her sister wasn't as far off as she thought.

Jess jumped at the chance for another sleepover. They cleared the kitchen table and sat opposite each other with an Adele CD playing softly in the background. Lucy was on the laptop with a cup of tea by her side. Jess was on her tablet with half a bottle of wine already inside her.

First, they registered on the site and added some basic information about Nicely Knitted Celebrities. Then Jess posed the knitted figures that Lucy had available for sale, photographed them and listed them. They placed Ed under a desk lamp on the kitchen worktop and tried to create a live concert feel; Thor they took onto the concrete patio and had him smashing up a few stones like a god; and Jess inventively hung *Twilight*'s Edward Cullen from a tree, so he looked swoopy and vampirey. Lucy decided to part with most of them, saving Poldark, and hoped their removal would make her living room less knitty and more grown-up. Between them, they came up with some fun descriptions for each figure and a price. Finally, Jess set her up with a PayPal account.

'Make sure you check the site regularly,' Jess said.

'Of course. I don't want to let down my hundreds of potential customers.'

'I'm liking the new positive attitude, babe. You really are a butterfly emerging from your chrysalis. Everything about you has more oomph. I'm not sure where it's come from, and there was nothing wrong with the old you, but the new you is kinda cool. So how about letting me give you Union Jack nails? I have the stuff with me.'

'One baby step at a time. But I wouldn't mind you having another go at a make-over.'

'Really?' Jess leaped up and scampered out to collect her overnight bag from the hall before Lucy could change her mind. 'You won't regret it, Luce. I can show you how to bring out the blue of your eyes.'

The myrtle oil Lucy ordered arrived Friday morning, in a small brown bottle with a white cap and a pretty olive-green label. She unscrewed the lid and took a sniff. It smelt a bit like bay leaves: peppery and camphory. Placing her finger over the open neck, she tipped the bottle forward then back, and cautiously licked the tip of her finger. It had an unpleasant, bitter taste. Dark chocolate, she decided, would mask the myrtle and feverfew. Combined with cherry perhaps – a traditional combination. Now was not the time to experiment with new flavour sensations.

Arriving at work, still mulling over the next spell, she witnessed Adam arrive five minutes after her to find his desk and chair had been wrapped in cling film. The more frustrated he became trying to remove it, the harder it got. Tugging at sections only made them stretch and shrink to tight plastic strips. He eventually sat down with a large pair of scissors and snipped through it all.

'Why do you do it, Daniel?' Lucy asked him when he rang the office for some safety information on the new range of Tramp'O'Bounce trampolines. Digging a hole in your garden and dropping in a trampoline frame was the new big thing after the flurry of personal injury claims from the trampoline craze of recent years, but customers had been slow to embrace this supposedly safer alternative. 'Cling film? Really?'

He didn't even bother to deny it. 'Because he makes it so easy and so much fun. The only downside is I don't get to see his cross little face. Bet he was furious this morning?'

'That's an understatement. He was so angry that when he'd finally liberated his desk, he picked up a pencil and accidentally snapped it in half. He's only got fourteen spares.'

There was a chuckle down the line. 'I keep waiting for a phone call from the Black Widow with some sort of official reprimand; I've already had my knuckles rapped over the Tardis incident – apologies again, Luce – but it hasn't come yet. Perhaps she's saving it for my annual review. Tally up the black marks and all that.'

Lucy sighed. It appeared her careless comment had become Sam's official nickname and she really regretted saying it in front of Adam.

'To be honest, I think he covers for you every time, Daniel.'

'I don't know why.'

'Probably because underneath all the bluster and bravado, he's actually a really decent bloke.'

Chapter 25

Lucy called in after work to ask if Brenda still had feverfew growing in her cornucopia of a garden. Brenda opened the door looking flustered and Lucy realised she had company. A neighbour was standing in the hallway behind her.

'Sorry. I'll come back later. It's not urgent,' said Lucy.

'No, please come in. Go through to the living room. I was just seeing Marjorie out.'

Lucy made herself comfortable in her favourite chair, or rather her favourite chair saw to it that she was comfortable, although she couldn't help but eavesdrop on the conversation taking place in the corridor.

'Don't worry, Brenda. It doesn't matter.'

'It does matter. I can't understand how it happened. I can only apologise.'

'It didn't smell right when I opened the bottle. Even our Ron thought so. But I appreciate the refund. I would have been equally happy with a replacement. It's always worked so well before. And I don't like going to Dr Hopgood, as lovely as he is, because, well you know, it's in an embarrassing place.'

'Goodness only knows how I missed the tea tree oil out. Lemongrass smells quite different. But like I said, I'm running the medicinal side of things down now. I'm getting too old to be fiddling about with plants and brewing potions. My eyesight isn't what it once was.'

Lucy knew there was absolutely nothing wrong with Brenda's eyesight, even if other things had started to fail her friend. But she was saddened to think Brenda was stepping back from her alternative remedies. It was the thing that kept her animated and busy.

'Such a shame. I know several people who rely on you for help when the medicine from the doc doesn't do its job. Looks like I'll have to dig out the inflatable cushion or brave showing the young doctor my nethers.'

The ladies laughed. Lucy heard the front door close and Brenda reappeared in the doorway.

'Coffee?'

'I prefer tea, if you don't mind.'

'How do you take it again?'

Brenda placed an old-fashioned wooden tray on the nest of tables. She was using her favourite Thirties bone-china tea set, and the matching cake plate was laden with a tempting pile of caramel squares. Where Lucy's mother might have gone for delicate understated flowers, Brenda went for garish orange and purple daisies that jumped off the cup and practically slapped you around the face. It was why Lucy had knitted the purple and orange blanket for her friend, and she was beginning to feel that the daisies would be her choice too.

Lucy looked down at her white blouse and wondered why she never wore clothes that reflected her love of the bold and beautiful, because she certainly embraced it in other areas of her life (the lime green feature wall in her bedroom being testament to that) but she suspected it was her general unease at being the centre of attention. *No more*, she thought to herself. The colours she loved shouldn't be reserved for a bedroom wall or a knitted blanket that she gave away. The next thing she knitted would be bright pink. And she would wear it.

'So, how are things?' Lucy asked.

'Apart from adding an excessive quantity of lemongrass oil to Marjorie's boil treatment instead of five drops of tea tree, you mean? Thank goodness she had the common sense not to apply it or she really would be reaching for the inflatable cushion.' Brenda started to pour and Lucy was disappointed to find it was ordinary tea with no hints of bergamot or lemon. A dainty cup was slid towards Lucy and then Brenda poured one for herself. 'Marjorie aside, I think we both know that things are far from okay, don't we? You of all people. You who know me better than anyone.'

Lucy blushed. 'I'm worried about you.'

Brenda added a touch of milk from the tiny matching jug and stirred her tea.

'*I'm* worried about me. I've been making up Marjorie's lotion for years, as she's unfortunately prone to infections in that area, and suddenly I've put some random ingredient in that could have given her a nasty burn if she'd applied it as I directed.'

'Don't beat yourself up. Everyone has forgetful moments, even me.'

Brenda gave her a Paddington Bear hard stare.

'Perhaps more so the older you get,' Lucy added, trying to be diplomatic.

'I have some pretty powerful herbs and oils in my pantry, Lucy. Some of them are not meant to be ingested. I could kill someone.'

There was a silence.

'Caramel square?' Brenda offered up the tea plate. 'Shop-bought,' she clarified and they both giggled as Lucy took one.

'I'm visiting my parents this weekend.' Lucy paused to find the correct phrasing. 'George said he'd pop over while I'm gone to see if you need anything doing or any shopping picking up.'

'Ah, George. That's our sexy neighbour, right?' Lucy nodded. 'He's such a dear. It's kind of you both, but I can manage, you know.' Lucy looked her straight in the eye. 'Okay, okay,' and Brenda put her hands in the air in capitulation. 'The company would be good. I'm sticking to traditional tea though. Don't want to poison your future paramour. Or accidentally administer a remedy for piles.'

'Try not to overwhelm the poor man.'

'I shall be on my best behaviour.' There was a pause. 'Probably.'

After they'd drunk their tea, Brenda took Lucy into her garden. Not a sunny day but a warm one; thin white clouds slowly drifted across the sun but didn't look substantial enough to deposit rain. Lucy wished they'd thought to have the tea outside on the little bistro set. It was a lovely space and made you forget that you were on the edge of a large town. The boughs of the trees overhead were as thick as a man's leg; drooping foliage created tunnels and hidey-holes; and large, leafy plants tickled at your feet as though they wanted to play. Like the mysterious armchair, the garden also welcomed Lucy and invisible arms embraced her every time she visited.

Brenda found a small pot of feverfew, telling Lucy to keep it as it was a useful plant for headaches, which Lucy already

185

knew from her own research. Suddenly looking weary, Brenda flicked some dead cherry blossom from one of the cast-iron seats and sank into it. She took a couple of deep breaths and placed her fingers on the table like a piano player. Absent-mindedly, she ran her fingers back and forth along the edge, almost as if she was trying to read a hidden Braille message. Her face shut down for a moment, and Lucy suspected her friend had temporarily forgotten she was there.

'I always feel so at home in your garden, and as though I am somewhere else rather than here. Does that make sense?' Lucy pulled her friend back to the present.

Brenda took a moment to adjust to her surroundings. She stroked the table one last time and stood up. Looping her arm through Lucy's, she gave a her a wrinkly grin, her bright blue eyes seeming all the more blue because they matched her cobalt-coloured smock. Taller than Brenda, Lucy noticed a good inch of hair growth where the purple needed recolouring. Again, uncharacteristic behaviour. Brenda had always been on top of the monthly beetroot and blackberry home-made hair dye.

'Yes, and it's important that you know this garden loves you very much, Lucy Baker.' There was a swelling of tears in Brenda's eyes that didn't quite spill over the bottom lid, before they were hastily blinked away. 'Because it will still be here, long after I'm gone.'

Chapter 26

'You're late, Lucy. You know I always serve promptly at one.' Her mother was holding a pale pink embroidered hand towel and air-kissed her daughter before drying her hands, to make the point Lucy's arrival had interrupted something.

'My darling baby girl,' said Dad, throwing his arms around his daughter as though she was a lifebuoy, which in a way she was. 'You must come and see the headlight unit now that I've fitted it. It looks fantastic.'

'Lunch *first*, Paul.'

'After lunch, obviously. Your mother has been cooking and baking all morning. We can sneak out to the garage later. I've also fitted the replacement BMW badges you got me for Christmas. Lovely thought, they really finish it off. I'm on the home straight now. Not long until she's fully restored.'

'Shoes,' chastised her mum, as Lucy stepped over the threshold.

'So, I said how much I sympathised,' Sandra continued, oblivious to the glances being exchanged across the white, pressed linen tablecloth. 'As if her son will ever amount to much. He's still temping at Pickard's and he's thirty. I said our Emily was

187

a regional manager for WHSmith now, troubleshooting for the company nationally. We all know she'll make director by the time she retires, so she had a narrow escape with that boy, I can tell you.'

'They were only about fourteen, Mum. I don't think it was serious.'

'Well, I doubt Jayne will see grandchildren any time soon. I did show her the most up-to-date photograph of the girls on my phone. She didn't say much. I think she's jealous. Emily said—'

'So how are you, love?' interrupted her dad.

'Fine.'

'How's work?'

'Stressful.'

'That doesn't sound like my Lucy. I thought you liked it there.'

'I do, but changes are afoot. The new general manager is very efficient. She'll spot a weak link at twenty paces.'

'Perhaps now is the ideal opportunity to look into another more lucrative career?' offered her mother. 'Something with good long-term prospects and a decent pension scheme. It's never too late to think about returning to education. If only you'd considered clearing, you could have had BA after your name, like Emily. Looks so much better on the CV. The better your qualifications, the better the pay.'

'Actually, Mum,' Lucy said, suddenly aware of the locket almost glowing against her chest, 'I'm determined to succeed at Tompkins – I've just got a lot on my plate at the moment.' Although not overly concerned about Brenda in the immediate future, there was something making her feel uneasy, poking her in her dreams and trying to wriggle into her thoughts during the day. She felt she was missing something and it bothered her. 'They are a decent bunch of people and the work is interesting and varied. It's a job I can leave at the office and allows me to have a life outside work; a challenge without being all-consuming.'

'And financial reward isn't the only reason for choosing a career, Sandra,' her dad added.

'Don't I know it? I have cursed Mother Nature on more than one occasion for making women the child bearers. I was working my way up at the library and had hopes for promotion, but, no, I went and fell in love at an early age with a man who had less ambition than a dishcloth – no, disrespect, love.' She reached out for her husband's arm, as if saying that would make her comment acceptable. Having Emily at twenty had certainly put a stop to Sandra's plans for world domination, but it was easy to blame others. There was certainly nothing preventing her from re-entering the workplace now if she chose to, but she'd found other roles to fulfil that need, and sometimes Lucy felt her mother enjoyed speculating about the career she could have had more than trying to redress it.

'But you wouldn't change anything?' Lucy said to her mother, noting the crestfallen look her dad often wore around his wife.

'Of course not! I love you, Paul. And I love my daughters. But I look at Emily and wonder how I would have fared if I'd had those opportunities. Modern women can have it all: a career *and* a family. It wasn't possible thirty years ago because the necessary childcare facilities weren't in place. Wanting the best for you all isn't a crime, surely?'

'Depends whose definition of best we are talking about,' mumbled her dad.

Perched on an old chrome bar stool that her dad had picked up from a boot fair, Lucy finally felt at ease. Her legs were dangling in mid-air and reminding her of childhood when her tiny feet never reached the floor. There was a smell of engine oil and sawdust. Rows of spanners hung from hooks along the wall, and a solid pine workbench ran the length of the garage, dotted with oily rags and random screws. An open tin of Swarfega sat on the bench, revealing its dark green, gelatinous contents. Lucy adored the smell and associated it with happy weekends spent alongside her father when she was young. She loved being his Chief Spanner Handerer – a job title she had coined at an early age and one that had stuck into adulthood.

It was cool in the garage, and despite the long strip light above them flickering and buzzing, it felt gloomy because it was so bright and sunny outside. They had brought cups of tea out with them in her mother's garden mugs. (Sandra had transferred the tea from the best china when she realised where they were heading.) Her dad took a swig and then replaced the mug on the bench, looking every inch the mechanic in the navy blue overalls that his wife insisted he wore when he was, as she referred to it, 'tinkering'.

'So now the headlight unit is in, I'm almost there. I'm still keeping me eyes peeled for an original gearstick as the leather always get worn. But, with the badges on, there isn't that much left to do.' He stood back to admire his beloved metallic green BMW M535i. 'I promised my twenty-year-old self that I'd own one of these one day, and now look – nought to sixty in over seven seconds, fourteen-inch alloy wheels and an impressive two-hundred-and-eighteen-brake horsepower. She was a real Q-car of her time; a family saloon with a sports-car heart.'

He stroked the bonnet like you might ruffle the hair of a favourite child.

'It's wonderful, Dad. You have a real talent for mechanics. Perhaps you'd have been happier with a job that gave you dirty hands and a sense of achievement, instead of banking, which we both know you hate.'

'Ah, but you weren't around in the Eighties.' He let out a sigh. 'They were a time of prosperity and growth. The increased use of computers created a demand for an educated workforce and people aspired to the yuppie stereotype: sharp suit, mobile phone, plenty of disposable cash. Careers advice at school consisted of filling in information about yourself on some form and the careers teacher allocating you a suitable career. I'm sure she only had a list of about ten jobs: banking, retail, teaching, the emergency services, the military... And my dad was old-school. You got an education and then got a job – one that paid the bills and they could tell the neighbours about with a sense of pride.'

'It's never too late, you know.'

'Can't see that going down well with your mother though. Can you?'

'Perhaps not. Thank goodness she has Emily.'

'She loves us all, sweetheart. Emily is in her mould, that's all. But the saddest part of that is, out of the three of us, I'm not convinced Emily isn't the most unhappy.'

This statement sat uneasily with Lucy, who wriggled about trying to find the stool stretcher with her toes and frowned. She'd had her own doubts about Emily but had assured herself they were groundless. Perhaps not. That was the problem with living so far apart. When they were children, they'd always been able to spot each other's unhappiness. It was a sister thing. But you couldn't see the truth in someone's eyes down the phone or over the internet.

'But Emily is living the dream,' said Lucy.

'Oh, Luce. Take off your Sandra glasses and look at your sister again. Call her, speak to her properly, perhaps even pay her a visit. I've got a feeling she's going to need her friends soon. And her family.'

Chapter 27

Lucy devoted Sunday morning to the Big Birthday, not wanting to be accused of favouring her father, since the pair of them had been out in the garage until quite late the night before. She sat with her mother and listened to the party update. Invites were now with the printer and Sandra had been consulting with a local florist about centrepieces. She had a plan of the tables and was running through possible seating arrangements three months in advance, with the assumption that no one would dream of refusing. Thankfully, talk of napkin swans was avoided.

With the help of the locket, Lucy wasn't dreading the event as much as before. Hopefully the successful local businessman and homeowner George would be on her arm, and her mother could wave him in front of anyone she felt the desperate need to impress. And despite a couple of minor hiccups at work, she still had the time and determination to make a success of that area of her life as well. Her mother commented several times on her smarter appearance (despite her initial reluctance, a bit of make-up did make her feel bolder and more attractive) and she was resolved not to be found lurking behind the aspidistra with her dad but flitting about and embracing her inner social butterfly.

They hugged goodbye on the pavement outside the family red-brick detached suburban home, later that evening. Sandra felt she'd fulfilled her motherly duties to perfection; Lucy was full of delicious home-cooked food and reminded of her daughterly obligations. As they embraced, Lucy noticed her mother's reluctance to let go.

When Lucy eventually returned to Renborough, having to park further away from the flat than she would have liked, she was exhausted. The traffic had been unusually busy for a Sunday and sleep the previous night had been restless. Those Regency lords kept morphing into George and taking liberties with her maidenhood. What was it with her brain? It seemed obsessed with that man at the moment.

Trudging along the pavement towards her flat, with her wheelie suitcase and her knitting bag, she decided to stop at George's to see how Brenda had been in her absence. Although frankly, after a long car journey, the last thing she felt like doing was biting her lip in front of Mr Call-a-spade-a-spade.

'Ah, Lucy. Erm...would you like to come in?' he asked, seeing her standing at his door with all her luggage and a weary face. She recognised he was trying to be more sociable so accepted his offer.

They stood together in his spacious kitchen, one of the few rooms she'd not been in before as the layout meant the utility and kitchen were both accessed from the hall. (In fact, in her flat, the back utility was her bedroom, and in Brenda's it was still the original pantry.) A red tea caddy with a circular glass window, a super-shiny chrome kettle and a small bottle of virgin olive oil were the only three items on his worktop – it beggared belief. It was as if he was living in an IKEA show-room. All it needed was a wicker basket of fake fruit and a plastic loaf of bread across a huge wooden board and she would have believed it.

'There is something different about your eyes,' George said, squinting as he handed her a glass of mineral water. 'Are you wearing make-up?'

'Yes,' she said, flattered that he'd noticed.

'Hmm... Prefer the natural look myself.'

'Good job your opinion of my cosmetic overload wasn't the reason I called then.' She was used to the lack of any emotions showing in his face but was ever hopeful of finding some indication he regretted the bluntness of his comments. It was not to be. She consoled herself with the knowledge should he ever say something flattering, it would at least be genuine. 'I was calling to see how you got on with Brenda while I was away.'

'Ah, yes, Brenda,' and his eyes crinkled slightly around the edges. So he did have some softer emotions lurking, but it took a flirty seventy-nine-year-old to unleash them. Or a stray cat. 'I popped in on her like you asked. Yesterday was a bit of a disaster. She wouldn't open the door and didn't seem to recognise me. I've not known her long, but she has spoken to me several times. On reflection, I think she'd been asleep. She seemed disorientated. I told her you'd asked me to call and she kept repeating, "I don't know any Lucys." It was awkward.'

George shrugged his wide shoulders, and Lucy felt an awkward lump rise in her throat. To hear Brenda had forgotten her, albeit temporarily, was hard.

'So I tried again a bit later and was more successful. She invited me in and made me a cup of some dodgy-tasting tea. She didn't mention my earlier visit, so I didn't bring it up. I called back that evening with two portions of fish and chips from town, and she was on better form. At one point I swear she was flirting with me.'

'That's because she's got a *massive* crush on you.' Lucy coughed as she realised she'd said it out loud and George went a becoming shade of pink. 'No accounting for taste.'

'Anyway,' George said, getting the conversation back on track, 'she ate well, because I stayed and had my meal with her.'

'I appreciate that.'

'It's fine. I'm not totally heartless, you know. Today she was up and about by the time I called; dressed and singing to herself as she answered the door. She seemed glad of the company and we sat in the garden for a long time, talking about the Yellow Crows. Did you know her husband was the drummer? Interesting lady, and although I didn't contribute much to the conversation, I enjoyed spending time with another human being – my own mother aside. We got through an entire dairy-free carrot cake.'

This was a side of George Lucy hadn't anticipated and it was quite appealing. He may not be a talker, but apparently he was a listener, and one who was not averse to spending time with old ladies.

'I know I'm unusual in that I like my own company but being widowed all those years must be hard. Does she have family?' he asked.

'There's no one. And, apart from me, I'm not sure she has any other close friends left alive. That's what happens when you hurtle towards eighty. Someone has to be last. And people around here have always been slightly wary of her, imagining she has all sorts of mystical powers and can see into their souls. Or maybe even turn them into toads.'

'Touché,' and his lips twitched as his eyes narrowed. 'She does have a knack of making you feel like that, though. Even if it is nonsense.'

'I agree. Did you know, many years ago she helped the police discover the location of a buried body? She has never talked about it to me, but several of the locals have mentioned it in passing. There is something about her not of this world, but I've never once felt uncomfortable about it. She is my best friend and I love her. Which is why...' Lucy's voice tailed off as she thought about what the future had in store. She sighed. 'I know it's dementia, more to the point *she* knows it's dementia, and that it is only going to get worse.' Although she remained composed as she said this, a tear escaped and dribbled a salty path down her cheek.

Without saying anything, George closed the space between them and wrapped his arms around Lucy, and for a moment she allowed herself to mould into his embrace. The soft cotton of his shirt and the clean smell of his soap, mingled with some undoubtedly ludicrously expensive aftershave, were comforting. His arms were like the boughs of the ancient trees in Brenda's garden and just as solid.

After a few moments, George cleared his throat and his arms went stiff. She realised he felt the embrace had gone on long enough and she pulled herself upright, but another tear crawled from her eye to her chin. Lucy lifted a hand to wipe it just as George swung his arm up, possibly also to brush away the tear. Their arms bumped.

'Sorry.'

'No, I'm sorry,' he said. 'I'm not good with emotions. Not had much practice with people.' He forced a smile. 'Only-child thing. Bit of a loner.'

'I'm not exactly Renborough's It Girl myself.'

'Only child?'

'No, but the inadequate one. Anyway...' Lucy looked at her watch to signal that she needed to leave, and to avoid any probing questions about her last statement. 'I should make a move.'

'Your other mad friend paid me a visit while you were away,' he said, following her down the hall. 'Knocked at the door and invited herself in. She doesn't get the whole "I'm busy right now" thing, does she?' Lucy thought George was hardly in a position to comment about the subtleties of the English language. 'I swear she talked *at* me for an hour, but in a far more intrusive way than Brenda. Would you believe she even asked what my salary was?'

'If it was Jess – probably,' Lucy said, rolling her eyes and wishing that however well-meaning Jess's intentions were, her friend would leave her to work this thing out by herself.

Chapter 28

'So, Daniel said he was sorry *again* and handed me a huge box of posh chocolates. Prefer Cadbury's myself, but I suppose he was trying.'

Jess was upstairs at Lucy's desk first thing pretending to query customer discounts.

'I don't think I'll ever understand men,' said Lucy. 'Talking of which, George mentioned you stopped by at the weekend?'

'Yeah, I totally forgot you were away and called in after picking up some shopping for Mum. I'm such a scatterbrain. You weren't there so I thought I'd pop in on your hunky neighbour and see if I could lay some more groundwork for you. Big you up. Talk about your outstanding qualities. That kind of thing.'

'Thanks, but I'm doing enough damage in that area for the both of us. How is your mum?' Lucy asked, not wanting to dwell on George for too long.

'Still doing shifts at the chicken processing factory and still getting through boyfriends like they were the bloody shifts.'

'I'm sorry.' Lucy recognised she was lucky to have a stable home life growing up. Jess'd had a tough time as a kid.

'I need to get out of there, Luce. I've tried so hard to put money aside for a deposit, but you know me – I'm not great with finances. Ironic, as I work in the accounts department. I do love her, but she's holding me back. And perhaps if I got out, she'd have to up her game and start acting like a responsible grown-up.'

Jess's eyes flashed across to Richard Tompkins' office as a serious-faced Sam strode towards them both. She gathered her folders and was out the door before their boss got within reprimanding range, but Sam had bigger fish than Jess to fry.

'Have you seen the file Daniel dropped off yesterday afternoon for the supermarket ClickIn order, Lucy? Adam doesn't have it and I've just had their MD on the phone double-checking delivery dates as they are going nationwide on the nineteenth?' Lucy shook her head. 'He wants the superhero units in their twelve hundred stores the week before, so I checked and the order hasn't been processed.' Sam was clicking the end of her pen in and out as though that would speed up the recovery of the file. 'It's delays like this that make me determined to update our system. The reps should be able to access it from their laptops, not be phoning in orders or dropping paper copies off. This company hasn't moved on from the Nineties.'

'We talked about the order when I arrived this morning, but I assumed he still needed it for some reason and would pass it over later. Either that or he'd given it to someone else to process.' Lucy noticed the usually calm and together Sam pulling at her bottom lip with her teeth.

'Damn. I don't want us to look unprofessional or people will take their business elsewhere. Our entire contract with a *national* supermarket hangs on this. They are used to dealing direct with manufacturers, so Tompkins having the exclusive UK distribution was a major coup. If the order turns up, let me know immediately.'

Lucy double-checked the papers on her desk but knew Adam hadn't handed the order over, so focused her search elsewhere, even checking the company's photocopier – a place missing documents had turned up on previous occasions.

A Mexican wave of unease travelled through the office as Sonjit distributed the mid-morning coffee. Pat dialled Lucy to say Connor had overheard Adam talking about redundancies to Richard, and she also mentioned she'd spotted Daniel was fiddling about at Adam's desk that morning, so Lucy rang him to rule out every possibility.

'Please tell me you haven't pulled one of your stunts and hidden the order when you were in the office earlier?' she said, the pornographic screen saver and cling film incidents still fresh in her mind.

'No way. My little pranks are harmless. I certainly wouldn't muck about with work stuff. This affects me as much as him. In fact, more so. He's just misplaced it. It'll turn up. However, if he gets a bit of a shock later, that might have something to do with me.'

'Now is not the time for you to be pulling stupid pranks, Daniel. You really need to grow up.' Surprised at the anger in her voice, Lucy ended the call abruptly and bashed away at her keyboard like a frustrated concert pianist. By this point, tensions were so high no one could even be bothered to reunite Igglepiggle and Shaun the Sheep, who stood bereft, staring at different corners of the office.

A little while later, Adam shot up from his chair with a small shriek. Daniel had rigged up a simple circuit with some crocodile grips and an old camera capacitor to give him an electric shock as he touched the metal handle of his desk drawer. Sonjit was straight on the phone to Daniel and everyone but Sam, who was in Richard's office, heard her tear him off a strip or two. But what was interesting, thought Lucy, considering Sonjit always had a smile on her face when she bantered with Adam, was the angry thump on her desk when she told Daniel how close she was to reporting him.

'Dare I ask if there's been any sign of the file?' Sam asked, returning from another private conversation with Mr Tompkins.

Lucy shook her head as a thought occurred to her. 'The ClickIn shipments come over weekly. The order needs to be placed before five o'clock today to catch the shipment.'

'Yes. Thank you, Lucy. I am fully aware of that.'

Lucy blushed.

'I'm sure you had it last,' Adam said to Lucy. He'd been darting around the office like the steel ball in a pinball machine all morning, as if the file was an animate object he could catch out by rounding a corner with sudden speed. 'I'd bet my grandma's grave on it.'

'I honestly didn't see the file after our conversation,' Lucy said, for the umpteenth time.

'Well, there's a damaged link in the chain somewhere and I'm determined to winkle it out before the guillotine blade falls. I don't want my head in a basket.' Adam spun around and began to do another aimless circuit of the office.

'I know we don't want to admit to the supermarket that we've misplaced the order, but I was wondering if I could ring their office and say I wanted to double-check the figures,' Lucy suggested. 'If I did it with a junior member of their office staff, rather than you or Mr Tompkins having to speak to someone at the top, perhaps it would go unnoticed? There was a lady there called Rachel who I got on with quite well when they altered Daniel's appointment. We both knit.'

'That could work,' said Sam. 'Good thinking. Leave it until two, just in case it turns up, and then make the call. And can you pull Daniel into the office first thing tomorrow? We've come up with some temporary procedures to ensure this doesn't happen again.'

Daniel was not impressed. 'But I'm playing golf with a customer just outside Romford tomorrow.'

'Golf? I think this is more important, don't you? You need to be here at nine.'

'Get you, Little Miss I Can Be Bossy When I Want To. What's happened to the compliant little girl who blushed every time I entered the office?' When she didn't bite, he continued, 'Then I suppose I'll have to reschedule.'

'Stop moaning, Daniel. It's only golf. You can do that any time.'

'You don't understand the politics and etiquette of the wider business world, my little sales office superstar. It's not merely a game of golf. It's networking and cosying up to the client. But don't worry your pretty little head about the complicated aspects of my job. You sit in your comfy office, with tea and coffee to hand, air-conditioning and your en-suite toilet facilities.'

'If you want to swap places, Daniel, you name the day, because, quite frankly, I would rather be out and about launching tiny white balls into sandpits, than up here sorting out everyone else's mistakes. If you want to liaise between disgruntled warehouse staff, demanding bosses and impatient customers, be my guest.' Her unusually angry tone surprised even her.

'Fair point. See you at nine.'

* * *

Rather unreasonably, Lucy thought, Adam suddenly decided to send her on an errand. They'd run out of C5 envelopes and he apparently needed to get something in the post that afternoon.

'Don't stand there so *stationary* – get it? Stationery? Stationary? Get accounts to give you some petty cash and pop to that independent office supplier in town. There's a love.'

'Can't it wait until the delivery tomorrow? Or use the smaller envelopes and fold whatever it is in half?' Lucy suggested.

'I don't know why you're whingeing. You never used to make so much fuss about the things you were asked to do. You must appreciate I can't possibly nip out as the place would totally fall apart without me. Pat would probably have a coronary if she had to undertake that amount of exercise – no offence, Pat-a-Cake. Sonjit is up to her...' Adam's hands were at nipple level, but he declined to name the exact level of her workload. 'And Connor, well, it isn't really a man's job, is it?'

Lucy decided to run the errand as a chance to escape outside was a bonus. The air-conditioned office made her temporarily forget that summer was so close she could practically reach out and touch it. She could see the sun through the window across from her desk, but it wasn't until she was outside that she could feel it sink into her skin and warm through to her very bones. It made her realise what an artificial environment she worked in. She rolled up the sleeves of the red cotton top she'd bought on impulse last week. And then, because no one was looking and she was on an isolated footpath that cut through the back of the industrial estate and into town, she did a Miranda gallop.

* * *

Returning to the office feeling brighter and fresher, she handed Adam the pack of white envelopes.

'Well, well, the troublemaker returns.' He stood with his hands on his hips, tapping his left foot. 'Sometimes, Lucy-Lou, I think your brain is as woolly as that knitting you spend every lunch hour doing.'

Lucy gave a nervous smile. Adam was often cryptic, but he'd lost her this time.

'You have some serious explaining to do, young lady. Guess what I found on your desk, under a pile of jumbled papers, while you were gone?' he said in a voice that was certain to attract the attention of every single person in the office.

Lucy's heart thumped and fell to her feet.

205

Chapter 29

'I don't understand.' Lucy's mouth went dry.

'I think it's perfectly obvious. I handed the order to you this morning and you lost it in that total pigsty of a desk.'

The comment was unfair. Her desk was much more organised since Sam had been working there. Full was not the same as untidy.

'I *knew* I'd passed it over to you. Fancy making me doubt myself.'

'The missing order has been found?' asked Sam, standing up and walking over to them.

'Oh yes. And everyone was *so* quick to point the finger at me...' Adam crossed his arms, the foot still tapping away.

'No one accused you, Adam. You were the last person who remembered having the order, that was all.'

'Well, it turns out it was young Lucy here who had it all along, under the pile of English translations for the Fizz, Boom, Bang sets.'

'Oh dear, Lucy, how unfortunate, but luckily you had a plan B up your sleeve – well done. Crisis over. Back to work, everyone.'

As Sam walked over to her desk, Adam muttered, 'Even

though you're responsible for this cock-up, you still come up smelling of pineapples. Unbelievable.'

Feeling down that evening, Lucy didn't even have the enthusiasm to get on with Brenda's birthday present – an idea that had come to her when she'd flicked through the Elliott Landy book with her friend earlier in the week. Sprawled across the sofa, the comments from her dad about Emily were bothering her like a wasp buzzing around a jam pot and refused to be swatted away.

She checked Facebook for any clues that things were not as rosy as she had previously assumed, but her sister's posts were all upbeat and motivational. So she called her.

'I'm so pleased you've rung.' Emily sounded tired.

'Just wanted to see how you were doing. How's the bump?'

'Oh, you know, not much has changed since I saw you last. The news is official as I'm thirteen weeks and the scan looks healthy. I can cope with feeding the cat now without vomiting all over the kitchen floor at the smell of tinned cat food, but this third pregnancy is still an absolute pig. I don't know how I get through the long days at work though. Give it a couple of months and I'm going to have trouble getting behind the steering wheel. Not good when I'm averaging four thousand miles a month.'

'How did work take the news?'

'To be honest, it's rather awkward. They weren't too enamoured by the request for a third round of maternity leave...'

Lucy thought she heard her sister's voice break, and decided she needed another face-to-face to reassure herself Emily was coping.

'I know it's short notice, but I wondered if I could come down and see you? I haven't seen my nieces in weeks and I could do with a change of scene. Say if it's not convenient. I don't want to add to your stress.'

'Oh, Luce, that would be wonderful. Could you? Could you really? Stu's got some work thing this weekend but let me have a word with him and I'll get back to you. It would be lovely to see you. A bit of girl time would be good.'

'You sound stressed. Are you sure things are okay?'

'I'm fine,' she sniffed. 'It's the hormones. I have a wonderful life, an adorable husband, a fab job and two beautiful girls. I'm being silly and self-centred. What's not to love?'

Oh dear, thought Lucy, *Dad was right*.

Visiting Emily would mean two weekends away in a row and Lucy's first thought was Brenda. Now they had the diagnosis, Lucy noticed the forgetful moments and blank looks more. A Facebook memory had flashed up in the week: Brenda sitting next to her supporting the Renborough primary school coffee morning a year ago. The photo shocked her because until that point she hadn't realised how gaunt Brenda had become in those twelve months. What would another twelve months bring for them both?

'I'm going to visit my sister this weekend, so I won't be able to pop in.' She tried to make the announcement sound casual, but Brenda wasn't fooled.

'And you're worried I will take a naked walk up to the town hall with a flowerpot on my head while you're gone?'

'No, I'm worried that you'll make a move on Gorgeous George, and once he's had a taste of the best, he'll abandon the rest. I'm not sure he can cope with the predatory advances of a sexually liberated woman who made the Sixties her own.'

Brenda chuckled and dropped her defensive attitude. 'I always liked your sense of humour. And as for Gorgeous George – don't tempt me.' She wiggled her eyebrows, but her smile vanished and she let out a long sigh. 'It's so important to laugh when all you really want to do is cry.'

'Please don't say that...'

'There, there.' Brenda patted Lucy's arm. 'I don't want you worrying, or feeling that I am somehow your responsibility...'

'No, never that. You are my friend.'

'I know, I know. And you mean more to me than any person alive.' There was a pause as a strong emotion bubbled in Brenda, but she successfully combated it and swallowed, refocusing. 'But back to the hunky...erm...' She scrunched her hands into tiny fists in frustration, searching for a name she had only recently used but was now temporarily camouflaged in her brain and refused to step forward.

'George?' Lucy offered.

'Yes. George. George.' She repeated the word a couple of times, trying to lodge it more securely in her memory. 'He's a lovely lad and a good listener. I told him that as much as I loved the beautiful flowers, his time was worth far more to me, and he said he was starting to realise that. Apparently, he's making an effort to spend more time with his own mum.'

'Those of us who don't have enough money to buy ourselves out of trouble every time things go pear-shaped learned that years ago,' said Lucy, notching up another reason why he wasn't a great match for her. 'I expect he will pop by to say hi. I think he gets lonely, rattling around in that big house with no real friends or family visiting. Perhaps you could invite him in again. I think he works too hard.'

Brenda threw her a stern look. 'If you are trying to convince me that I will be the one doing George a favour, it was a nice try. But I'm not gaga quite yet, Missy. It's wonderful that you care so much, and I think *George* genuinely cares too.' She emphasised his name almost to prove to herself that she could remember it. 'But what I really want to hear about is where we are up to with the locket. Have you given him the feverfew tea yet?'

'To be honest, I've been so preoccupied with other things, I'd forgotten all about it.' With everything at work, and her worries about Emily, the locket had slithered to the bottom of her list of priorities.

'Well, get on it, my girl. There are a few spells to complete yet, and I want to see a conclusion to all of this before...' She trailed off.

'Of course. In fact, I'll nip into town now for the cupcake ingredients. It's not late. I can have them baked and around to him within a couple of hours. He won't know what's hit him.'

'Love,' Brenda said. 'Love will have hit him. And it is more powerful than a speeding train.'

'Why would you randomly bake me cupcakes? It's not my birthday, for goodness' sake. Your excitable friend insisted on plying me with some foreign liqueur and a home-made flap-jack at the weekend. And there was that woman from the WI who tried to force-feed me cheesecake when I first moved in. What are you all up to? Everyone seems to want to shove cake at me. It's hardly like I need fattening up. Are you all after something? Or is there some weird cult operating in the area that I'm unaware of? First you fatten us up, then you sacrifice us to the Neighbourhood Watch God or something?'

Lucy hadn't realised Jess's impromptu visit to George had involved bringing her own refreshments. And home-made flapjack. That was a first for Jess.

'It's a thank you for looking in on Brenda last weekend.'

'Not necessary.'

'I know. But please take them. They're dairy-free.'

He made a grumbly sound but took the plastic container.

'I know it was a bit of disaster, but I was hoping you could do the same again this weekend?' Lucy asked.

'Ah. Bribery. The truth will out. You'd better come in. You can help me eat them.'

There was a pause. George cleared his throat and tried again.

'What I meant to say was: would you like to come in for a cup of tea and share these delicious-looking cupcakes? I would very much like it if you would.'

Lucy grinned and skipped over the threshold.

Sitting on the black leather corner sofa in his minimalist living room with Scratbag on her lap, Lucy waited for her host to make an appearance with the promised tea. This room really needed a woman's touch. Actually, it really needed *someone's* touch. A solitary geometric abstract hung over a bare mantelpiece that didn't even have a clock on it. Having spent so much time surrounded by so much *time* at Brenda's, the absence of timepieces was noticeable, and the silence unsettling.

The locket was warm against her skin and she could swear she felt a tiny electric tingle as George returned with two mugs awkwardly clasped together in one hand and the plastic box of cherry and chocolate cupcakes with their dubious magical properties in the other. Scratbag immediately abandoned her lap and made for George, rubbing around his legs. Breaking into a smile at the sight of the cat, possibly the first unguarded one Lucy had seen him give, George unceremoniously deposited everything on the coffee table, some of the tea slopping over the edge and onto the glass top. He could have at least put the cakes on a plate, she thought. Her mother would have turned purple and collapsed on the floor at the thought of presenting them in a plastic tub.

Despite a cursory rub of his nose, George bent over to pet Scratbag behind the ears and the silence was broken by a loud, rumbly purr. There was an awkward pause as Lucy and George caught each other's eye and both looked away.

'I like the picture,' she said, pointing to the abstract.

'I don't. I only bought it because I couldn't stand looking at the bare wall any more. It looks like bits of Swiss roll. Twelve hundred pounds is a lot to pay for a picture of chopped-up cake, but I was in a hurry.'

'When I look at it I think of colourful balls of wool stacked in the cubbyholes of a yarn shop. It's really eye-catching.'

'If I ever change it for a decent picture, you can have it.'

'You can't give a twelve-hundred-pound painting away.' There it was again – George's flippant attitude towards money.

'Why not? You like it. I don't.'

Lucy sighed, and momentarily wondered what it must be like to have the kind of money where you thought nothing of giving away an expensive painting, like you might pass on a spare can opener to a friend, because you happened to have two.

'So, how's the knitting going? The furry muffs?' George asked.

'Twiddlemuffs. They're for people with dementia: knitted tubes with ribbons, buttons and twiddly bits for people to, well, twiddle. It keeps anxious hands occupied and alleviates stress. I'll drop you off some leaflets and perhaps you can take them into work?'

'Of course, but you do know that a muff—'

'Yes, thank you. But, historically, it was a perfectly acceptable word for something you put your hands in to keep them warm. I popped along to Renborough Hospital last week to drop off some more and it was so heartening to see an old gentleman with one on his lap, fiddling away. The nurse said it's drastically cut down on his wandering.'

'How very community-spirited of you. Hmm...these actually look rather good.' He reached over for a cupcake.

'Gee, thanks.'

George devoured it in two bites and then grabbed a second, which he practically ate in one. He didn't comment on a bitter taste, so adding extra cherries and using a high cocoa content chocolate had worked.

After a couple of minutes, he began to look slightly uncomfortable. He pulled a face and stretched open his mouth, sticking out his tongue.

'Are you okay?' she asked.

'Not sure. What's in these?'

'Don't tell me you are allergic to something else?'

'My mouth feels tingly. I get this sometimes with apples, but then I'm not a big fruit eater as a rule.' He was still contorting his face and his cheeks were flushed. 'I feel a bit sick.'

'You did stuff them in rather.'

'Oh, tho it's my fault you've put thomething poithonous in these bloody caketh? *Are* you trying to poithon me?'

213

'No, no...' blustered Lucy. 'I don't understand.'

'My tongue is thwelling. I can feel my thwoat getting tighter.'

George's face had gone pink and slightly blotchy, and he looked really unwell.

'Oh. My. God. I need to get you to the hospital. *Right now*. At this time of night we can scoot through town in five minutes. I'll grab my car keys.'

'I don't like the look of that. Come with me.'

A passing nurse whisked a blotchy George through a set of double doors before they'd even approached the triage desk, not realising Lucy was with him, so she slunk into a chair at the back of the Renborough Accident and Emergency waiting room and sipped at a watery coffee. Trying in vain to stop her bottom sliding off the shiny plastic chairs – a rainbow of green, red and bright blue, bolted to the floor in military rows – she gazed around at the unfortunate souls who had found themselves at hospital on a sticky June evening.

Rows of tired faces, many with traces of blood and pained expressions, sat awkwardly on the hard chairs with body language suggesting they understood they were there for the long haul. Most were on their phones, playing games of Candy Crush Saga and Clash of Clans to see them through the lengthy wait.

Lucy was finally called over and directed to resus, where she found a noticeably less pink and swollen George lying down with his gigantic feet dangling over the end of the hospital bed.

'I didn't expect you to wait for me. I assumed you'd gone.'

'I couldn't leave you. I felt responsible. Anyway, how will you get home?' She walked over to his bed and stood awkwardly before him.

'I can call a taxi. Don't think I'm going anywhere for a while though.'

'Well, I stayed. Wish I'd thought to grab my knitting bag. I could have knitted some furry muffs while I was waiting.' She smiled. 'So what's the story?'

'They gave me an adrenaline injection and I've been on oxygen for a while.' He indicated to a mask by the bed. 'Turns out I'm allergic to cherries, on top of everything else.'

'Sorry, George. I had no idea.'

He sighed. 'It's okay. Neither did I.'

Chapter 30

As George suspected, he was kept in overnight for monitoring. He was given further medication and was having bloods taken when Lucy eventually left that evening. Still feeling guilty, she insisted he told her when he was being discharged so she could collect him, and he rang early the following morning. Lucy contacted work and asked for the morning off so she could bring a friend home from hospital. Adam assumed she meant Brenda and Lucy chose not to correct him.

The journey back, Lucy realised later, was one of the longest conversations she'd ever had with her neighbour. His answers were initially blunt and brutally honest ('Are you feeling better now?' 'No.'), but the longer they were confined to the intimacy of the car, the more relaxed his conversation became. She negotiated her way around the bypass and back through town. Apart from catching his enormous knee every time she went for the gearstick, she felt more comfortable with him than at any point before.

As they waited at the high street traffic lights, he finally began to open up.

'I know you think packaging is boring, but it really isn't.' Where had that statement come from? He certainly didn't need to justify anything to her. 'And it's not like it was part of my life plan. I studied economics at uni and was a qualified financial risk analyst when my father dropped dead at fifty-two. I put my life on hold to oversee the sale of the company.'

George shuffled in his seat and Lucy glanced over at his strong profile as she pulled away from the lights. He did have lovely eyes.

'Five years on and the company is growing, my team are a great bunch, and somehow I'm hooked. It's a fascinating industry, especially at a time when everyone is pushing for less plastic and biodegradable alternatives. We intend to be market leaders in this area.'

Lucy decided he was suffering after-effects from the hospital drugs because now he'd started talking, he didn't stop. Most un-George-like behaviour. Normally she'd have joined in with some comment, but she was interested to see where this was leading. There was something endearing about his stilted attempts to be conversational.

He cleared his throat to fill the pause. 'And you won't believe it, looking at the size of me now, but I was a three-pound, fourteen-ounce premature baby and spent most of my childhood as the runt of the class.'

She glanced over. 'Correct. Don't believe it,' she said.

'Honestly. My growth spurt didn't kick in until my late teens and then, oh boy, did it kick in. With unflattering NHS glasses until I was old enough to switch to contacts, and a lactose intolerance that meant I was the butt of dairy-based jokes ad nauseam, socialising never came naturally.'

Was that it? Was he trying to be sociable? She felt flattered and was aware of the locket under her top. Had she done enough with her potentially life-threatening cupcakes to move the spells on? Because as she got to know George better, she was starting to hope the locket did possess magic properties after all. George Aberdour as a boyfriend was starting to appeal. Big time.

As they pulled into Lancaster Road, George asked, 'Why do you drive this horrendous banana yellow car?'

'Because I ordered a pretty metallic blue one, but there was a mix-up at the garage so I settled for this.' Lucy didn't mind the colour now as much as she had at first. At least she could always find it in a car park.

'I'm guessing you didn't make a fuss? Try and beat them down in price for their mistake? Get angry and demand a refund?'

'No. It wasn't worth it.'

'You are such a pushover.'

'Was. I think I'd probably stand up for myself better if it happened now.' She pulled up alongside his Audi and performed a passable parallel park in front of Brenda's house.

'Thanks for the lift,' he said, squeezing out of the car like a grown-up getting out of a pedal car. 'I like talking to you. It's good to have a friend.' There was a slight crinkle around the eyes and Lucy willed him to give her his heart-stopping smile. 'Although, and don't take this the wrong way, don't ever bake me Thank You cupcakes again.'

'I know he could have died and everything, but it is *sort* of funny,' said Jess, after Lucy had filled her in. 'More importantly though, did it work?'

She was at Lucy's flat again, inviting herself over for the evening to watch *Dirty Dancing* for a hot-man fix and to try and persuade Lucy to let her experiment on her face with autumn colours. Lucy had never been so popular with her friend. Jess had abandoned her usual full-on dating regime and was content to spend most of her free time at the flat, even if a lot of it was spent at the living-room window.

'Despite the allergy disaster, it seems so.' The first thing Lucy had done after dropping George home was check the locket.

'So you've got the next spell then?'

'Yes.'

'And?'

Knowing she would be like a dog with a rawhide chew until she'd shown her the locket, Lucy placed her knitting on the coffee table, dragged the chain over her head and handed it to Jess.

'You know I can't open it. C'mon, Luce. Stop being a tease.'

With no problem at all, Lucy opened the locket and passed it back. Jess read out the spell.

> *A drop of his blood on a linen square*
> *To carry your true love everywhere.'*

'The poor man has had to rescue me from a fire, nearly caught me trespassing in his house, and was almost killed when I poisoned him. Now, *now* I'm supposed to impale him with something sharp and take the very blood from his veins. He would be totally justified in having me arrested. Or having some sort of restraining order put in place, at the very least.'

'The police is about the only emergency service you haven't had to involve, apart from the Royal National Lifeboat Institution, of course,' said Jess.

'To be honest, until all the spells have been revealed, I'm not ruling either of them out.'

Rain was forecast for the rest of the week, which Lucy thought was bad sportsmanship for June, but temperatures were noticeably warmer, so she dug out some summer dresses in anticipation of the coming season. She was starting to wear more colourful clothes, no longer worried that her wardrobe would draw attention to her, and had even found time during her lunch hours to crochet a vibrant pink, short-sleeved cardigan. Her grandmother's button tin had yielded some wacky mismatched buttons to complete the look. Derek and Roy had both commented how pretty she looked, which had in turn put an extra bounce in her step and an attractive flush on her cheeks.

Work was hectic, but Lucy thrived on being busy. She was getting in early and leaving late, and found herself singing out loud and smiling at everyone, even Adam. Although after her trip to A&E she felt more like punching him, because he spent the remainder of the day making tedious jokes about her poisoning everyone and how glad he was it wasn't her day to do the tea round.

'So, I had this dream about you last night...' Daniel was in the office for the monthly sales meeting, which meant an office full of reps milling about waiting for Richard Tompkins to call them down to the conference room. He leaned over the partition and wiggled his eyebrows at Lucy.

'Really? Do tell me *all* about it. In explicit detail.' She put her chin in her hands and looked up to him with wide eyes.

Daniel jerked his head back. 'Oo, she has fight,' he said, not fazed by Lucy's response. In fact, his body language suggested it had only excited him more. Lucy heard Pat's chair squeak backwards and, along with the rest of the office, witnessed Pat stand up and face up to Daniel over the top of the partition.

'You...' She faltered but found her voice. 'You are a male chauvinist pig and I've had enough. Stop with the sexist comments or I'm going to report you.' And then she sat back down.

There was an eerie silence and a few uncomfortable glances until Sam burst through the main door, Richard Tompkins in tow, and announced the meeting was about to start. The reps filed out, Daniel giving Pat a nervous glance as he passed, and the low hum of the sales team started up again.

Lucy dialled Pat's internal line.

'Way to go, Pat,' she said. 'Appreciate the support.'

'No problem. I've been watching you stand up for yourself a bit more lately and it inspired me. I should be thanking you. I've already put my foot down at home. John doesn't know what's hit him. Mind you, the sex has improved. I get to do the tying up now. It's been a revelation.'

As was that, thought Lucy, eyebrows almost hitting her hairline, as she switched the line to take an incoming call.

Sam started to work her magic on the limp carcass that was Tompkins Toy Wholesaler. Each department had been visited, observed and was now being evaluated. Everybody knew that the company was behind the times; one look at the photo-copier could tell you that, so they were expecting change, but most were hoping Sam would be gentle with them. Teaching the old dog new tricks was okay as long as you explained the trick several times and didn't shout if he got it wrong. Nervous whispers and hushed speculation was rife as Sam shut herself away to collate the data, and Adam was asked to help drag the huge desk back into her office so she could do so in peace.

As part of her final assessment of the company, and after a promising start shifting the old and damaged stock, Sam decided to do a complete stocktake, even though the company usually only undertook them annually. This meant overtime, which was generally welcomed, but also cross-examinations over missing, damaged and faulty stock, which were not.

Persuading most of the staff to stay late one evening, Sam paired everyone up and allocated each pair a section. Lucy found herself with her new general manager but didn't feel as nervous as she would have been without the locket to see her through. They worked together on the mezzanine floor at the back of the warehouse, counting Disney jigsaw puzzles, and Lucy respected her boss for getting her hands dirty. Richard Tompkins usually took a supervisory role in these situations. You wouldn't find him heaving heavy boxes out from dark corners or scaling shelving to count lime green alien space hoppers.

'I think we can have this wrapped up in half an hour. I'm sure you've got someone waiting for you at home,' Sam said, perching on a pile of pallets while she caught her breath.

'I live alone. I don't even have a cat,' Lucy answered, thinking briefly of Scratbag and how lovely it would be to come home to someone or something.

'Friends to socialise with then?'

'Not so much midweek. Sometimes a small crowd of us go out after work, although Jess and I usually do something together on a Friday or Saturday.' She didn't want to sound like a sad loser who stayed at home most of the time. She also didn't mention Knit and Natter. Or her seventy-nine-year-old best friend.

'I don't go out at all,' Sam said. Lucy looked up and noticed her focus intently on the stack of fifty-piece Jungle Book puzzles. 'Too busy carving out my career to have a social life.'

'But you are good at your job; general manager at such a young age.'

'Nice of you to say, but I'm in my thirties. Suddenly not so young any more. And when I pause for breath and look around, I don't really have *anyone* – never mind a boyfriend. Sometimes I go to work-related events, or stay away for conferences, but there's been no man for two years. And no close girlfriends. School friends tailed off over the years and the women I come across in a professional capacity seem to see my success as a threat.' She hesitated. 'Do you remember me asking you if the other ladies in the office were unkind to you?'

'Yes, but they really aren't,' Lucy assured her.

'I had a lot of trouble a few years ago when I worked at a London-based firm. I hadn't been in the job long when I got promoted and it didn't go down well with some of the staff who had been there considerably longer than me.'

'But if you got the promotion, you were the best person for the job.'

'You know how women can be? There was never anything I could put my finger on, but there was a lot of whispering and giggles. I wasn't included in things and they were uncooperative and forgetful when it came to carrying out my instructions.'

'It was only jealousy.'

'Absolutely. And I decided to ride it out, convinced it would die down, but it went on for months. In the end, it prevented me from doing my job properly and I had to resign. I couldn't prove anything, but I kept encountering delayed orders and a lot of work to rule – that kind of thing.'

'So you let them win?' said Lucy, suddenly feeling quite indignant on her behalf.

'Yes.' Sam sighed. 'I let them win, in a way. But you have to choose your battles, Lucy. And I've always been in it for the long game. Although I'm not sure I appreciated the social cost when I set my career goals.' Another sigh escaped from her scarlet lips.

Lucy couldn't bear to see Sam, someone she was slowly warming to, look so sad.

'You could come out with Jess and me sometime, if you like,' Lucy blurted out.

'If that's a genuine offer, I'd love to.' And Sam gave her a half-smile. 'I don't know this area well, as I moved up for the job, so you'll have to show me some of the places you hang out.'

Hmm, thought Lucy, *I'm guessing The Yarn Shop isn't the sort of hang-out Sam had in mind.*

'You said she could do what?' Jess spluttered out a mouthful of Sprite as she coincided the morning coffee run with Lucy's turn on the sales office rota.

'Come out with us.'

'Are you mad?'

'I didn't think she'd actually say yes. Besides, I felt sorry for her. I don't think she's got any friends.'

'She's our boss, Lucy. Technically more yours than mine, but still. What do you plan to sit around talking about?

224

Because if she starts harping on about the new accounts software she's having installed next week, I might just swing for her. I've got to go to Bedford for a two-day training course. There was absolutely nothing wrong with the old system. This new one is going to make extra work for our department and possibly fry my already shrivelled brain in the process. Bloody woman.'

'I didn't think it through. I'm sorry.'

Pulling in to the last kerbside space at the top end of Lancaster Road that evening, Lucy noticed a well-dressed lady standing outside number twenty-four. She was tall and graceful, with legs up to her elbows, and she was wearing the sort of killer heels that would do a splendid job of aerating any bowling green lawn. Her glorious auburn hair fell down her back, inches from her Jennifer Lopez pert behind, and swished from shoulder to shoulder as she tried to peer through the frosted glass to spot any sign of life from within. She looked vaguely familiar, but then Lucy wasn't great with faces.

George was rarely back before seven o'clock, so Lucy suspected the woman might have a long wait. The stranger continued to alternate between knocking and peering as Lucy walked past.

'He's not usually home until later. Can I take a message?' she offered.

The woman looked Lucy up. Then down. Then up again.

'Yes. He's not answering my calls. Can you tell him his wife is trying to get in touch with him?'

Chapter 31

Lucy was so shocked to discover George had a wife that she went home and knitted seven rows of flesh-coloured stocking stitch for the new Poldark she'd started, without even taking off her shoes.

It was her first Etsy order – a private request for a Poldark – and she'd read it through three times, still stunned someone would pay good money for something she rattled off as she watched the television. Reluctant to sell her prototype, but so pleased with the result, she'd listed Poldarks as an option and had a lot of interest, but then the man was everywhere at the moment.

Two minutes later and she unpicked her work, because her mind was flitting around like erratic disco lights and she'd dropped a stitch in the first row. Why she was quite so flustered by this revelation about George's private life was a mystery. Perhaps because he'd come across as such a dyed-in-the-wool bachelor that she simply couldn't imagine him having a relationship with a woman, let alone marrying one. It would mean having to communicate. Not one of his strengths.

Brenda was equally caught out by the news when Lucy went over later to check she'd eaten, taking the half-knitted Poldark with her.

'I don't know how I missed that,' she muttered to herself. 'It explains the muddiness and swirls I can often detect in his aura. Although I still can't quite believe it.'

'That's the end of the spells then. I can't follow them now,' Lucy sighed, her mother's Big Birthday tapping her on the shoulder.

'Don't be so hasty, young lady.'

'But he's married, Brenda.'

'He's married but living alone. I wouldn't say that was a happy marriage, more likely the end of a failed one.'

'If you've brought me something to eat – I don't want it. If you've set something on fire – I'm busy. And if you have another mammal carcass to beautify – I've run out of hair gel.' George peered over the rim of his glasses at the girl on his doorstep. He was clutching a bundle of papers and looked quite harassed.

It had been hammering down all evening. While Lucy understood the farmers needed the summer rain for their crops to flourish, she wished it would have the courtesy to do so overnight, and not in the day. Or in June. She wiped the strands of wet hair away from her eyes and took a good look at George's stressed face. Not the faintest trace of a smile.

'I'm merely here to pass on a message.'

'Let me guess: you want to borrow a cup of cornflakes to make breakfast for the unemployed, blind, suicidal alcoholics?'

'No. Your wife is trying to get hold of you.'

'BLOODY WOMAN,' he shouted and shut the front door with unnecessary force.

Not one hundred per cent sure if he meant her or the wife, Lucy turned towards her flat and stomped back along the pavement, not caring if she caught a few puddles along the way.

The pounding knock on her front door a few moments later reverberated through her flat like the aftershocks of a minor earthquake. She was comfort-kitting; doing row upon row of knit one, purl one to try and stop herself from hitting something. Where others turned to chocolate, she turned to mass twiddlemuff production. Poldark required more concentration than she had heart for at that moment.

The banging got louder. If she ignored him for much longer, the door would be off its hinges. She laid the knitting on her seat and turned down her Angry Music – a Linkin Park CD left behind by her last boyfriend. Walking down the hallway towards George's oppressive silhouette in the frosted glass, Lucy felt something snap. How dare he shout at her like that! She yanked the door open and took a deep breath. There were a couple of things she needed to set him straight on.

'The only reason I was hair-drying that poor rabbit the other day was because *your* cat killed it and the distraught four-year-old owner wanted its pathetic bloodstained body back.' Lucy launched into her attack before George had even opened his mouth.

'Oh.'

'Yes – oh.' Her hands went to her hips.

George took a deep breath. 'I came round to apologise. One of the line managers walked out on me this afternoon, I'm in the middle of very overdue staff reports, and Karen showing up was an irritating end to a stressful and exhausting day. My behaviour was absolutely and completely inexcusable.'

'Oh.'

'Yes – oh.'

She sighed. 'Then you'd better come in. *I* don't like to leave people standing on my doorstep when it's raining. I don't think it's very polite. Tea?'

'Please.' He smiled.

'My goodness, George Aberdour, you said please. There's a first. You'll have to have your tea black. I don't have any fancy non-dairy, cherry-free, not-been-within-six-inches-of-an-apple milk,' Lucy said, stomping down the hall.

She thought she heard a chuckle, but when she glanced back, his face was as straight as a professional poker player's.

'I'm not allergic to milk. I'm lactose intolerant. If I have too much it causes bloating, discomfort and...other things. A small splash in a cup of tea won't kill me.'

'Shame,' she mumbled.

'Okay. I deserve that.'

He followed her into the kitchen and pulled out one of her battered pine kitchen chairs, as she filled the kettle from the tap. She turned back to face him, leaning her bottom on the edge of the worktop with her arms crossed, not prepared to sit anywhere near him for fear of thumping him. Not emotions she usually had to put a lid on.

'She's my ex-wife,' George said.

'You don't have to explain anything to me.'

'She's been my ex-wife for over a year and we haven't lived together for two years.'

'Honestly, it's not my business.'

'She took me for a lot of money in the settlement. I nearly lost *my* business.'

The kettle flicked off. She opened the top cupboard and rummaged around, looking for two mugs that matched but pleased that the cupboard itself was ordered and tidy. Not

229

that she cared what George thought about her cupboards. Was a failed marriage supposed to excuse his rude behaviour? Not as far as she was concerned.

'We weren't together for very long before it became apparent we weren't compatible.'

Lucy fished two teabags from the Tetley Tea removal van caddy someone had dared to give her mother and Lucy had taken off her hands. She popped them into the mugs.

'You've apologised and that's fine. Perhaps we could not talk about your ex-wife, please?' She opened the fridge and pulled out the plastic carton of milk. 'But can I just check? When you said "bloody woman" on the doorstep – you were talking about her, right?'

'Ah.' There was a moment while George replayed the scene from Lucy's point of view and looked momentarily embarrassed. 'Yes. Sorry. Ambiguous. I was furious that she'd tracked me down. It was the last straw balanced on the back of a very fragile camel. But stupid George's usual lack of social skills meant I messed up again. Sorry. Friends?' He looked up so hopefully, like a small child – or rather an oversized child sitting at a primary school table – that Lucy's heart thawed the tiniest bit.

'Okay, friends,' she agreed.

'The subject of my ex-wife is officially off topic and shall forever remain so. My problem. Not yours. But thank you for passing on the message.'

They clinked mugs and he smiled. Actually smiled. His mahogany brown eyes twinkled and she noticed small creases folding around them as two tiny dimples appeared either side of his mouth. If only he knew what difference a simple smile made to his face, she thought. But then, as he seemed generally off women at the moment, perhaps it was for the best. He clearly had no idea quite how magnificent that smile was and would totally fail to cope with the undoubted stream of lovestruck women throwing themselves at his size-thirteen feet should he choose to employ it more frequently.

The conversation moved on and he enquired about Brenda. She, in turn, asked how Scratbag was settling in. After a surprisingly pleasant half an hour of small talk, George drank the last of his tea and she stood up to take his mug.

'I would offer you a more grown-up drink as it's nearly nine o'clock, like a glass of wine or a beer, but I don't generally keep anything in, I'm afraid. I can only offer you another tea.'

'No problem. Not every evening needs to end with alcohol because, believe me, when it does, it often ends badly. As for the tea, thanks anyway, but I must get back. I've got a job vacancy to fill and a bundle of personnel reports to go through before the morning. They're taking longer than I anticipated.'

His chair was clumsily scraped back, and then he stood up and paused.

'Thanks for the chat. Never have been great at the whole socialising thing. Then with what happened to my father, and the business, and... Well, I need to start making more of an effort with people.' And he graced Lucy with another of his knee-wobbling smiles. Something inside her fluttered. Perhaps ensnaring him wouldn't be such a hardship after all. He would tick most of the boxes on her mother's potential son-in-law list: good-looking, tall, successful businessman with his own excessively tidy home. Not that *she* was thinking of him as a potential husband, but her mother didn't need to know that.

'Perhaps you need to be a bit more spontaneous and make

an effort to have a life outside work,' Lucy said. 'Embrace opportunities as they present themselves? That's a good way to make friends. Try to say yes to things. You never know what they might lead to, or what friends you might make along the way.' Persuading him to be open to offers that came his way would be in her favour when it came to asking him about the Big Birthday.

'Perhaps.' He didn't look convinced.

A drop of his blood on a linen square, she remembered and began to look around the room for something sharp, but it wasn't thought through. She could hardly launch herself at him with a corkscrew. How on earth was she going to extract some of his blood without getting arrested in the process? Or smashing down these carefully constructed bridges that were finally enabling them to spend time together?

'Then, as part of a concerted effort to be more sociable, perhaps Brenda and you would like to come round? Like a belated house-warming? Tomorrow? At seven?'

'That would be lovely. Thank you.' And she followed him to the front door, resisting the urge to pick up the sharp, pointy antique letter opener that was balanced on the radiator as she passed.

Chapter 32

'And I thought, you're really lax about doing this locket thing because you think he's so rude and unpleasant, that you probably hadn't got the linen yet. I assume it's got to be the proper stuff and isn't the same thing as any old scrap of cotton.' Jess handed Lucy a square of fabric.

'Yes, they come from different plants. Oo, it's tiny. I didn't think you could buy it in small squares.'

'I bought a metre, but I was going to use the rest for a cushion cover or something.'

'But you don't sew.' Jess simply didn't have the patience for needlecraft – her disastrous flirt with knitting had shown Lucy that.

'If you're going to start cross-questioning me about this then I'll keep it and you can buy your own linen.'

'Sorry. Thanks.' Lucy folded the square up and tucked it between her mug and the rim of the tray. It was Connor's day to do the teas and coffees, but he was off with man flu so Lucy happily volunteered. The rota was working well; Adam even included himself, although it took him twice as long and they got through three packets of biscuits on his day, rather than the usual two.

'So what's the plan?' Jess asked. 'I was thinking: invite him over for a meal, start chopping up the onions, wave the kitchen knife about a bit and sort of slip.' Jess was leaning her chin on her hands and grinning as she sat at the table, waiting for the kettle to boil.

'Are you mad? The man would have me in a head lock and be on the phone to the police before I'd taken my first step. I was thinking more of a discreet prick.'

'Back to Daniel again.' Jess winked.

'With a sewing pin.'

The kitchen door opened and Richard Tompkins gave one of his charming smiles. For an older man, he certainly still had it. Jess stood up and started riffling through the cupboards to look busy.

'Ah, Lucy, could you make me up a separate tray with the decent coffee for the conference room? We have a garden centre chain coming in to discuss the Tramp'O'Bounce with us in half an hour and we need to make a good impression. Daniel is hoping to swing by as well to try and persuade them to order a few more of our lines – garden centres seem to sell everything these days from cookery books to headphones. So, including Sam, we'll need coffee for four please.'

'No problem. Shall I pop across the road to The Teaspoon and get some pastries? It would look better than a plate of broken Rich Tea. I can take the money from petty cash.'

'Splendid idea. He's come to squeeze us dry, of course, because he knows he can source similar products from other distributors, but I've always found the personal touch works wonders.'

Lucy's mouth suddenly went dry. She'd had the germ of an idea bouncing about in her head for a few days and realised it was now or never. Her right hand went to the locket and she took a deep breath.

'I'm not thinking specifically of this customer, but perhaps we could encourage customer loyalty with a bribe?' Lucy began. It was Jess's joke a few days previously, how everyone except her lit up at the thought of a glass of wine, which had started her thinking.

'Go on. I'm listening...'

'I thought we could offer, say, half a case of wine for buying in pallets rather than boxes, depending on the product, or spending over a certain amount with us. I think giving people something tangible, something they can enjoy outside of their work environment, means they forget about the monetary value and feel their business is appreciated. It's like giving someone a gift, which always makes the receiver feel special. I looked into the wholesale prices of several suppliers and if we bought in bulk, each case would work out a fraction of the cost in real terms, rather than upping the trade discount we give to the customers.' Now that she was saying the words out loud, her confidence flagged. 'Oh, it's probably a stupid idea...'

'No, let's see if it's got legs.' Richard was nodding. 'Give me some hard figures and outline what you're thinking, and I'll take a look.'

As he left the kitchen, Lucy was left open-mouthed, surprised how easy it was to be brave.

Jess pulled a cheeky face. 'Please, sir. Pick me, sir,' she teased. 'I want to be your best friend, Ricky.'

'He's not Ricky. His golfing buddies always ask to be put through to Dick.' Lucy measured out spoonfuls of supermarket gold roast into the cups and added the hot water, her head spinning with ways to present her idea in a professional manner.

'Oh, Ricky, Ricky, Ricky.' Jess was singing into a silver teaspoon and winding her lithe body around one of the plastic chairs in a provocative manner. 'I know you've always thought of me as a little mouse of a girl, but I've grown a pair and am set to take the world of toy distribution by storm.'

Lucy wasn't impressed with Jess's impersonation of her and closed the cupboard door rather forcefully. 'He's Mr Tompkins to us.'

'Ricky to his lovers.' Jess wiggled her eyebrows.

Lucy picked up the tray containing the office coffees, balanced it in one hand and fumbled for the door. She stepped back cautiously, turning her head to Jess.

'You're wrong. Richard Tompkins is a Dick.'

She turned back to face the hallway and her heart sunk to her ballet pumps as she stood nose to nose with Sam.

'What can I get everyone? Tea? Coffee? A soft drink?' offered George.

'I brought a bottle of my home-made sparkling elderflower. Much more appropriate for house-warming drinks, wouldn't you say?' Brenda had a touch of rouge on both cheeks and a smear of pale blue eyeshadow. There was a sparkly necklace hanging low over her chest that matched the sparkles in her eyes. This was the Brenda she knew and loved. George was proving a good tonic for her friend.

'Then I'll look for some appropriate glasses. Through here, ladies,' and he gestured towards the living room.

'His emotional energy is a lot more positive than when he

first moved to Lancaster Road,' said Brenda when they were alone. 'His aura is changing too; the green is less muddy and more vibrant. Ah, here comes my little friend.'

Scratbag wandered into the room and made a beeline for Brenda. He sniffed her outstretched hand and leaped onto her lap. She bent her head over his upturned nose.

'Interesting. Thank you, Scratbag.'

'Don't pretend the cat is communicating with you. Honestly, Brenda, sometimes I suspect you are a massive fraud.'

Brenda smiled and edged her face closer to the curious cat. 'What's that, Skippy? The little boy has fallen down the well? And George is falling for our Lucy?' The cat was nuzzling her hand now, and Brenda was getting in the swing of her role play.

They were laughing as George entered with a tray of goodies.

'Excellent. Cake,' said Brenda.

'Yes, a fancy non-dairy, cherry-free, not-been-within-six-inches-of-an-apple sponge cake,' George said, looking over at Lucy as his dimples put in a fleeting appearance. 'Goes better with tea than elderflower wine, but still.' He poured three small tumblers of the wine, apologising that they were the only glasses he owned, and then chose to sit on the sofa next to Lucy, rather than in the remaining empty armchair.

'Welcome to the neighbourhood. I think you may have found your true home here. And your little lodger absolutely adores you. He told me so,' Brenda said, looking at Scratbag and raising her tumbler.

'It's odd, but ever since he's been around I've felt calmer and decidedly less stressed,' admitted George.

Brenda threw Lucy an I-told-you-so look. 'Animals have

that effect. And good friends. How is the allergy now?' she asked.

'Better. Sitting on my lap is okay as long as I don't stroke him because that makes fur fly everywhere. I'm even managing the contact lenses occasionally.'

Shame, thought Lucy. The glasses made him look sexy.

'I think my body has accepted the thing that I'm allergic to isn't going away, but I'm still popping the antihistamines.'

'It's a lesson you must heed, young man. Sometimes you must make sacrifices to get the things in life you need – even if you don't realise how much you need them until they are a part of your life.' Brenda tipped her head back and emptied the tumbler, pushing it hopefully towards George for a refill.

While Brenda and George continued to chat, Lucy pulled her bag towards her feet. She turned her body away from his and rummaged inside for the packet of sewing pins. Mumbling odd words to make it seem as if she was participating in the conversation, she slipped a pin from the packet and concealed it in her hand. The linen square was folded in the front pocket, ready for action.

'Shall I pass the cake?' Lucy offered, standing up and wiggling the pin so the point protruded slightly from her fingers.

The plan: pass the plate around, pretend to slip and scratch him, apologising for her sharp nails. Run to her bag for a 'handkerchief' – *et voilà*!

The reality: as she turned, the cake slid from the plate and into George's lap, her fake stumble became real as her feet twisted together and she landed across his knees, on top of the cake, and in his outstretched arms.

'I am *so* sorry.' Lucy looked up into his cross-looking deep brown eyes, their crossness magnified by the lenses of his glasses.

'Hmm. I'll fetch a brush.' George helped her stand upright and picked up most of the large lumps of mashed cake to put them back on the plate. He brushed the remaining crumbs from his clothes and onto the tray.

'What was that gymnastic display in aid of?' asked Brenda when he'd left the room.

'The next spell. I totally mucked it up though; blood on a linen square.'

'Oh yes!' Her eyes twinkled with excitement. 'Let me help.'

'No, really, I can manage...' George reappeared with a dustpan and brush, which looked small in his massive hands. 'Oh, George, let me do that.'

'I insist. Sit down.' He sounded teachery cross.

As they both bent forward, their heads collided, but George came off worse as Lucy caught his nose with the back of her head. He put his hand to his face as a trickle of blood came from the left nostril.

'Lucy, the poor man needs a tissue,' Brenda said, almost smiling.

'Of course,' and she dashed for her bag. Despite George putting his hands up to his face, doubtless wondering what damage she could possibly inflict next, she managed to dab his bloody nose with the surprisingly to hand handkerchief.

As he went to the kitchen to look for something cold to stem the bleeding, Lucy stared at her mysterious friend.

'Did you do that?'

'Are you implying I could somehow control your collision or get blood to flow from his nose. Ridiculous.'

Lucy stood with her hands on her hips, looking down at

her favourite old lady in the whole world, who still had a sparkle of something undefinable shooting across the irises of her eyes. She graced Lucy with a 'butter wouldn't melt if my face was on fire' look.

'Hmm.'

Chapter 33

Parked between her sister's BMW and her brother-in-law's top-of-the-range Mazda, Lucy's little yellow car looked like the Trotters' three-wheeled van. Before she'd even lifted her suitcase from the boot, a flash of fuchsia pink came running out of the house and crunched across the freshly raked gravel drive.

'Auntie Lucy!' Rosie, her four-year-old niece, was by her feet and out of breath. 'Can I pull your wheelie case?'

'It's a bit heavy, but you can take my special bag in for me,' and she handed her the floral knitting bag.

'Oh goody. Can we do more knitting? Alicia at school is very jealous of my Elsa doll and she said she's going to get her mum to buy her one, but I said she couldn't because it was made by my auntie and it's the best and she only makes them for me so she couldn't have one and then she cried and called me mean, but I didn't care because I had an Elsa doll and she didn't.' She sucked in a hearty breath.

Emily appeared behind her chatty daughter carrying the younger Grace in her arms, who was wriggling to get down and calling, 'Oo-cy, Oo-cy' – unable to pronounce her aunt's name properly.

'Stuart?' Lucy asked.

'Golf course.'

'Ah.'

'Grrr more like. Come in. We've been baking. Just for you.'

Inside the large family kitchen-diner, with the glorious smell of cake coming from the cream-coloured range cooker, Lucy parked her suitcase by the kitchen door and slid into one of the high-backed oak dining chairs that matched the huge refectory table.

'*Weee* did make cakes,' said Grace, tipping her head to one side and making sure Oo-cy was listening.

'You didn't do much of the *actual* caking,' said Rosie. 'Mummy and I did. You just licked out the bowl and then tipped over the bag of flour and Mummy said bugger and then I thought she was going to cry but she didn't and we had to clean up *all your mess*.' She stood with her hands on her hips and her head to one side, as she reprimanded her baby sister.

'Did *too* help with cake.'

'Did not.'

'Did too.'

'Girls,' sighed Emily, 'let's not quarrel in front of Auntie Lucy. Why don't you go upstairs and put on those special princess dresses as we have such an important guest? And then when you come back down the cake will have cooled and we can have a tea party.'

With thundering feet and excited chatter, the girls rushed from the room to transform themselves into magical and glamorous grown-ups.

'Tea?' Emily offered.

'Let me make it. You look exhausted.' Lucy was worried by

her sister's pale face and inability to look her in the eye. 'Did you really have a bag of flour all over the floor?'

Emily nodded and then shrugged.

'You wouldn't know. This kitchen looks immaculate.' Lucy reached a tentative hand across to her sister's arm.

'It looked like a scene from *The Snowman* half an hour ago.' And with that Emily burst into tears, which only subsided five minutes later as the thunder of visiting princess feet was heard returning.

'So we're hoping, all being well, Ems can get back to work by February. The nursery takes from three months. It's the same one we used for the girls. You can't afford to be out of the game for too long or your colleagues start to undermine you.'

The girls had long since gone to bed and Stuart was nursing a cut-glass brandy balloon, swirling the dark liquid around the glass and inhaling the pungent aroma, but only occasionally taking a sip. He was sitting on the sofa next to his wife, the other arm draped casually around her shoulder.

'The thing of it is, we couldn't afford the mortgage on this place without the two incomes. I think we both agree we don't want to sacrifice the standard of living we've become accustomed to, and we all know you have to work hard in order to play hard.'

Stuart had indeed spent his life working hard. He was older than Emily by almost seven years and was a salaried partner with a small firm of solicitors just outside London. He came from money and consequently knew all the right people in all the right places. Lucy had no doubt he would end up as an equity partner eventually – his family connections alone made him an invaluable asset to the firm.

Emily, Lucy realised, hadn't contributed much to the conversation. She looked tired and had her head on Stuart's shoulder, her eyes flickering as she fought to keep them open.

'Are you ready for bed, button?' asked Stuart.

'Mmm,' mumbled Emily.

'Off you go then, sweetheart. Lucy and I can amuse ourselves.'

Emily stuck out her belly and heaved herself out of the sofa. Even though there was no sign of a baby bump yet, her body was clearly changing.

'Oh, how I love that woman,' he said as she left the room. 'She's so amazingly capable. Lesser women would have fallen at the first hurdle.'

Horses can go down at any point in the race, thought Lucy. And it can often mean the end of their racing career when they do.

Chapter 34

Waking the next morning in the tastefully coordinated spare room, all shades of white and accent colours, Lucy was temporarily at peace with the world. The tweetings of busy birds, the clean, crisp air that circulated the room and the pleasing lack of traffic noise through the open window reminded her that she was a country girl at heart.

She pulled the pale blue sheet up to her cheeks and inhaled the scent of the expensive laundry powder. Closing her eyes, she retreated back to the bizarre yet comforting dream of her in a Julie Andrews-style Alpine dress, running down a lush, green hill, towards George. He was standing uncomfortably at the bottom in enormous lederhosen made from curtain fabric and holding a goat. Once she realised she was muddling Captain von Trapp with Peter the goatherd, she opened her eyes again and focused on reality. And then a part of her wondered what she would have done with George if she'd made it to the bottom of the hill.

The room had been redecorated since her last visit, even though it had seemed perfect to her before. The small pine bookcase that stood under the window contained the sort of books that Lucy felt she should have read, and Emily wanted people to think she *had* read, but neither of them ever would:

A Brief History of Time, One Hundred Years of Solitude, Lord of the Rings. She wondered where her sister kept the Regency romances and light-hearted romcoms – probably tucked away in a wardrobe where their mother wouldn't stumble across them. A cream upholstered Chippendale-style chair stood in the corner, which Lucy could see no purpose to. And a pale oak Victorian chest of drawers was to the right of the door, with nothing but an antique gilded vanity mirror standing on top. Lucy knew all the Heathcote & Ivory lined drawers were empty because she'd checked.

As she lay in the crisp, ironed, high thread count cotton sheets and stretched out her toes, she listened to the noises of bustling family life drift up the stairs: the non-stop chatter of little girls, a boiling kettle and the hum of a television playing away to itself.

There was a rumble of feet on the staircase and then Grace burst through the door.

'Oo-cy, help?'

Lucy shuffled to her elbows and peered over to her youngest niece. She was holding a Princess Belle doll that appeared to have her opulent golden ball gown stuck halfway over her head.

'Of course. Jump up here next to me and I'll see what I can do.'

Grace snuggled up next to her aunt, daring to poke her toes under the white duvet cover and then looking up at Lucy with wide eyes.

'Snuggle in then,' and Lucy lifted the edge so she could wiggle in further.

Managing to dress Belle in a more satisfactory manner, the pair were happily chatting in the bed when the door was pushed open slowly and Rosie's head peered into the room; at first cautiously, and then with a flash of horror across her eyes.

'NOOOOOO...' she wailed. 'Mummy said I could wake Auntie Lucy. She said it was my job and only I could do it because I was her biggest girl and it wasn't a job for baby sisters because they aren't old enough and I would do the bestest job with my tray,' and she threw herself down on the cream carpet and began sobbing uncontrollably.

Within seconds Emily tapped at the door and entered.

'Oh dear. What have I done?' Lucy asked.

Emily sighed and knelt down next to her increasingly hysterical daughter, stroking her hair but getting kicked and screamed at in return.

'It's not your fault. Rosie has been begging to be the one who woke you this morning since she found out you were coming. She's been downstairs all morning making you a breakfast tray to bring up and it was her thing. Bless her, she even went into the garden and picked some cornflowers to put in a small white china bud vase she found in the sideboard.'

Hearing the reasons for her distress spoken out loud only seemed to increase Rosie's sense of injustice and her cries increased in volume and ferocity.

'What I don't know,' Emily said, eyeing her youngest daughter, who seemed to have slid further down the bed as this conversation progressed, 'is whether my two-year-old did this on purpose or not.' Grace locked eyes with her mother and then cast them downwards, picking up the doll from the duvet and thrusting it in front of her aunt, trying desperately to draw everyone's attention back to the doll and away from the escalating drama. 'Come on, Gracie, let's leave Auntie Lucy to get dressed. Rosie, are you going to bring the beautiful breakfast tray up or not? Because if you aren't, I shall do it.'

Rosie was quieter now but still had her head buried in the carpet. She didn't answer.

'I'm going downstairs and I will wait exactly five minutes. If you don't appear, I shall bring the tray up to Auntie Lucy. It isn't her fault your sister barged in, and she's probably starving by now. It will be such a shame if you aren't the one to present it to her after all your hard work.' And leaving Rosie with that thought, Emily and a reluctant Grace left the room.

'The worst of it is that I feel like throwing a Rosie tantrum most days but the social expectations placed on adults mean I'm not allowed to.' Emily had a wry smile on her face and a weak white wine spritzer in her hand. She glanced at her drink. 'And I can't even drink properly to take the edge off. Bastard pregnancy.'

They were sitting in the south-facing conservatory at the back of the house. The double doors were flung open and the girls were playing on the lawn, the earlier incident seemingly forgotten. Rosie had reluctantly presented the tray at the last moment, and Lucy's enthusiasm over the breakfast from her eldest niece had smoothed everything over.

Mouth-watering smells of roasting meat wafted from the kitchen and Stuart kept half an eye on his daughters while he practised his golf swing across their perfect lawn, insisting the sisters had some alone time to catch up.

'You don't mean that. When the little one is here and your family is complete, you will sit in your lovely garden, surrounded by your precious children and realise it was worth it. It's got to be better than sitting in a rented square of concrete, next to a shabby old shed, surrounded by knitting patterns and a microwave meal for one,' she joked.

'Oh, hon, it's a grass is greener, if ever I saw one. Don't look at me and think I'm sorted – that my life is some kind of fairy tale. This is the first time in ages we've had a proper family weekend and it's only because you were coming. You have to work hard to have beautiful things, but if you are working so hard you aren't ever here, who gets to enjoy them? Everything comes at a price. But I don't want to talk about me...' She put her glass on the low wicker table and turned to her sister, hitching her feet up on the chair. 'I want to know what's made my little sister look so...different.'

'Me? I'm the same as I ever was.' She was aware of the locket beneath her T-shirt.

'I don't think so. You are positively glowing. Even Mum said she'd noticed a change in you. You are standing straighter, your eyes are animated and you seem more...colourful somehow.'

'Perhaps I do feel different,' Lucy admitted. 'I suppose I'm standing up for myself a bit more and caring less about what people think. I don't want to be in the shadows any longer. It's not that I crave the limelight, but I desperately want to succeed at work, and that's not going to happen while I let myself get pushed around and spend half my day making tea and coffee for everyone in the office. It's amazing what happens when you start to assert your authority.'

'Good for you, little sister. Look, don't feel obliged, but there are two bags of clothes I sorted out for charity, which you are welcome to riffle through. I know my colouring is darker than yours, but we are the same shape. Some of it's a bit formal – suits for work and some posh dresses that I've done to death either at work functions or playing the gracious hostess to help further Stuart's career – but do take a look.'

The biggest smile spread from Lucy's flushed cheeks to her wide eyes. 'I'd love to. Thanks, sis.'

After a ridiculously elaborate meal that Emily insisted on largely preparing herself, the sisters remained at the dining room table while Stuart magnanimously loaded the dishwasher. Grace had crashed halfway through the meal into her plastic bowl of mashed-up meat and vegetables. She was lifted into the living room, where she slept on the sofa covered in a Barbie blanket and clutching Belle tightly in her chubby hands.

Rosie was sitting at the table beside Lucy, head down and tongue out, as she tried to loop a strand of emerald green wool around the fat crochet hook to produce a simple chain. Unlike most four-year-olds who had barely mastered the control of a pencil, she had pretty good fine motor skills and was doing extraordinarily well. The green chain was now a couple of inches long, and despite Auntie Lucy sorting out a few tangles, she was determined to make it long enough to tie in Elsa's hair.

Emily twisted around for the third time to check the time on the wall clock, and Lucy started to wonder if she had outstayed her welcome.

'Do you need me to go? I don't want to intrude into your family Sunday afternoon.'

'No. Far from it. I want you to stay until the last possible minute. It's just Stuart has a solicitor friend popping over this afternoon. Something work-related. I thought I'd introduce you. He's a nice bloke, Luce.'

Lucy choked on the mineral water she was sipping. 'Are you trying to set me up?'

'No. Well possibly. Look, Mum mentioned—'

'Oh no you don't. You and our manipulative mother are not going to manage my life. I'm twenty-five, Ems. I'm doing okay.'

Emily lifted her hands defensively. 'I'm sorry. I know. In some areas of your life you're more sorted than me. Mum said you'd refused to make the swans. Wish I could say no to her sometimes. You're a brave girl.'

'Nonsense. I am getting more confident and it's having surprising results, but I've never been as totally driven as you. I don't think I would be able to remain as focused on my career, and still juggle five hundred and sixty balls in the air with my free hand. Something would have to give, possibly my sanity.'

Emily stared at her clasped hands, resting across her folded knees, but didn't respond to Lucy's comments.

'Ems?'

Nothing.

'Ems?'

'What? Sorry. I think Gracie has woken up. Excuse me,' and she wandered into the hallway.

As Stuart lifted Lucy's suitcase into her boot, and the girls skipped around her banana-coloured car singing a random version of 'Yellow Submarine', Lucy took her sister's hand and met and held her eyes.

'If anything happened to you, Emily, this family would

collapse. Promise me you'll put yourself at the top of your to-do list.' The weekend visit had done little to dispel Lucy's concerns about her sister.

'I'll try, but it's not always that easy.'

'Nonsense. If I can say no to mother's napkin swans, you can say no to the things that don't matter outside your immediate family. I'm always on the end of a phone or a car ride away. If you need me for *anything*, just ask. Promise?'

'Promise.'

Emily pulled her baby sister towards her and hugged her as if she was about to depart on a twenty-year mission to Mars. Lucy stroked her sister's back and wondered when she'd suddenly become the strong one.

Chapter 35

Brenda was full of tales about her weekend with George, the highlight of which was being taken to some posh hotel near Peterborough (she was frustrated with herself but couldn't remember the name) for afternoon tea with his mother. So much for just popping in – it seemed he'd taken it upon himself to become her personal chaperone.

'It was all tiddly sandwiches and dainty cakes,' she enthused. 'As soon as I'd poured a cup of tea, someone swooped in and replenished the pot. I felt like royalty. Or a modern-day pop star, which is practically the same thing I understand.' She patted her hair, which was up in a bun, and her cheeks flushed pink. 'Such a handsome man. He told me I looked beautiful when he knocked on the door to collect me. And his mother was such a gentle, quietly spoken lady. I had the most wonderful afternoon.'

Okay, Mr Aberdour, another house point, Lucy thought begrudgingly. *Keep this up and I might* want *you to fall in love with me*. And then she noticed Brenda staring at her and, wary of Brenda's uncanny insights, tried to focus on the things he did that made her cross.

'So tell me more about his mother,' Lucy said, just in case she kept him on. Some future mother-in-law...erm, mother-of-the-boyfriend information might be handy.

Head high and gigantic sunglasses perched jauntily on the top of her head, Lucy strode into the office Monday morning and slipped elegantly into her seat, crossing her ankles and flicking her loose hair over her shoulder. The linen square was in her handbag, and instead of being tucked away under her clothing, the locket swung on its chain from side to side, across a pretty silk top in a deep shade of purple.

She'd spent the previous evening trying on the clothes her sister had given her. They were all items she'd never have bought for herself; either because of their distinct Look at Me factor or the price tag, but wearing them now added to her new-found confidence. As well as acting like an assured member of the sales team, she looked the part.

The office was quiet as it was still early, but Adam was in the corner, wrestling with an awkward ring-binder. He did a double take as Lucy entered and it didn't take long for him to sidle up to her and perch a bottom cheek on the edge of her desk.

'Well, a good and most impressive morning to you, young Lucy-Lou. Power dressing for any particular reason? Hoping for promotion, are we? My job is taken, I'm afraid. Well, unless there's a promotion on the cards for me as well. Ha ha. We all want to climb the slippery ladder of success, but most of us don't rely on dressing provocatively for the boss to do so.'

He stretched out an elbow to rest on the partition board but his reach wasn't quite long enough and he slipped.

'Sam is a woman, Adam.'

'Well, yes, but I wouldn't assume your leanings. Or hers for that matter. I've said it before, and I'll say it again: anyone is welcome at Tompkins. We are an inclusive company and your race, religion and sexual persuasion are irrelevant. In fact, we could do with a gay in the office. Or the warehouse. I'll mention it to Sam when we think about recruiting Christmas staff later in the year.'

Lucy switched on her computer and entered her password to indicate she was busy.

'Anyway, Lucy-Lou, wanted a word. You know that you do all that knitting?'

'Yes.' She wasn't sure where this was going.

'Can you knit *anything*?'

'You aren't going to ask me to knit a pair of long trousers, are you?' She regretted saying it immediately, but Adam didn't seem to get the dig.

'Not sure why anyone would want knitted trousers, unless they were woolly-minded. Ha ha. But seriously, I was thinking publicity and, even though it's months away, I was wondering if we could pull together and knit a little nativity scene for reception? Something home-made and original? Sales of the starter knitting kits have really taken off for the eight to twelve age range. Might even be worth talking to Kiddicraft and getting some sponsorship? Between you, me and the bedpost, I don't think Sam the man has taken a shiny cloth to me. I thought I'd up my game.'

'Hmm.' Lucy considered his suggestion. 'How about knitting a sort of nativity scene but one where the figures were replaced by well-known toys? Maybe the three bears instead of the three kings? That sort of thing?'

'I'm liking your thinking. Link it more to what we do at Tompkins. Serious sucky-up points for me – and you, of course – if we could pull it off.'

'I'll give it some thought and get back to you.' It was an interesting idea, and one she would enjoy brainstorming.

'That's my girl,' Adam said, and Lucy thought for one horrible moment he was going to ruffle her hair.

People began to arrive for work and sit down at their desks. Lucy put on her headset and took a call. Adam looked around for someone else to engage with, but everyone was suddenly extremely busy, so he meandered back to his desk.

'What the ACTUAL bloody hell?'

Everyone looked up as Adam shouted at his computer.

'Cress. Bloody cress?' He was waving his keyboard around and pointing at it. Closer than most, Lucy could just about make out a faint green edging to the keys.

Sam walked over to the ranting sales office manager and peered over her red-rimmed reading glasses.

'You do know that persistent teasing is a form of bullying in the workplace, don't you? This is something we can discuss, if you wish to take it further?'

'No, I've got this. It's a one-off,' Adam said. 'And anyway, it's not like we even know who the perpetrator is.'

Taking a file downstairs to copy before lunch, Lucy bumped into Sam in the Tardis.

'I'm nearly done and then it's all yours,' said Sam and she looked admiringly at Lucy's smart suit. 'Look, I have no right to ask this question, so don't feel you have to answer, but are you looking for another job?'

Lucy frowned.

'Forget I asked,' Sam said, gathering her papers and lifting the lid to take out the master copy.

As she left Lucy to the photocopier and returned upstairs, Lucy replayed the question and wondered if it had somehow been Sam's coded way of telling her she should be.

Coming out through Brenda's gate having shared a fish and chip supper, Lucy stopped to stroke Scratbag, who was sunbathing on the low wall between Brenda and George's houses. Chloe, the little girl from across the road, was coming along the pavement carrying a clear plastic bag of hay. Her arms were wrapped around it but her hands didn't meet and she could barely see over the top.

'This is for my new rabbit.' She stopped in front of Lucy and held the bag up for Lucy to appreciate. 'She's so much nicer than Turnip. He was a bit bitey sometimes, but Bunny Snuffle-Paws is a licky rabbit.'

'Wow, a new rabbit. You'll have to show her to me sometime.'

'You can come and play with her whenever you like.'

Lucy looked across to the mother who was a few paces behind Chloe. Her face said it all.

Chloe dropped the bag at her mother's feet as she drew level with them both and reached up to pet Scratbag.

'Flipping rabbit,' the mother whispered. 'I didn't wish Turnip ill, but I was a teensy bit relieved when he passed away. I'm the one who was cleaning him out and feeding him. Same old, same old. I give Bunny Snuffle-Paws a week and then she'll be abandoned to my care, like Turnip.'

'Then why on earth did you get her another one?' asked Lucy.

'I didn't. The man at number twenty-four turned up saying he'd heard the sad news about her rabbit and thought he'd get her a replacement. He also gave Chloe a special pet carrier, a huge bag of food and some rabbit treats. Lovely idea and all that, but I wish he'd run it by me first.'

George buying his way out of trouble again.

'I suppose he meant well,' she said in his defence, and leaned over her own gate to unlatch it. 'Great name, by the way. Don't you love the naming skills of a child?'

'Chloe didn't name her. The man from number twenty-four did.'

Chapter 36

'Is everything all right?' Lucy had been summoned to her elderly neighbour's by phone the following evening, so rushed straight over, wondering what she was going to find.

'What a lovely surprise,' Brenda said in a much louder voice than was necessary.

Oh dear, another muddled moment, thought Lucy. *She's forgotten she called me over.*

'We were having a cup of tea and a sticky bun. Well, one of us is having a lactose-free cookie, but I just adore sticky buns and he remembered. Wasn't that thoughtful? Come and join us.' She pushed open the living-room door to the sound of tinkly chimes and there, in Lucy's favourite chair, sat George; his large thighs squashed together by the wooden arms and his height making the whole thing look much smaller than it was. Brenda gave her a conspiratorial wink from the doorway. 'Just giving him a nudge in the right direction, dear. I can't wait around for you two to get your act together any longer,' and she scuttled down the hall towards the kitchen.

'Lucy.' He leaned forward to stand, but she put her hand out to indicate he should remain seated.

'I'll sit over here, out of your way, as every time we meet you seem to end up injured.'

'Yes, you are rather like an unpredictable tornado leaving destruction in your wake.' He gave a half-smile and there was a definite and undeniable appearance of both dimples.

'Is that chair big enough for you?' she asked. Goldilocks was sitting in her chair and baby bear didn't like it.

'Yes. It's surprisingly comfortable. And warm.'

'Like it's got a heated seat?'

'Yes.'

Something equally warm flooded Lucy's heart; she trusted the judgement of that old, worn-out chair. She looked across at George and was glad she was persevering with the spells. They looked at each other, neither of them able to tear their eyes away, but neither of them able to think of a single thing to say.

The clocks took over the conversation they were unable to have as the living-room door opened. Brenda, with an extra bun on a pretty tea plate, looked at the faces of her two young neighbours and grinned. She handed the plate to Lucy and joined her on the sofa.

'So, who's been trying to ease their guilty conscience by playing fairy godmother then?' Lucy asked to break the silence.

George looked confused.

'Replacing Chloe's rabbit.'

'Ah, that. Well, Scratbag is my responsibility, so I felt accountable for his actions. It was the least I could do.'

'Chloe's mum said you chose the name?' She bit her lip to stop herself smiling.

'I blurted out something that sounded about right. What do I know about naming a rabbit?'

The atmosphere was strained and Lucy couldn't pinpoint why. George clearly felt the same as he searched for a conversational topic. 'You look, erm...different.' George looked at Lucy properly now that he'd drained his cup. 'Very professional. You'll be getting highlights, lowlights, manicures and leg waxes next. And fake tans.' The last comment was made with a sigh.

'Stop trying to change the subject. You are in trouble, Mr Aberdour. Wait until you're a parent. I'll turn up with a drum kit for your son's third birthday. A big one.'

Not quite understanding the conversation going on, Brenda looked between the pair of them like a Centre Court spectator.

'Our magnanimous neighbour has been buying presents for little girls to ease his guilty conscience,' Lucy explained.

'That sounds wrong,' George huffed.

'And now, in further efforts to ingratiate himself to the Renborough community, I find him wooing the most eligible lady in the street.'

'Oh, he quite often pops in now, don't you, dear? I suspect it's my sexual allure.' George choked on his freshly poured cup of tea and the tips of his ears went beetroot red. 'Like so many men, he is drawn to my raw animal magnetism.' Brenda tossed back her head and gave a George a cheeky wink. He dropped his eyes and studied the laces on his brown brogues.

It was news to Lucy that George had been visiting Brenda other than the two weekends she'd asked him to keep an eye on her, but it was nice to know he was being a good neighbour. She might even have to look for a bigger house point chart for him.

'Now, to this hand.' Brenda reached out for George's hand and took it in her own. Lucy noticed for the first time that he had a square beige plaster across the back of it. She watched Brenda peel it back gently to reveal a nasty cut underneath. 'It's not infected, just deep. A dab of TCP should do the trick.'

'TCP?' Lucy said. 'Not chamomile and honey smeared on a calendula leaf? Or a potato poultice?'

'So you have been paying attention. Perhaps I should have trained you up, but too late now. Most of the herbs and spices have gone, Lucy. I was serious when I said I was getting too old for this healing lark. Anyway, TCP has been around for a hundred years.'

'But it's not a natural remedy. It's a man-made product.'

'Fetch an aloe vera leaf then,' Brenda sighed. 'There should be a pot on the kitchen windowsill. But I've told you: I'm winding all this down. I don't want the responsibility. You'll have to do it, Lucy.'

Fetching the plant from the kitchen, Lucy could see Brenda had cleared out an awful lot. Shelves held empty bottles, there were spaces where the large jars and tins had been, and the rows of various drying herbs were noticeable by their absence. It didn't smell the same either; whereas before your nostrils were greeted by repeated wafts of fragrant herbs, sweet honey or fresh flower scents, now all Lucy could smell was the slightly meaty aroma of a cooked dinner. It wasn't an unpleasant smell, but it wasn't the exotic, comforting smell of the kitchen that she'd felt so at home in for the last two years.

She carried the plant back to the living room, the chime above the door tinkling as she nudged it open with her bottom, and snapped off one of the fleshy, green leaves. Kneeling in front of George, conscious of his proximity, she reached out for his mighty hand. Why she should feel so intimidated all of a sudden was bemusing, but she was acutely aware of both the warmth of his fingers as they lay across hers and his intense stare. As she dabbed the broken end of the aloe vera onto the wound, she asked how he'd managed to injure himself.

'Don't ask,' came the familiar blunt reply.

So she didn't.

Jess was away from the office at the start of the week, training on the new accounting software, but as they only saw each other for occasional coinciding tea and coffee runs, Lucy didn't miss her as much as she thought she would. The company was rushed off its feet with summer orders, and she enjoyed the grumpy banter of the warehouse crowd at lunchtime.

Sam let it be known that staff changes were afoot, but so far this had only involved swapping two guys around in the warehouse, as she felt their skills would be better suited to each other's jobs. She had been proved right and both were happy with the move.

Sam was filing papers in the corner near Pat and Lucy's desks, when she came across an old newspaper article from the late Eighties. It covered the launch of the company and in the grainy photograph, she could make out Vernon and Richard Tompkins. They were the only two original members of staff, although the total staff had been ten back then, and was nearer forty now.

'Wouldn't it be great to come up with something news-worthy to get us back in the paper?' Sam said. 'I skimmed through a copy of the *Renborough Chronicle* at the surgery the other day and the most exciting story they were running was about a local man who's scooped some national prize with his Polish Frizzle. They are crying out for news, so perhaps we should give them some, even if it's just an office sponsored walk for charity.'

Lucy immediately thought of the nativity scene she'd discussed with Adam. Han Solo and Princess Leia would make a good Joseph and Mary, and R2-D2 might be fun for the baby, as anything with *Star Wars* on had been selling well for the last fifteen years. Although it seemed ridiculous to be thinking about Christmas in June, Adam was right to plan ahead. To knit that many figures would take several weeks, and the toy industry, like most of the retail world, would be gearing up for Christmas by the end of August.

'News? I can give them news,' said Adam, who as usual had wandered over to involve himself in whatever was going on without him. 'How about organising a topless calendar, Calendar Girls style? Although Pat would need an enormous—'

'Adam, my office. Now,' said Sam, putting the newspaper cutting back in the file and tucking it under her arm.

There was a hushed silence as the sales staff watched Adam trail behind Sam. No one spoke for a moment. The door to Sam's office swung shut.

'I hope he doesn't get in massive trouble,' said Sonjit. 'I kind of like him, despite everything.' There were general mumbles of agreement.

'The problem is, he doesn't realise when he's overstepped the line,' said Connor. 'It's like this big act to make us like him and to be one of us, but he's our boss. Does he *need* us to like him?'

'Perhaps,' said Lucy, and she thought about the short trousers and the mysterious home life. 'But what he fails to grasp is we'd like him a whole lot more if he stopped trying so hard.'

'He was wonderful last year when Mum was at the hospice,'

said Sonjit, 'and he's always so understanding when people have to leave work early for sick kids, that sometimes I think he must have a family, or perhaps even a wife.' She sighed and looked briefly across at Adam.

Lucy realised they knew very little about him. He was often in a rush to get home, and occasionally said "we" when referring to things he'd done outside work, but he never mentioned anyone specific.

Adam and Sam stood facing each other behind the full-length glass of her office window as the sales team tried to watch without making it obvious that's what they were doing. Sam had her hands on her hips and Adam, who started the conversation with a nonchalant shrug and head high, left her office five minutes later looking at his shoes before slumping into his chair.

Lucy's internal line buzzed.

'There's no way he's married,' whispered Pat. 'A wife would never let him leave the house in those trousers.'

Chapter 37

All afternoon, Lucy played with ideas for the knitted nativity, conscious of Sam's plan to get the company into the local paper. The more she thought it, the more she was convinced it could work. If she made the figures on the same scale as her knitted celebrities, perhaps she could even use a couple of them. The three bears could bring traditional toys as gifts: a drum, a toy car, and perhaps a small toy soldier. All easy enough to knit. The seating could be temporarily removed from reception, the scene could be set up there, and the figures could be auctioned off after Christmas for charity. If the local papers picked it up, it would be great publicity.

As she left the building later that afternoon and stepped out into the bright sunshine, a large black Audi swept into the car park. Lucy paused. What was *he* doing at Tompkins? She couldn't even remember telling him where she worked. The locket was clearly more powerful than she realised.

Conscious of her appearance, she smoothed her hair and adjusted her top. Lingering by the door, she waited while he parked, locked the vehicle and walked over to her.

'George, what a lovely surprise.' She felt slightly breathless all of a sudden. She kept forgetting how big and powerful he was until she stood near him. That damn aftershave wasn't helping. Her legs wobbled.

'Ah, Lucy. *Now* I understand. I really wish you hadn't interfered.' He looked irritated and cross. And then he walked straight past her and into the company building, leaving Lucy totally bemused.

Passing Brenda's gate on the way home, Lucy noticed her friend's silhouette moving behind the glass of the front door, so she walked up the path and knocked. She could do with offloading about George's strange behaviour that afternoon.

'Glad you called by.' Brenda gave her a big smile as she opened the door. 'Haven't seen you for a couple of days and I wondered how you were doing.' Lucy felt a tiny stab in her heart. She'd been with Brenda that morning, as she was every morning. 'I've been a busy bunny today and have some exciting news. Come in and let me tell you all about it. In fact, would you like to stay for supper? I walked into town and got a huge piece of haddock – far too much for one. We can share it.'

'That would be lovely. Just let me dump my bags and change out of this suit. Give me five minutes.'

'I'll be up on the third floor, but I'll leave the door on the latch. I've been in Jim's studio this afternoon, reconnecting with him. I only popped downstairs briefly to answer the phone. Wish I hadn't bothered. Stupid PPI.'

Reconnecting? Not a séance or a Ouija board, Lucy hoped.

Ten minutes later, she stood in Brenda's hallway and heard the boom of a bass drum, a flurry of lighter beats and a tinkling cymbal drift down from the top of the house.

Like a child from Hamelin blindly following the music of the piper, Lucy climbed the first flight of stairs and the drumming got louder. She paused on the middle landing, where the bookshelves housed a combination of books about herbal remedies and Seventies Mills and Boons. A turquoise and green glass bauble hung in the landing window, casting a beautiful rainbow on the pale wall opposite.

Boom-boom, tish. Boom-boom, tish. The drums were working up to a dramatic crescendo as she reached the top floor and rounded the corner. There was only one door on this storey. The partition walls had been taken down and the whole floor turned into one relatively soundproofed home studio, except when the door was left open like today. It was the room Brenda always escaped to when she was missing Jim and, although it wasn't the first time Lucy had been up there, it was the first time she had heard Brenda play. As she entered, she saw her friend sitting behind the drums, her wavy purple-streaked hair flying about her shoulders as her head bobbed about in time to the beat. Her eyes were closed as she lost herself in an imaginary world.

Boom, tish, boom, tish, BOOM.

Brenda finished with a flurry of arms and swishing hair, and finally opened her eyes.

'Have a seat, my dear,' and she indicated to a battered leather armchair next to the drum kit. 'I used to sit there when Jim was playing. Sometimes he'd have some of the guys up here with him. It was called jamming back then, but I expect that's an old-fashioned term nowadays. Often he'd sit up here alone with headphones on, accompanying an old track. He'd just bash away, the same beats, over and over.'

'I didn't know you could play.'

'I only tinker with the snare drum, high hats and bass, but you don't live with a drummer for forty years and not pick up a few things. I can't really play. It's just waving some sticks around, but it's a great stress reliever.' She laid the drumsticks carefully across the snare drum. 'He loved this set: Ludwig Mod Orange, but the colour has faded a bit. It was his favourite. End of the Sixties. I think his very first drum kit is still here somewhere, boxed up.' This was all information Lucy had heard before but she smiled and looked interested.

The black and white photo on the wall of Brenda and Jim caught her eye. It was taken in the late Sixties after one of the Yellow Crows' sell-out concerts. Brenda looked so young and so alive. She was in a bold print tunic top and flared jeans, with her long dark hair framing her face and fake lashes that almost met her eyebrows. In a way, she hadn't changed. She was just as vibrant at seventy-nine, and not just because of the wild hair. Jim, with his equally mad hair, was gazing at the petite girl by his side, not at all bothered by the all-seeing eye of the camera. It made Lucy feel warm inside to share this moment in time, even though it was fifty years on, with two people so clearly in love.

'I miss him terribly, Lucy.' Her voice cracked.

'I know.'

Brenda slid off the stool, came over to her friend, bent down and gave her the tightest hug. There were muffled sniffs and Lucy kissed the top of her head, returning the hug but even tighter.

'He's worried about me, you know. He knows what's going on and has been telling me for months things weren't right, but I was too stubborn to listen. I can feel him, more so up here, but he is always with me.'

Not quite sure where she stood on matters of the afterlife, Lucy was always in awe of the incredible connection Jim and

Brenda had. Was it possible to believe it went beyond the grave? Theirs was a once in a lifetime love, for all its freedoms and non-conformity. Whether Jim was still a presence somewhere in the ether or an overwhelming strong memory that Brenda couldn't let go of in her own head was completely irrelevant.

Later, they sat together at the kitchen table. Lucy had prepared the dinner as Brenda seemed to have retreated to a distant world, possibly one where she could be with Jim. Pushing the mashed potato around her plate and not eating properly, Lucy gently reminded Brenda to put the food in her mouth. There were long silences when the kitchen clock was the only sound, but now the room was devoid of its familiar aromas, the clock was a comfort.

'You had some news for me?' Lucy said, trying to reconnect.

'Did I?' Brenda stared at the fork in her hand as though she couldn't work out how it got there, and then she scooped up a piece of the white fish and put in in her mouth. 'Oh yes.'

'So...' Lucy prompted.

'So, you know I turn eighty in a couple of weeks? Well, I've decided to have a birthday party after all. It was talk of that great big bash your mother is having that started me thinking.'

Lucy had asked her friend what she wanted to do for her birthday a few months ago but Brenda had only wanted a quiet get-together, which Lucy had planned to organise on her behalf nearer the time.

'A little tea party or a bigger function?' Although Lucy was no longer as petrified by the thought of a big affair as she had been the previous month.

'The biggest I can afford. I'm hiring that company on the high street – Party People, I think they're called. They did that elaborate wedding for Marjorie's granddaughter last year. I may not have many close friends, but I do know a lot of people. I'd like to do something to mark what is, after all, a fairly impressive landmark. I may not still be here to celebrate ninety... Or be with it enough to know what's going on.'

Lucy couldn't bring herself to contradict Brenda's last statement so chose not to comment.

'Money isn't an issue and I don't want the stress of trying to do it myself. The nice young lady from the shop is coming to finalise everything next week. All I have to do is say what I want and they will make my wishes come true.' She tapped her fork in the air as if it was the magic wand of a fairy godmother.

'What a wonderful idea,' said Lucy. 'But let me help. It's not right you should be doing this by yourself.'

'My dear, this is exactly why I kept it to myself until now. It's a gift to all my friends. Marjorie was faffing around and offering to make a cake, a lovely thought, but she's not in great health at the moment and it's what I'm paying Party People for. They take the worry out of it all.'

'But—'

'You should know by now there is no point in arguing with me when my mind's made up.' She threw Lucy a surreptitious glance as she scooped up the last of her mashed potato. 'That hunky George will be there. I've already asked him to keep the date free...'

Lucy felt her pulse quicken and reached into her jeans pocket to feel for the linen square. The spell said to take it everywhere. She absent-mindedly caressed the edge of the fabric. What exactly were her feelings for George? One minute she felt an undeniable attraction, the next, he made her so cross she wanted to stamp on his head. Even Jeremy Vine and his swingometer couldn't keep up. But all of that was unimportant because it clearly mattered so much to Brenda.

'So, it's just a question of who you will get to see to the horses. But I'm sure that stable hand you hired won't mind some extra hours. He seems like a nice boy.'

'I've decided to see the spells through to the end. If it works, George can accompany me to The Big Birthday, and if he behaves in front of my mother I may even keep him on until Christmas,' Lucy said, winding a strand of orange wool around her needle.

Jess was staying over again, tired from the software course and looking forward to returning to the office. To be fair, she was contributing to the meals and providing the wine, but as she consumed most of it, that was fair enough. As much as Lucy enjoyed having her friend over, she was starting to feel they were flat sharing in all but name. While she understood Jess's desire to escape home, if she cut down on the wine, shoes and expensive make-up, the rent money was probably there.

'But you don't fancy him, right?'

Lucy's eyes flicked left before she forced herself to look at her friend again. If Jess had asked her that question the day before, she might have admitted he was growing on her, but his unexplained bluntness outside the office the day before rankled.

'No, I told you, he has an irritating tendency to say what he thinks without a filter, and I can't see what Brenda sees in him – great lump with his silly glasses. He reminds me of that huge man from *Pointless*.'

Jess had her new gel nail kit spread out over the fire-damaged coffee table. She was grumpy because Lucy refused to have her nails painted so was trying a black and white zigzag design on herself. Her left hand was currently stuck under the LED lamp to set the polish. Lucy was busy with Brenda's birthday present, now Poldark had been finished and posted. It was still a wonder to her how quickly the Etsy shop had taken off. Six of her existing figures had been sold, even though posting Thor had been a bigger wrench than she'd anticipated. Several more enquiries had come in regarding Poldark commissions, but she hadn't committed to knitting any more as she wanted to get Brenda's birthday present finished in good time and then start on the toy nativity, assuming Sam went for it.

'Have you got the next spell then?' Jess asked.

Lucy slipped the locket out from under her top without taking it off and leaned forward to show her friend.

'Yup. And it's a corker.'

Chapter 38

'Take five possessions from the chosen man
Place at the points of a chalk-drawn pentagram.'

'I remember pentagrams from my white witch days: five-pointed stars. I think each point represented something: air, earth, fire and something or other,' said Jess.

'Do you think the objects have to relate to the points?'

Jess shrugged. 'It doesn't say, but you could check with Mrs Witchy Knickers. So you've got to get your hands on some things from his house then? Good job he gave you the key.' She removed her hand from under the light and selected the top gel coat. After unscrewing the lid, she began to apply it carefully down the length of each nail. The smell of the polish hung in the air. At least it masked the faint bitter smell that still lingered from the fire.

'I feel uneasy about being in the house when we aren't supposed to be. And stealing things? It doesn't feel right.'

'You aren't stealing; you're borrowing. Anyway, it's for his ultimate happiness and a lifetime with the woman of his dreams.' Contemplating this, Jess perked up a bit. She screwed the cap back on the bottle and replaced her hand under the light to set the polish.

'Not totally convinced that's me, to be honest. I think he'd prefer someone less knitty, less clumsy and substantially more glamorous. You're probably more his type.'

'Hmm.' Jess seemed distracted by her drying nails and bent forward to look at them more closely.

Sitting back into the chair and casting off the last stitch from her needle, Lucy smiled to herself. 'A thought has just occurred to me.'

Jess looked up.

'Perhaps there is a whole gaggle of women who have been following the spells to get their hands on George and one by one, they've taken all his possessions. They are sitting on the points of hand-drawn pentagrams in gardens all over Bedfordshire.'

'It's one explanation, but it does highlight the real issue.'

'Which is?'

'He hasn't got much left to borrow.'

Lucy caught up with George later that week. Having spent the first few weeks trying to avoid him, she now actively looked out for him when she was in the street. She was in luck; he was leaving Brenda's house as she was heading in. Another kind act that counterbalanced his inexplicable rudeness outside the office. What had he been up to at Tompkins? He was hardly the type to stock up on teddy bears.

'Hello, Trouble,' George said, eyes serious and face dark.

'I have no idea what you're talking about.' They both put their hands up to the gate at the same time, and for a moment they touched. George removed his hand first.

'Come on, Lucy. Telling Karen where I lived?'

She shook her head. 'I've only met your ex-wife once, and that was outside your house, so it wasn't me.'

'You don't seriously expect me to believe that; she's been dating your boss for months.'

Adam was dating Karen? Was that his big secret? Although Adam was growing on her, she wouldn't have pegged him as Karen's type. But then, it took all sorts.

'However, as it turns out, her tracking me down wasn't as awful as I'd feared, so I forgive you.'

How very gracious of him to forgive her for a crime she hadn't committed. She was about to make a sarcastic remark, but he stopped her in her tracks with an unexpected compliment.

'Besides, I can't stay cross with you for long. You're my favourite...correction, *second* favourite neighbour.'

'Right,' Lucy said. 'I have four bottles of white I'm investigating as part of this idea I put forward to Mr Tompkins. I've outlined the proposal, but I want to check they aren't totally undrinkable first. You know a bit about wine, well, more than I do at any rate, so we are going to do a taste test.'

Jess sat at Lucy's kitchen table with her head resting on her hands, amused by the market research they were about to conduct. It was Saturday and Lucy had offered another sleepover, as the research would not be ideal combined with driving. Jess didn't need asking twice.

'Go you! I never thought I'd see you work your way through four bottles.'

'We aren't going to drink all four,' Lucy gasped.

'We aren't?' Jess stuck out her bottom lip.

'No. We are going to have a *small* glass of each and I'll note down if they are any good.'

'Shall I get out the measuring jug and we can limit ourselves to 50ml of each?' said Jess.

'Great idea... Oh, you were being sarcastic.'

'I preferred the first one – the Pinot,' said Jess as they took their first sip of wine number three.

'Okay, I'll jot that... Oh dear, where did I put the notebook. Oops.' The notebook and the assortment of knitting magazines and junk mail that were piled neatly at the end of the table slipped to the floor as Lucy spun around faster than her brain could process. She bent forward without her bottom leaving the seat. Her hair swished about the floor like a delicate golden mop as she swayed her head from side to side. 'Oo, I say. The blood has rushed to my head and made me feel quite peculiar.'

'Not sure that's the rush of blood, love.' Jess laughed. She bent over to help her butter-fingered friend collect the papers.

'Right.' Lucy slammed the notebook back on to the kitchen table with a little too much force. 'Where were we? Need to double-check this one and we can finish off with number four.' She picked up her glass and tipped the remaining wine into her mouth. 'Next!' she said, like a regular at a bar.

Jess opened the remaining Chardonnay and poured two generous measures.

'Chin-chin,' said Jess, raising her glass.

Lucy stuck out her chin and wiggled it around. 'Bottoms up,' said Lucy, in response.

Jess stood in the middle of the kitchen, flicked up her

pleated, cotton skirt and bent forward to reveal her polka dot cotton pants.

'Tits out,' Jess shouted, now fully into the swing of the toasts. There was the barest flicker of a pause and then both girls stood up to face each other and flashed their bras. The girls collapsed back into their chairs in hysterics as though this was the funniest thing *ever*. For Jess, who had never seen Lucy even wear a low-cut top, never mind flash, it possibly was. 'What's the verdict on the wines then, Luce?'

'Erm, it's a bit fuzzy. Give me a sec.' Lucy waved the notebook about in front of her in an attempt to focus on the page.

'Oh, pass it here,' and Jess took it from her. 'Lucy! For wine number one you've put eight out of ten; number two you've described as B minus; three is two stars, and four you've written "top hole". How on earth can we compare them with that random scoring system? And who says top hole? Honestly.'

Absent-mindedly turning her wine glass around in her hands, Lucy drained it but caught the foot of the glass on the tabletop as she put it back down. Wine slopped over the edge, but Lucy didn't notice. 'Let's do it. Let's do it right now.'

'Do what?' asked Jess.

'Nick his stuff. Well, technically *borrow* it for a day or two.'

Lucy scraped her chair across the floor and wobbled to her feet. She reached out for the nearest bottle, poured herself a glassful and downed the contents, then looked across at Jess.

'C'mon, slowcoach. Watcha waiting for?'

'So how is this gonna work?' Lucy grabbed her friend's arm as they stumbled along the pavement towards George's house. The she hiccupped. 'We haven't gotta plaaaan.'

Lancaster Road was deserted, so Jess motioned Lucy to follow her through George's side gate.

'Worry not, young Jedi, for I know the ways of the masters.'

'Smashing.' Lucy promptly fell over a low-growing lavender bush and disappeared from view. She stumbled to her feet moments later with a dead twig fascinator elegantly protruding from the side of her head.

'Although—' Jess put her hands on her hips '—it involved you keeping him talking at the front door while I crept in the back and shoved a few personal items up my top. We may have to consider a role reversal as I'm clearly better placed to engage him in intelligent and coherent conversation.'

'But we didn't bring the key.'

Jess swung George's key ring from her index finger. 'The real question is whether you can sneak in the back and pocket a couple of things without crashing and banging about like a drunk. I'll head out the front as I have a plan to lure him out of the house, but be quick.'

'Absolutely,' and she nodded the nod of an earnest child for an unnecessarily long time and rested a finger on her lips. 'Mum's the word.'

Jess dangled the key and Lucy put out her hand. As Jess released it, Lucy swayed and the key fell straight to the ground.

'Oops,' she said.

After several jabs at the keyhole, Lucy slipped through George's back door. Her foot caught the high threshold on the way in and it was nearly 'slipping through' the literal sense.

'Let me guess: more sugar for the homeless, disabled orphans?' She heard George and Jess talking as the utility door was half open and George wasn't exactly a quiet speaker.

'Or have you come with another bottle of that foreign Mirto stuff? Or whatever it was called. Wait, I've got it, you're going to attack me again?' The last bit of the conversation didn't quite make sense in Lucy's muddly, blurry head, but she was focusing all her efforts on being silent.

'I've got a slow puncture. I drove over to see Lucy, but I think she's out because I can't get an answer, so I wondered if you had a pump I could borrow to get to a garage safely?'

There was a further muffled interchange and then the front door slammed shut.

Excellent thinking. Right. So now all she had to do was... What did she have to do? She couldn't quite remember... Oh, that looked fun; George had a novelty tin opener in the shape of a pig near some tins of posh cat food. She spun the snout around a couple of times and then remembered she needed to focus.

Five things – that was it. She was here to borrow some of his personal possessions to place on a penta-thingy. Casting her slightly unfocused eyes about, she saw some folded laundry near the tumble dryer. She took a sock from the top of the pile and stuffed it down the waistband of her jeans. Everywhere else in this room was tidy and bare, apart from cat-related items and a packet of washing tablets, which she didn't think were personal enough to make the spell work, because it was now vitally important to her that it did.

Tiptoeing down the hall, she grabbed a posh ballpoint pen as she passed the side table, then she opened the living-room door. Scratbag jumped up immediately and began to make an inadequate meowing sound.

'Shhh.' She put her fingers to her lips and tried to persuade him to be a willing accomplice in her subterfuge.

'Where, oh where, are this man's personal belongings?' she asked the cat.

Opening cupboard after cupboard, she looked for items small enough to secrete about her person. She picked up a gold tiepin from the mantelpiece and found a leather bookmark lying about, which she stuffed in her back pocket. By now, she'd lost count and it was like a real-life version of Buckaroo.

She poked her head around the edge of his black and white brocade curtains to see Jess leaning casually across her bonnet and George bent down by the nearside front tyre. He was too close to her friend's bare, bronzed and very shiny legs for Lucy's liking and there seemed to be an awful lot of giggling going on. On Jess's part at least.

Lucy hurried into the kitchen and grabbed some things that were small enough to stuff down her bra. Deciding, if she was quick, she still had time to pop in the downstairs cloakroom, she found a toothbrush, a small pot of hair gel and some nail clippers in the white mirrored wall cabinet.

As she turned back towards the utility, the front door swung open and two pairs of eyes stared in her direction.

'What the blazes...?' said a startled George.

Chapter 39

Lucy stood, frozen to the spot, every item of clothing bulging with the contraband items. Her face flushed puce.

'Luce, what a surprise to see you here. I thought you were out,' Jess said, but it wasn't an Oscar-winning performance.

All Lucy could do was hiccup.

'What *exactly* are you doing in my house?' George asked. 'And is that my toothbrush sticking out of your top?'

'Erm…' She reached out for the bannister knob to steady herself. Everything felt even more wobbly – must be all the rushing about. The blood in her body was coursing around faster than a greyhound on a dog track. The shock of being discovered in such an embarrassing position made her heart pound so hard it nearly exploded inside her. Things went rather dark, really fuzzy, and then the carpet came up to meet her.

Smack in the face.

Opening an eye and then quickly closing it again, Lucy felt her feet swaying about with nothing solid to rest them on. She felt nauseous, like the motion sickness she experienced as a child if she tried to read in a moving car. She could feel herself being cradled and something solid around her back and under her knees.

'Honestly, dump her on the sofa. I can take it from here. Let me move Ed Sheeran over.'

Lucy rolled onto the sofa but kept her eyes closed – she felt less spinny that way – and tried to focus on the voices around her.

'She stinks of alcohol. She told me she didn't drink. And what the bloody hell was she doing in my house?'

'I've absolutely no idea but I'm sure there is a—'

'Yeah. Perfectly rational explanation. Is that one of my socks sticking out of her trousers?'

'Erm, possibly.'

Lucy risked a peek and put her hand out to George, who was still within grabbing distance. She wanted to apologise, to explain and, if she was honest, she was quite up for a feel of those impressive biceps that had held her so firmly and so safely.

'It *is* my sock.' George bent over her slumped body and reached for the sock, pulling it from her waistband like a magician removing a silk scarf from a sleeve.

Not used to the general lack of control that accompanied alcohol consumption, and the tempting freedoms that were part of the heady package, Lucy threw her arms around his neck and pulled him closer.

'You are *absolutely gorgeous*, George Aberdour. Especially with those big, old silly glasses on. They do it for me, even if you are a *very* rude and abrupt man a lot of the time.'

For the briefest of moments he was within millimetres of her mouth. She could smell his aftershave again; she remembered it from when he'd tumbled on her during the fire. His warm breath was playing with her hair and her small hands gripped his muscular arm. Then suddenly he jerked himself out of her hold.

'I suggest you sober her up and drink plenty of water so you don't wake with a nasty hangover. I've got very little tolerance for drunks. Excuse me.'

After a moment, the front door closed and Lucy tried to wriggle upright. Jess walked back into the room having seen George out.

'I said that whole you're gorgeous thing out loud, didn't I? I didn't mean it – I'd probably fancy Adam if he walked in right now – but it sort of just spilled out.'

'You'll have to play the "I was so wasted I can't remember a thing" card.'

'But I will remember it. I'm mortified.' The shock of the moment sobered her up. She put her hands to her cheeks and let them drag slowly down her face, so she looked like a cross between Edvard Munch's 'The Scream' and a remorseful panda.

'Just tell him you can't, then you can both pretend it didn't happen. Problem is, we've now got to come up with another plan to get our hands on his belongings.'

'Ah, there you have underestimated your ever so slightly, tiny bit tipsy, best friend...' and Lucy reached down to her socks and pulled out the tiepin, the posh pen, and some loose change. Then she produced the bookmark from her back pocket and, after a further rummage in her bra, a small tub of hair gel and a pair of nail clippers fell onto the sofa cushions.

Sunday morning a delicate Lucy sat hunched over her knees, wrapped in her crocheted blanket, on the back step. The searing sunshine was attacking her light-sensitive eyes and she couldn't possibly contemplate consuming any food. At least she hadn't embarrassed herself further by being ill, but she felt as though a hundred stampeding wildebeest had done a dozen circuits of her head – in stilettos.

Jess drew a pentagram in pavement chalk on the tiny square of concrete that had pretentiously been called a patio when the property had been listed in the *Renborough Chronicle* two years ago. She always seemed better prepared for the spells than Lucy.

Sipping a sugary tea and waiting for the painkillers to kick in, Lucy watched Jess dust her hands off and walk over to the tub of borrowed items.

'I'm guessing it doesn't matter which bits I put where.' Jess placed each of George's belongings on a corner of the star.

'Shouldn't I be doing that?' Lucy moved to stand, but her legs were uncooperative.

'It's fine. Anyway, you were the one who took them and you're sitting right next to the pentagram. We'll soon know if we've done it wrong because the locket won't change.'

'Good point. Now what?'

'Not sure,' said Jess, hands on hips and surveying her handiwork. 'It didn't say anything about saying any magic words or how long to leave them. Guess we're done.'

Chapter 40

Despite the lovely weather, Lucy drove to work on Monday for two reasons. Firstly, she had to wait for George to leave and then sneak back into his house to return his belongings. And secondly, she didn't have the energy to walk, probably because she'd barely eaten anything the day before.

As soon as she stepped into the office, Adam called her over.

'The Black Widow is out on the road with Daniel tomorrow and she wants you to go with her. Don't ask me why. It's going to leave us a man down in the office, but she implied it was for general note-taking. I made it clear I wasn't prepared to let Connor go, but then note-taking is more of a girl...' He paused. 'Note-taking wouldn't be his thing. By the way—' he was shaking his right hand to try and remove the piece of Sellotape that had stuck three of his fingers together '—I meant to ask how your elderly neighbour is getting on?'

'She's doing okay. It's kind of you to remember.'

'Look after her, Lucy-Lou. You never know how long they have left. And just tip me the nod if you need any more time off.' He removed the offending tape, scrunched it into a ball, and then tried to shake it from his left hand.

He was a kind man, underneath all the bluff, Lucy realised. Perhaps that was what attracted Karen.

Wearing another of her sister's tailored suits, Lucy was waiting in the office promptly at eight the following day. Decidedly Duplicitous Daniel swung his company car into the car park five minutes later and Sam emerged from Richard's office, where they had been deep in conversation since before Lucy had arrived.

'I've got a notebook.' Lucy waved a spiral reporter's notepad at Sam. 'And some pens.'

'Right.'

'So what sort of thing do you want me to note down?'

'Lucy, I think you can make that decision for yourself, don't you?'

Why did she always feel about thirteen years old when she was with Sam? Perhaps she was trying too hard.

'Are we good to go?' Sam asked.

'Absolutely.'

'Let's see how Daniel spends his days then, shall we?'

Daniel, it seemed, was far busier than either of the two ladies had anticipated. Sitting in the back of his company car, Lucy hid in the shadows and listened to him talking about the various aspects of his job, and then his plans for the day. If he was to be believed, he often didn't get home until gone seven.

Initially singing along to every tune played on the Radio Two breakfast show, half an hour in Sam politely asked if the radio could be turned down or off. Preferably off.

'Of course, m'lady. Your wish is my command.' But five minutes

287

later he was absent-mindedly humming the *Thunderbirds* theme tune.

'So where first?' asked Sam, possibly to stop the humming.

'I've got a couple of independent toy shops lined up this morning, and then we need to head south so that I can assess a claim for water-damaged stock. If we have time, I'd also like to call in on some newsagents. I think the new range of Pocket Money Toys would appeal to them.'

'And how many calls do you make in an average day?' Sam continued her questioning, an open folder on her lap.

'It varies, depending on which area I'm covering. You have to take into account travel time, but generally I would try to see about seven customers. If I'm in a big town I can see more. There are three independent toy shops, several large chains, and a handful of general retail outlets that buy from us in Bedford town centre alone.'

Lucy diligently wrote down, 'Seven calls a day average,' and then looked up from the notebook, feeling nauseous. She would have to remember the conversations from the car and write them up later or she would make herself travel sick, but she wanted to make sure she gave Sam a full and detailed report.

J M Toys, their first call, was a large, old-fashioned toy shop with an eclectic window display and an air of tradition and respectability. It had a Hamleys feel about it as you walked in; a wooden train set was set up on a low table for children to play with and an enormous stuffed teddy sat in the far corner of the shop. According to Daniel, the bear had been there since the Seventies when the shop opened.

There was a high counter on the right and a pretty dark-eyed girl sat behind the till point. Her coal-black cornrows swung from side to side as she talked, the brightly coloured beads clicking as they collided. She recognised Daniel and smiled, picking up the phone to call her boss from the back of the shop.

Lucy walked over to a display of superhero fancy dress costumes and started to look through them, feeling excited and nervous at the same time.

'Graham is a good bloke. Usually uses us, unless it's something we can't supply, like Lego. Carmichael's offered him the same discounts, but I like to think we have a more personal touch. It's all about the networking, Lucy.' Daniel sauntered over to Lucy, as they waited for Graham to appear.

A bespectacled middle-aged man appeared from a doorway to the right of the till point in an open-neck shirt and green chinos.

Daniel shook down his cuffs and adjusted his tie. 'Watch and learn, ladies. Watch and learn.' And he walked over to the man and gave him a hearty handshake. 'Graham, how's the lovely Melanie? The twins must be looking forward to starting secondary school in September. You'll have to dig out some recent photos. I bet they've grown.'

Graham's face beamed. 'They really have. Tommy's goalkeeper for the under-twelves next season. And I'm back in Melanie's good books after your idea for our anniversary. Thanks for that – worked a treat.' He winked at Daniel and then looked over to Sam and Lucy expectantly. Sam was already striding towards the men with her hand outstretched. Lucy lagged back, unsure of her role in all this.

'I have two of Tompkins Toy Wholesaler's most delightful ladies with me today. This is our extremely competent new general manager Sam Mulligan. And this vision of loveliness is Lucy from the sales office.'

Graham shook both their hands and steered them to the door marked private at the back of the store. 'Lucy? Were you the one who sorted out the Hear Me Growl Tyrannosaurus Rex mess a few weeks ago?'

'Yes. Sorry about that.'

'Nonsense. Regardless of where the error was made, you sorted it quickly and without fuss. And it's not the first time you've helped us out of a hole. Keep your eye on this one, Sam,' and he winked at her. Lucy smiled, stood a little straighter and a little taller.

'Oh, I am,' said Sam, without the hint of a smile.

Despite feeling under scrutiny from the ever-watchful Sam, Lucy enjoyed her day. Lunch at a country pub had been on the company, even though she'd been scribbling notes down through most of it. Her respect for Daniel had increased, despite the humming. It seemed his little pranks were not confined to Adam but were weirdly welcomed and even encouraged by some of the customers. Mind you, Lucy was discovering that the people running these toy outlets were little more than big kids themselves. It was a happy section of the retail world, and Daniel, with a trick up his sleeve and a song to woo the ladies, was well liked. And a damn good salesman.

Standing in the staff car park at half past six, Sam and Lucy watched Daniel pull away.

'You did well today, Lucy,' said Sam.

Lucy didn't feel she'd actually done anything, other than trail around and look interested, but she was pleased to hear Sam's words.

'I enjoyed it. It's good to see a different side of the company.'

It helps me understand how all the departments work. I've certainly got more respect for the reps now.'

Sam nodded. 'Look, we never did organise that drink.'

'Sorry. I hadn't forgotten.' But she was rather hoping Sam had.

'How about grabbing one now? Are you up to anything tonight? If we meet in town, we can both drop our cars home and walk in.'

'On a Tuesday?'

'Yes, Lucy. Let's live dangerously and have a drink on a work night.'

'Okay, give me an hour, there's someone I need to pop in on first, and then we can hit the town,' and she looked down at the locket, thrilled her new boss wanted to spend time with her outside of the work environment, and feeling she could conquer the world.

Chapter 41

Sitting in the garden of The King's Arms, Lucy slipped her mobile back into her pocket as Sam approached the table with a bottle of house red and two wine glasses on a circular metal tray. Unable to persuade Jess to join them, she was entertaining her boss alone. It would have been a terrifying thought only a few short weeks ago, but she was almost looking forward to it.

'Just a small one for me,' she said, as Sam poured the first glass.

'Sharing a bottle is hardly debaucherous behaviour, Lucy.'

'I've recently had a bad experience with alcohol in front of a particularly unimpressed young man. Not my finest hour.'

'And you like him, this man?'

Lucy grinned, not bothering to deny it. She couldn't admit the truth of it to Jess, sensing she would somehow be disappointed with her, but with Sam she felt at ease. Despite her authoritative air at work, social Sam was a different beast. Her face was full of smiles and her shoulders were less hunched.

'Ah, I did wonder. You've been noticeably perkier at work recently.'

'Have I?' Lucy didn't think George had anything to do with

her perkiness; she wanted the locket to give her confidence in her work life, more than her love life. Getting herself a boyfriend had only ever been a by-product, although quite an appealing one of late.

Lucy smiled and placed her hand over the locket.

Taking a sip of wine and avoiding Sam's eye, Lucy asked whether she had anyone special in her own life, wondering if Sam would be prepared to share such intimate details with her.

'Not for a long time. And when there was, I put him very low down on my ridiculously long list of priorities. Only appreciated him when he was no longer there. It's not that I need someone. I can be me and I can be fulfilled without a partner, but I *want* someone. There's a subtle difference I didn't appreciate until recently. So, tell me about your man?'

'Not mine.'

'Not yet.'

'No, not yet. But soon.' Lucy took another sip of the wine and felt it slip down, warming as it went.

'Great attitude. What's the plan?'

Resisting the urge to say, 'Perform a string of dubious spells so the magic of a mysterious Victorian locket can trap the poor sod into falling for me whether he wants to or not,' she said, 'Wear him down, I think.'

'Good plan.' Sam smiled.

The pair talked about friendships, family, careers and knitting, but Lucy wasn't quite ready to present Sam with the nativity idea. It was a collaboration with Adam, still in its formative stages, and she wanted to get it right before pitching it. Sam was, however, keen to hear about the Nicely Knitted Celebrities, impressed Lucy had set up the site and how successful it had become, and expressed an interest in ordering a Poldark. *Honestly*, Lucy thought to herself, *I should have called the site Nicely Knitted Poldarks.*

After a pleasant couple of hours at the pub, Lucy walked along the river and back into town, which was her quickest route home. As she headed along the high street, she saw a badly parked car in one of the disabled bays outside the cinema. There was an older lady in a wheelchair and the back of a man bent forward trying his best to untangle the strap of a black leather handbag from the wheels.

'You...twit. I told you not to... Hang it on the back.' Her speech was slow and deliberate.

'I'm doing my best, Mum,' the man replied.

Lucy felt sorry for him as he struggled to lift the wheelchair without tipping out the occupant and wanted to see if there was something she could do.

'Can I help?' Lucy asked, now level with them.

The man turned and the blue glow from the neon signage of the cinema caught his face.

It was Adam.

The colour drained from his face and his eyes momentarily flashed wide. Realising he couldn't bluff his way out, he cast his eyes downward. Lucy's heart went out to him. She didn't want him to feel embarrassed because he was out with his mother, and thought it sad he never talked about her: whether she lived locally, or even the fact she was in a wheelchair.

'We're fine. Thank you.' His response was curt.

She didn't want to intrude on his personal life, but the strap detanglement was a two-man job.

'Don't be...silly, Adam. Let this young girl...help or we'll be here all...night.'

'Hi, I'm Lucy. I work with Adam.' She put out her hand to introduce herself and gave the white-haired, rosy-faced old lady her biggest smile.

'Ah, he never talks about work. Nice to...meet you, Lucy. Now...do you think you could help retrieve my handbag? Men make such a...fuss over the simplest of tasks.'

'Of course.' Lucy tipped the chair forward slightly and Adam was able to liberate the strap.

'I'm not complaining really. He's a good boy. Not many men his age...would move in with their mother...after a debilitating stroke...and look after them.'

Chapter 42

Before Lucy had taken the key from her ignition the following morning, Adam was hovering by the driver's door and trying to catch her eye. He even lunged to open the car door but thought better of it. Taking a step back, he waited for Lucy to gather her handbag, knitting and lunch, and exit the car in her own time.

'Lucy...'

'Good morning, Adam.'

'About last night...'

Lucy pressed the button on the key fob and it gave a cheery beep.

'I mean,' he continued, 'our private lives should stay that way, don't you think?'

Lucy took a deep breath, pulled her sunglasses down from the top of her head to rest on her nose and swung her handbag over her shoulder. She stood in front of Adam and bowed her head slightly to peer over the rim of the sunglasses. She wanted to make sure he was listening.

'I totally agree. I wouldn't dream of discussing your personal life with other people, but would expect you to extend me the same courtesy. I wouldn't tell people if you'd accidentally administered something to a friend and had to drive him to

A&E. Or gossip if you'd been caught in an embarrassing situation in the stationery cupboard that was not your fault...'

Adam swallowed hard. 'Ah, yes, see your point. Unforgiveable. I hope you won't hold my indiscretions against me?'

'Of course not, but I would like to discuss a couple of other things whilst I've got your attention. I don't like being the one sent down to the Tardis to do the photocopying all the time,' she said.

'No, well, Pat could do that. Or Connor. Seems unfair that it's always the new girl, eh?'

'And perhaps it would be a good idea to let Sam know it was my idea to split the ClickIn order up to get it done in time? I hope you aren't going to take all the credit if the nativity idea comes off as well?'

'Of course not. I was just trying to demonstrate we were a team and all that. But you're right: I'll mention how it was you who took charge of the order and how we've worked together with this idea to get the company publicity. Perhaps we can talk about it some more, polish it up and present it together.'

Her slightly raised shoulders slumped slightly and she gave him a genuine smile.

'Thank you. And as for your mother – I think you'll be pleasantly surprised if you opened up to people at work. You are doing such a kind and thoughtful thing and it can't be easy.' She thought about her own situation and how the coming months would only get more difficult with Brenda's care. 'I really admire you,' and she reached out a hand to touch his arm and then walked towards the office, without any rolling, flipping or handstands in her stomach at all.

* * *

It was an important day and Lucy wanted to be taken seriously. She chose clothes that made her feel confident but that were businesslike, and took time over her hair and her make-up. Mr Tompkins arranged to see her first thing to talk about her idea for the wine promotion. She slid into her chair, unaware of the admiring glances from her colleagues. Connor ran his hand nervously through his hair. He had a girlfriend but it clearly didn't mean he couldn't appreciate a good-looking woman when she was in his vicinity.

As Sam walked past, Lucy waved her notebook in the air. 'Here are the notes I took yesterday.'

'I don't want them.' Sam wrinkled her brow and shook her head dismissively. 'Put them in your desk or something.'

Great. She wasted my entire day taking notes for nothing, thought Lucy. Oh well, at least she had the meeting with Mr Tompkins to look forward to.

Opening her drawer, Lucy pulled out a blue folder, pushed her handbag under the desk with her foot and slid the chair out again. She was surprised not to experience a ripple of nerves, but he was a kind man and she had nothing to lose.

Richard Tompkins gestured for her to sit and leaned forward over his desk, interlacing his fingers as she briefly pitched her idea. Afterwards, she passed him the blue folder. He flicked through the pages and nodded his head.

'I like this idea in principle. We save money by not giving customers the final five per cent, but they still get, like you say, something tangible. It might work with the independents but not the bigger chains. I think we should investigate further.'

'You do?' She beamed at him.

'Absolutely. Well done, Lucy.'

*   *   *

Life was good, mused Lucy. Work was going well; she had the respect of her colleagues and was starting to make her mark in the company. There was the distinct possibility of romance bobbing its six-foot-four head over the horizon. Brenda seemed to have accepted her situation and Lucy suspected she had a comfortable care home lined up for when the time finally came. With all the excitement about the imminent eightieth party, Brenda was more sunny and upbeat than she'd been in a while. And although Lucy wouldn't go so far as to say she was looking forward to her mother's Big Birthday, she was at least no longer dreading it. If things continued on this trajectory, she was heading for those twinkly stars she had been standing on the ground and admiring for so long.

Sadly, life took one look at the projected graph of Lucy's happiness and decided to throw in a few random coordinates.

Chapter 43

Not knowing what life had in store, Lucy remained keen to get her man. The pentagram must have worked, because when Lucy finally checked the locket, it revealed the next spell.

'A night beneath the stars together
Ensures this love will last forever.'

All the spells had been difficult but this one was going to be particularly tricky. How could she persuade George to spend a night in the open air with her? Because she assumed this was what the locket was asking her to do. Perhaps she could lock him out of his house last thing at night? But knowing him, he'd just book a room at an expensive hotel until a locksmith sorted it all. Or could she convince him it was for charity? Something along the lines of a sponsored camp-out? Again, she felt sure he would happily and generously donate to the charity without feeling the need to participate in such an idiotic activity. So how was she going to pull it off? It wasn't as if she could just ask him. Especially as the last time she'd seen him had not been her finest hour, and he was probably still furious with her. She looked down at the locket. Or was it?

'You know we were talking about being more spontaneous and living a life outside of work?' Not giving him a chance to answer, she gabbled on, 'So I wondered if you'd like to do a bit of camping out beneath the stars on Saturday?'

'What?' George stood on his doorstep, towering over her, and doubtless wondering what his bonkers neighbour was going on about now.

'You know? A couple of deckchairs and study the constellations? Or even grab a sleeping bag, a big Thermos of tea and a couple of packets of dark chocolate digestives and discover our inner Bear Grylls? We don't need a tent. Just us and the universe above us. It will be fun.'

'Instead of getting into a proper bed like any sensible person and having a perfectly decent night's sleep, you mean?'

'Yes.' Lucy stood up straighter, tipped her head up, and looked George in the eye. 'Instead of the sensible option.'

He wriggled under her piercing stare, remembering their previous conversation.

'No, Lucy. I will not lie on the hard ground, with no adequate protection from the elements, and be food for the mosquitoes, when there is a bed and a decent roof ten paces from us. Total and utter madness.'

Just as she started to slink away, he raised an eyebrow. 'And anyway, I'd probably wake up to find you'd made off with my sleeping bag...'

Ah, she was rather hoping he'd forgotten about her drunken escapades. Obviously not.

* * *

'I understand from Richard that you have put together a proposal giving cases of wine to customers who are pushing for extra discount?' Sam stood at Lucy's desk the following morning, as Lucy tried to gauge her boss's mood. As usual, Sam was giving nothing away.

'I thought it might encourage customer loyalty but cost the company less than half the discount in real terms. Some of the independent guys would be tempted, I'm sure.'

'And you went over my head and straight to Richard? Didn't you consider discussing it with me first?'

Lucy's heart sank to her brand-new, heeled court shoes.

'It wasn't like that. We were talking in the staff kitchen and it just came up. He asked me to put my ideas down.'

'Well, I've just had a meeting with him and he assumed I knew all about it, because that's how the office hierarchy works, Lucy. You talk to Adam or me first with any concerns or ideas, and we take them to the top.'

'I'm sorry.' Running it by Sam hadn't even occurred to her, but she could see how it might be seen as going over her head.

'I don't like being the last in the loop, Lucy. I've spent enough of my working life being on the outside.' Sam returned to her desk.

An uneasy feeling bubbled. *Why did she pretend she wanted to be my friend*, thought Lucy, *when she clearly doesn't like me very much?*

Friday evening, as she was leaving Brenda's house, Lucy was accosted by George on the pavement outside. Before he got the chance to speak, Lucy started to gabble an apology.

'The other night, when you found me in your house—'

'There's no need to revisit that. Everyone's allowed to overdo it occasionally. Perhaps I need to embrace my wild side more often than I do. I was wrong to blow up. And by way of an apology, and in an attempt to inject some much-needed spontaneity into my life, I was thinking about your totally ridiculous and utterly madcap idea from the other day and I thought why not?'

Lucy scrunched up her face and frowned, petting Scratbag's black, furry head as he leaped onto the wall next to her.

'The all night under the stars thing?' he clarified.

This was a shock. She'd been racking her brains to come up with a plan to lure George under the night sky and had even briefly considering drugging him, she was getting that desperate. And now here he stood, agreeing to it voluntarily.

'I'm trying to be more sociable, but I still say it as I see it, I'm afraid, so I was typically blunt when you suggested it the other day. It was so out of the blue. And quite frankly more outrageous than a Marvel super villain's plans for world domination. And then I mulled it over. The more I get to know you, the more I have to reassess my definition of normal. You're really odd—'

'Thanks.'

'But I'm learning that odd isn't a bad thing. Perhaps I need to be more odd.'

'Believe me, you already qualify.'

The much-sought-after and orgasm-inducing smile that he only broke out to coincide with the appearance of Halley's Comet and every fourth blue moon appeared from nowhere and Lucy had to grab the wall to stop her giddy legs collapsing.

'I like having you as a friend. You're like the sister I never had. I suppose I was old-fashioned and thought males and females couldn't be just friends, with no hidden agenda, but I think with you I can.'

Lucy hid her inward sigh and broke out what she hoped was an equally orgasm-inducing smile. And then adjusted it slightly, feeling orgasm-inducing wasn't terribly appropriate from a sister substitute.

'So, sleeping bags and flasks tomorrow at nine o'clock then?' she rallied.

'Yes,' he said. 'But not in your grotty back garden. Come to mine. I'm going to drive us somewhere rather more picturesque.'

Filling Jess in on the next stage of the spell, Lucy nursed a small gin and tonic in the garden of The King's Arms. It was a refreshingly cool Friday evening after a long, sticky week.

'For Pete's sake, that's not playing fair.' And Jess pulled her mouth into a tight line. 'A night under the stars? How are you supposed to pull that off?'

'It's my worry, not yours, but I'm sorted. I asked him outright and he said yes.'

Jess looked impressed. 'Wow. You really are rocking this confidence thing. So he just agreed? No questions asked?'

Lucy nodded, not wanting to admit he'd shot her down the first time.

'Can I join in? It'll be fun.'

'If we were hanging out in my back garden, I would have said yes. But he's taking me somewhere and it's a surprise.' She tried not to look too excited. After all, Jess didn't need to know she was warming up to him until she had something more positive to report.

Jess's shoulders dropped and she turned the stem of her wine glass around slowly in her fingers. 'When?'

'Tomorrow.'

'What time?'

'Why all the questions? You nagged me to get a grip with the locket and now that I'm behind it, you don't seem to trust me.'

Chapter 44

George swung the Audi into a narrow unmade road and after a few hundred metres the car came to a halt. They stopped in front of a metal barrier that prevented them from continuing their journey, but there were far worse places to be stuck, Lucy decided. Beside them were pretty splashes of scarlet field poppies on the low bank that edged a wheat field. It was still a pale green, waiting for the summer sun to ripen it to a deep golden colour before harvest. A dry, dusty smell drifted in through her open window and a slight breeze rippled through the fine hairs along the back of her arm.

The drive had taken twenty minutes, with Lucy chattering away and George making the occasional terse comment, but often smiling at her as he did so. She knew he thought she was silly and ditzy, but she liked being with him. Even if this locket thing failed to have him jumping her bones or getting down on bended knee, it had enabled her to form a friendship with him that she was starting to treasure.

'Where are we?' she asked.

'Somewhere I used to come with my dad when I was little. Stay here. I won't be a moment.'

Wriggling in his seat to retrieve something from his pocket, he opened the car door and walked to the barrier. There was a large padlock holding the barrier arm down, but Lucy saw the glint of something shiny in his hand and realised he had the key. He heaved the metal arm up, hung the padlock temporarily on the loop and came back to the car. The process was repeated in reverse after they'd driven through, and he returned to the driver's seat, but didn't pull off immediately.

'I thought someone else was coming, but it looks like they've turned off. It's usually only members that come down the track this far. Bit of a dead end. Right, let's go.'

The sandy track had occasional potholes and large, loose stones across it, and was very bumpy going.

'Members? So are we at some kind of club? It's not a pagan cult, is it? You're not taking me to some isolated spot as a sacrifice to the Neighbourhood Watch God you were so worried about when everyone plied you with cakes? Because if it's a virgin sacrifice you're after, you may have to rethink.'

'I'll use you as a cult offering another time. Tonight, my little suspicious friend, we are at a private members' fishing lake.'

'You fish?'

'I used to. More often than not, I played with the tub of maggots, racing them across the ground, while my dad untangled my line. But it wasn't about the fishing – it was about being with him in this beautiful and isolated place.'

'I can see that appealing to you.'

'Absolutely. In fact, with my social skills, it is exactly the sort of after-hours hotspot I should be frequenting. The fish don't seem to mind my poor manners and taciturn nature. Maybe I'll take it up again.'

They followed the track down a slight hill and Lucy could see a body of water to her right, the light from the low sun glinting off the surface. Dark silhouettes of bushes and trees lined the bank and some impressive bulrushes stood in groups like oversized kofta kebabs. The water followed them down the track, travelling companionably beside them as they made their way to their destination.

'That's a river, not a lake,' Lucy said.

'It doesn't lead anywhere and the water is stagnant. Lakes don't always come in convenient circle shapes, you know,' he said. 'There's some truly magnificent fish in there. Pike as big as a man's leg. There are also deer, foxes, often a swooping barn owl illuminated by the moon, and otters about – although the latter are unwelcomed by the syndicate.'

Lucy looked at him.

'They decimate the fish population.'

They drove in silence a while longer and then he pulled into a rough parking area by a large shed.

George got out and opened the boot, gathering up their sleeping bags, roll mats and rucksacks with his massive arms. Lucy followed mutely. He pressed his key fob and the indicators flashed as the car beeped and locked itself.

'Boathouse,' George said, indicating to the shed. 'But we aren't taking out a punt at this time of night. One reckless step at a time for me.'

They walked past an area near the bank that had obviously been cleared for fishing because Lucy noticed a wooden platform protruding into the dark water. There was a squawk as George took hearty man strides into the undergrowth and disturbed a bird, and then a plop as it jumped into the water.

He found a secluded spot, sheltered at one side by a lopsided willow, where the trunk grew over the water as if the tree was peering from the bank to look at its own reflection. George swept some dead twigs and large stones to the side with his foot and spread out the roll mats, placing the sleeping bags and rucksacks on top.

They smiled at each other and George gestured to the closest mat. As Lucy knelt down and leaned forward to spread out her sleeping bag, the locket swung out from her top, nearly smacking her in the face.

'What's in the locket?' he asked, noticing it catch the light.

Lucy's heart started a slow thud. She could hardly show him.

'Just an old photo,' she muttered.

'I've noticed you wearing it before. Family heirloom?'

'Brenda gave it to me.'

'She's obviously fond of you, but then you're so good to her. Not many people would give up their time to look after an old lady who wasn't even related to them.' He sat down and dragged his rucksack across the dusty ground towards his feet.

'But she's not just any old lady.'

'I know,' he said, tucking his enormous feet under his knees. 'Odd, slightly scary but endearing. Like you, in fact.'

'I'm not scary. Or odd.'

'Most of our encounters result in me suffering some kind of life-threatening injury. And you do knit. And give dead things make-overs.'

'Point taken,' Lucy said, quite liking the endearing bit and settling down opposite George.

'So how long will you manage until she needs proper care?' he asked.

'The doctor said she was in the early stages. I'm sure we'll cope for the next few months with no problem. The condition often plateaus for a period and then there is a sudden deterioration. Maybe with medication she'll even see a short-term improvement. Mind you, getting her to take any medication won't be straightforward.'

'And then what?'

'I don't know.' She cast her eyes around, looking for a distraction. For want of something to do, she pulled at a long stem of grass and wound it around her finger. 'But she's assured me that part is all taken care of. I think she has somewhere in mind – a place she will be happy when she needs more care. She seems at peace with it all and relatively cheerful at the moment, what with the birthday party to look forward to. But I don't want to think about what the future holds right now. We're managing. I can work it around my job and it's not like I have a massively demanding social life. And all the neighbours, including you, Mr Aberdour—' she gave a shy smile '—are so kind and helpful. We'll muddle through.'

'Yes, it's one of the lovely things I've noticed about Lancaster Road; everyone cares without being in your face. There's a sense of community without it being imposed upon you. That student lad from the flat above yours took in a parcel for me the other day, and Chloe's dad offered me a spare ticket to the football for nothing – not my bag, but a kind thought.' There was a pause. 'So what happens if you get a boyfriend?' George didn't look at her as he asked this but copied her by pulling up a piece of grass and fiddling with it.

'He'll either adapt or be out on his ear,' she said, surprised at his line of questioning. She hoped she sounded like the sort of girl who had lots of offers but could quite happily move on to one of the many suitors waiting in the wings if a boyfriend proved difficult. George looked up to hear her answer. Their eyes locked and the silence was louder than it should have been. Her heart somersaulted and stood up for a wobbly finish.

'You are a very giving person, Lucy Baker. And an interesting one.'

He leaned towards her, placing a hand next to her outstretched leg. His body tilted and he came closer.

He's going to kiss me, she thought. *Oh. My. God. The locket has worked.*

Her tongue flicked over her lips and she closed her eyes...

She felt a shoulder catch her arm and opened her eyes again to find George reaching for the Thermos.

'Tea?' he asked.

Chapter 45

It was a pale crescent moon that watched over the two friends as they lay together, full of hot, strong, soya milky tea and far too many dairy-free chocolate biscuits. They crawled into their sleeping bags and lay on their sides, facing each other. George was propped up on an elbow, looking quite handsome in the moonlight. It caught his features, highlighting his strong nose and large eyes. He was in the glasses again. In fact, he'd been wearing them since she'd made that drunken comment, although it was probably a coincidence.

Knowing she wouldn't sleep comfortably with the locket around her neck, she took it off and tucked it in the top of her rucksack with her phone. George assured her the only people within a three-mile radius were a handful of all-night fishermen, waiting patiently for fishing alarms to beep, and certainly not wandering around the lake looking to steal antique silver jewellery. Lucy wondered if she'd seen a fisherman earlier as there had been a flash of torchlight deep in the undergrowth when they were drinking their tea, but George thought it was more likely to be the reflection of an animal's eyes, perhaps a deer or a fox, especially as it was promptly followed by snapping twigs and rustling. But animal or fisherman, it hadn't disturbed them and had promptly disappeared.

'Cold?' George asked.

'No. You?'

'A bit. But I have this,' and he reached into the side pocket of his rucksack that Lucy was sure he had purchased purely for this excursion, as she could still see the price tag hanging from the front zip. (Sixty-four pounds for a diddly rucksack? They saw him coming.) 'Fancy a stiffener?' He produced a silver hip flask and started to unscrew the cap.

'I thought you didn't drink?'

'What makes you think it's not Ovaltine?'

He held it out to her and she sniffed.

'That's whisky,' she spluttered.

'It's for medicinal purposes. It's the excessive consumption of alcohol I find unsettling. People drinking it like tea to get them through the day and relying on it to solve life's problems. We're hardly going to get drunk from this small flask. Go on. It'll warm your cockles.'

Lucy took a tentative sip of the spicy, burning liquid and tried not to cough. As it travelled down her throat, it left a warming sensation that quickly spread to other parts of her body, like dropping a pipette of water onto a piece of blotting paper. Soon, her cockles felt well and truly toasty. Then George put the flask to his own lips and took a swig.

The sky was cloudless and the blue-black of the night was punctuated with dots of brilliant white. The soft breeze had cooled since the afternoon and the air had the clean but damp smell from being near water. A bat swooped out from a tree and circled above them, silhouetted against the pale light from the moon.

George rolled onto his back and looked up at the twinkling stars, scattered like tiny fragments of broken glass overhead.

He remained silent and, after a while, Lucy also rolled over and looked up. They lay together in mutual companionship for several minutes, Lucy feeling the residual tingles dance through her body from the whisky.

'She had a drink problem,' George said suddenly from nowhere.

Lucy turned her head to look at him, but he was still staring straight up into the night sky. She waited for him to elaborate.

'Karen,' he clarified.

The muscles tightened in her stomach. That explained a few things then, like his angry reaction to her drunken escapade and not particularly being a drinker himself.

'She was always a bit highly strung – either up in the clouds or deep, deep underground, but she was the first woman who was serious about me. Girlfriends always seemed too much like hard work and my previous relationships had been very casual. But she was determined. She didn't give up, even though I was monosyllabic and offhand.'

He adjusted his position and turned his head to hers.

'She pursued me with a passion worthy of a tiny, hyperactive puppy after an oversized, unsociable bone. And I was flattered. And then somehow I found myself married and things started to change. Living together, I realised we weren't compatible.'

He glanced away.

'Sorry, you don't want to hear this...'

'I do. I was wrong to make her off topic. Friends should be able to talk about things with each other. I'm sorry I said I didn't want to talk about her before.' Lucy brushed a fluttering moth away from her face and sat up on her elbows to prove he had her full attention.

'She wanted to be out all the time, preferably spending my money, and she liked a drink. Not in an alcoholic, breakfast-is-forty-per-cent-proof kind of way, but when she partied – boy, did she party. I tried to make it work; after all it takes two to say I do. I wondered if it was my fault, being busy with the company, so I made an effort to be around and even tried talking to her, and you know what a big deal that is for me. But she never wanted me when I was there, only when I wasn't. What started out as small things to get my attention escalated into increasingly dramatic gestures. She would go off in the car, knowing the fuel was low, and drive until the tank ran out, calling me at four o'clock in the morning to come and rescue her. Or simply not come home at all, with her phone switched off so I couldn't contact her...'

He tailed off and rested his arm across his eyes, like he was shutting everything out. Lucy, however, was delighted he was finally letting her in.

'And then, on my mother's birthday two years ago, she got so ridiculously drunk I had to leave the restaurant early and take her home. She refused to come to bed, told me I was boring and no fun to be with, and that she'd only married me for my money. Possibly all true, but still hurtful. So I said I was going to sleep at the office and I left her to sober up.'

There was a pause, as though he was searching for the right words or struggling with a memory. Lucy risked a glance at his face, but it was so dark now all she could see was shadow.

'It's the smell...'

'Of what?' Lucy prompted.

'The bitter, acrid smell of smoke. Sometimes when I shut my eyes, I can still smell it. She maintains it was an accident, but I got a phone call at half three that morning. She was hysterical, sobbing down the phone, saying how sorry she was and how it was all a terrible accident.'

'Oh my goodness. There was a fire?' There was a second crippling blow to her stomach as she realised getting drunk and setting fire to her coffee table were possibly the worst things she could have done to the poor man in her efforts to win him over.

'By the time I got back, there were four fire engines and an ambulance along our drive. She was wrapped in a blanket and a paramedic was sitting with her, holding an oxygen mask to her face. Half the neighbourhood gathered as the blackened roof timbers protruded from the rubble of our home like a recently unearthed skeleton of some ancient dinosaur. Everything was so bloody black. The following day, returning to the house to assess the damage, I realised there was nothing left. Absolutely *nothing*.'

He moved his arm and stared back up at the stars.

'She'd promised me months before that the smoke alarms had been checked. I don't know whether she lied or simply forgot to replace the batteries, but a midnight craving for a bacon sandwich and an easily distracted drunk woman don't mix. The fat caught, quickly followed by the oven housing. Neither alarm went off and the fire was able to rage through the house unchecked. She was lucky to get out alive.'

Lucy was now cross-legged and upright. What a horrific experience for Karen, and for him.

'It marked the end of our struggling relationship. A quick divorce and I found somewhere to rent until Lancaster Road caught my eye. None of it was amicable at the time, but, as you know, she got back in touch recently and her life seems

316

to be on a steady path now. She's with Richard and seems genuinely happy. They invited me out for a meal the day I was at your office. I think she wanted to prove that she's changed and for me to see she was no longer a threat.'

Karen was dating *Richard*. Of course, that made considerably more sense. She looked familiar because Lucy had seen her at Vernon's retirement party, if only briefly. And Jess had talked about Karen visiting Tompkins, so she suspected it was Jess who had divulged George's whereabouts.

'It was closure for us both and I think we've parted friends. I tried to tell you all this the other day, but you were grumpy and told me Karen was off topic. It just spilled out tonight.'

'Sometimes it's good to talk.'

George looked thoughtful. 'Yeah, I'm starting to realise that. I'm glad I've got a friend like you. Someone who is happy to spend time with me with no ulterior motive. Perhaps I can start to trust women again and appreciate they aren't all after my wallet or my exquisitely toned body.' He put up an arm like a bodybuilder might and flexed a bicep.

Lucy chewed at her lip and kept quiet.

Shortly afterwards, she fell asleep, dreaming of perilous fires and George launching himself on top of her. She stirred in the early hours when his bear-like snoring invaded her dreams and found he had shuffled nearer, his huge body curled protectively around her tiny frame, as if she was something of his that he didn't want anyone else to steal.

Waking with a start, and a dull ache in her lower back where her hips had been resting awkwardly on the hard ground, she noticed George was out of his sleeping bag and sitting next to her, with the locket in his hand.

'Erm, that's mine,' she said, reaching out a lazy hand.

'It fell out of your bag. You didn't zip it up properly. It feels warm, probably from being near your phone.' He turned it over in his big hands and moved to press the catch. 'May I?'

'No.' She sat up in horror, not wanting him to see inside. 'You won't be able to open it. It only opens for...'

Despite having fingers the size of dried salamis, the catch popped and the top flipped open. Lucy felt her cheeks flush.

'*A night beneath the stars together, ensures this love will last forever,*' he read aloud. 'What is this?' He looked puzzled.

'Just a silly locket Brenda gave me. It's meaningless. Some old poem from long ago.'

'Is this what you were doing? Dragging me out to the middle of nowhere because of a poem in a locket?' His eyebrows met in the middle.

'No. And *you* dragged me out here. I was going to sit in the back garden.'

'*Do* you have feelings for me, Lucy?' He turned to her, frowning and confused.

Her forehead felt hot and her chest was thumping harder and faster than his stupid knock at her front door.

Lucy grabbed the locket from his open hands and slipped it over her head. The pounding from her heart subsided and she looked him straight in the eyes.

'No,' she said. 'I do not. How ridiculous.' She scrabbled around, gathering up her belongings, tripping over the end of her sleeping bag as her feet became tangled in the material. 'I'd decided that despite your abrupt nature you were a decent man, who had rescued a cat and was kind to Brenda, so I thought we could be friends. Clearly, you suspect me of all sorts of underhand dealings and I was wrong.'

'Well, I'm not sure I—' George began, but as she snatched up her rucksack, Lucy's phone started to buzz.

'Hello?' she said, glad of the distraction.

'Am I speaking to Lucy Baker?'

'Yes.'

'It's Renborough Hospital here. Brenda Pethybridge was admitted early this morning. She's had a fall and you are listed as her next of kin.'

Chapter 46

'It was silly. I was clearing out the racks in the kitchen, stacking up empty jars and I tripped over the broom handle,' Brenda explained.

'At four o'clock in the morning?' squeaked Lucy.

'Well, obviously I didn't realise it was quite that early. But, anyway, I managed to shuffle on my bottom to the phone.'

'You should have asked me to do it. You're lucky it's not more serious.' Lucy was upset her friend hadn't thought to ask for her help.

George had driven Lucy straight to the hospital and now they both stood at her bedside; a tiny lady on a big white bed with a flappy diamond-printed hospital gown tied loosely around her. Lucy was impressed to find she had already been X-rayed as it was a Sunday, after all. There were no broken bones, but the nurse said she was badly bruised down her left side and the consultant wanted to run a few more checks before they discharged her. This news had not gone down well with Brenda, who insisted she was fine and Lucy should take her home immediately.

'They can't keep me here against my will, you know,' she muttered.

'But if I stay with you, and they don't keep you overnight,

it would make me feel better to know you had been thoroughly checked. It would stop me worrying.'

Brenda snorted and Lucy took that as an 'Okay, if I must'.

Nearly halfway through another week already, thought Lucy, as she sorted through the accumulated papers on her desk. Being organised and tidy was harder than it looked.

The hospital had discharged Brenda late Sunday afternoon and George returned to pick them both up. Lucy and George drifted back to their good friend roles, neither of them mentioning the locket. Brenda was stiff and sore from the fall but didn't make any fuss. Lucy was hopeful that her friend's desire to pack up the kitchen was the first step in her plan to look for more suitable housing – perhaps downsizing or sheltered accommodation. It made her sad to think there would come a day when she didn't live next door, but was relieved her friend wasn't fighting the inevitable, even though whenever she approached the subject, Brenda shut her down.

There was a clatter from behind the partition as Pat dropped something, and Lucy returned her focus to the spring clean before Sam noticed how messy her desk was. Sam and Adam had been in with Mr Tompkins most of the morning. Adam came out of Richard's office first and walked to Lucy's desk.

'Heads-up, Lucy-Lou, it's a no.'

'What's a no?' Lucy asked.

'We ran through your idea for the wine as an alternative to discounting and we aren't going to fly with it.'

'Oh, okay,' Lucy said, her stomach collapsing. 'Any particular reason?'

'It was a good idea, but there were some issues, and basically it was vetoed by The Black Widow in the end.'

Lucy's blood froze in her veins as Sam's head loomed into view behind an oblivious Adam.

'I'm known as The Black Widow, am I? Who thought that little gem up?' Sam asked, looking around the office.

Six pairs of eyes swivelled in Lucy's direction. Her heart sank to her shoes and out onto the colourful carpet tiles.

The week showed no signs of improving for Lucy. In fact, it was about to hit rock bottom and head straight through the magma, towards the earth's solid iron inner core.

Pat spoke to her on the internal line to say she suspected something big was afoot, as there was lots of activity downstairs in the conference room – the official name for the office opposite the accounts department that held a large oval table surrounded by chairs. Not that the company conducted many conferences. It was mainly used for the reps' meetings and to hold the sizeable buffet for the annual office Christmas party.

Adam's internal line buzzed as he wrestled with the binder of revised company policies that Sam had positively insisted he should be the one to proofread. As he tried to balance the phone between his ear and shoulder and unclip one of the pages, the binder slipped off his knee and the sheets spread gloriously over the floor in front of him like a paper path. A few choice expletives came from his mouth as he crawled around on the floor to gather them all up.

'Lucy-Lou? Actually, no, Connor?' Adam corrected himself. Connor's head peered around the corner. 'Would you mind grabbing the laptop from Sam's desk and running it down to the conference room? There's a love...erm, I mean there's a good chap.' He was making an effort to be less sexist, thought

Lucy, but as Adam himself might say: you can't expect a leopard to change his spots before the shops shut.

'I'll do it,' she volunteered. 'I was going down to the Tardis to do some photocopying anyway,' and she waved a sheet of paper at Adam to prove it.

'Make the most of escaping into the time machine,' said Sonjit, as she slipped out from her desk and walked over to help Adam. 'That big old-fashioned beast of a photocopier has been served its notice. Posh, new, whizzy machines are coming next week. One for in here and one in accounts. From what I understand, they can do the lot: printing, scanning, photocopying, paper aeroplane folding...and they are a fraction of the size. I bet within the year she's replaced us all with fancy software,' she grumbled.

'Thank you most kindly, lovely lady,' Adam said, as Sonjit started to retrieve scattered papers. Lucy noticed the pair of them briefly lock eyes before Sonjit returned to her paper gathering.

'You're welcome, Adam,' she replied, and then lowered her voice. 'I was, erm, wondering what you were doing after work tonight? I have this friend who has just opened a restaurant in town and is looking for some early online reviews...'

Lucy smiled to herself as she collected Sam's laptop and headed for the conference room. She'd seen that one coming, even if Pat now looked more shocked than someone who'd dropped their hair straighteners in the bath.

When she got downstairs, Lucy noticed the conference room door was ajar, but before she was close enough to knock or push it open, she heard Sam's voice float out into the corridor.

'I've narrowed it down to four suitable candidates for Lucy's job and I will be interviewing in here after lunch. If we keep the applicants downstairs away from the sales office, we can avoid some of the gossip. You know how quickly it spreads around here.'

Lucy's hand stopped in mid-air and everything in her world ground to a slow stop, including her heart.

'Excellent. Get in some new blood and shake the company up a bit at the same time,' she heard Richard Tompkins respond. 'It's about time young Lucy moved on.'

Chapter 47

She only had herself to blame, Lucy thought, sitting back at her desk and staring at the screen. She was trying to be someone she wasn't and even a magical locket couldn't override that. Who had she been trying to kid with her half-tidied desk and her jumped-up ideas?

It made sense that Sam would be looking to replace her. As far as her new boss was concerned, she'd called the managing director a dick, her The Black Widow and chosen to spend her lunch hour in unsuitable company. She took unauthorised time off work to look after a neighbour, had been caught in the Tardis with Daniel, and had shown an unworkable customer incentive scheme to Richard Tompkins over Sam's head. Sam was looking for dynamic achievers to shake the company up. Not a disorganised office junior with ridiculous ideas above her pay grade.

But what hurt Lucy most as she digested the news was Sam's efforts to socialise with her. Had it all been merely a ploy to catch her out somehow? She'd genuinely looked up to her new boss and now felt betrayed and very sorry for herself.

I won't cry, I won't cry, she repeated in her head.

She focused on the order she was typing up and concentrated on her work to take her mind off the impending dismissal. She might as well give the job her all while she still had it. And perhaps Adam would present their idea as planned, and continue with the nativity scene. The lovely ladies at the Renborough Knit and Natter were already on board. It was a fun idea and deserved to go ahead, with or without her.

Sam walked through the office a while later and stopped at Lucy's desk. Aware of her boss's smart navy blue suit hovering by her side, she couldn't quite bring herself to turn and face the inevitable music. She typed frantically on the keyboard to indicate that she was super busy and couldn't *possibly* be disturbed.

Sam tapped her on the shoulder and leaned forward to speak to her in hushed tones. 'Can you come and see me in my office tomorrow? About ten o'clock? I need to speak to you about something, but I'm tied up all afternoon downstairs in the conference room.'

'Ten o'clock. No problem,' Lucy said, still tapping away and without turning her head.

Sitting in the downstairs staffroom with Derek and the others at lunchtime, Lucy's face was longer than the A1. Roy attempted to make her break a smile by talking about his drunken weekend escapades, but it fell flat. Eventually, and realising all was not well with their usually chirpy lunchtime companion, they persuaded her to open up.

Derek thumped his hand down on the table and tea slopped over the edges of their Balamory promotional mugs. 'That's not right – you're an asset to the company, love. More lively than Pat, bless her. And harder working than Adam. He wouldn't know a hard day's work if it danced naked in front of him with "this is what a hard day's work looks like" stamped on its forehead.'

'Please don't say anything. I haven't even been told officially yet. I'm not supposed to know and I don't want to get in any more trouble than I already am. I'm going to need a decent reference, after all.'

'You'll be fine, lass,' said Roy. 'Even though in the last few weeks you've not been yourself and gone all posh and bossy like the other one.' He smiled to indicate he was joking. 'Wherever you end up, you'll shine. Don't think of it as a negative. It could be just the kick up the ar— bottom that you need.'

'I'll miss this place.' Lucy looked up at the calendar, expecting to see Miss July and her unfeasibly perky breasts and spray-on tan but instead saw Renborough Animal Rescue's cat of the month. She sighed.

'And this place will miss you,' Derek said.

'I'm glad Brenda wasn't kept in at the weekend,' Jess said, perched on Lucy's desk. 'Although you do realise this could be the start of more frequent falls for her, don't you?'

Jess had been off sick Monday and Tuesday with a rotten summer cold. Not someone who was often ill, Jess told Lucy it had been brewing since Friday and she'd finally succumbed over the weekend after staying out far too late Saturday night.

'We'll deal with each one as it happens,' Lucy said. She wasn't sure if she was executing the best thought-out plan in her life: to take each day at a time, and not to worry too much about what the future held. But as no one could give her answers or timescales, it was the only plan she had.

Because Sam and Richard were still busy in the conference room, no one questioned Jess being upstairs. Adam was also absent, having nipped to the Tardis. Although he had every possible colour of highlighter, about fifteen spare Biros and enough staples to adorn the wall displays of all the primary schools in the county, the Tardis was next to the conference room and Adam didn't like being out of what he referred to as The Managerial Loop.

Unlike the warehouse lads, Jess was chatting away, oblivious to Lucy's low spirits.

'But, despite dashing off to hospital Sunday morning, you got to spend the whole night under the stars, like the locket said?'

'Yes.'

'And?'

'It's finished. That was the last spell.' She'd been buzzing when she'd found the final words and realised the spells were finished, but it wasn't important any more. Losing her job had taken precedence.

'Fantastic,' said Jess, with a huge smile. Her leg started to bob up and down, as it often did when she was excited. 'And the words changed?'

'I'm not in the mood to talk about this right now, Jess.'

'I know what you mean. The accounts office is in total chaos and the new software is causing us a major headache, not helped by me being off for two days. But did it?'

'Did it what?'

'Say any more?'

'Oh, just take it,' Lucy said, tugging the locket over her

head and passing it to Jess. There was a pause as Jess looked to Lucy for the necessary assistance.

'For goodness' sake. Give it here.' Lucy opened the catch and showed Jess the inscription. With all the drama over Brenda on Sunday, it wasn't until Monday she'd even thought to check it.

> *'When his lips now meet with thine*
> *It seals a love to last all time.'*

'So, do you reckon that means you have to go out and kiss him, or he'll be so in love with you now that he'll turn up and kiss you?'

Lucy rested her head in her hands and sighed. 'Right at this moment, I don't care.'

She loved her friend but the stupid locket was the last thing she was worried about. Why was Jess so obsessed with the damn thing that she couldn't see Lucy was desperately unhappy? Well, if Jess hadn't picked up on her mood, she didn't feel inclined to spell it out to her.

'What are you going to do if it hasn't worked? If you were right, and it was all mumbo jumbo?' Jess persevered.

'You've changed your tune. You were the biggest advocate of the locket and now you're implying that it might not be magic after all?'

'What I mean is, are you going to be terribly disappointed if he doesn't fall in love with you? Or falls for someone else? I mean, you aren't really into him, are you? It was just to keep your mum quiet and have someone to take to the Big Birthday.'

'I don't understand. Where are you going with this?'

'I don't want you to get hurt, that's all. You don't even like the man, do you? He's a great lump with silly glasses, who you find unpleasant and rude – remember?'

'No.' Lucy swallowed. 'I don't even like the man.'

It was as if Scratbag knew she'd had the worst day ever. He came towards Lucy as she swung her legs out of the car, rubbing his head around her ankles and nuzzling up to her outstretched hand with his soft, shiny head. George had stopped by that morning to say he would be away overnight at a conference in London and would she mind feeding the cat, so she suspected Scratbag's affections were merely a form of cupboard love. She promised she'd be over later and he seemed content with that.

Brenda was hobbling around and still very sore down her left side but was generally buoyant and chatty when Lucy checked in on her. As they passed the living room, Brenda rushed to pull the door closed but Lucy could see the tiny Edwardian writing bureau in the corner was open. Brenda was clearly catching up on correspondence as paper and pens were scattered across the fall of the desk.

'Wish I'd kept some of the lavender oil now as I don't want to be fiddling about in the garden cutting chunks of witch hazel off. All I need is to slip with the knife and put myself back in that bloody hospital again,' Brenda said, referring to the treatment of her bruises. 'I'm not going to miss this party for the world. And if I have a bit of bruising to live with, so be it.' She pulled out a kitchen chair for Lucy.

The kitchen looked even emptier now. All the shelves on the tall dresser were completely bare and the floor had been swept.

'George took the bottles and jars to the recycling centre for me today before he left for his work whatsit, and even ran the broom over the floor,' Brenda said, following her eyes.

'On a work day?'

'Yes, we had a late breakfast together. He turned up with a couple of bacon baps, saw the bottles stacked up and said he could easily pop past the bottle bank on his way to the conference. He stayed for about half an hour. We had a lovely time, apart from when he accidentally put one of the boxes on top of his spectacles. He said a few inappropriate words, nothing I've not said myself in times of great stress, but they were totally justified. They're his only pair, so I hope he gets on okay today. He told me he'd taken next week off, as he needs a break, and that he was going to take his mum away for a couple of days.'

'But he won't miss your party, will he?' Lucy felt disappointed at the thought he might not be there. Despite the tension at the end of their camp-out, she was certain there was a connection and was hopeful the locket was about to perform its final magic and bring them together.

'George promised to be there, don't worry. He returns tomorrow afternoon and is heading straight back to work. Certainly not a shirker, that one. Is that why I picked up a muddying of your auras when you walked in then? You were worried about him missing the party?'

'No, the muddy auras are because my boss is about to let me go.' The rising lump in her throat was audible but she swallowed it back down.

'Oh, Lucy.' Brenda slipped into a chair on the opposite side of the kitchen table and concern crossed her face. 'Are you certain?'

'They've been interviewing for my job today.'

'Oh, my darling. At least you have George. I'm certain he is yours now. Sometimes I can pick up things clearer than others. Where are you with the spells? Have you done the three hairs under the bed yet?'

From her dementia research, Lucy knew it was kinder not to continually correct sufferers, so she simply said, 'The spells are finished. Just the final kiss to go, I think.'

'How did I miss the last couple of spells? Oh, never mind. So, tomorrow it is then? You can ambush him when he returns from work.'

Or hijack him before he even makes it home, decided Lucy. Not that she was suddenly keen or anything.

Back in her flat, putting the final touches to Brenda's birthday present (never had she eaten so much Camembert, and all to get her hands on the boxes), Lucy became aware of the locket as she worked. It no longer felt warm to her, instead it felt cold and hard and heartless. She leaned forward to reach for the scissors from her knitting bag and it swung in front of her face, taunting her. As she sat back up, it slapped abruptly against her chest.

Stupid locket. It had given her this magical self-assurance that just wasn't her. All the new-found confidence had done was get her into trouble at work. By raising her head above the parapet, she had put herself in the firing line, quite literally, although Sam would probably phrase it differently to soften the blow. Now she had to drag her sorry backside into work tomorrow and sit in front of her traitorous boss while she was told, no doubt very politely, that they were going to let her go.

She walked over to the fireplace and knelt down in front

of her large basket of wool, but the end of one of her needles tangled in the chain of the locket. She looked down crossly at it, as if it was totally to blame for her approaching unemployment, and wrestled it free without realising she had inadvertently loosened one of the links. The chain of the locket caught on her sleeve as she rummaged about in the basket, the weak link parted and the locket slid into her lap. A few minutes later, as she stood up to return to the sofa with her wool, it fell into the gap between the rug and the hearth, and nestled there quietly, waiting to be found.

Barely five minutes later, the phone rang. It was her mother.

'Is Emily with you?' Her mother sounded anxious and flustered.

'No, I haven't seen her since my visit. Why, what's happened?' Lucy panicked. 'Please don't say something has happened to the baby.'

'We don't know.' Her mother's voice was unusually fragile.

'How can you *not* know?'

'Because Emily has gone missing.'

Chapter 48

Emily had dropped the girls off to preschool and nursery that morning, then sent Stuart a text telling him she was going off radar and he would have to leave work early to pick them up from the childminder. She hadn't answered her calls or made contact with him for the remainder of the day. By five o'clock, having duly collected his daughters, Stuart was frantic and started to call people, asking if they knew where she was. Shortly afterwards, another message came through to say she was fine but needed a bit of space and would be in touch.

Lucy felt shell-shocked, and as if she had somehow let her sister down, even though she'd been contacting her every day since returning from her weekend stay.

'I said I'd ring you and a few other family members, but this is most unlike her. I can't think what's happened. She is such a capable woman and this whole episode is totally out of character. Stuart tried her best friend and then me, and we both believe the only other person she would turn to if she had problems is you. You've always been so close,' said Lucy's mother.

Yes, she'd picked up signs that all was not heady blossom and flowering shrubs in her sister's garden of life, but the shoulder she offered hadn't been taken, so she assumed Emily was just low and exhausted from the pregnancy.

'I can promise you she's not here, but I'll contact you immediately if she gets in touch.'

Twenty minutes later, Lucy opened the front door to her pale, puffy-eyed but surprisingly calm sister.

'I can't do it any more.'

Emily was sitting on Lucy's sofa, hugging Wolverine to her chest as if he was a favourite teddy and she was a three-year-old girl.

'Something inside snapped. I dropped Rosie and Gracie off, and was walking back to the car thinking of all the things I had to organise for the girls and the jobs that needed doing about the house. Work were expecting me in for nine and I suddenly could see the future stretching before me, where the most precious things in the world to me, my girls, were occasional visitors as I negotiated this chaotic, rush hour of a road alone. I slumped into the car and thought how much easier Stu has it. He gets up, eats the breakfast I've made him, puts on the shirt I've ironed, goes to work without having to worry there might be a call from the nursery or the preschool to say a vomiting child needs collecting, then he comes home, eats the food I've prepared, reads the girls a story and goes to bed. Don't get me wrong, he's not a bad man, but he is simply that – a man. He doesn't think about the endless meals that have to be cooked, how the dirty washing magically reappears clean, ironed and back in his wardrobe. He doesn't juggle the complicated lives of two small children with doctor's appointments and the application of head lice treatments. I know that we have a cleaner, but trust me, if it wasn't for her, I would have gone under much sooner.' She was on her soapbox, but telltale tears were building.

'You know he loves you more than anything?'

'Yes, but he's the one piling on the pressure. He constantly reminds me how hard we need to work to afford our large house, big cars and fancy holidays abroad. But what if that's not what I want? What if all I want is to be there when my girls get home from school and to be able to give them my time? Not the latest Boden summer dress or expensive toys?'

'Oh, sweetheart.'

Lucy leaned forward to embrace her sister and reassure her everything would be okay.

'You know you've got to call home? They're beyond frantic,' she said as she squeezed Emily tight.

'I know. But I needed to escape for a while and think about my next move without someone asking for projected sales figures, or a child begging me to wipe their bottom. And a mean part of me wanted Stu to see what it's like – juggling five hundred and twenty-three balls in the air while someone casually tosses you a flaming baton to see if you can catch it between your butt cheeks.'

Stuart took the news surprisingly well, largely relieved his wife was safe and well. Sandra was less understanding. Lucy sat next to Emily as she made the call and heard her mother's voice drift out from the phone.

'But why? You have *everything*.' Lucy could almost picture her wringing her hands.

'I can't live this life any more, Mother. I can't be all things to all people. I can't have a demanding career and a young family and do a good job of both. I know there are people out there who can, and I take off my hat, coat and shoes to them, but I'm not one of them. Not any more.'

'I thought it was what you wanted?'

Lucy put a consoling hand on her sister's knee and Emily gripped it for dear life.

'No, Mother, it was what you wanted. I was living the life you so badly wanted for yourself. Don't get me wrong, in no way am I blaming you. I'm a big girl and I have made my own decisions. Well, here is another decision I've made. At lunchtime today I handed in my notice.'

The other end of the phone went eerily quiet.

Adam was cross-legged and highly animated, swinging his chair from side to side as Lucy walked through the sales office door on a bright but pleasingly breezy Thursday morning. She'd left her sister in bed (insisting the sofa was more suitable for the non-pregnant member of the family) and reassured her she could stay as long as she needed to. She rang her dad and warned him that Mum showing up on the doorstep wouldn't make Emily return home any faster, but he was one step ahead and hatched a plan to point Sandra in Stuart's direction, certain he would be glad of help with the girls until Emily got her head together.

The summer weather contrasted starkly with Lucy's icy winter mood, which had only been temporarily shelved the previous evening because Emily's crisis had been greater than her own. She hadn't mentioned her impending dismissal to her sister and her spirits had deteriorated even further after breakfast when she realised she'd lost the locket. Despite a thorough search, it was nowhere to be found.

'Good morning,' Adam chirped.

'Morning,' she replied, feeling that it was about as far removed from a good morning as the planet Neptune was from Flat Twenty, Lancaster Road. She slung her bag under her desk and sat down.

Pat stood up briefly to hand her a home-made cupcake on a white china saucer, but returned to her seat before any meaningful eye contact had been made. Pat, Lucy realised, was a silent but effective force in the office, keeping everyone together and happy. Lucy tucked it in her drawer to have after the meeting. She would need something to cheer her up and a small, swirly mountain of pink frosting might do the trick.

The white plastic clock on the wall seemed to be going backwards. As Lucy watched it meander its lackadaisical way around to ten o'clock, her short-spin-cycle stomach was not helped by Adam's chirpy pen tapping and irritating smirk. Did he know? she wondered. And was he laughing at her? Could this somehow be linked to her accidental discovery that he was a carer to his disabled mother? Perhaps he was pleased she was leaving and hoped his secret would go with her. Perhaps he'd even had something to do with her losing her job?

Finally, Sam walked past and peered over her glasses.

'Ten minutes, Lucy. My office.'

Lucy nodded as her stomach completed the final spin and gave a clunk to signal the end of the programme.

When she stood up ten minutes later, she let her hand trail across the edge of her desk as if she was leaving a dear friend. Crunch time.

Chapter 49

'So, Lucy, assuming the jungle drums have been beating out their gossipy rhythm since yesterday. Do you know why I've called this meeting?'

'Erm, I think so,' Lucy mumbled. *I mustn't cry*, she thought. Why had the locket gone missing when she needed it most?

'Good. It should make everything a bit easier if we are working from the same file, as it were.' As usual, there were no signs of emotion from her efficient and professional boss.

'When do you need me to clear my desk?' Lucy tried to match Sam's professionalism.

'I was thinking by the end of next week to give you an overlap with the new girl. It would be great if you could oversee a transition period for her. Daniel found her actually; she was a temp at TopToys, so she has some background in our industry.'

'That's not a problem,' Lucy said, but was inwardly thinking Tompkins Toy Wholesaler were taking not only the Mickey but the Minnie, Goofy and Daffy as well. Perhaps if she'd been wearing the locket, she might have told Sam exactly where to stick the suggestion she trained up the girl taking her precious job. But she merely forced a smile and cleared her throat.

'And then we should be good to go the week after that.' Sam looked down at the papers in front of her, ticked something with her silver pen, and turned the page.

'Erm, will you be able to provide me with a reference? If it's not too much trouble? I know things haven't worked out and there have been some unfortunate incidents recently, but I am a hard worker and I'm not asking you to lie or anything, just focus on some of my good points. I mean, I enjoyed designing the promotional fliers, I have a good relationship with most of the customers and...'

Sam frowned and bent forward to inspect Lucy more closely over the rims of her red glasses. She took them off, folding the arms across the lenses, and placed them on the large expanse of table between them. 'Do you think I'm letting you go?'

'Aren't you?'

Sam chuckled to herself, put her hands together as if in prayer and rested the tips of her fingers on her lips. 'So you think you're in here for me to fire you, and yet you are perfectly happy to retrain your replacement?'

Lucy's eyes darted from right to left a few times, as if an explanation to the confusing situation might suddenly pop up in the office and wave at her. She was missing something, but it was pretty damn camouflaged.

'This certainly explains why I was ambushed by the warehouse staff last night. It was like being subjected to the Spanish Inquisition. Five of them stood where you're sitting now, a semicircle of burly men making me feel even smaller than I already do and begging me to save your job, which was never in jeopardy in the first place. I've never seen so many grown men get emotional. How I hate the Chinese whispers of the workplace. Often destructive and usually totally unfounded.'

'I'm not being sacked?' Lucy was confused.

Sam shook her head.

'I don't understand. I have to work late to catch up, my desk is in total chaos – so much so I lost an important order – you caught me in the cupboard with Daniel, and overheard me refer to Mr Tompkins less than respectfully...'

'No, you *choose* to work late. You are conscientious and hard-working. Yes, your desk looks like a tip, but it doesn't stop you doing your job properly and, anyway, I have my own theories about that missing order. Even if I'm wrong, everyone makes mistakes. It's how you deal with them that matters.' She gave a brief but encouraging smile.

'But you were so cross when I approached Mr Tompkins with the wine idea.'

'No, I was surprised you hadn't mentioned it to me but not cross. And although the idea wasn't workable, Mr Tompkins and I were both impressed that you had been thinking about the issue and presented your idea in a professional manner. That's the kind of employee we are looking for. We need people who want to see the company succeed. I'm not sure what kind of ogre you think I am. Possibly one with eight legs?' She raised her eyebrows at Lucy. 'But I'm actually an okay person. Even though, as you know, I don't have any friends to back up that statement.'

'You have me,' Lucy said, and Sam smiled.

'You've got massive potential, Lucy. You can mix with everyone, from the managing director – who I happen to know is very fond of you – to the warehouse lads – who would quite literally get on bended knee to save your job. And this is a massive advantage.'

'But I don't understand. You've given my job to someone else.'

'I have other plans for you, Lucy Baker,' and she opened the desk drawer in front of her and took out a small plastic box. She slid it across the desk towards Lucy, who picked it up and opened the lid. Inside, there were two hundred printed business cards.

Lucy Baker
East Anglian Area Sales Representative
Tompkins Toy Wholesaler.

Chapter 50

'Daniel's going to cover inside the M25 as Trevor has been headhunted by a manufacturer but was totally upfront about it, so I've had notice. It's the trickiest area, but Daniel is more than up to it. He occasionally displays inappropriate behaviour in the office, which I am addressing, but he's extremely good at what he does. Why on earth did you think I'd taken you out with him for the day?' Sam asked.

'Adam said it was to take notes for you.'

'Ah, I wondered why you were so diligently scribbling everything down. I probably said something like I wanted you along to come and observe Daniel. I swear that man hears what he wants to. So, is it a yes?'

'If you think I'm up to it. But I'm still in shock. I was sure after all my disasters I was heading for the door.'

'Lucy, I know people think I'm some sort of career-driven robot, but I am human, and a lot sharper than you give me credit for. The whole Dick thing for example: just because I didn't roll around on the floor laughing doesn't mean I can't appreciate the funny side.'

For something Sam professed to find amusing, she merely raised an eyebrow and shook her head gently from side to side at the memory. Honestly? She'd be a good match for George if Lucy hadn't already earmarked him for herself.

'Haven't you noticed how Daniel asks *you* to get the warehouse staff or drivers on side when things have gone pear-shaped?' Sam continued. 'He knows, as well as I do, that those men would do anything for you. You are going to breeze this job, Lucy, and we'll need to watch that you aren't headhunted like Trevor.'

Lucy took the top card from the pile and turned it over in her fingers. Her name was there, in black and white, shouting success and the start of a promising career. Her hand went for the locket, as it had done so many times over the last few weeks, but it wasn't there.

'Thank you,' she said, reaching across the desk to shake Sam's hand. 'I appreciate this fantastic opportunity.'

Walking back into the office, Lucy couldn't have felt higher if she'd been smoking one of Brenda's hand-rolled Sixties joints. The plastic box was carried carefully, as if it contained a precious jewel, and gently placed on her desk. She pulled on her headset and logged into the system, but halfway through the first call (an angry customer who'd just discovered the sound synthesiser chips in his order of thirty My Pretty Princess dolls were repeatedly yelling, 'Take cover! Incoming tactical nuke!') she opened the lid, took out a card and pinned it to the edge of her board.

The background chatter and diligent tapping on keyboards was disrupted as the office door was flung open with some force and Daniel burst through the door. His face was difficult to read. Eyes wide and sucking in a deep breath, he headed over to Adam's desk. Adam looked momentarily intimidated and slunk into his chair, almost visibly cowering from an imagined blow. Daniel's hand shot upwards and came down with a flourish.

'High five and *massive* respect,' Daniel said, as his open hand came towards a hunched-up Adam. He managed to reciprocate the high five before it became an accidental palm in the face. 'Mr Csar? Yes, it's an unusual name, but I've got a customer called John Dungworth and I don't hold it against him. So I undertake the two-hour drive down to London to meet Mr Csar who has expressed an interest in ClickIn, and I stand there in reception, insistent that I have an appointment with him at nine o'clock. The receptionist – nice one, by the way, she was obviously in on the whole thing – asks if I have a first name. Lou, I say, Lou Csar. And she asks me to repeat it. And then the penny drops. Quite frankly, Adam old chum, I didn't think you had it in you.' And Daniel went for another high five, one Adam was prepared for this time.

'Right, well...' said Adam, getting out of his chair and standing up to tower over his nemesis. 'Never underestimate a sales office supervisor, that's what I say.'

Daniel shook his head but was smiling. 'Six-a-sodding-clock I was up this morning. You got me good and proper. Let's call it quits, shall we?'

Adam and Daniel stood together and shook hands, before Daniel wandered down to Sam's office.

Adam walked over to Sonjit's desk with a huge grin on his face, they exchanged a perfect high five, and then he circled back to his desk and sat down with a flourish, slightly adjusting himself as his bottom nearly missed the chair.

'So, as a result of all the observations and assessments, which I know everyone found intrusive and time-consuming, I have been able to work out ways to save the company a considerable amount of money. I can halve the stationery budget for a start,' and Sam threw a wry glance at Adam. 'There are ways to reduce waste and manage time and resources far more efficiently. With some money invested in modernisation – don't even get me started on that great hulk of a photocopier – I think we can give the competition a run for their money. And after the success of ClickIn, Richard is already in talks with another international toy manufacturer for exclusive import rights to their new range of outdoor games. Therefore, I am pleased to announce there will be no redundancies.'

Everyone gathered to hear Sam's prognosis for the company, to be told the news of Lucy's promotion, and the appointment of a new member of sales staff. Even Daniel had been called in.

'It has become apparent, however, that the photocopier is not the only outdated thing in this company and some of you need to address your behaviour in the workplace.' She spun to Adam, who was hovering to her left. 'Adam, I am sending you on a one-day employee training course next week in Peterborough. The fact I have been required to send you on this course is noted in your staff record, but your attitude towards it, and subsequent behaviour, is in your hands, and will be equally noted. The morning session covers a variety of topics, including a module on workplace harassment – which I expect you to pay particular attention to – and there are a variety of team- building exercises in the afternoon. I suggest you take a pair of trainers.'

Daniel smirked as Sam handed Adam a leaflet covering the course details. 'Monkey bars and raft building. You're gonna love it, mate.'

'Perhaps the two of you could car share?' she suggested, and she handed Daniel an identical leaflet.

It was interesting how the office chatter across partitions, over lunch and in the corridors was no longer critical of Sam, but instead there was an air of respect for the general manager, and a feeling of optimism and enthusiasm.

Jess rang Lucy on the internal line that afternoon. 'Well done with the promotion. I'm so proud of you. Gonna miss sneaking up to see you though.'

'To be honest, I still can't believe it. All I need to do now is bag that grumpy neighbour of mine and it will be a week even my mother would be proud of. He's back from London this afternoon; knowing him he'll head straight to the factory, but by the end of today I should know whether Brenda's locket has worked its magic.'

Dropping off her handbag, lunch bag and knitting bag, and quickly changing out of her work clothes, Lucy put on a pretty floral dress and white pumps. If there was going to be a big moment in her life, this would be it, and she felt she should dress for the occasion. The only thing missing from her ensemble was the locket, which still hadn't turned up. She could have done with the extra confidence, but her promotion had given her a temporary boost.

She knew where the E.G.A. Packaging factory was as she had driven past it on several occasions, so she jumped into her car and nipped around the one-way system, certain George would still be there. He was rarely home before seven o'clock and suddenly she couldn't wait that long.

The car park was full when she arrived, but she eventually

found an obscure parking slot to the side of the factory, near the warehouse delivery entrance. She took her mobile from her pocket, found George's number and sent a text.

Can you spare a few minutes? I'm at the factory. I'll come to reception. Lucy x

She toyed with removing the kiss but it was innocuous enough. She put kisses on the end of her texts to Jess, so he shouldn't read too much into it. And anyway, she was about to launch herself at him, full pelt, and plant the world's biggest and most heartfelt smacker on his lips – if her toes could tip up high enough.

Right, she told herself, *here goes nothing…*

And then she dropped the phone down that ridiculous gap between the edge of the driver's seat and the gearstick casing. It slid on its side and wedged itself just out of reach. She spent several minutes squeezing her fingers down to try and poke it out but eventually managed to flick one end up with a knitting needle (they were breeding in the glovebox) and yanked it out.

Taking a quick look in the rear-view mirror, she wiped under her eyes and pinched her cheeks. It would have to do. This bold action would either seal it or not. But she was a tiger now, not a mouse.

She got out of the car and brushed her skirt down, thankful no playful breezes were going to whip it up and cause embarrassment. As she turned the corner to walk towards reception, she was surprised to see Jess walking towards the factory and noticed her car abandoned outside the open gates. George appeared from the building and was striding towards her with purpose. He looked like The Incredible Hulk, only decidedly less green, and was a man on a mission – not to be stopped by anyone or anything.

Standing on the path in her simple cotton dress, her hair about her shoulders, Jess looked as shocked as Lucy at the approaching tank of a man. She was quite beautiful and it was easy to understand why men found her attractive. Jess stood her ground, and when George reached her, he took her into his arms, almost lifting her feet from the ground. No words came from his mouth, but then this was George and conversation had never been his thing. He bent to meet her upturned face. Dropping her down to the path, he cupped her head in his large hands and brought his lips down onto hers with a force and determination that spoke of uncontrollable passion. Jess slid her hands about his waist and the kiss continued; their bodies moulding together and their lips searching and finding responses from each other.

Lucy tore her eyes away and her heart crumbled as if someone had removed the last supporting Jenga block from the wibbly-wobbly tower that was her life. She turned and ran back to her car, without once looking back.

Chapter 51

Lucy crashed through her front door, relieved to find Emily was still out. Her sister had left the flat that morning to meet with her boss and told Lucy she'd return for her bits and pieces later, as she was ready to return home. Not able to face Brenda quite yet (she had some serious sobbing to do first), Lucy got out her knitting. It was easier to lose herself in the repetitive nature of row upon row of simple stitches, letting frustrated tears fall onto her work, and the television play a backdrop to her misery.

Perhaps, thought Lucy generously, Jess had rejected George. To be fair, she hadn't hung around long enough to witness the end of the encounter. Jess had always maintained she didn't fancy George and that he absolutely wasn't her type. Perhaps after the initial shock of being so dramatically swept off her feet, she had pulled away and told him his advances were unwanted.

Knit one, purl one, knit one... Her needles clicked as her fingers automatically formed the stitches without the need for her to focus. If Madame Defarge could knit code as she sat by the guillotine, surely her anger and deep unhappiness could be worked into her own knitting? The tension of her stitches increased as her hot hands fumbled with the wool, and it became harder and harder to push her needle through the loops.

So much for the locket helping her to find her true love. It had been an unmitigated disaster from start to finish. She'd followed all the spells and yet George had chosen Jess. Lucy cursed as her shaking hands wobbled the needles and several stitches were dragged off the end. She was getting herself into a state and it wasn't going to help matters. Taking a deep breath, she carefully fed them back on. It was all so unfair. Jess wasn't even interested in George. She had some mystery man that she'd set her sights on. Someone she didn't feel she could share with Lucy yet.

Lucy frowned and placed the knitting on the sofa beside her. Then she picked it up again, shaking her head. She looped the wool over the needle but stopped mid stitch, laying it beside her again.

There was no doubt in Lucy's mind that the locket *was* magic; the changing inscriptions were proof enough of that. So perhaps it had worked after all. Perhaps she should consider the possibility that someone else had been performing the spells alongside her own disastrous efforts. Perhaps someone who had been with her every step of the way, someone looking for a wealthy boyfriend to get her out of her unhappy domestic situation...

No. Lucy shook her head. Jess wouldn't do that. She'd been so helpful. In fact, every time the locket had changed, she positively insisted on knowing the next spell...

Lucy put her hands to her face as realisation dawned and explanations for her friend's actions offered themselves. She had generously bought Lucy the beeswax candle, but who was to say she hadn't bought one for herself? Every time a spell was completed, she had begged to be included in the next part. Lucy rubbed her temple. Which spell had come after the candle? The hairs, that's right. Without invitation, she had shown up and insisted on helping her get the hairs under George's bed, which Lucy had done herself, so how could Jess have undone that?

Lucy stood up and started to pace the living room as if the act of taking each step would bring her closer to the solution she was muddling through in her head. Of course, Jess had returned to close the wardrobe. Lucy's shoulders slumped as she remembered each of the spells: Jess turning up at George's with food when Lucy was away, the unexplained cut on George's hand and Jess placing all the items on the pentagram. Events suddenly made uncomfortable and gut-wrenching sense.

She pressed the speed dial for Jess and walked over to the large front window as she waited for her friend to pick up. She mustn't assume, she kept telling herself. There could be a perfectly rational explanation. Someone else could have undone the spells and Jess's keen involvement could be what she had believed all along – the genuine desire to help a friend. But with the nagging doubt gently tapping at the entrance to her brain, she needed to get a straight answer one way or another. The ringtone buzzed in her ear and she watched a curious Scratbag leap up onto her front wall and stare at her. She moved away from the window.

Jess finally picked up. 'Lucy, I'm glad you've rung. I need to speak to you—'

'I saw you and George outside the factory earlier,' Lucy interrupted.

'Yes, we saw your yellow car pull away. Oh Luce, I need to apologise—'

'Did you undermine the spells, Jess?' Lucy asked, cutting through her friend in a deliberately calm voice.

'Yes, and I'm so sorry.' Lucy's stomach slid down to her knees. 'But—'

'Why?' It came out as a whine. 'You told me he wasn't your type.'

'Come on, Luce, he's *everyone's* type. You told me even Brenda has the hots for him and she's old enough to be his grandma.'

'So you're telling me you've always been attracted to George?'

'From the first moment I saw him I thought he was bloody hot, but you kept insisting you weren't interested. You were so grumpy and negative about him, whereas all I could see was a big, strong man who wasn't short of a bob or two, and had a sexy alpha-male thing going on. You didn't want him, so I thought I'd do the spells and have him.'

Trying to stay calmer than she felt, Lucy's eyes started to prick with gathering tears.

'You've lied to me, time and time again, and manipulated me. How could you do it? That's not what friends do.'

'But you don't understand—'

'I understand all right. You betrayed me, so you are no longer my friend. There's nothing more to say.'

'But, there's something important—'

'Stay out of my life, Jessica Ridley. I don't want to hear it.' Lucy hung up.

Within seconds, her mobile was buzzing. Seeing it was Jess calling, she blocked the number.

Anger fizzed up inside her like bubbles in a dropped Coke bottle. All it needed was someone to open the lid and she was certain she would explode up the walls. She wasn't the

353

sort of girl to hit things but had been known to launch the odd Barbie doll or high-heeled shoe at her sister when they were growing up. Throwing the mobile at the sofa, still rational enough not to launch it at anything that would permanently damage it, she watched it bounce off a surprised Wolverine and slide down his legs to the floor. Sinking to her knees, Lucy let the building emotions escape, and a small gathering of woolly celebrities could only watch as a heartbroken young girl sobbed her heart out on the fireside rug in front of them.

Emily returned to the flat as the daylight ebbed away.

Lucy had been curled up in a tight ball for the last hour, a thick crocheted blanket enfolding and comforting her tiny body, as she stared like a zombie at the TV.

'I've been into work and thrashed out the details, and then Stu met me for lunch,' Emily called from the hall as she closed the front door and walked into the living room. 'We both said things that needed to be said and cleared the air. I'm going to return...' She dropped her handbag on the sofa arm and rushed over to her sister. 'Luce? What's wrong?'

If Lucy had harboured any thoughts of concealing her dark mood from her sister, they vanished within seconds. They knew each other too well.

'Man trouble. Don't worry about me. I'll get over it.'

'I didn't even realise there was a man.' Emily nudged her sister's feet with her bottom and nestled beside Lucy. 'I know I've been wrapped up in my own problems, but I'm still here for you, you know?'

'I know, but there's not a lot to tell. I like someone. He likes someone else. Simple. In fact, I shouldn't be wallowing over him because I've had some good news today. I've been promoted to East Anglian Area Sales Representative. I get a company car and a sales-related bonus.' She tried to sound upbeat about the job that only a few short hours ago had been such marvellous news, but she couldn't.

Emily smiled but the smile was fleeting. 'I, more than anyone, know that the heart is a much harder beast to satisfy than the head. Come here, you, let's hug it out.'

So Lucy let herself be crushed and comforted by her big sister and the tears fell again for the big, silly neighbour who had broken her heart.

Lucy plastered a bright smile and perhaps a little too much make-up over her face before visiting Brenda the next morning. Emily had returned to the bosom of her family the night before, after a sisterly chat and lots of chocolate helped them to put the world to rights.

Before Brenda's door had swung open, the old lady's arms were outstretched and concern for Lucy was apparent across her face.

'My darling girl, what's wrong? I've hardly slept. I felt all was not well with you and it's made me restless. Come out of the rain and talk to me.'

It had been hammering down since four a.m., as if the heavens could feel Lucy's pain and decided to have a good old blub in sympathy. Being back in her own bed hadn't resulted in a better night's sleep. She watched each flash of lightning cut through the black and into her own troubled heart. Crawling from beneath the covers in the dead of night, she opened a window in a desperate effort to rid herself of the suffocating heat and her suffocating thoughts. The cooling, clean, damp air was a welcome relief, but her mood plummeted again when she realised the locket was still missing. If ever there was a time she needed it, it was now. How could she face Jess without it?

Brenda's bony hands reached out and guided her through the door and into the living room. The antique wooden mantel clock ticked away as they settled together on the sofa, bypassing the amiable chair.

'Scratbag told me all was not well and I could feel your unhappiness as if it was my own.'

'Scratbag did not come over and talk to you,' Lucy said, dismissing a fleeting image of the cat chatting away with Brenda over a saucer of muesli, but the hint of a smile danced across her eyes.

'You don't have to speak words to be able to convey a message. Anyway, it doesn't matter how I know. I just know. Come on, young lady, tell me what's going on.'

Lucy told her friend what she'd witnessed between George and Jess, and Jess's subsequent admission. Brenda was scrunching up her wrinkled lips and shaking her head as Lucy relayed Jess's betrayal.

'I thought there was something going on. The chair didn't like her much, remember? And she was a difficult one to read. I'm sorry. I should have spotted it and done more to help.'

'Don't be silly. It's not your fault.'

'Oh dear.' Brenda's eyes fell to her liver-spotted hands. 'This is all putting rather an unexpected spanner in the works and I'm running out of time for things to adjust themselves.' She looked up and caught Lucy's bemused expression. 'What I mean is, I wanted everything to run smoothly for the party. It's only days away now. George is invited, you know. I don't want there to be any awkwardness.'

Lucy took a moment to consider her feelings. 'I promise nothing will spoil your party,' she said. 'We're all grown-ups and it's not his fault either, not really.'

'But you do have feelings for him, don't you, my dear?'

Lucy sucked in a breath and exhaled the truth she'd known for several weeks. 'Yes,' she replied. 'I'm not sure how I would feel without his huge frame stumbling around in my life, throwing itself over me at inopportune moments and scooping me up when I do a face-plant on his hall carpet. You may have to work hard to get a smile out of him, but when you get one, it takes your breath away. You were right about him all along. He's a big softie underneath and one heck of a sexy man on top.' She put her hands over Brenda's. 'I think I've been in love with him for quite some time, but my heart forgot to email the message to my brain. Either that, or the message went straight into the junk folder.'

Chapter 52

Triple-checking there was absolutely nothing she could do to help Brenda with preparations for the birthday party on Saturday, and being told repeatedly that Party People had it all in hand, Lucy started to plan the toy nativity in earnest. They'd finally presented the idea to Sam and got a thumbs-up. Adam took on the role of finding sponsors and liaising with the local papers when the time came. Pat was keen to get involved and offered to make the stable, as her husband could do wonderful things with plywood and she was handy with a paintbrush. All Lucy had to do was coordinate the knitting of about thirty figures in as many weeks. Just about doable with the help of the Knit and Natter, and just as well she didn't have any distractions, like a social life or a boyfriend. She decided on the donkey from Shrek, Shaun the Sheep, Kung Fu Panda and a smattering of Minions to help fill the stable. Brenda's present had been finished earlier in the week and was now boxed and wrapped, ready to hand to her in the morning, so Lucy was free to focus on the office project.

Having managed to avoid both Jess at work and George at home, Lucy was unexpectedly cornered by him in the road on Friday. He'd obviously been waiting for her to return because his front door opened as soon as she pulled into a kerbside space. She was surprised to see him during daylight hours, but then remembered he'd taken the week off.

'Lucy, I need to talk to you,' George said, trailing after her as she strode towards her flat. 'I've been talking to Jess and it upsets me that you're quarrelling. Have you got a moment? I think you may have misunderstood the—'

'Sorry. I can't do this right now.' Her cheeks flushed scarlet and she ran up her path, into the flat, and firmly closed the front door behind her. She simply couldn't face justifications from George or pleas for them to remain friends, because being that close to him again had reminded her how strong her feelings for him were.

Lucy and Brenda, with more than two generations between them, sat together in the garden later that evening, enjoying the last of the sun as the trees started to cast the tiny patio in shade. It seemed to Lucy that all the birds within a two-mile radius were sitting on Brenda's roof or roosting in her trees that evening. There was a fragrant honeysuckle dousing them with its scent and Scratbag was rolling around at Brenda's feet, hoping for a tummy rub.

'You'll wear the locket tomorrow, of course? To indulge an old lady?' she said.

It was time to come clean.

'Oh, Brenda. I didn't know how to tell you, but I've lost it. I've had the flat upside down and everything. I'm so sorry. You trusted me with it and I've let you down.'

'Tish. I gave it to you, Lucy. If it's lost, then it's lost. It's just a locket.'

'How can you say that? It's a very special locket. One I need desperately to help me get through bumping into George in the future, which is sadly inevitable as he only lives a hop, skip and a big, manly stride away.'

'You don't need it, although it has a way of appearing when it's required. I doubt it has gone far. Perhaps it's resting for a while; after all, it has had an unusually busy few weeks.'

Lucy's hands went to her stricken face as she realised a further complication. 'And I'll need it to help me with my new job. How can I talk to all those people and persuade them to buy from Tompkins without it? I only got the job in the first place because of the confidence it gave me.'

Brenda gave a sigh and reached for her hand. 'No, Lucy, you didn't. You got the job because your boss saw your potential and you deserved it. The locket had absolutely nothing to do with it.' Brenda looked somewhat sheepish. 'The truth is, my dear child, it is a powerless, if somewhat attractive, lump of metal.'

'But it made George fall in love with Jess.' Lucy knew she sounded like a petulant child but she didn't care. Stupid locket making her lose such a lovely man to someone else.

'Tish. That locket can no more make someone fall in love with you than I can mount the broomstick in the pantry and sail through the night sky.'

'You're saying the locket isn't magic?'

'Well,' Brenda conceded, 'there are elements about the locket that it would be difficult to explain to a man of science.' She avoided Lucy's eyes and ran her fingers up and down the edge of the garden table, watching as a ladybird landed on her hand and quickly flew off again.

'Like the words changing?'

'Yes, but that's visual magic not emotional. I told you, Lucy, magic can't go against the natural order of things. It can't make someone behave out of character. It can't make someone fall in love with you. Or create a confidence in someone that doesn't exist. That was all you. I just had to get you to believe in yourself. A bit of trickery on my part, but it was for the greater good, and you came out of your shell. You've lost faith in your abilities because you've lost the locket, but they haven't gone anywhere.'

Lucy's spirits were lifted for about a millisecond before a devastating thought struck her and tumbled to the floor to sit beside the jagged pieces of her heart.

'But that means George *chose* Jess over me. That no magic was involved and he still wanted her.'

'You have to talk to him, Lucy. The eye is not always the best judge of what is going on.'

Lucy returned to the flat having decided that she was definitely, absolutely, and without a shadow of a doubt able to move on from George. She could be the bigger person and gracefully accept he had chosen the pert breasts, tanned legs and Union Jack talons...erm, fingernails over her. Friends would be manageable. Eventually.

Deciding to get in quick before her mother rang with the weekly update, she called to check up on her sister.

'I can't thank you enough for letting me crash while I got my head together. Stupid hormones,' Emily said.

'Don't be silly. I was flattered you felt you could come to me. Any further news?'

'Only confirmation of the things I'd discussed with work in the week. They've written my absence off as sick leave and I return on Monday, but in a reduced capacity. I'll take my maternity leave as early as I can, but they know I'm not returning. Now I've made the decision, I don't feel under so much pressure and can enjoy the remaining few weeks. Stu's been really supportive. He's even been talking about down-sizing the house, but we'll see. You?'

'It's Brenda's eightieth tomorrow and George will be there. It's okay, I've shed my tears and moved on, but I don't want things getting awkward for either of us. It's all a bit raw, and if he brings Jess, I don't know how I'll react. Maybe high-five her...in the face...with a chair.'

Emily laughed. 'Even the New You isn't that brave.'

'Maybe not then. I don't want to lose her as a friend, but I think I'm allowed to sulk for a bit. Although, avoiding her at work this week hasn't been easy.'

'You go to that party and you shine, my darling, regardless of who's there. Brenda needs you and, anyway, I wouldn't give up on George completely. Remember how long it took me to get Stuart? And as Dad always says, "It ain't over until your mother says it is."'

'Happy birthday,' Lucy said and bent down to kiss Brenda, an enormous gift-wrapped box in her arms.

'Oh, my dear, I didn't want you to get me anything. At my age, there is nothing left I either want or need. But thank you.'

Lucy carried the box inside and placed it on the coffee table. With some help, Brenda pulled away the pretty striped paper and opened it. Lucy lifted out the present in all its component parts and, moving the box to the chair, arranged it on the table between them.

Tears fell from Brenda's eyes as she surveyed a miniature replica Ludwig Mod Orange drum kit and a six-inch-high knitted Jim, with his wild hair and tiny drumsticks. Sat to the side, in a knitted armchair, was a Brenda of yesteryear in a colourful tunic top and flared trousers. Although the photo upstairs was black and white, it had very much been the inspiration and Lucy had allowed herself some artistic licence with the colours.

'It's perfect,' Brenda said. 'Absolutely the most wonderful thing I have ever been given.'

Brenda sat caressing and fiddling with the figures while Lucy made them both some tea and toast. When it was time to leave, Lucy reminded Brenda she would meet her at the hall later that evening, making up a feeble excuse not to be part of the lift Brenda was getting from George.

'It's going to be a wonderful party,' said Lucy.

'Yes,' Brenda replied, 'it will be the party of my life.'

After four stressful wardrobe changes, Lucy stood outside the village hall that Party People had chosen as the venue for Brenda's eightieth. The dress she finally decided on was a simple grey corsage waist dress from Emily in a chiffon fabric that swished gracefully about her legs as she walked. She felt comfortable and feminine, no longer so keen to give out the Look At Me vibe. There was music and chatter permeating the air and pulling her in. She smoothed the front of her dress and took a deep breath.

Brenda approached her as she entered. The streaks in her hair were a vibrant purple and had clearly been dyed at some point during the day. As all of her potions and lotions had disappeared from the kitchen, Lucy wondered if she'd splashed out on a hairdresser, something she wouldn't normally have dreamed of. Looking resplendent in a Sixties pink and purple psychedelic maxi dress, Brenda put her fragile hands up to Lucy's face and her bell sleeves hung elegantly in mid-air like colourful pennants. There was a long row of black glass beads around her neck, catching the lights circling the room, and she smelt of rose petals and vanilla.

'Sorry I'm late.'

'Please don't apologise. The important thing is you are here. The party can start properly now. Come and mingle.' Standing on tiptoe, Brenda kissed her beloved friend's cheek with her soft lips. They held each other for a moment without the need for words, and then separated to face the room.

The hall was beautifully decorated, silver helium eights and zeros announcing Brenda's milestone rising up from each table on purple ribbons and secured by shiny foil metallic weights. A giant disco ball hung from the high ceiling and scattered elegantly gliding spots of light over everyone, the beams catching faces and bouncing off reflective surfaces as they swept the hall. Swags of purple and silver organza hung from the walls, interlaced with fairy lights, and a Sixties tribute band were mid-song on the wooden stage that protruded into the rectangular hall. They were playing a Rolling Stones cover and the bouncy lead singer had a powerful, punchy voice that filled the room with happy sounds.

It was heart-warming to see how many people had turned out for the party. Some Lucy recognised: those who'd popped into Brenda's over the years with troubled faces but left clutching small bottles and discreet paper packages with calmer, hopeful looks. There were neighbours, like Chloe and her mum – the younger of whom was skipping around the hall, trying to stamp on the dancing lights as they slid across the floor. A couple of the Knit and Natter ladies waved from the far corner, and Lucy recognised the young Dr Hopgood sitting at a nearby table with a pretty brunette she assumed was his wife.

And then there was George, his back to the hall, talking to someone she didn't recognise. So he hadn't brought Jess along then, she thought, unless she was joining him later. No, neither of them would be that unkind. They were both good people, people she loved in different ways who had followed their hearts, unfortunately at the expense of her own.

'The hall looks amazing,' Lucy said, forcing a smile. 'Party People have done a super job.' She turned her body towards the band so that George was deliberately obscured from her eye line.

'You've got him all wrong,' Brenda said, noting her body language. 'I told you to talk to him.'

Lucy bit her bottom lip to stop it trembling. 'I'm sorry, Brenda, but I don't think I can just yet.'

'I love you so much, but sometimes you can be a silly thing. He brought me here tonight, you know? We had such a lovely chat in the car. You need to listen to him, sweetheart, and hear what he has to say.'

'Chat about what?'

'I'm not saying any more. I've done far too much interfering where you two are concerned. I must step back now.' Brenda looked across at George who was bent forward listening earnestly to an older gentleman, and she let out a wistful sigh. 'He really brings out the carnal side of me. I don't know how I kept my hands off him in the car. What a body.'

'I know.' Lucy was almost whispering. The pair embraced and Lucy felt her friend hang on for dear life, only to break apart when a waitress tapped Brenda on the shoulder to inform her they were opening the champagne in ten minutes.

'Do the rounds. Say hello to some people and then I'd like you to say a few words,' Brenda said to Lucy.

'Me?' Her eyes widened in horror.

'Yes. I can't think of anyone better, can you? I can hardly toast myself. You only have to say a sentence. Then I can look suitably flattered and thank everyone for coming.'

'But I don't have the locket.'

'And we have firmly established, Lucy, that you never needed it.'

Chapter 53

With ten minutes to kill, and George to avoid, Lucy headed over to where Dr Hopgood was sitting. He introduced his wife and pulled out a chair for Lucy to join them.

'Brenda really is a marvellous and surprising lady,' he said. 'In many ways, it is a shame she showed up on my radar so late. I would have liked to get to know her sooner.'

'She's certainly a character, and she *definitely* knows how to throw a party,' said Lucy.

'Yes, weeks in the planning, I understand. My sister works for Party People and Brenda was in the shop sorting it out within days of my tentative diagnosis. But I often find the people with a positive mental attitude in life heal better and live longer.' He stopped as a waitress put three glasses of champagne on the table in front of them. 'Apparently no expense has been spared. Only the best champagne, a band from London, exceptional buffet food and an open bar. For someone who isn't a big social mixer, she's pushed the boat well and truly out into the middle of the ocean.'

'I suppose she wants to mark her milestone birthday in style while she can enjoy it as much as everybody else. She may not make it to the next one.' As Lucy spoke the words, they jabbed at her emotions and made her heart crumple.

'Talking of which,' said the doctor, 'my ongoing efforts to get her to talk about her long-term options have been constantly brushed aside. There are lots of things she can put in place to help with her day-to-day living: handrails and better lighting, and painting things like doorways to give a contrast between objects and background. She could undertake some form of regular exercise to improve the strength in her arms and legs. There is a lot of support out there for both of you, but she won't entertain any of it at the moment. I'm hoping she'll come back to me after the excitement of the party has died down, because at the moment she's avoiding some important decisions.'

'I don't think she's ever looked healthier or happier,' said Lucy. 'Look at her face; she's on top of the world.'

'Yes,' Dr Hopgood replied, 'that's what worries me.'

'If I could have everyone's attention please,' Lucy said in a voice that was never going to be heard above the music or the chatter.

She cleared her throat and tried again.

'Excuse me,' she said, grabbing a fork from the table nearby and tapping it on an abandoned wine glass. The hall chatter died down and Dr Hopgood signalled to the band to stop. Nearly one hundred faces turned in her direction and there was a palpable hush. Ignoring the thud of her panicking heart and the tremble in her knees, Lucy took a steadying breath, intending to say a simple toast, but the words flowed from her mouth in an unstoppable stream.

'Ladies and gentlemen.' She paused to compose herself,

irrationally conscious of George. 'As some of you know, I moved to Lancaster Road two years ago, and it immediately felt like home. Brenda made me feel welcome from that very first day and has continued to play a huge part in my life ever since. She is a mother figure when I feel homesick and a listening ear when things get tough. We have giggled together over romantic heroes and sat in contented silence whilst we pursued our separate hobbies. Always supportive and never critical, she is everything a friend should be. And through the books, knitting needles and jars of herbs and spices, she has become one of the most important people in the world to me. She is a giver, a listener and a rainbow in our dreary world. I hope she will continue to shine around us, tiny rays of colour touching all our lives, for many years to come.'

The audience nodded and mumbled in agreement.

'So, would you please raise your glasses and toast one of the most special and wonderful people I know. To Brenda.'

'To Brenda,' the whole room chorused, getting to their feet and raising their glasses to toast a lady they were all fond of, even if they would always remain slightly wary of her.

A sense of accomplishment gushed through Lucy. Standing in front of a hall full of people and delivering a toast, albeit a short one, was not something she could have imagined herself doing a few weeks ago.

Walking towards her, champagne glass in hand and eyes that held unbidden tears, Brenda stood at Lucy's side and reached for her hand, refusing to let her return to her seat.

'Thank you, Lucy. I'm not sure I deserve such a glowing tribute, but it means the world to me,' Brenda said, turning to the roomful of guests.

She spoke eloquently for a few minutes, refusing to release

Lucy and keeping a firm hold of her hand. She talked briefly of her childhood, of losing her mother, of Jim and how he was her everything, and their sadness at not being able to have children. There were tales about her wild groupie days and then she finished with some words about the importance of friendship.

'People are the thing that make this life bearable. They are the cause of our laughter and sometimes our tears, but living alone in this world would be unthinkable. I have been blessed with many wonderful friends during my eighty years and I want to raise a glass to all those who have touched my life, whether they are still with us or not.' She raised her own glass and there was a moment when many of the people in the hall silently followed suit. 'I think eighty is a splendid age to have reached, and I can honestly say I have enjoyed every single one of those years. So, I beg you all to do the same. Go home to the ones you love and tell them every day how they light up your life, so they can hear those heartfelt words spoken out loud. Words are powerful, more powerful than we sometimes realise, so if you take one thing away from tonight, I'd like you to all to try and live your life by my three favourite words: Be Kind Always.'

Neighbours and friends reached out for each other's hands and threw smiles across the tables. For one perfect moment, the hall was imbued with feelings of love and happiness.

'And now I would like to dance the night, and my cares, away. I hope you will all join me,' she said. 'George, shall we?' And she looked over to an unsuspecting George, who was leaning awkwardly against the architrave of the fire escape. He put his glass down, walked over and took Brenda's arm from Lucy. He opened his mouth to say something, but before he could speak Lucy slipped away to the other side of the hall, content to let someone else have the limelight now she'd done her bit.

It was a touching sight: great big George trying to pull off a clumsy version of the foxtrot with a fragile Brenda barely coming up to his chest. The band were playing a cover of The Yellow Crows' 'London Lady' – a haunting rock ballad that had proved to be their biggest chart success. As they took their first faltering steps, Lucy wondered who the London Lady was. Could it even have been Brenda?

'She makes me smile, holds me for a while, and everything's okay – my London lady,' the lead guitarist crooned into the microphone.

George held Brenda gently in his arms, her tiny frame supported by his sturdy body. He wasn't a natural dancer, thought Lucy, mainly due to his size, but he wasn't bad. She watched his lips move as he counted the steps; slow, slow, quick, quick. The pair moved slowly but with purpose. Brenda closed her eyes and allowed herself to be led. Lucy knew her friend would be thinking of Jim, perhaps even imagining herself to be dancing with him at that moment.

A quiet ripple of applause echoed around the hall as the song came to an end. Brenda put her hands up to George's chest and ran them across to his arms. *Incorrigible flirt*, thought Lucy. A slow dance with George was a dream come true for Brenda, who was motioning for him to come closer as she whispered something in his ear. He smiled and whispered something back, took Brenda's left hand and softly kissed it. She tugged at his collar, pulled him towards her and got away with some crafty lip-to-lip contact. Blushing, George led her to the side and pulled out a chair for her. Then he scanned the faces of the guests and finally met and held Lucy's eyes.

No, she thought. *No. I don't want to hear his stupid explanations or pathetic pleas to remain friends. Not tonight.* And she turned away, making for the open doors at the rear of the hall. An inner voice told her she was being cowardly, but she knew, now that she understood the locket was not the source of her courage, that she was being brave. Brave enough to draw a line under the whole affair and walk away with her head held high.

Outside, she made for the comforting shadows of a nearby cluster of elderflower trees, and let the welcome fresh air dance around her hot, cross body as a lively cover of a Beatles song drifted from the hall. There was a bench beneath the trees and she walked towards it, heading for a place she could be alone for a while. She would gather herself together, paste on a fake smile and then return to enjoy the party.

'Lucy?' George's voice came from behind. She carried on walking. 'Don't walk away. Please.'

She stopped but didn't turn and heard his footsteps pound on the concrete path as he sped up to close the distance between them. He was now directly behind her and she felt an electric pulse jump the gap between their bodies like the blue sparks she'd watched her dad test on his cars over the years. Still she didn't turn.

His voice was soft and low, washing over the top of her head like a gentle wave. 'Why won't you let me explain?'

'You don't have to explain anything to me. I'm your neighbour, not your mother.' It wasn't said unkindly.

'And my friend?'

'Of course.'

'You saw me with Jess.' It wasn't a question, but she answered it nonetheless.

'Yes. Not that I think Jess is your type, but it's not my concern.'

'Ah, well, there I'd have to disagree.'

'She *is* your type?' Her tone was disbelieving as she turned to face him. Why were they even having this pointless conversation? She didn't want to hear about his future with Jess, their planned two point four children and their cottage in the country.

'Not that bit, you daft woman. The bit about it being your concern.'

'Well I—'

'Oh, do be quiet and listen to me before I get even more nervous than I already am. Jessica Ridley is not my type because Lucy Baker, of Flat Twenty, Lancaster Road, is. So much bloody so that I've been unable to focus on work since she persuaded me to camp out beneath the stars for no apparent reason other than it suited her and she wanted me to live a little. Quite frustrating, because I was doing okay at the living thing until she crashed into my work-orientated life. But I've only gone and bloody fallen in love with her.'

It took a moment for her brain to process the words she'd heard, and George talking about her in the third person wasn't helping. When her brain finally staggered into the moment, she looked up into the eyes of the six-foot-four bear of a man, who had taken her hand and was bowing his head in earnest, trying to make eye contact. She could smell his distinctive aftershave, almost taste the champagne that had touched his lips.

'Not that I would have said a few weeks ago that my type might include a crazy, pyromaniac knitter who has a tendency to poison perfectly respectable individuals and randomly roams the neighbourhood, indulging in her drunken kleptomaniac tendencies. As for the rabbit – let's not even go there.' His eyes twinkled, despite his attempt to stay deadpan.

'I don't understand.' Okay, so perhaps he did like her, but she was damned if she could work out why. After all, she'd been assured it was nothing to do with the locket. Surely he didn't like her for her unexciting woolly self?

'Personally, I blame Scratbag: meeting you in the first place, needing your help to feed him, which meant we kept seeing each other, drawing my attention to your plight on the night of the fire. And then, of course, he's the reason I buggered everything up.'

She shook her head. 'I still don't understand.'

'Has anyone told you before how similar you and Jess look? How a man with more allergies than Sneezy from The Seven Dwarfs, who has broken the glasses he has to wear because of his stupid itchy eyes, might walk up to the girl he's fallen for and take her in his arms – the only truly romantic gesture he's ever undertaken in his whole life, might I add? – only to find he's buggered it all up and is kissing the totally wrong girl?'

He'd mistaken Jess for her. Her mouth formed the word, 'Oh,' but the word didn't make it past her lips. Poor Jess.

'Because, stupid blind fool that I am, I was kissing the mad one who, while she's okay in very small doses, unfortunately reminds me of Karen and really wasn't my cup of soya-milky tea.'

Lucy was experiencing the warm glow that she thought,

374

until that point, had come from the locket. Perhaps love had that effect as well.

'With a failed marriage behind me and the social skills of a cantankerous hermit, I didn't want or need anyone in my life. And then you and Scratbag reminded me that it's not healthy to be on my own. I suspect Brenda might have had something to do with it all as well, but you never can pin down what she's done or said. All I know is, every time I go to see her, I come away with a feeling she's been messing with me somehow.'

'She wouldn't do you any harm because her chair likes you too much.'

George frowned but didn't ask her to elaborate, as Lucy gave him an encouraging smile.

'What did Brenda say to you on the dance floor just now?' she asked.

'Something along the lines of, "If you don't tell her that you're in love with her, so help me, you'll regret the next curiously flavoured cup of tea you have at my house."'

'And what did you reply?'

'That I was on it. And then I told her, if I was twenty years older, it would have been a toss- up between the two of you.' His fabulous, orgasm-inducing dimples came out to play.

Life is full of special moments that you wish you could bottle up and save forever like one of Brenda's potions. For Lucy, this moment needed a huge jar and an airtight stopper. And as she closed her eyes, she imagined an enormous glass bottle on a high shelf in Brenda's pantry, her spidery handwriting clearly labelling the bottle The Moment You Knew You'd Found The One.

As George's lips collided with hers, and one of his shovel-like hands slid up her back and pulled her tiny body closer, Lucy Baker left this world for a brief moment and found a special place in the ether she shared only with George.

And Brenda Pethybridge, inside the hall listening to Marjorie talk about the charming Dr Hopgood, looked to her right and lost track of the conversation, because suddenly she knew her final job on this tiny planet, millions of miles into an infinity of space and time, and floating in a universe no man could ever fully comprehend, was finished.

Chapter 54

The party went on until two o'clock in the morning, the last guests leaving when Brenda finally admitted defeat and asked to be taken home. She kept Lucy and George close to her for the remainder of the night, like precious children that she couldn't bear to part with, holding their hands firmly in her own. There were no moments of forgetfulness, no muddling of names and no distant moments.

George drove all three of them back to Lancaster Road and they saw Brenda safely inside. Lucy and George kissed again under the deep orange glow of the street light until Scratbag appeared like an uneasy parent to check the courting couple. George chivalrously offered to walk her to her front door. She joked about his long journey home and they reluctantly parted.

For Lucy knew she was many things: kleptomaniac, poisoner and pyromaniac amongst them, but her mother had not brought her up to behave like a floozy.

The dream was disturbing. Lucy was running through a series of dimly lit corridors. Sometimes she glimpsed an indistinct figure in the room at the end, but by the time she got to the door it had either closed or the room was empty. All she could hear were the echoes of her footsteps bouncing off the walls and her own panicked breaths. Someone was calling out to her in a soft sing-song voice. She stopped running and walked to the end room. A woman sat in a high-backed chair, but this time she didn't disappear as Lucy approached. The woman had no face, but Lucy knew her. She knelt at the woman's feet and a hand stroked her hair. In the nonsense way that only dreams work, Lucy realised she was lost but also knew she was found. And then the woman started to disappear, turning to shadow and memory. The dividing line between her dream world and reality began to blur.

'Brenda?' she mumbled as her eyes focused on her familiar room. Fear built to an inexplicable crescendo. The room was dark, but a peeping light from the gap in the curtains gave definition to her furniture. Her eyes struggled to focus on the table lamp and she reached out to switch it on. She waited a moment for the feeling of relief that usually floods through your body when you realise it was all a dream. But it didn't come.

She didn't know what was happening or why, but she did know that she had to get to Brenda immediately.

Chapter 55

Dawn was breaking as Lucy unlocked her front door and stepped into the cool morning. Low light bounced off the treetops and an unusually large crowd of birds gathered on Brenda's roof. Scratbag appeared from behind the low wall and started his pathetic meow. He came to her feet and put his little catty paws up on her knees, before dropping to the path again. Scurrying towards Brenda's house, he stopped and turned, as if to check she was following. Something was going on and the omniscient Scratbag knew it.

After knocking a few times and getting no answer, Lucy tried the door handle. To her surprise it wasn't locked and the door swung inwards. A hanging chime above the door-frame tinkled as the door was pushed into the hallway. Scratbag watched her enter and then turned back down the path, as though he'd done his part and it was time for him to leave.

The first thing that hit her was the silence. Not just the absence of voices or the usual noises made by someone moving around, but a no-ticking-clocks silence. There were always at least a dozen chattering away in Brenda's house and now there was an eerie nothing.

'Brenda?' she called, passing the open living-room door

and noting that the wooden mantel clock had stopped at eight minutes past four.

She walked into the kitchen and the hands on the bright orange, square, battery-operated wall clock also read eight minutes past four.

A faint smell of alcohol lingered in the air and two vintage green champagne saucers sat on the kitchen table next to a dusty, dark green and gold bottle of Bollinger Special Cuvée. A bottle Brenda had perhaps been saving for a special occasion, and her eightieth birthday would certainly qualify. One glass was empty, the other full, but its bubbles had long since dissipated. And then Lucy realised the one person in the whole of her friend's crazy and magical world she would want to be with might be there to share the moment, but wouldn't be able to lift the glass.

'Brenda? It's Lucy,' she called again, as she moved back into the hallway and stood at the foot of the stairs. The poor woman probably hadn't gone to bed until the early hours and here she was expecting her to be up and about at silly o'clock the next morning. It was perfectly reasonable to assume Brenda was sleeping off the champagne and excitement of the night before.

Yet Lucy knew inside her troubled heart that something was wrong. She took the stairs in twos and bounded up the first flight. She went straight for Brenda's bedroom, now bracing herself for a lifeless body on the bed, but the bed hadn't been slept in and Brenda was nowhere to be seen. Since her last visit to this room, when she had collected clothes after the wandering episode, the room had changed dramatically. Most of the contents had been neatly packed into carefully labelled boxes. Brenda's old-fashioned handwriting detailing the contents of each: shoes, evening gowns, clutch bags, jewellery. Looking about her now, it appeared the only room that had remained untouched was the living room. Brenda hadn't wanted anyone to know what she was up to and must have been packing for weeks, but to go where?

Lucy's heart was thumping and her breaths were forced, each exhalation threatening to release an unstoppable flow of emotions. She realised the most precious room to Brenda was on the third floor: Jim's studio. Her stomach flipped over completely and for a moment she thought she might be sick. Not running but walking now, she climbed the last flight. She took each step one at a time. The thumping of her heart so powerful she feared it would break through her ribcage and bounce out onto the floor in front of her.

It was as she rounded the corner that Lucy finally found her dear friend sitting in the old, leather easy chair that stood next to the precious Ludwig Mod Orange drum kit. Motionless and pale, there was no movement from her chest. No gentle up and down to reassure the frightened Lucy that all was well. On the floor in front of her were the knitted drums Lucy had presented her with only the previous morning, arranged perfectly to mirror the real kit, but the tiny knitted Brenda and Jim were nestled together on her lap. One lifeless hand rested protectively across the pair of them, keeping them safe. And, more importantly, together.

Brenda was still wearing her psychedelic party dress, her purple-streaked hair wild about her shoulders and her eyes closed as though she was listening to her sweetheart serenade her with his drums one last time. Maybe, thought Lucy as she fell to her knees and let the unrestrained tears fall from her eyes, gasping for each painful breath between sobs, he had.

Chapter 56

'When I locked up Brenda's house yesterday, I found this poking out from her bureau.'

George had been by Lucy's side since her heartbreaking discovery, his repeated gentle kisses seeing her through the awfulness of the day, and his strong, silent presence a comfort. She uncurled herself as he passed over a cream envelope with *For Lucy Baker in the event of my death* written across the front.

Trembling, she took it, traces of lavender and rosemary drifting from the stationery as she held it close. She pulled a large knitted blanket from the back of the sofa and slid into it. The tears fell again and only when she felt she could focus through the blur, did she finally open the letter, noticing the tiny forget-me-nots dotted around the edge of the pretty paper. It wasn't dated, but Lucy had her suspicions as to when it had been written. And why.

Dear Lucy – the daughter I never had,
This is one of the hardest letters I have ever had to write.
I don't know when you will be reading this, but I know
that if you are, then I have left you.
I am sitting outside at the little bistro set in the garden

– the garden that we both love and loves us back. The honeysuckle is in full bloom, wrapping me in such a delicious and heady scent that I feel alive and content, but I can also smell damp soil from the summer rain we had briefly this morning. I am reminded of all the seasons in a year, and also the seasons of my life.

I think I have made a difference. I have tried to live a life to help others and spread a little sunshine in the world. Even after losing Jim, my focus has always been a positive one. But the news that I may spend the next few years slowly deteriorating and become a burden has been a bitter pill and one that will be hard to swallow. Perhaps I will pass peacefully in my sleep. One can but dream…

I hope you are shedding a tear for the peculiar old lady who was a small part of your life for the last two years, or perhaps longer by the time you read this. Is it wrong to be a little pleased that I will be missed and there is someone left behind to truly grieve? Had I not met you, lovely Lucy, I fear only a handful of locals would gather at my grave, commenting on the odd woman who they visited for help with their ailments and charms for their happiness, but never really got to know. The real tears will come from you and from George. For that, however twisted my logic may seem to you, I thank you both.

Two years ago, you came into my life – a quiet, unassuming girl but one with so much potential. I've watched you blossom in that short space of time and have such high hopes for your future. I know now that you'll be fine. My last project on this earth was to ensure your future with George and I believe my work there will reach a happy conclusion. Call it magic, call it a gift, call it a curse

*– I am determined to stay around long enough to see you
and George realise what I have known from the beginning.
Treasure each other. Love is the greatest gift.*

*Whatever you put out into the universe, Lucy, will come
back threefold. I believe you will live a good life and be a
light for others. I'm not asking you to embrace my beliefs
or follow them, but don't be scared of things you do not
understand. Remember that your courage and your confidence come from within, and that you can do magical
things without needing magic.*

*I have left you a little something in my will that I know
you will cherish and take excellent care of. It will help to
keep me alive in your thoughts and memories. Again, a
little self-indulgent of me, but I don't believe you are ever
truly dead while you remain alive in the memories of those
you loved and who loved you in return.*

*They will say I was lucky to have lived a full life, but
remember, Lucy, you make your own luck – which I think
you knew all along.*

*Air I am, fire I am, water, earth and spirit I am. Look
for me, Lucy, for I will never be far away.*

*Forgive me for leaving you, darling girl, but no one can
live forever.*

Brenda x

Moving the letter to the side to preserve it from her streaming
tears, Lucy looked up into George's concerned face and passed
it over. He perched on the edge of the sofa and read Brenda's
words.

'That's beautiful, Lucy. I know it's painful right now, but
you can revisit these words when you're stronger and take

strength from them. You were so lucky to have found each other. I know you made a massive difference to her life these past two years.'

Lucy shook her head from side to side, still unable to accept the harsh reality of her friend's passing. 'I don't know how I'll manage without her.'

'She'll always be with us – floating about, probably, if I know her, and keeping her beady eye on us. That's probably why she left you something in her will,' he said, folding up the single sheet of paper and slipping it back into the envelope. He handed it to Lucy, who gripped it tightly with both hands. 'A reminder of your friendship. Something you can look at and remember her by.'

'Perhaps it will be one of the clocks,' she said. 'I hope so, even if they did all stop mysteriously at eight minutes past four.'

'I noticed that. It's odd being in her house without the symphony of ticks and tocks. It makes me think of that song "Grandfather's Clock".'

'Yes,' said Lucy. 'I think they died with her.'

George leaned over and slipped his big arms around his precious girl and held her tight, glad that she didn't look up to witness his own emotional struggle.

'Skipping all the legal jargon, her will is very brief. She leaves everything in its entirety to you, Lucy: the house, the contents and some not insubstantial savings.'

George had a comforting hand on Lucy's shoulder as she sat in the offices of Pickering, Pickering and Blythe – an old firm on the edge of Renborough that had been going since about 1420 or something equally ridiculous. Mr Rutherford looked as though he was an original member of staff, with his white Einstein hair and Dickensian suit, which made the Apple Mac on his leather-inlaid desk look somewhat incongruous.

Brenda had been buried the previous week in a beautiful wicker (and very environmentally friendly) coffin. The service was held at the graveside by an enthusiastic and incredibly well-informed humanist celebrant. Brenda had arranged it all, and not that long ago it turned out. The funeral had been paid for and her instructions were quite specific. No flowers. Donations to Dementia UK. And absolutely and unreservedly no black.

'No.' Lucy was quite definite there had been some mistake. 'She said she'd left me *something* – an ornament, a book, maybe even a piece of jewellery. She definitely said "a little..." Oh my goodness.' She lifted her hand to her open mouth as realisation dawned.

The solicitor smiled. 'As per my client's instructions, I was asked to wait for the penny to drop, or at least give you a few moments in the hope that it would. I was then to read the following short letter to you...

'Dear Lucy,

'My last message from beyond the grave, I promise, unless you have another stray cat appear. That might be me. I'll see what I can do. Maybe with lilac eyes.

'Forgive the twisted humour of an old lady and take a moment to remember our conversation when you gave me the Elliott Landy book. You were so struck by the sentiment at the time, that I couldn't resist...'

And then the solicitor and Lucy said together, 'Sometimes a little something can mean everything.'

Epilogue

'Ah, Sheila, I'd like to introduce you to my daughter Lucy. She is a high-flying rep for a national toy wholesaler. They really couldn't manage without her. And this is her boyfriend George, who owns E.G.A. Packaging. You might have heard of them? They are hoping to expand into the European market soon.'

Sandra's friend put out her hand to shake Lucy's. 'So lovely to meet you. Your mum talks about you all the time. Are you local?'

'Lucy and George both own *enormous* Georgian houses on the outskirts of Renborough – the *nice* end of town,' answered her mother on her behalf. 'But, quite frankly, she could be as poor as the proverbial church mouse and I would still be immensely proud of her. She is kind, she is generous and she is a simply *marvellous* sister and daughter. Did I mention she knits these amazing celebrity figures and has her own successful online shop? It's been such a success, she's had to enlist the help of her knitting group, and they still can't keep up with the demand. And do keep your eyes peeled in the local press as Christmas approaches. I think we may have a minor celebrity in the making.'

Before Sheila got an opportunity to comment on any of

387

the information she'd been bombarded with, Sandra continued, 'Oh, and look, there's Emily – my eldest. Another great success, but in a different way. She's a full-time stay-at-home mum to my two beautiful granddaughters, with another one on the way in November, and I couldn't be prouder...'

Sandra steered Sheila towards Emily, giving her husband a tinkly wave as they passed him deep in conversation with Jess's new boyfriend – a car mechanic from the MOT centre in town. They were discussing what might be causing the rattle under the bonnet of his beloved BMW, but he paused to lift a hand to his wife and gave her a huge grin.

'She's parked outside, if you want to take a look? Little beauty – M535i, 1980 and I did all the work myself.' The young man nodded enthusiastically, so Paul fished the keys from his suit trouser pocket. He was enjoying this party so much more than he'd thought he would.

Jess gave her friend a cheeky wink, and Lucy beamed back at her. They'd had the painful talk over two Danish pastries in The Teaspoon Café the week after Jess's betrayal. It was silly, Lucy realised, to quarrel over a man, and Jess had cried such floods of apologetic tears that her pastry was soggy and inedible by the end of their talk. With Brenda gone, Lucy couldn't bear to lose another friend, and so she did exactly as Brenda had bid everyone that last fateful night – she had been kind and would always continue to try her best to be so.

Lucy watched her nieces hiding underneath the pressed lined tablecloth of the buffet table, a whole bowl of cheesy puffs smuggled into their den, and smiled as she felt George kiss the top of her head. He slipped his arms about her waist as they stood at the side of the large dining room at Mortlake Hall and took a moment.

'She's here, you know. I can feel her,' George said.

'I know,' said Lucy, and she reached for the silver locket. It had turned up the evening of Brenda's funeral. Brenda had been right – it did have a way of appearing when it was needed. Popping the catch, she revealed the final words she'd discovered that night.

'True love is the real magic.'

And fifty miles away, curled up on the sofa of number twenty-four Lancaster Road, Scratbag stretched out his front paws and sat up. He pricked up his tatty ears, turned his head in a south-westerly direction and let out a perfect meow.

Lucy Baker's Dairy-Free Cherry Muffins

Ingredients (makes 9)

200g self raising flour

1 tsp baking powder

140g caster sugar

125ml sunflower oil

2 eggs

100ml water (you may need to add a little more if your mixture is too stiff)

100g cherries (stoned and halved if fresh)

1 tsp vanilla essence

Method

1. Preheat the oven to 160°C and place 9 cases in a muffin tin.

2. Toss the cherries in 1 tbsp of the self raising flour.

3. Sift the rest of the flour and baking powder into a large bowl, then add the sugar and vanilla essence.

4. Lightly beat the eggs then add them, along with the oil and water to the dry ingredients. Stir well to combine.

5. Stir in the cherries then divide the mixture evenly between the muffin cases. (Reserve a few to place on top before cooking as they have a tendency to sink)

6. Bake in the centre of the oven for around 25-30 minutes until the muffins are golden and well risen and a skewer inserted into the centre comes out clean.

7. Leave the muffins to cool for 5 minutes in the tin then place on a wire rack to cool completely.

The muffins will keep for a couple of days in an airtight container.

Acknowledgements

There are a whole host of people who have supported me and my writing dreams over the past few years. I may spend my days in isolation at the keyboard but I am surrounded by so many friends in real life that to name everyone individually would be impractical. Please know that each and every one of you has made a difference. The following are just some who deserve a special mention. To any I have forgotten – please forgive me.

Firstly, I would like to thank Victoria at Avon for championing my book and making my author dreams come true, but also the effervescent Katie, who so competently took over the reins as editor when Victoria moved on. You were both so enthusiastic about Lucy Baker's story that it quite bowled me over. Also, thanks to my amazing agent, Louise Buckley, who gently guided me through some tricky moments.

Big thanks to Clare Horton and Paul Dye for donning their nursing and firefighter hats respectively, to help with research, and Sarah Cox – knitter extraordinaire – whose woolly Harry Hill inspired the Nicely Knitted Celebrities. Like Emily, I wouldn't know which end of the needle to poke in the wool. Any mistakes in the research are mine and mine alone.

I would like to give a special shout-out to Sharon Teague,

who got me up to speed on social media over the past few years, and supplied me with truly marvellous graphics to that end. She has patiently sat through various brainstorming sessions and let me bore her with entire story outlines. You deserve more wine, love – just the one bottle, mind.

To everyone in the Romantic Novelists' Association, but particularly my two NWS readers, the sage and encouraging Heidi Swain and my virtual office buddy, Clare Marchant (who meets me every morning at 9 a.m. by the virtual water-cooler). To my fellow NWS member, Mary Anne Lewis – Siam Son, my friend. Your courage humbles me. And to my darling sister, Linda, for introducing me to the RNA in the first place, and for being the most brutal but totally stupendous beta reader.

To Jacqui Lawrence and Shirley Bearman for having such unstinting faith in me at the start of my journey, and to my darling husband, who can never remember the title of anything I'm working on, but has never once questioned why I want to write. And not forgetting Leo, my thirteen-year-old son, who insisted on reading his mum's book and #totes loved it. Not my target audience but, hey, I'll take it.

An extra special mention to the amazing Ann Warr-Wood, my neighbour and good friend, and my very own Brenda. I love you.

To each and every reader out there who has taken a chance on my debut novel – I hope you've enjoyed it. Please find me on social media and let me know what you think. I want to be the best writer I can possibly be and you can help me learn.

And finally, Julie Harrington. She knows why.